Down Down Down

Down Down Down

Ted Darling crime series

'deadly mind games with a killer'

LIVRES
LEMAS

L M Krier

Published by LEMAS LIVRES
www.tottielimejuice.com

Cover design DMR Creative
Cover photo Neil Smith

DOWN DOWN DOWN

ISBN 978-2-901-77321-4

Contents

About the Author

L M Krier is the pen name of former journalist (court reporter) and freelance copywriter, Lesley Tither, who also writes travel memoirs under the name Tottie Limejuice. Lesley also worked as a case tracker for the Crown Prosecution Service.

The Ted Darling series of crime novels comprises: *The First Time Ever, Baby's Got Blue Eyes, Two Little Boys, When I'm Old and Grey, Shut Up and Drive, Only the Lonely, Wild Thing, Walk on By, Preacher Man, Cry for the Bad Man, Every Game You Play, Where the Girls Are.*

All books in the series are available in Kindle and paperback format and are also available to read free with Kindle Unlimited.

Contact Details

If you would like to get in touch, please do so at:

tottielimejuice@gmail.com

facebook.com/LMKrier

facebook.com/groups/1450797141836111/

twitter.com/tottielimejuice

http://tottielimejuice.com/

For a light-hearted look at Ted and the other characters, please consider joining the We Love Ted Darling group on Facebook.

Discover the
DI Ted Darling series

If you've enjoyed meeting Ted Darling you may like to discover the other books in the series. All books are available as ebooks and in paperback format. Watch out for audio-book versions, coming soon:

Acknowledgements

I would just like to thank the people who have helped me bring Ted Darling to life.

Beta readers: Jill Pennington, Kate Pill, Karen Corcoran, Jill Evans, Alison Sabedoria, Emma Heath, Alan Wood, and The Dalek, for editing assistance.

Police consultants – The Three Karens.

Thanks for all the expert advice on the work of the Fire Service and Fire Dogs to George, to Matt and Fire Dog Kai.

Language advice: Manuel and Jenny (Spanish), Lyndsey (Welsh).

Prison service advice: Ron and Cynthia.

Expert tree advice: Becky and Philip at Jodrell Bank.

Special mention for Hilary for all her kindness and patience in updating me on Stockport and suggesting locations for cover photo-shoots.

And a very special thanks for all Ted's loyal friends in the We Love Ted Darling Facebook group. Always so supportive and full of great ideas to be incorporated into the next Ted book.

To service animals everywhere.
Thanks to you and your handlers
for everything you do for us all

Author's Note

Thank you for reading the Ted Darling crime series. The books are set in Stockport, Greater Manchester, and the characters do use local dialect and sayings. Seemingly incorrect grammar within quotes reflects common speech patterns. For example, 'I'll do it if I get chance', without an article or determiner, is common parlance. Ted and Trev also have an in joke between them - 'billirant' - which is a deliberate typo. If you have any queries about words or phrases used, do please feel free to get in touch, using the contact details in the book. I always try to reply promptly to any emails or Facebook messages. Thank you.

Chapter One

Ted Darling snapped awake at the first sound of distant sirens. A light sleeper, he'd had a more restless night than usual. He had yet another day of meetings ahead of him and was worrying about whether he'd got all the figures which he would need.

He listened attentively, trying to identify from what he heard the level of the incident and whether or not it might involve him or his team.

Fire appliances. Two of them, on bull tone, and not all that far away. He couldn't yet hear either police vehicles or ambulance sirens, so it was hopefully a minor incident.

But he was awake now, although his mobile phone on the side table showed it was not yet five o'clock. He knew he wouldn't get back to sleep. He might as well get up and phone the station for information.

Ted, lying on his back, was as usual confined to a few inches of space right at the edge of the bed. His partner Trevor was fast asleep, one arm and a bent leg draped possessively over Ted. Adam, the smallest of their seven cats, was curled into a tight ball. A warm, furry presence in the space between Ted's shoulder and his cheek. The rest of the feline family members were scattered randomly about on top of the duvet.

Adam opened mismatched eyes and yawned widely as Ted slid carefully out of bed. Trev made a low sound then burrowed more deeply into the mattress, showing no signs of waking.

Ted didn't bother to pull on any clothes as he padded

silently out onto the landing, shutting the door behind him. He phoned the station and asked for the duty inspector. He and his team would only be involved in a fire incident if a serious crime had taken place. Arson, especially one involving casualties. Insurance fraud.

'Hello, Irene,' Ted said in surprise when he was put through. 'I thought you'd gone off on leave.'

'Don't rub it in, Ted,' she groaned. 'I had done. Gone off to do last-minute shopping and packing. Got called back in. Roly was meant to be on duty. Came in, started his shift, then the poor bugger collapsed and was rushed to A&E with his appendix on the point of bursting. He'd been complaining for a few days of having gut ache but I thought he was winding me up. I'm covering the graveyard shift then Kev's relieving me at seven, so I might still have time to get to the airport. If not, I might be needing the services of a good divorce lawyer, if you know of one.

'Anyway, what are you doing awake at this ungodly hour? Why aren't you sleeping the sleep of the righteous while you can?'

'I heard the sirens. Wondered if it was anything for us. Is it, do you know?'

'As far as I know at the moment it's just a derelict property gone up in smoke. Fire Service are attending, but it's off the main road so they've not even requested help with road closures or diversions or anything. So I'd say no, at the moment, nothing for the pay-grade of a mighty Detective Chief Inspector. Go back to sleep while you can – you lucky bastard. I'll let you know if anything changes. Although god knows why you think they gave you a DI and two DSs on your team, if you insist on doing everything yourself.'

Ted smiled to himself as he ended the call. She was right, he knew. His job these days as DCI was largely management and admin. But he missed the hands-on, front-line action. He was drawn to it. He decided to take a drive past the scene of the fire on his way in later. Irene had given him the exact location and it was not much of a detour. It left him with a couple of hours to kill before there was any point in doing that. He decided to put his sweats on and go for a run for an hour or so round the nearby recreation ground. That should clear his head in time for the meetings which lay ahead.

The fire was well under control when Ted arrived. Fire-fighters were already packing up one of the appliances, getting ready to leave the scene. Ted approached the nearest person, his ID in his hand.

'Who's OIC here, please?' Ted asked him.

The officer glanced at Ted's card then looked around.

'George is. Over there, in the white helmet.'

Ted went over to introduce himself to the officer in charge. He knew the man by sight but no more. The Watch Commander looked from Ted's details to him in surprise.

'A DCI already? Blimey. Are you lot gifted with second sight? I was just about to call it in to flag it up as suspicious.'

'I don't live very far from here and it's barely out of my way. I heard the sirens, so I thought I'd drive by and see what's what. Any casualties?'

'Luckily no, it's an empty building. Not even any squatters, although it's not secure.'

'But you suspect arson?'

'Way too early to be certain of anything. But I've seen plenty of fires and more than my fair share of deliberate ones. Do you know much about arsonists, Ted?'

Ted shook his head. 'I've only come across a handful so far.'

'They're an interesting breed. Often very intelligent and highly manipulative. I'm sure you've heard that they love to revisit the scene of their crimes. They'll often stand and chat to fire crews, although we haven't seen anyone here this morning. Another thing I can't yet confirm, but I suspect the fire was set to start after the perpetrator had left the scene.'

'And one more thing that's not uncommon with them is they will often have their own MO. An individual signature way of starting a fire. It will be very distinctive, when you know what you're looking for. Unique, too.

'Like I said, it's far too soon for certainties. The Fire Investigation Officer is on his way and I've already raised with him the possible need for a fire dog, once the scene is safe for them to work in. They can quickly pinpoint the source of the blaze, indicate various patterns we'd expect to find in arson cases. That would confirm my early suspicions.

'Now, my brother Eddie is also in the service. We're a right old pair of boring buggers. When blokes get together for a drink or a meal out, they usually talk football. Or politics. That sort of thing. Me and Eddie, we swap fire stories. He's up in Preston. I remember him telling me about an arsonist on his patch who left distinctive doughnut patterns with his starting methods. Very precise and specific sizing. Almost as if it was carefully measured out. That's what I think I see inside that building, but it's up to the Investigation Officer to take it from here. We're clearing the scene now ready for them to come in and work.'

'So you think it's the same arsonist, changing his patch?'

'That would be the logical conclusion to draw, wouldn't it? Except that, as far as I know – and it's not long ago that me and Eddie were discussing this – his arsonist is still inside serving a very long stretch for a fire which took the lives of a family of four.'

It was nearly the weekend. Ted's team were restless at the start of morning briefing. They'd had a hard couple of weeks and those not working over the weekend were looking forward to a break. Knife crime was on the rise. It seemed they'd no sooner finished with one incident and the associated paperwork than there was another young person wounded and bleeding.

Luckily, to date, although there were serious injuries, there hadn't been a knife-related fatality.

Ted was attending the briefing so he could update on the possibility of an arson case to open. At least it felt like proper policing before he left for the Headquarters building at Central Park with both of his immediate bosses, Superintendents Debra Caldwell and Jim Baker.

Ted's DI, Jo Rodriguez, was in charge of the briefing so Ted left him to it to get things started. He noticed that one of the team members, DC Virgil Tibbs, was absent. Jo began by explaining the reason.

'I got an early call, boss. A severed leg found. All wrapped up in bin liners. It had been in the river but got caught up on some tree roots. A jogger out for a morning run spotted it and phoned in. The roots had torn some of the wrapping, so he could see part of a foot sticking out.

'I sent Virgil because he lives nearest to where it was found. He called to update me from the scene and he's on his way back in for now. The limb's gone off for forensic examination, so of course we don't know at the moment what sort of a crime we're looking at. But there's clearly a crime of some sort. You can't just accidentally throw out a severed limb with the household waste.'

On cue, the office door opened and Virgil came in. Always the joker of the team, he risked saying, 'I legged it back here as fast as I could, boss. Whoever dumped the limb seemed to have hopped it before I got there.'

DC Jezza Vine gave a snort of laughter which she quickly disguised as a cough. Ted was a good boss but he did expect his officers to show respect at all times. Jokes in dubious taste were always pushing the boundaries in his presence.

'All right, everyone, settle down. Whatever happened behind this incident, the limb is part of a person and that deserves a bit of respect. First job involves trawling through any and all CCTV right along the river, and the approaches to it, if there is any, for any signs of anyone dumping something suspicious. And you get that job, Virgil,' Ted told him.

'Yes, boss,' Virgil responded meekly, then went on, 'Anyway, from what I could see of it, the limb was reasonably fresh and seemed to have been cut off with some sort of a power tool, I would say. It looked to me like it could have been a man's leg but all the toe nails had fresh nail varnish on them. Bright red.'

DC Maurice Brown started to speak. 'Daddy Hen' had a heart of gold but was always lacking in the tact department. 'So does that mean it belonged to a ...'

'Maurice, engage brain very carefully in gear before going any further,' Ted cautioned him. 'It means nothing until we have more information to go on. And if my memory serves me right, I recall you turning up to work with purple sparkly nail varnish on your fingernails one time.'

'Aye, boss, but I'd been playing princesses with the twins and couldn't find any of that remover stuff ... Oh, I see what you mean. That could have been my leg in the Mersey if my ex had carried out some of her threats of what she wanted to do to me.'

That brought a general ripple of amusement. Even Ted had to smile. He was going to have to leave them to it shortly to set off for his meetings, leaving Jo in charge, but he needed to say his piece before he left.

'I've also got a possible case for us. There was a fire not far from where I live this morning, early. I spoke to the officer in charge and he's flagging it up as a likely arson. We're quiet enough at the moment,' he looked to Jo for confirmation as he said it.

Jo signalled his agreement so Ted continued, 'So we might as well make an early start on both potential cases. If it turns out that either or both of them isn't for us, then we can write it off as useful training. Starting with finding out what offences are involved in disposing of human body parts in a public place. Not something I could quote off the top of my head. Jezza, that's one for you as you clearly find it amusing.'

'Yes, boss.' Jezza gave him her sweetest smile then switched into serious mode as she asked, 'By the way, is there any news from Spain yet, speaking of remains? Any ID on all of the victims found under the swimming pool?'

Ted and Jezza had been out to Spain just before Christmas on a historical case involving a paedophile ring. It had been a harrowing one for both of them, which had brought them closer together.

'I've been in regular contact with DI Balewa and DS Reid since we got back. They've been out there most of the time, apart from a quick trip back to catch up. In fact, I spoke to Josie this morning, before I went to the fire scene.

'Not all of the remains found by the Victim Recovery Dogs have been identified yet. But it has now been officially confirmed that one of them was little Storm Moonchild. Although she disappeared from Josie's patch up in Bury, the discovery of her body and the circumstances around it mean that the case belongs to the Met, as part of their whole historic child abuse investigations. But at least it brings closure of a sort, now she's been formally identified.'

All the team members were quiet for a moment. Although it wasn't their case, they'd all been affected by what Ted had told them about it. Especially the discovery of children's bodies buried under the foundations of a swimming pool. Children who had appeared in extreme porn films found on the property, sometimes with their deaths recorded on film.

The silence was interrupted by DS Mike Hallam's desk phone ringing. He answered it quietly and listened, making notes, asking the occasional question. When he ended the call, he looked up to report on its contents.

'Right, another severed body part found. On the other side of town from where the leg was discovered. A hand and forearm. Parcelled up in the same way, in bin bags, but found stuffed into bushes on the edge of a park this time.'

'Boss, do random bits of body like this need a post-mortem, like a complete corpse would?' Jezza asked. 'And will that need to be done by a Home Office pathologist, in case it does turn out to be a murder case?'

'Another nice bit of legal research for you, Jezza,' Ted told her. He knew the answer but it was good training to let Jezza find out for herself.

'We'll need CCTV checking for the new dump site as well now,' Jo told them. 'Steve, you and Maurice can help on that one. Let's see if we can't get a lead on what's going on, preferably before any more bits of body turn up. '

'Any nail varnish on the fingers, Mike?' Ted asked. 'That might help us establish a link between the parts. I'm hoping we're just dealing with one body here. That's bad enough. I don't want to think we have more than one dismembered body to come to light.'

'Impossible to say, boss,' Mike told him. 'The hand was missing all its fingers and the thumb. Initial reports from the site say they look to have been removed with something like a pair of heavy-duty bolt cutters. Whoever the poor victim was, let's hope that was done when they were already dead.'

Chapter Two

'So you're saying there's a possibility of a copycat arsonist on our patch?' Superintendent Debra Caldwell asked Ted. The car in which they were travelling was winding its way through traffic, heading for the M60 and Central Park, the force headquarters.

They were going in Jim Baker's official car. He had a driver for the occasion so the three of them could work on the way, going over figures they would be presenting at the various meetings. Ted had taken the opportunity of having both his bosses in one place to flag up the news of what was probably an arson case.

Ted, in the front passenger seat, opened his mouth to reply to her question but Jim Baker was ahead of him.

'Of course the other bloody possibility is that someone cocked up the first case and the wrong person is inside doing time for crimes they're innocent of. If that turns out to be what's happened, you might find yourself doing the digging into what went on there, Ted. Now you've shown yourself to be rather good at that sort of thing.'

'I don't know anything for sure yet, but the OIC said he should be able to let me know within about twenty-four hours. Once the Investigation Officer has been in, and the fire dog, if he decides to call for one.

'It's several years since the arsonist with the same MO was sent down and we've not so far heard of anything with a similar signature. Steve's running a check on that. I don't want to start getting ahead of myself but that did make me wonder if it was someone who'd been inside with the original arsonist, learned about his methods and decided to try it for himself when he got out.'

Once on to the motorway, the traffic was more fluid so they made good time. Knife crime was one of the subjects on the agenda for the day's meetings. Ted had spent some time before the morning briefing updating his figures to reflect the week's cases and to include yet another incident from the previous night. The statistics made grim reading.

The force's Assistant Chief Constable (Crime), Russell Evans, was chairing the proceedings for much of the day. As soon as he saw Ted arriving with Jim and Debs, he made his way over to them.

'Ted, you and I need to find time to talk at some point today. Debs and Jim too, probably. There's the usual indifferent buffet on for lunch so we can find a quiet corner to get together before that. I'll come and find you.'

With that, he was gone, working the room, greeting people, catching up with news, before it was time to call the first session to order.

Jim Baker and Debra Caldwell were both much taller than Ted. They turned inquisitive looks towards him which inevitably meant they were looking down at him. It gave him an uncomfortable flashback to his school days. Doggedly standing his ground, chin lifted in defiance, as one teacher or another was reading him the riot act when he believed he was in the right.

'What's that all about?' Jim Baker rumbled. 'It sounded ominous. What have you been up to?'

'I genuinely can't think of anything I've done or not done that the ACC would have heard about.'

Ted found himself distracted for the rest of the morning, wondering what Evans wanted to talk to him about. It left him not paying as much attention as he normally would to the proceedings.

'Right, Ted, this only came to my attention this morning, although I saw your report at the time, of course. I'm guessing you've not seen it yet.'

The ACC handed printouts to each of them. The first session had finished and they'd adjourned to another room. A long table had been laid along one wall laden with various uninspiring collections of sandwiches, limp quiche and pizza of dubious vintage.

The heading on the single page they were each given related to something called Mercado International Life and Finance. The page in question was subtitled, 'Mind the Money'.

As Ted scanned it quickly, he was shocked to see a blurred but, to him, unmistakable enlarged mobile phone shot of Trev on the terrace of the Spanish hotel where they had stayed for the case Ted had been on. It was clear from his posture that Trev was gyrating wildly with DI Josie Balewa, who had both hands on his hips, low down.

'Only hours after a joint operation between Europol, Spanish, and British police had uncovered the bodies of several abused children, two detectives on the case were partying the night away at a nearby hotel. One of them, a Detective Chief Inspector from Greater Manchester police, Ted Darling, had flown his husband out to Spain to join him, a source told *Mind the Money*. His husband, a civilian with no police connection, also took part in a raid on an armed suspect's house, which resulted in several arrests. The husband is pictured here dancing with a second GMP officer, DI Josie Balewa, from Bury.'

Jim Baker flapped the page in his hand and said, 'Well, this is a load of old bollocks and a total non-story, Russell. I knew about Trev being out there. He was acting as unofficial interpreter until the liaison officer got there.'

'Boss, thanks, but that's not quite accurate,' Ted told him, then addressed the ACC. 'Sir, I didn't know myself that Trev was coming over. He turned up out of the blue on the Saturday and I didn't tell Jim until the Monday. I should have informed him earlier, of course.

'Once DC Vine and I had finished what we went out there to do, we happened by chance on the other suspect, Ian Maxwell. When I realised the risks involved, I immediately sent DC Vine back, so Trev was worried about how I would manage without an interpreter.'

'But did Trev go on the raid?' Evans pressed him.

'Not strictly speaking,' Ted was trying not to be evasive, but all too aware of what it sounded like. 'He drove me there because it was his insurance details on the hire car, not mine. I didn't go with Josie and Jock Reid because I knew they'd be staying longer than I needed to. But Trev stayed in the vehicle, away from the action, at all times.'

Superintendent Caldwell, the Ice Queen, was still scan-reading the article.

'I don't understand why this has appeared. It seems to be some sort of internet scandal sheet making allegations of financial irregularities. Largely unsubstantiated, if this article is representative. So why is this even of interest to them?'

'The Press Office picked up on it. They have alerts set up for anything which may be relevant or of concern to us. Of itself, it's something and nothing. The only worry is if, for any reason, it gets seen and picked up by any of the nationals and turned into some sort of "Dodgy cop partying in Spain at the taxpayers' expense" sort of nonsense. You know how much the gutter press like to turn on the police at the least opportunity. Especially on a big case.

'Our people have dug into the site and the person behind it. It's some Brit ex-pat, operating out of Gibraltar, who publishes this pile of crap, supposedly to warn people away from investing in dodgy property deals and finance. Ironic, since both he and his chums offer exactly that. He apparently hosts property exhibitions where people can go and snap up their future home in the sun. He claims to vet anyone dodgy and not only to refuse them exhibition space but to publish some salacious report about them. Warning people off. He's as slippery as an eel. No one's yet managed to sue him successfully for libel, so he keeps on going.

'We're assuming he must have had a tip-off from the hotel about police presence there in connection with the raid.'

He looked to Ted for confirmation as he spoke. Ted nodded, remembering how Trev had told one of the hotel staff that he was Ted's husband. Ted's name would have been on the hotel records, as would both Josie's and Jock Reid's, in all probability. A staff member might have seen the possibility of making some money on the side by selling the information.

'Ted, you're usually sharper than this. Letting your Trevor go anywhere near the scene of the raid was always a risk. I wish you'd got a lift with someone and walked back or got Trev to drop you off and pick you up well away from the action. But it is what it is. The Press Office advice is to say nothing unless and until it goes any further than this, then consider our options carefully.'

'Sir, I only billed the Met for the agreed nights in the hotel. Because it was my decision to stay on, I paid for the rest of the time myself. Delaying my flight cost nothing because it was a flexible booking, and Trev paid for his own flights, car hire and fuel. Like I said, I didn't know he planned on coming over or I would have told him not to. But his presence there was in no way at the public expense and I can prove that, should it be necessary.'

'I hope it won't come to having to justify anything but let me have the paperwork, just in case. I wish idiots like this bloke – what does he call himself, David Mercado?' the ACC jabbed an angry finger at the byline on the article, 'would realise that officers are entitled to some down-time, especially on a case like this one. And god knows, Josie deserves to let her hair down more than most, with what she's been through in her lifetime.

'Let's hope this is the last of it and no one picks up on this load of old rubbish. You don't need me to tell you, Ted, that if anyone tries to contact you directly about this, you don't speak to them at all, other than to refer them to the Press Office. Let's all just keep our fingers crossed in the meantime.'

The mop, meticulously wrung out to avoid streaks, glided slowly and rhythmically the width of the long corridor as the man worked.

Left to right. Then a precisely executed circle.

Right to left. Another circle.

Then back into the bucket to rinse and start again.

All the time the prisoner worked, he kept up a low humming to himself. A Sixties country classic. Just the chorus and the short brass refrain. Repeated over and over, on an endless loop.

There was nothing distinctive about the man. The sort easily forgotten. He looked to be in his forties or thereabouts. His colouring was bland. Mousy hair, thinning on top. Hard to describe. Easy to overlook as he blended into the background.

Another man came walking down the corridor towards the mop-wielder. Thirties. Tall and gangly. The sort of stride which bounced him up and down as he walked. The sort of face which smiled at everyone. He was wearing a dog collar.

'Hello, William. Hard at work, I see,' he greeted the prisoner brightly. 'And doing a first-rate job as usual. Well done. Really, jolly good job.'

The man paused in his mopping and humming. He lifted strange light grey eyes towards the priest.

'Hello, padre. Thank you. I try my best. If a job's worth doing, it's worth doing well, I've always believed.'

'That's the ticket. Absolutely so. And the chapel is certainly looking cleaner than ever with you as our Red Band.

You have just the right positive attitude. Work hard, keep your nose clean. That's the best way to survive in here. That's what will impress a parole board.

'Now, I just wanted to say that when you've finished your cleaning in the chapel after here, I wanted to talk to you about a new Listener assignment for you. A young man, Joey Barrow. His first time inside and he's utterly lost, poor lad. I've cleared it with the governor to talk to you about him. Your training and attitude is exactly what's needed to help him. He's Catholic, too, like you and me, so I feel you're the best person to reach out to him. Then I can hear your confession at the same time, as you requested.'

'I still have all of this corridor to clean first, padre. I can't finish until the job is done. But I'll certainly get permission to talk to you after I've finished the chapel. I have, as ever, many sins to confess.'

His grey gaze looked searchingly into that of the priest as he added, 'I wonder if you have, too.'

It was late when Jim Baker's driver dropped Ted and the Ice Queen off back at their own nick. The meetings had run on. And on. There were plenty of grievances to be aired. Constant pressure to improve clean-up statistics with ever-dwindling resources.

The ACC had listened to his officers and allowed them time to express their feelings. Things were bad enough without them believing they were not being given an audience by the top brass. He'd at least done them the courtesy of hearing them out and promising to do what he could, although he warned them it might not be much.

Both Ted and the Super headed for their respective offices before they could even think about going home. Ted had sent a swift text to Trev to say he was likely to be late. Again. If Trev wasn't used to it by now, there was no hope for them.

Ted found a note from Jo on his desk but no signs of any of

the team still at work. The note said, 'Another bit of body. Upper arm this time. Phone me for an update when you get back.'

All Ted really wanted to do was to clear his desk as soon as he could, go home, change out of his suit and relax. Instead he got his phone out to call Jo.

'How did your day go?' Jo asked him to begin with.

'No change. The usual tune. Get better results with fewer resources. So tell me more about our mystery body parts.'

'The latest was just the upper arm, sectioned at the shoulder and the elbow joint. It was found in a skip, roughly halfway between where the other two bits were dumped. A site that's had some recent development on it, hence the skip. Someone was rummaging for anything useful and played the honest citizen by letting us know what they'd found.

'We've been trawling Mispers for any likely matches, although we really haven't got much to go on. No obliging tattoos or anything else distinctive on any of the bits uncovered so far. Nothing showing up on CCTV of anyone dumping black bin bags of anything, let alone body parts, for the first two. And no CCTV near this latest dump site.

'We don't yet know for sure whether the remains are male or female. Professor Nelson's taking an interest herself now, though. She says it will make a fascinating case study for her forensic pathology students. So that's all to the good for us.

'Oh, and the fire officer from this morning phoned for you. He said to tell you the investigation officer is also pretty sure the blaze was an arson. They've had the dog in today and the handler and dog will be working over the weekend, so he'll update you on Monday, hopefully.'

Ted's good intentions of clearing his desk abandoned him. He'd been planning to come in at some point over the weekend. He decided things could wait until then. He sent Trev another text to say he was on his way. He was in need of some good hot food after the offerings at lunchtime.

'You look shattered. Hard day?'

Trev was in the kitchen, preparing the meal, when Ted arrived back after the short drive from the station. Trev paused to hug his partner as he was taking off his jacket and pulling off his tie, fending off young Adam who immediately vied for his attention.

'Long meetings. Not much progress. And this, which the ACC dumped on me.'

Ted pulled the computer printout from his pocket and handed it to him. Trev started to read it, then looked at him in horror.

'Oh, god, Ted, I'm so sorry. I've screwed things up for you and that was never my intention.'

'With any luck it will be a five-minute wonder which no mainstream press takes up and I can forget all about it in a day or two. But in the meantime, I need to furnish the ACC with proof that your presence there wasn't funded in any way by the public purse. I've got the hotel receipts from what I paid, but I'm going to need your credit card statements to show you paid for your own flight and the hire car.'

'Oops.' Trev looked guilty. 'I was rather hoping to hide those from you until I'd got things a bit more under control.'

Chapter Three

'Another bit of a body found late on Saturday. An upper leg this time, from hip to knee. Dumped in a stream on the opposite side of town and once again, it floated up to the surface where it was spotted by a passing jogger,' Jo told the team first thing on Monday morning, for the benefit of those who weren't yet up to date with the latest development in the case.

'Apologies to those of a delicate nature, especially so soon after breakfast. But the reason the jogger spotted it as possibly being of interest was that something had torn the bin bag wrappings open and had made a start on the limb inside. We don't yet know what but possibly a stray dog, or foxes. Maybe even rats.'

'Anything from pathology yet?' Ted asked him. 'Any further forward with identifying features? Do we at least know the gender?'

Jo shook his head. 'I imagine it's been a bit like a jigsaw puzzle for them, getting it a bit at a time. And with the weekend intervening, I doubt we'll get that for a day or two yet.

'The only early indicator we've got is that it appears the body parts had been kept in a domestic deep freeze before being dumped. And once again, it looks as if this latest part was removed using some sort of a power saw. Professor Nelson has promised she's going to give it her full attention today, while she's got some students with her, so we might know more by end of play.'

They were in the main office. Jo had put up a map of their area with the body part dump sites to date marked on it. They were wide spread.

'And before you ask, boss, no. No sign of any witnesses, nothing suspicious on camera in the immediate area. So we're still pretty much in the dark. And so far, trawling through missing persons isn't helping us a lot without a definite confirmation of sex or approximate age. Not even size or build at the moment, although I imagine that with a full leg now, it might bring a clue as to height. Always supposing the limbs are all from the same body.'

'Of course, for the two found in water, they could have been thrown in anywhere upstream and floated down to where they were found,' Mike Hallam pointed out. 'They weren't weighted down with anything. Just wrapped and dumped.'

'Theories, anyone, please?' Ted asked, looking at the map. 'Even far-fetched ones, as they may be all we have at the moment.'

'Has to be a murder, surely, boss?' DS Rob O'Connell began. 'If it was natural or accidental, would anyone go to this much trouble to dispose of a body?'

'They might if they felt guilty about it,' Jezza suggested. 'Or if they were convinced that they would be considered as a suspect and weren't sure if they could prove their innocence.'

'Sir,' DC Steve Ellis began, hesitant as ever. 'I know it's too soon to tell for sure, with only four parts for now. But three on Friday, one on Saturday, none yesterday. Someone who works, but not on Sundays, disposing of them on their way to and from work?'

'But look at the spread pattern, Steve,' Virgil told him. 'A bit far-flung.'

Steve was turning pink, as he often did, but was sticking to his guns. 'Yes, but think about the probable tools involved here. Power saw and bolt cutters. That could be someone doing some sort of site maintenance, which would involve them travelling from place to place.'

Ted nodded approvingly. 'Very good point, Steve. None of it gets us very much further for the time being but that's definitely something to keep in mind.'

Ted let Jo wrap up the briefing then spoke again.

'Last Friday's fire is now confirmed as an arson, so we will be involved. No casualties, thankfully. But it could potentially be an interesting one. The Watch Commander I spoke to on the scene is coming in this morning, with the Fire Investigation Officer, to talk us through what they know so far. He's also bringing video footage of the fire dog working, to give us more idea of how their investigation is run. They'll be here at ten and we'll use the briefing room. Inspector Turner and some of his officers from Uniform will be joining us.'

Ted's desk phone was ringing when he went back into his own office. He'd muted his mobile for the briefing. Glancing at it as he headed for his desk, he saw there was a missed call from Professor Nelson, the forensic pathologist. Hopefully she had an update for him.

'Edwin, what an utterly fascinating case you've presented us with,' she began breezily, with no preamble. 'It's going to be an intriguing one for my latest little clutch of students.'

'Morning, Bizzie, glad to hear it. By any chance are you phoning with any information for me? I know it's early days but we've not a lot to get started with at the moment.'

'I was principally phoning to say I do hope you and Trevor will come to our handfasting. Douglas and I have decided it's about time we did something a bit more formal. He practically lives at my house now. I'll be sending out invitations shortly, of course, and I do understand that your job means you can never be sure. But I'd be delighted to have you both there.'

'I'm sure Trev would love to be there and I'll certainly do my very best,' Ted assured her, reluctant to admit that he wasn't quite sure what he was being invited to. He hoped Trev would know more than he did.

'Excellent! It really would mean a great deal to me. I've come to look on you both as good friends.

'Now, to the gruesome bits, so I hope you're not munching on a bacon roll or anything. I think initial reports suggested that the dismemberment was carried out with some sort of a power saw to take off the larger limbs, then something like bolt cutters to amputate the fingers, which I gather haven't been found yet.

'Based on what I've seen so far, I'm not convinced those are the correct implements, but I need to do some experiments to be sure. That's where my young students get to help with the exciting bits.

'Basically, under the very strictest supervision, they will be allowed to play about with trying to reproduce the wounds using various implements. But – and here's where I'm going to stick my neck out somewhat – I have an inkling already.

'I'm not a gambler, but if I was I would be going for a chainsaw and tree loppers. And if that's the case, the very good news is that we might be able to get something further for you to work from. With any luck, we may find microscopic traces of trees and other vegetation lodged in the wounds, left behind by those tools. And with the amount of science now available to us, we might even be able to identify the species of trees or shrubs those traces came from.

'Then if by any stroke of good fortune they were anything at all unusual, they might just give us a geographical pinpoint for where the tools had been used. Now that could potentially be of great help to you, I would imagine. But don't get your hopes up too high, too soon. All of that is going to require some specialised research, which may well take some time.'

'Right, everyone, my name's George Martin. I was Officer in Charge at Friday's fire. This here is the Fire Investigation Officer, Hugh Parry. We're here to explain to you the ins and outs of why we know this was an arson, as well as why it looks like it's going to be an interesting one. Hugh.'

'First off, apologies if I'm teaching my grannies to suck eggs, but I'm going to assume none of you knows everything there is to know about arson. So I'll explain on that basis. As George said, this is an interesting case for a number of reasons. I'm going to be showing you video footage of the fire scene, which we can now confidently call a crime scene. In particular, you'll see Fire Dog Ellie at work with her handler, Matt.

'We use specially-trained dogs who can find traces of flammable liquid, which helps us to pinpoint exactly where the fire started. Because said liquids continue to evaporate after the fire is out, we try to get the dog in as soon as it's safe for it to work, and certainly within the first twenty-four hours.

'The usual sequence of events is that as soon as the fire is out and the Stop message has been sent back to Control, the FIO – me, in this case – goes in for a first look. Sometimes it's fairly obvious from early on when a fire has been set deliberately. If you look at the screen, you can see what jumped out at George right away, and at me as soon as I got there.

'This was an old building; a former warehouse. A lot of timber about, not all of it in the best condition. Downstairs, which was the source of the fire, you can clearly see a curve pattern on the floor. Like part of a circle. The edge of a doughnut, if you like. Keep that thought in mind. It's significant.

'This was on a bare wooden floor so the pattern showed up far more. If there'd been carpeting down, especially synthetic fibre, that tends to melt and mask the pattern. The carpeting can actually create false pool burns which can confuse inexperienced eyes.'

The man paused and looked at Ted. 'Is this all right? Not too basic and too much of an information dump for you?'

'Interesting and vital,' Ted assured him. 'If we're going

after an arsonist, we need as much information on their methods as you can give us. Please carry on.'

'Right, so here's the footage of Ellie working the scene, once all the crew have been withdrawn. She gets a free run with no distractions and she will indicate on any accessible flammable liquid traces. If there are traces she can't get at, she'll show heightened interest in those areas. You'll see she's wearing special boots to protect her from anything like broken glass, and any hot spots.

'Once she's done her initial search, we can start excavating the site to see what's uncovered, and the dog will come back at various points to search further.

'This fire took hold quite quickly because of various broken windows which gave a good air entry. In fact one of the windows on the ground floor was wide open, which we suspect is how the perpetrator got in. And out again. But we responded fast and got control of it early on.

'Watch the way the dog is working. Some of the cross members in the ceiling came down, but you can see that she's basically working in a circle rather than any random kind of a pattern. That becomes significant later on in the video. After she'd done all her initial searches, we started to clear some of the fallen timber from where she was indicating then let her search again.'

The dog they were watching was a black Labrador, clearly enjoying her work from the way her tail was threshing as she searched. The FIO explained that she was working off her own initiative and would later be redeployed with more targeted searches.

'You'll probably remember from your school science lessons that it's the vapour which burns, not the liquid itself, so the dog can still find traces of that.

'Jumping forward slightly here, you can see the dog searching again after the fallen timber has been cleared. Now you can see very clearly that she is following a perfect circle. I can tell you, because I measured it, that it had a diameter of exactly one old-fashioned yard. Three feet precisely.'

'Ring of Fire,' Jezza said, half to herself.

When several pairs of eyes turned her way, she gave one of her characteristic shrugs and said, 'Sorry, it just gave me an earworm. The Johnny Cash song. Probably no significance at all. I'll shut up now.'

'It is significant, to a degree. I'll come on to that. Not only a perfect circle, which would indeed cause a ring of fire, but an extra dollop of flammable liquid at each of the four cardinal points. Very precisely done. I checked with a compass.

'Dollop is a technical term we Fire Officers like to employ,' he added with a smile.

'So what flammable liquid are we talking about? Petrol?' Jo asked. 'Sorry if that's an idiot question but this is actually the first arson case that's come my way.'

'A good question, and one we're often asked. It's a good sign because it shows I haven't yet sent you to sleep. Generally, arsonists favour a heavier liquid than petrol. Paraffin, white spirit, that sort of thing. A diesel/petrol mix is quite popular and effective and again, significant in this case. Potentially. It used to be possible to trace the exact type of fuel with petrol branding, but those days are gone now, unfortunately.

'So now you're probably going to want to know how the fire was started and why we see a link between it and the historic one for which someone is serving time. And he is still inside, we checked. And as George was able to spot that link early on, I'll hand back to him.'

All the officers present were listening attentively. Arson was not all that uncommon. Fires which took lives, especially. It had the benefit, as a murder method, of being a contactless crime. A way of getting revenge on a victim whilst remaining at a safe distance.

'Thanks, Hugh. And this is where it gets really interesting, in terms of a possible, yet seemingly impossible, link to the older crime for which, as Hugh said, the perpetrator is still serving time.

'On screen now is the man we're talking about. William Warren. Aged forty-two. He taught science at a comprehensive school near where he lived. Currently serving life with a recommended minimum of fifteen years. He's done seven years so far. He has always denied being guilty of the crime. The jury couldn't agree but in the end he was convicted on a majority verdict. He's made a few attempts to appeal but not successfully. Insufficient grounds. I won't go into all of that here as that's something you can do yourselves.

'Those dollops Hugh mentioned are significant here, because that's something which was never disclosed in public. So that tends to suggest that Warren has been talking to someone about his MO. That's unlikely, as arsonists tend to be proud of their signature and keep it to themselves. Even if Warren wasn't guilty, he could still pass that information on because he would have seen it through disclosure to his legal team.

'The other possibility, of course, is that someone other than him started the blaze he's doing time for.

'Remember we're talking here about a fire which killed four people. Mother, father and two teenage boys. Both pupils at the school where Warren taught, and he'd apparently had a run-in with both of them. Not just at school but near his home as they lived not very far apart.

'On the occasion of that fatal fire, it was started by a method which was quite common in the Seventies. Particularly in Ulster, for example. A box of matches with a smouldering cigarette in it. That gives the arsonist a good few minutes to have left the site before the cigarette burns down far enough to ignite the matches and set off the fire.

'Any smokers amongst you?'

There was a pause then Jo raised a hand, looking sheepish.

'Promise not to tell the wife, but I have been known to have the odd small cigar. She thinks I gave up years ago.'

George laughed. 'Your secret is safe with me. And for the purposes of this case, we're only interested in cigarettes. An EU directive aimed at reducing the number of fatal fires caused by smouldering cigarettes, particularly with people smoking in bed and nodding off, means that method is no longer effective. Normally.

'Cigarettes now are what's called RIP – reduced ignition propensity. That means that you have to keep taking a drag to keep them burning. Once you stop smoking them, they go out.

'Now we get to the part which sounds as if it belongs in some very dodgy fiction book.

'As has been said, it's the vapour which burns, not the liquid. Our arsonist set his matches and cigarette timer on the floor close to the open window. Presumably to make sure he would have a quick getaway if it went up before he intended it to. When the matches ignited, it's likely they caused a vapour deflagration resulting in a rapid spread of fire at higher level. This meant that in this case, the matchbox on the floor burned much less efficiently, eventually smouldering and going out.'

He reached into his pocket to pull out something in an evidence bag which he held aloft.

'All of which means that a portion of the cigarette remained intact. You can see the breaks in the paper of RIP cigarettes. This has none, which suggests to me it could well be a cheap knock-off brand imported from somewhere not compliant with EU safety standards.

'The best news of all, as far as the investigation goes, is that, with a bit of luck, the arsonist's DNA is on this fag end from where he put it in his mouth to light it.'

Chapter Four

Inspector Kevin Turner went upstairs to Ted's office as they were both getting ready to knock off at the end of the day. Ted's first thought was that he might be going to suggest they go for a drink together, as they sometimes did.

Instead, Kev began with a wide grin, 'I thought you might need a hand with your body parts case. I can't give you one, but I can offer you most of a second arm.'

Ted groaned in mock despair. 'I've already had to jerk Virgil and Jezza's chains for jokes in bad taste at the expense of whoever the poor victim is.'

'It's just a bit of 'armless fun, Ted. Anyway, I've been working on that gag for ten minutes since I got the call, but I didn't want to try it out with anyone else present. This time the arm was amputated at the elbow and it's just the upper arm that's been found. Same as the others, wrapped in bin bags, chucked in the water again. In a canal lock this time, up past Marple.'

'Any news yet about gender from forensics?'

'I was hoping to hear something today but nothing so far. They're probably backed up from the weekend but we might get a result tomorrow. It's slowing up searching through Mispers, until we know what gender it is we're looking for.'

'I know it's occurred to you as it has to me, but we're going to need reinforcements if we've got this arson case and now a possible murder enquiry with no ID. When is it Maurice starts his parental leave?'

'The twins are due at the end of the week, so he's booked it to start then. I just hope they don't keep him waiting. And you're right about needing extra officers. I've asked to talk to Jim and Debs tomorrow and I'd value your input.'

'I think we can both predict the outcome, in the shape of a big fat no. But we might as well try. Right, let's both run for it now before there's another major incident,' Kev told him, then laughed as a phone in the main office started to ring. Ted was the only one still in.

'You bugger, you made that happen,' Ted laughed as he went through to answer it.

'A caller asking for the Chief Inspector. I'm afraid I didn't quite catch the name, although I asked him to repeat it. Mr Mac-something, I think.'

'Serious Crime,' Ted said, his tone neutral, as the call was put through.

A man's voice with a slightly nasal intonation and an accent Ted couldn't place spoke in his ear.

'I want to speak to DCI Darling. My name's David Mercado. I write ...'

'I'm DCI Darling. I know who you are and what you do, Mr Mercado, and I have nothing at all to say to you. The correct procedure is for you to phone our Press Office at Central Park, as I'm sure you're aware. You'll find the number on the website ...'

'It might be in your best interests if you spoke to me directly, Mr Darling.'

Ted's voice was always quiet, polite, measured. Now his tone turned glacial.

'Are you threatening me in some way, Mr Mercado? I wouldn't recommend you do that.'

Mercado tried to cut in to say something but Ted wished him good evening and put the phone down. Hard.

Then he did something he hadn't done for some time. He went back to his office and kicked seven bells out of his waste-paper basket until it was a mangled wreck. After that, to save her the hassle, Ted pre-empted the reproachful note from his long-term cleaning lady by writing one of his own and leaving it in the middle of his desk for her to see.

'Mrs Skinner. Sorry. It was either the basket or me on an assault charge. Please sort out a replacement and I'll pay for it. Thank you.'

Trev was laying the table in the kitchen when Ted got home. He'd sent a text ahead to let his partner know he should arrive back in time to eat something. Trev gave him a brief hug then went to start putting the meal together.

'I sorted out my credit card statements for you. They're a bit scary, but I promise to get things back on an even keel as soon as I can. First, though, I wanted to ask if you would mind if I take Eirian away for a few days over half term.'

'Eirian?' Ted queried, stooping to stroke each of the cats in turn, although Adam was at the front of the queue as usual.

'Ted, you are hopeless sometimes,' Trev rolled his eyes theatrically. 'I did tell you, but you clearly weren't listening. Shewee doesn't like her nickname any more and as she currently hates her mother more than usual, she doesn't want to use her Irish name, Siobhan. Like me, she has an Irish name and a Welsh one. So as she currently hates her father slightly less than her mother, she's now using the Welsh one. Eirian.'

Despite sharing the same parents as his sister, Trev refused to acknowledge them as such if he could avoid it. The bitterness he felt at having been disowned by them when he came out ran too deep.

'Sorry, you did say and I forgot. Of course I don't mind, but when is half term? Is it near Valentine's Day? Only I'm always letting you down and promising to make it up to you. So I thought I'd book that day off. It's on a Saturday this year so we could perhaps even have a weekend away somewhere, if you like.'

'That would be perfect. Half-term starts on the Monday and we can't go before then because Eirian is competing at the weekend.' Trev's face fell for a minute as he went on, 'I had promised to go and watch her, then take her to Paris. And don't look like that. It will be a budget trip. Laurence has a flat there which we can use so we won't have hotel bills to pay or anything.'

'Will Laurence be there?' Ted asked, trying to sound casual.

Trev laughed, giving Ted's hand a squeeze as he sat down at the table, putting food in front of each of them.

'I do love it when you get jealous. You have remembered that Laurence is female? And that even if she wasn't and was the fittest bloke in the world, I wouldn't be interested. Anyway, she won't be there until the Friday and we're planning to fly back on the Saturday, to get Eirian back to school.'

'I don't know why you even put up with me, when I forget what you tell me from one day to the next. Look, here's an idea. Why don't we both go down to the West Country for that weekend? Spend time together in the evening and in the day time we can go and watch She … Eirian competing. As long as we get some quality time together over a nice meal, there's no reason why we can't do both.'

'Ted, you'll be bored witless at horsey events all day. You know you will. But it's really kind of you to offer. Can you even guarantee getting the time off?'

'Irene reminded me the other day that I've got an excellent DI and two first-rate DSs. And I know I have. So there's no reason why I don't pull back occasionally and let them get on with it. I won't be bored, honestly. I may not know much about it but I like watching the horses, now I know which end is which. And you know me – I'm a people watcher. You find us somewhere nice online and I'll book it. You'd better rest your credit card, by the sound of it.'

'That's fabulous, thank you. Oh, and not long after that

half-term, I'll have to be grown-up and sensible and work longer hours. Geoff's got to go into hospital for an operation. Minor, he said, although I didn't ask the details in case it was something a bit personal. So I'll be in charge of everything at work while he's away. I've not got the definite dates yet. He's still waiting for confirmation.'

The prison officer with the group in the chapel kept glancing at her watch in anticipation. Val Johnson was looking forward to handing over to the night shift and knocking off. Which she couldn't do until all her charges were back in their respective cells and locked up for the night. She hoped her partner had the kids sorted out by the time she got back home. Homework done, clothes put ready for school the next day. She hoped, too, that there would be something to eat when she finally did get back. It seemed a long time since her last meal break and she could eat a scabby donkey by now.

It sometimes felt like she spent all day looking after kids, with the prisoners. Big ones, but still in need of constant watching. At least this lot were seldom any trouble. To even be considered as Listeners to support other prisoners they needed to be trusted and to have kept their noses clean. Warren was the only lifer amongst them and he was generally polite, well-behaved and no real trouble. The only query hanging over him was those occasional episodes of his. Even the medics couldn't say for sure which ones were genuine and which weren't, so they couldn't be ignored.

'Can you wind things up now, father, please? Only it's nearly bang-up time so we need to go.'

The chaplain glanced guiltily at his watch and said, 'I'm so sorry, Ms Johnson, I hadn't realised how late it had got. Well, thank you everyone, for your presence here this evening. And a special thanks to Mr Warren. From listening to him, I hope you all now have a much clearer idea of what is involved in taking on a Listener role for fellow inmates, and that each one of you will go ahead and become one yourself. Thank you again.'

'Right, come on, you lot, let's be having you. Line up ready to go.'

The officer was already on the radio to the control room, giving her call sign and requesting permission to move twelve prisoners from the chapel back to their wing. Control would check that corridors were clear to avoid any possible confrontations, before giving the go-ahead to make the transfer.

'You too, Warren,' she said, above the noise of the other prisoners standing up, pushing chairs back, starting to talk to one another as they shuffled towards the door. Warren had gone over to the chaplain to say a few words.

'I'm just coming, Ms Johnson. I just wanted to thank the padre ...'

'Now, Warren, and I mean it. It's not up to you to decide.'

She was speaking into her radio again, confirming with Control that they were just about to leave the chapel, her eyes on Warren and the chaplain. With the call still connected she suddenly said, half under her breath, 'Oh, bloody bollocks, Warren, not now, for god's sake.'

Warren had turned to look at her and gone rigid. Then he slowly crumpled to the floor as his knees buckled. His eyes rolled back into his head, his jaws were clenched and his body started to twitch and convulse on the wooden floor.

'Oh, fuck,' the officer said, raising a laugh from IC Comms. Then she moved rapidly to take control of the situation. 'Everyone stand still, shut up, and wait for further instructions.'

She spoke again into the radio, requesting Healthcare response for a Level One medical emergency. Then she made her way across the chapel to where Warren continued to writhe on the floor. The chaplain was hovering over him in evident panic.

'What's happening? Is he all right? Should we try to put something between his teeth in case he bites his tongue?'

'No, don't touch him, father. No physical contact. Help is on its way and should be here in minutes. If you could just move some of those chairs back a bit so he doesn't bang his head on them.

'The rest of you stay there and don't move!' she barked sternly as she saw a couple of the prisoners making to come over to them to see what was happening. She turned her attention to Warren who was still squirming and shaking on the floor. She spoke through gritted teeth, almost under her breath. 'This better be a genuine one, Warren. I won't be amused if you make me late clocking off for no good reason.'

The chaplain was bobbing about on the spot. Clearly worried. Not knowing what to do.

'Is it a seizure? Does he have epilepsy? Should I pray for him?'

Val was trying to stay calm and polite when she could happily have slapped the pair of them. Warren if, as she suspected, this was one of his Oscar-winning false attack performances. The chaplain for flapping about like a useless budgie.

'I can't discuss a prisoner's medical condition with you, father, and certainly not when there are others present. Assistance will be here very soon now, but if it would help you to pray, then please go ahead.'

'Will he know that we're here? It must be very worrying for him. Should I speak to him? Or just pray?'

'Oh, I'm sure he knows we're here, so perhaps the sound of you praying would be reassuring for a man of his faith.' Then, under her breath, 'Thank fuck for that,' as she heard the door of the chapel open and the Healthcare responder arrived, medical bag in hand, accompanied by more officers. Reinforcements were sent as routine to a Level One, in case it was a diversionary tactic for something about to happen. One of them exchanged a glance with Val.

'I thought he'd settled down. Seems a long time since the

last one. Are you good to go now?'

'Evening, father,' the medic said politely, crouching down to assess the patient. Then, to Val, he asked, 'Our friend Warren, I see. How long's he been down?'

'Less than five minutes.'

'Okay. Warren? Can you hear me? You're quite safe now. I'm just going to move you gently into a safer position, but you're fine.'

Val spoke quietly again so the other prisoners couldn't hear her.

'If you're planning on shoving Valium up his bum can I at least get the others out of here first and get off home? I've not had my tea yet and I think that sight might just rob me of my appetite.'

The other officer grinned at her. 'Yes, we're fine here. It's not the first time I've dealt with him like this. And I don't think we'll be needing the suppository.'

'I'm quite happy to stay and help in any way I can,' the chaplain told him. 'I don't know if I could be of any use, but I'd be glad to stay on and I'll do anything that's required, if you tell me what to do.'

Val straightened up, back on the radio, checking she still had clearance to move the prisoners back to their cells. By the time she'd got them all safely back in the right place and written up this little lot, it was going to be much later than she'd hoped before she got home.

Warren's convulsions were starting to diminish as the other prisoners filed out of the chapel, being shepherded back to their cells. The medic was leaning over him to monitor his condition.

'All right now, Warren. Are you back with us yet?'

Warren's eyelids flickered a few times, then opened. His eyes still looked a little bleary, unfocused.

'Do you feel you could sit up now?'

The chaplain moved swiftly, reaching out a comforting arm

towards the prisoner, moving to support him as he slowly seemed to regain his faculties and struggled to sit up.

'Best not, chaplain. No physical contact. How are you doing, Warren?'

The prisoner was looking around him, seemingly bewildered. 'What happened?'

'Nothing to worry about. Here, let me give you a hand onto your feet and we'll get you back to your bed. A good night's sleep and you should be fine. Your kecks are clean and dry, at least. Do you think you can stand up?'

Warren looked up at them plaintively. 'Could you give me a hand, please? I feel a bit woozy.'

The chaplain was hovering again, eager as a puppy to be doing something useful.

The officer nodded. 'All right, Warren. Bend your knees up so your feet are on the floor. Chaplain, you and I will take one of his arms each. Put your foot there to block his   like I'm doing, look   then on three. One. Two. Three.'

They hoisted the prisoner with no effort. The officer let go of him immediately. The chaplain kept hold of his arm for longer.

'Do you think you'll be all right to walk back to the wing now, Warren?'

'Yes, Mr Smith, I'm sure I will. Thank you. I'm sorry for the inconvenience I've caused.'

'I can come with you, if you like? If I can be of further help? It's really no trouble.'

'It's fine, chaplain, thanks. We'll be all right from here, I'm sure. Won't we, Warren? You'll need to tidy up and lock up, I imagine. Don't let us delay you.'

As the officer was collecting his bag, Warren turned back to the chaplain. 'Thank you so much for your help and kindness, padre.' Then he dropped his voice so it was barely audible as he said, 'And for the soft gentleness of your touch. As ever.'

Chapter Five

'All right, Ted? Have you got a minute?'

Ted was surprised that DC Maurice Brown was the first team member into work the next morning. Maurice had many good qualities. Punctuality was not normally one of them. Ted hoped it wasn't going to be anything serious about the impending birth of Maurice's second set of twins.

'Yes, come in, Maurice. Take a seat. What can I do for you?'

'You know Owain and Killian are due to arrive at the end of the week, and I've booked leave? Well, as soon as I can nip out and leave Megan with them for an hour or so, I was going to put some money behind the bar at The Grapes and come and join everyone for a swift one. And I got to thinking.

'Rob and Sally have been talking about getting married for ages. But Sally's been considering stopping work, or going restricted part-time, because as you know they're down to foster or adopt a child. She wants to have more time if they do get given one. Which means money's tight, so they've put the wedding plans on hold.

'I just thought that if we're having a bit of a booze-up for the twins' arrival, why don't we make it other halves too and have a whip-round so it can be like a reception for the two of them, at the same time? It won't be the same, like, but it would show them we care about them.'

'You're a good man, Maurice.'

'Aye, well, we all know what it's like to want to do

something and not have the cash to do it. Shall I organise it?'

'I should think you've got enough on your plate already, getting ready for the little ones. Why not ask Jezza? She's good at persuading people and you know she'll keep it quiet. I'll have a word with Trev, see if he might like to do some baking for it. He loves any excuse to cook.'

The rest of the team were filing in now. Ted was a stickler for timekeeping so it was rare for any of them to be late. Certainly not without a good excuse.

Ted wanted to kick off with an update. There had been an email from Bizzie Nelson waiting for him in his inbox when he'd got in. It made him realise with a guilty start that in discussing Valentine's Day and half-term with Trev, he'd completely forgotten to tell him about the handfasting. Which left him still a bit in the dark as to exactly what it involved.

'Right, team, settle down,' he began in his customary way. 'Latest info from pathology is that all the body parts are from a male. Probably all from the same one, although that's a qualified probability at the moment. And the likely age range is forty to fifty, although again, that's still guarded and subject to further testing.

'There's also confirmation of the early suggestion that the parts had been stored in a domestic deep freeze. The timeframe for that is now provisionally put at three to six months. So that might help with identification. It rules out any more recent disappearances, but let's leave a wider margin to allow for error. Who's on Mispers?'

'Me and Steve, boss, and that should certainly help us narrow things down a bit,' Maurice told him. 'We've not really been able to do much without a lot to go on. We've just eliminated any very young ones, because of the leg size. We've concentrated on adults. Bit depressing how many there are. We can crack on a bit now, though.'

'And a bit more info from Professor Nelson. She's been experimenting with various tools with her students and can confirm that the saw used was a chainsaw and the cutters were tree loppers. Both fairly hefty design. Professional standard, she put it. So, Steve, back to your theory of someone travelling round to work in different places. It could still be correct. We just need to think a bit broader about the type of work involved.'

'It could still be site maintenance, boss,' Jo put in. 'There might be a need on some sites to keep vegetation under control. Road safety, perhaps?'

'Could be a landscape gardener,' Jezza suggested.

'Tree surgeon, sir,' Steve put in.

'Good. Useful suggestions to keep in mind, if and when we find out who the body parts belong to. We need an ID before we can make much progress, so let me know when we have something. Where are we up to with the arson?'

'The owner of the building lives and works in Brussels, boss,' Mike Hallam told him. 'I've tried calling the only number I could find for him but there was no reply. I left a message. The building is for sale but I don't yet know which agent it's with. There was no board up. I'm ringing round a few likely ones to see what I can find out.'

'Arson for the insurance, then?' Rob O'Connell suggested. 'Hardly prime property, unless it could be developed, so maybe get someone to burn it down and take the insurance money? That might have netted the owner more than selling it would.'

'He probably wouldn't get much of a payout if the building was left insecure,' Jo pointed out. 'It was lucky it wasn't being squatted or we could have had a fatality on our hands.'

'And what's the latest from the scene? Any update from there?' Ted asked.

'Fire Service are just finishing off then we have full run of the place to let Forensics loose. The cigarette end has gone off for DNA testing. With a bit of luck and a following breeze, it's someone with form so it will be an easy one to wrap up.'

'And can we get some more detailed info on the man who's

inside for the fatal arson, please. William Warren. The one who used the same MO as our arsonist. We need to start looking into that case. As you know, I don't like coincidences and this is too much of one on the surface. Steve, can you chase up the original files on it, please? I'd like to take a look at them. Just in case there was a miscarriage of justice and we have to reopen the whole thing.

'Right, I'm just off to see if we can get a few more officers, with two cases to run. Don't hold your breath, but I'll see what I can do.'

'Boss, this sounds a bit gruesome, but it's not meant to be. Going back to what the sarge said after the first body part was found. Are we assuming that the owner of these limbs is definitely dead? I mean, could it be some hideous torture thing going on? Removing someone's limbs without actually killing them?'

Ted was quiet for a moment, mentally kicking himself. 'You're absolutely right, Jezza, I should have checked that with Professor Nelson. I made an assumption. Something I'm always telling all of you not to do. Jo, please can you phone the Professor's department to check, with my apologies for not having done so at the outset.

'I rather thought – and now I sincerely hope – that such injuries inflicted on someone whilst they were still alive would cause catastrophic blood loss. Not to mention shock. Possibly resulting in fairly rapid death. But please check it out. I suppose it's just possible that the missing fingers were removed prior to death, for instance. No fingerprints, of course, but let's hope the DNA is on record somewhere, although we've no results back on that, yet.'

'Bloody hell, though,' Maurice put in. 'If it is something like that, what the hell are we looking at here? Some sort of gangland killing? It's more like the Kray Twins than anything I can remember happening in Stockport in my time here.'

'Trying to keep it realistic, then, Ted, how many more officers do you need?' Detective Superintendent Jim Baker asked.

He, Superintendent Caldwell, Ted and Kevin Turner were packed into the Ice Queen's office. It wasn't a particularly small room but Big Jim's bulk always made it look that way.

'A replacement for Maurice while he's on leave plus two extra officers,' Ted said promptly.

'Meanwhile, on the planet Earth,' Jim replied, pausing for a drink of his coffee. 'You can have a temporary replacement for Maurice, as you can't afford to be an officer down with potentially two big cases. As for any more, you know it's a numbers game. I'll shuffle around what I can from the officers at my disposal but it might have to be on an as and when basis. So don't get too attached to any of the reinforcements. You might have to give them back at any moment.'

'Before you ask, Kevin,' Debra Caldwell cut in, 'the same goes for Uniform.'

For once, even she was being informal in a small meeting. Ted suspected she was keeping it that way to soften the blow of having to warn Kev he might not get the extra officers he needed.

'There's going to need to be an awful lot of legwork on both cases, unless we get anything more solid to go on. And that's not meant to be a joke in poor taste. I've already got all the officers I can spare going door-to-door on both the arson and the potential murder. But I'm forever having to pull people off that to redeploy them elsewhere.'

'All right, everyone,' Jim cut in, 'to save us all a lot of time, let me just state once again, for the record. We all know that. We probably all heard about the recent case where officers had to be sent from more than a hundred miles away to assist another force with an arrest. So, Ted, Kevin, one more time. If Debs and I can find any more, you can have them. If not, you'll just have to do the other thing.'

Ted was saved from replying by his mobile vibrating in his

pocket. He pulled it out to look at the screen then said, 'It's the ACC.'

'You'd better take it, then,' Jim told him then added, his tone dripping in sarcasm, 'perhaps it's news of additional officers.'

'Sir.'

'We could do without your little friend in Gibraltar right now, Ted. I take it you've not been checking on his page?'

'He did phone last night, trying to speak to me. I simply referred him to the Press Office.'

'Did you log the call? Not that it would have made much difference, I don't suppose. Are you in front of your computer?'

'I'm in Superintendent Caldwell's office, sir.'

'Well, put this call on speaker phone, it's important. Debs, can you go to this Mind the Money site, please. Ted, whoever this Mercado bloke is and whatever he has against you, he's not letting go.'

The Ice Queen's fingers moved quickly over the keyboard, then she turned the screen so they could all see it. Ted put his phone on the desk and looked at the website, his heart sinking.

It was better footage than a mobile phone would capture. The video had clearly been shot with a decent camera, on a powerful zoom. It showed Ted, in his shorts, on the beach in Spain. Dancing with Trev. Going through their *Moondance* routine, as Trev had wanted to practise it again before they did it in public at the Christmas drinks do.

The accompanying article was predictable scandal sheet stuff: 'British police complain of manpower shortages and insufficient funds for proper policing. But one Detective Chief Inspector from Greater Manchester spent a recent Monday morning dancing on the golden sands of a Spanish holiday resort with his husband. According to information received by this reporter, the couple stayed in a hotel room paid for by the Metropolitan Police as part of a large ongoing operation into historical child abuse.'

It went on in the same vein for several paragraphs, ending with, 'This reporter contacted DCI Darling for his explanation but he refused to make any comment.'

'Are you sure you don't know this bloke, Ted? Not someone you've nicked in the past? Or investigated? He certainly seems to have a personal axe to grind with you. I had hoped it would all blow over. But we're clearly going to have to put out a short statement now to clear up a few inaccuracies in this rubbish. Let's just hope the nationals over here don't pick it up for any reason and run with it. You know how some of them like to trash the police at every opportunity. Setting aside the rights and wrongs, we all know how the mob turned their collective sights on that copper in Portugal and his long lunches. And look how that ended. So we need to be pro-active, I think.

'Ted, presumably you took the weekend off, which you're entitled to do, of course. What about the Monday, though?'

'Booked as annual leave, sir. Retrospectively, it has to be said. I'm sorry about this, and I honestly have no idea who this man is. I've sent you through the credit card statements, first thing this morning.'

'I've not had time to look yet. It's manic here today. With a bit of luck, it will all blow over and be a five-minute wonder.'

After the ACC ended his call, the meeting wound up. As Ted headed for the stairs, Jim Baker fell into step next to him, saying he needed a word with him. It sounded ominous.

As soon as they got to Ted's office and Jim shut the door, he said, 'Do you have any idea how bloody annoying you are, Ted?'

'Not really, but I suspect you're about to tell me. Is this still about the Spanish thing? Because I'm sorry it's all blown up ...'

'Only indirectly,' Jim said as he lowered himself carefully onto the spare chair which creaked in protest. 'But it is to do with that bloody video. Well, not that one. The one which went viral all over social media. I made the mistake of showing it to Bella. She loved it. Then, of course, she saw you and Trev do it live at your drinks do. So now she wants us to do a first dance when we get married. And speaking of the wedding, I hope you've remembered you agreed to be my best man.'

Ted started to speak again but Jim cut across him, 'You're doing it, whether you like it or not. But here's the thing. You know I have two left feet. You know too that I broke my leg last time I tried to dance so ...' He hesitated, then his words came out in a rush, all at once, 'Could you teach me something easy I could dance with Bella? To make her happy. Seeing you're so bloody good at it. And because I know I can count on you to keep your gob shut about it.'

'Me? I'm a crap dancer. That was Trev, leading me while I just stumbled about trying to follow him. If you want to learn to dance, it's him who needs to teach you. He's very good.'

Jim looked aghast. 'Trev? I can't ask him. He's ...'

'A gay bloke? Newsflash, Jim. So am I. I promise you, you'd be quite safe. He'd tease you and muck about a bit but honestly, he'd love to do it, I'm sure. I'll ask him, then we'll fix a time for you to come over. And seriously, I'm sorry about the crap from this Mercado bloke.'

The mop was once again gliding across the width of the corridor and back.

Left to right. Circle.

Right to left. Circle.

This time, the man dabbed the mop precisely in the centre of each circle before continuing his progress.

As before, he kept up the same humming, the chorus of the same country song, over and over. He seemed totally absorbed in his work, barely noticing as the chaplain came bobbing down the corridor with his distinctive rise and fall gait.

'Back at work already, William? I'm pleased to see you're

clearly so much better today. You gave me a bit of a scare last night. How are you feeling now?'

'Back to normal now, thank you for asking, padre. The devil finds work for idle hands, so I was keen to get straight back to work.'

All the time he spoke, he continued his mopping, not raising his eyes from his cleaning.

'I had to work hard to get the privileges I enjoy. In particular, that of being the chapel Red Band, which is very important to me. I appreciate our little chats as I work. Your words of comfort help me through the darkest days.'

He lifted his eyes as he said that and looked directly into those of the chaplain.

'Those and the touch of your hand. Always there to guide me.'

Chapter Six

Trev had clearly been hovering, listening out for Ted arriving home. He was there in the hallway, waiting, as soon as the key turned in the lock.

'Are you all right? I've been monitoring that Mercado's site and I saw his latest attack.'

He smothered Ted in a hug as he went on, 'I'm so sorry, Ted. I really am. I'd no idea it was going to turn out like this or I'd never have come to Spain. Is it going to be all right? Are you in trouble over it?'

Ted gently extricated himself from his partner's arms.

'It's fine. It'll all blow over. Don't fuss. I wouldn't say no to a quick shower and change before we eat, if there's time?'

'I can make time. Are you sure you're all right? Are we all right? Are you angry with me?'

Ted took both his hands and smiled at him. 'Seriously. We're fine. Honestly. You weren't to know. I have no idea who this bloke Mercado is or why he has it in for me. But the Press Office are sending him a short statement and that should hopefully be the end of it.'

'It must be my fault, talking too much to the hotel staff. Telling them we were married. I should have been more discreet.'

'Don't worry about it. I won't be long, I'll just grab a shower.'

'Shall I come and wash your back?'

'No, honestly, it's fine. I'll only be a minute.'

He took the stairs two at a time, leaving a forlorn Trev standing in the hall watching him go.

Ted was true to his word and back down in record time, hair still damp and floppy. Trev was busy in the kitchen sorting the food. Adam immediately attempted to climb up Ted's leg and had to be removed as gently as he'd done earlier with Trev's embrace.

Trev made to speak again but Ted cut across him. He appreciated his partner's concern but as far as he was concerned, there was nothing he could do about a press vendetta so he'd rather forget about it for now.

'With everything that's been going on, I completely forgot to tell you that Bizzie wants us to go to her handfasting. Whatever that is.'

'Oh, how wonderfully pagan of her! I shouldn't be surprised that Bizzie is doing something out of the ordinary.'

The food was ready. He put it on the table as he and Ted sat down.

'It's a commitment ceremony. Celtic in origin, I think. It used to be like a trial marriage. A couple were handfasted for a year to see if they were right for one another. At the end of the trial period, if they weren't they could just separate and go their own ways or they could confirm their marriage. Nowadays they seem to be quite trendy as an alternative form of public commitment. I've never been to one. It will be a fabulous experience. And you probably won't have to dress up.'

'That's good news. The less good news is that Jim is adamant he wants me for his best man. And you know that will be a church wedding, for Jim. He would have had Mickey Wheeler, of course, before everything that came out about him. But now he's stuck with me as the next best thing. So that will mean dressing up like a dog's dinner, no doubt. Not to mention all the church stuff.'

'Ted, you know Jim thinks very highly of you. He would want you there anyway.'

'And speaking of what Jim wants, he came to ask me if I could teach him how to dance, for the reception. Bella liked us doing our *Moondance* thing so she wants to do a first dance with Jim and he's even worse than I am. So I said you'd help him. Is that all right?'

'Of course it is. What fun! I'll really enjoy that.'

'Just, you know, don't tease him too much. You know what he's like. He's already uneasy at the idea of getting up close and personal with a gay man. He tries his best but ...'

Trev let out a shout of laughter as he picked up his knife and fork.

'Oh, bless him. I promise to behave impeccably. For me, anyway. But what larks, Pip.'

'Right, this is my attempt at an artist's impression. You have to remember I did drama, not art, at school. But I thought it would be helpful to start a ready reference of what body parts have come to light so far, and where they were found.'

At Jo's request, Jezza was standing in front of the white board for the morning briefing, marker pen in hand. Rather than use the crime scene photos, she'd sketched drawings of the different limbs found to date. Lines went from each to the margins of the board with precise details of every location. Every part was numbered in the order in which they were found.

'Number one was the severed leg, found in the river. Removed at the hip and with the foot attached, so we know it's a right leg. Male. And that the toenails were painted with bright red varnish. No distinguishing features.

'Next up, a forearm and hand, minus the fingers and thumb, found in bushes at the edge of a park. Here.' She pointed at a map of their area with cross-references to the items found.

Watching her, Ted was impressed. Talking to her on the flight to Spain, he'd been disappointed, from her career point of view, that she was no longer interested in going for promotion. Those feelings were tempered by appreciating what an asset she was to his team.

'Even without the digits it's been possible to establish that it's the right arm. Therefore from the same side as the leg, which may or may not be significant.

'On to body part number three. The upper arm from the skip on the development site. Also from the right side and, according to pathology, a match for the forearm.

'To even things up, Saturday's offering, number four, was an upper leg, hip to knee, which is confirmed as from the left side of the body. And finally, floating in the Marple Canal, most of a left upper arm, minus the forearm and hand.

'Now, putting my drama to good training, I'm going to segue to my glamorous assistant Maurice, with Misper findings. I thank you.'

She went back to her seat, clearly pleased with herself. The diagram was a good idea, especially related to the map. Ted was already having difficulty remembering what parts had been found
where.

Maurice stayed where he was to start presenting his findings.

'Based on the likely age range of the victim – forty to fifty – that's the age bracket Steve and I have been concentrating on. Like I said, it's depressing how many there are. For now, we've narrowed it down to a few possibles and one very strong likely contender.'

Now he got to his feet and went over to the white board to pin up a Mispers poster.

'This man. Name of Bartholomew Ignatius Byrne, poor sod. Born and bred in our area. Went to Catholic schools. Unsurprisingly, with names like that. Worked on the production line at the biscuit factory. Forty-three when he was last seen. Bit of a loner. No family. Lived in a one-bedroom council flat up Heaton Chapel way. Hasn't been seen in several months. His work reported him missing when he stopped showing up for his shifts and there was no word from him. That was very out of character for him so they became concerned.

'He was a good worker. No trouble. Kept to himself and got on with the job, which was why he was missed. Otherwise I doubt we'd ever have got to hear about him going. Eventually, when there was still no sign of him, Uniform went round and gained access to the flat. No trace of him. But also no sign that he'd moved on or wasn't planning on coming back. Food in the fridge, milk that had gone off long ago. And no sign of any disturbance hinting at foul play. There was a mobile phone in the flat which hadn't had much use and told them nothing.

'They tracked down the only known relative. A distant cousin living in Wythenshawe. She'd not seen or heard from him for years. They weren't on bad terms or anything. Just never kept in touch a lot and then any contact between them had rather fizzled out. She was able to fill in a bit more background about him, though, some of it useful in terms of circulating the poster.

'He wasn't considered as high risk for any reason, so there was no major operation to try to find him. It was out of character not to turn up for work or contact them, but still not enough to red flag the case as anything other than someone who'd gone off somewhere of their own free will.'

'Do we know anything about his state of mental health? We all know the figures for male suicides in particular are very high. He could simply have disappeared for that reason and not yet been found.'

'Hold your horses, boss, I'm coming to that. Steve and me have been doing as much digging into his history as we could so far. You're always telling us you don't like coincidences, so don't shoot the messenger. Our Mr Byrne was a bit of a little devil in his younger days. Nothing quite the wrong side of the law. Just kids' stuff. But he sorted himself out after he had a nasty accident mucking about at a bonfire party as a teenager. He was trying to scare someone by chucking a lighted firework at them. But he got his timing badly wrong and it went off in his hand. He's left-handed. He was lucky not to lose his fingers, but it left that hand and the forearm very badly scarred.

'He also suffered serious injuries to his left foot. Part of the firework landed on it. He had cheap knock-off trainers from the market and they caught fire and melted. Again, surgeons saved all his toes but they, the foot and the lower leg were also badly marked.'

Maurice turned to look at the white board as he spoke again.

'So we have a missing man in the right age-range for our body parts, and so far, our body's missing its left lower leg and foot, as well as the left forearm and hand. The parts of Mr Byrne that are easily identifiable. Coincidence?'

'Now make my day and tell me that Mr Byrne was on record and we have his DNA on file.'

'No can do, boss. He was never charged with anything. Spoken to by police on a few occasions when he was younger and before he straightened himself out. There was talk of an official police caution over the firework incident. In the end, according to case notes at the time which Steve pulled up, it was decided it would be a bad PR move because of how seriously injured he was. So he just got another talking to and appears never to have put a foot out of line since then.

'No pun intended there, boss, honestly,' Maurice ended hastily.

'Further details from the Professor, boss,' Jo put in. 'The fingers of the hand we found were amputated while the victim was still alive. She says there would have been considerable blood loss, not to mention shock. She's not yet able to say for sure whether that could have been a factor in the cause of death. She said she's not prepared to rule anything in or out at this stage without more evidence. But she did confirm that all the other limbs found to date were amputated post-mortem. All of which, of course, means we have no fingerprints to identify the victim by.'

'So in one way we need more body parts for further information. And we need to find out for sure if this collection of limbs belonged to Mr Byrne. If not him, then who? And where is he? We are still talking about one victim here, are we, Jo? Was the professor able to confirm that?'

'All from the same body, so that's something.'

'Boss, this is probably completely off the wall,' Jezza began, unusually hesitant, for her, 'but could there be any link with the arson case? Our possible victim having been involved in a fire-related incident in the past. I know it sounds crazy ...'

'Hard to see how, Jezza,' Mike Hallam told her. 'If our body was in a freezer for up to six months, then that person can't possibly have been involved in last week's fire.'

'Before we can consider any link we need to find Mr Byrne, if he's still alive somewhere. And we also need to know all there is to know about the arsonist who's serving time. William Warren. Who's on that?'

'Me, boss,' Virgil told him. 'I've not got all that far with it yet but I'm working on it. Warren became a suspect early on because of his link to the two boys who died. Several witnesses came forward to say there had been incidents between them and Warren had allegedly threatened the boys, although it was all a bit vague about what he had actually said. Some witnesses said it was nothing more than saying he'd put them in detention. Apparently Warren suspected the boys of having keyed his new car while it was parked at the school.

'Warren didn't fit the typical profile of an arsonist. They often start young. Setting fire to litter bins, garden sheds, empty buildings, that sort of thing. He had no criminal record at all. The only time his name came up was when he was in his early teens. A gang of lads at his own school tried to burn down the bike sheds when he was a pupil there. Some of them tried to blame it on him but he was younger than the others and played the "a big boy did it and ran away" card, so no further action was taken against him.

'Also, arsonists often return to watch a fire they've set. There's no evidence Warren did that, but – now here's the interesting part – he was not far away from the scene of the fatal fire. He did live nearby, but he was closer than that.

'The fire dogs aren't allowed to be used to search onlookers but the dog handler was just taking his along the road to cock its leg as Warren was walking past. The dog showed heightened interest in him so the handler flagged it up to the police.

'When officers went to his house to talk to him they found him in his garage, where there was a half empty can of petrol. He drove a diesel car. It was a diesel/petrol mix used to start the fatal fire. His story was that he'd bought petrol because he was going to mow the lawn of an elderly neighbour. There was an electric mower in the garage for his parents' home, where he lived. The person he named was a bit away with the fairies and denied all knowledge.

'Warren had no luck at all with elderly witnesses. His alibi for the time of the fire was that he was at home with his parents. But his mother had dementia and his father drank to deal with it. The mother couldn't be spoken to and the father claimed to remember very little about the night in question, so the alibi was flaky, at best.'

'At some point one of us needs to talk to Mr Warren. The parents, too, if they're still around. And to the prison staff to find out who he's had contact with. It's bound to be a long list if he's a lifer. Where's he serving his time?'

'Right on our doorstep, boss. In Manchester. So that part's easy enough. And he's still singing the same song of innocence and wrongful conviction, by all accounts.'

'So as the title says, Joey, as a Listener, I'm here for you to talk to. Anything you say to me is confidential and stays between you and me. Unless, of course, you ever want to take any of your concerns further. In which case I will do what I can to help you take whatever troubles you to the right person. But you can trust me. With anything.'

'Fanks, Mr Warren.'

Joey looked no more than a boy. Far too young to be serving time in a prison for adult males. His speech impediment didn't help with the image, making him appear even more childlike. It was no wonder the chaplain had referred him to Warren as at risk.

'You really are very welcome, Joey. It's what I'm here for. I imagine that, like me, you take some comfort in your faith?'

'Oh, yeah, Farver Archer is okay. He's been well kind to me.'

'He's always there to offer the spiritual hand of guidance, isn't he? A kind touch, a gentle gesture. Sometimes it's all we need, isn't it? A little physical contact with someone. To tell us we are still loved, despite our sins.

'But, you know, if ever that comforting hand were to concern you in any way ...'

He locked his grey eyes into those of the younger man and saw him shift slightly in his seat.

Bingo! He knew he'd hit home with his first shot at goal. This one was going to be easy.

Probably the easiest one yet.

Chapter Seven

'Who the bloody hell is this twat Mercado and why's he got it in for us?'

It was DI Josie Balewa's angry voice in Ted's ear via his mobile, with no form of greeting before she launched into the tirade.

'As if this case isn't hard enough without the shite he's been pumping out. I had to put a lead on Jock to stop him driving over to Gibraltar as soon as he heard about it and giving him a serious going over.'

'With any luck it will all blow over soon. The ACC's sorting it. Sending him a statement.' Ted tried to sound reassuring. He knew Josie's DS, Jock Reid, was her self-appointed guardian and protector. He could imagine how angry Jock would be at any slight on the boss he clearly held in high esteem.

'Easy for you to say. My gaffer's a right knobhead. Our regional scandal-sheet has got hold of it somehow. I suspect Mercado passed it to them. They're threatening to run with it. They phoned my gaffer for quotes, so now I've got him pecking my head while I'm trying to get on with my bloody job here and wrap things up.

'Anyway, what I was really phoning you for was to tell you that me and Jock are about finished over here. At least with our case. It's mostly down to the Met from here but finally we've got closure on little Storm, poor kid. The DNA on one of the bodies linked positively to samples found at the crime scene from when her mother was murdered. So at long last she can get a decent burial and that's something we can tick off on our books.'

'Were you able to get IDs on the other bodies? What was the final count?'

'Four in total. All little girls. Two others were identified. They'd disappeared from different holiday resorts along the coast. The fourth one is still unknown. According to Ramon, the feeling locally is that she could have come from a traveller family passing through the area. They wouldn't have been likely to report her disappearance to the authorities, so we may never find out who she was, poor little bugger. He also said there's just a chance the parents sold her to someone. Apparently it's not unknown for shit like that to happen.

'So me and Jock should be back this weekend, or early next week at the latest. We should have a debrief together, I reckon. Don't you? Have you got much on?'

'Sounds good. We have someone littering our patch with body parts. And an arson with the identical MO of someone who's inside doing life. The team's on top of both of them, so I can come out to play. Do you want me to come up there?'

'No, we'll come to you. Like I said, I get a lot of earache from my boss, so it's a case of any excuse to get out of the office when I can. I hope your body isn't another kiddy? I've had about a bellyful of murdered children. Enough for a lifetime, I think.'

'No, it's a middle-aged man, as yet unidentified, although we're working on a possible.'

'Well, if it turns out to be my gaffer, at least Jock and I have a solid alibi here in Spain. And the press have conveniently confirmed it. For me, at any rate. I didn't hire a hit man, either, although I've thought about it often enough.

'Sorry your Trev got dragged into it all. And sorry that the video shows me unashamedly groping his bum, but you can hardly blame me for that, can you?

'Anyway, I'll keep you posted when we're coming back and we'll get together.'

Ted was in work first, as he often was. The team members were starting to file in now. Jo came to find him before the team briefing.

'And another one to start the day, Ted. Found in woodland next to a park late yesterday evening. Bunch of kids messing about down there but luckily they did the right thing and phoned in to report it. Probably because one was a copper's son. My eldest, George. Who is now in serious trouble and grounded for the foreseeable future, because he was meant to be round at a friend's house while they did homework together. Not hanging about in the woods getting up to goodness knows what.'

'Do we know yet which body part it was this time?'

'We do and it's a bit grisly. According to my George, it was in the usual black bin liner wrapping and had clearly been there some time because it was stinking to high heaven. That's why the lads went to investigate. One of them poked at the wrapping with a stick and it split. When they saw what was inside it a few of them threw up but George was actually pretty switched on. He made all the others stand well out of the way while he phoned it in. That might just redeem him a bit, but I haven't said anything to let him off the hook yet.

'Forensics report it was the lower half of a human trunk, from the top of the hips down to where the legs join. And here's the grisly part. It's very clear that the dangly bits had been removed, once again with loppers or bolt cutters. So I hope to god that wasn't done while the poor sod was still alive.'

'We need to continue treating each of these various dump sites as individual crime scenes, which is where we're going to risk running seriously short of people to cover them all. Unless Jim comes good on his promise to find us some reinforcements. Have you sent anyone to this latest one yet?'

'Not a lot of point last night, in the dark. I thought I'd send Mike this morning. We're still trying to catch up on all of the other sites.'

'I might just tag along with Mike. I feel the need to get out from behind my desk for a bit.'

'Yes, I heard about the grief you've been having from this so-called journalist on his website, over the Spanish case.'

Ted stared at him. 'Are there no secrets in this place?'

Jo laughed. 'You should know better than that, Ted.'

'Well, because of all of that crap going on in the background, I want to get away at a decent time tonight to go to my judo club. And tomorrow for karate. Possibly again on Friday for Krav Maga, if I can. I've already murdered one waste paper basket this week and if I don't let off some steam, I can't guarantee that will be my only victim.'

Ted was about to follow Jo into the main office when his mobile phone rang. He glanced at the screen and told Jo, 'Jim Baker. You start, I'll come in and join you shortly.'

'Don't say I never do anything for you, Ted,' Big Jim said by way of greeting. 'I've got you two temporary new officers. One's coming later today, the other one you can have from tomorrow. Don't get too fond of either of them, though, like I said. They're definitely temporary loan only. You can't keep them long. Just until you make some headway on the arson and the body parts. I'm also going to suggest to Kevin that he gives you someone from Uniform, on a long-term loan until you get on top of things.'

'Kev's not going to like that. He's already struggling for numbers.'

'If he doesn't like it he can bloody lump it. I'll speak to him and square things. So, first off, coming today. Amelie Foster.'

'Emily?'

'No, Amelie. With an A. Looks about fourteen to me but you know what an old dinosaur I am. Fresh in, direct entry.

Knows all the theory and the regs inside out and back to front but very green on practical experience. But she's keen. Bloody hell, she's keen. For a horrible moment I thought she was going to hug me when I accepted her for your team. You know I always like to see them for myself, rather than rely on reports.

'The second one I didn't need to see as I know her from way back. Martha McGuire. A DS and a bloody good one with a shitload of experience ...'

'I'm sensing a but,' Ted put in.

'Only a small one. It shouldn't be an issue. She took quite a long career break to have a child and she's recently back. So she may not be entirely up to speed, especially with procedural stuff. She's recently finished her return to work programme and she's raring to go. I think she'll be an asset to you. She'll make a good Maurice replacement, in a sense, as she was always the mother hen of a team, even before she had her own kid.'

'And I'm guessing this is Hobson's choice? These officers or no one?'

'Got it in one, Ted.'

'Right, boss. Well, at the moment, I'll take anyone you can spare. We've had another body part find. I'm going out to look at the scene myself shortly, with Mike. I need a bit of hands-on. To see if I can't get a feel for what's going on.

'Oh, and I spoke to Trev. He's more than happy to help you. Not tonight, it's judo, nor tomorrow, which is karate, but whenever you're free after that.'

'What about Friday, after work? And I want you there as well, Ted.'

Ted laughed. 'For goodness' sake, Jim, he's not going to make a pass at you. You're seriously not his type. I was going to go to my Krav Maga club on Friday. But I'll try to be there for your lesson if you want me to.'

'I don't just bloody want you there. I'm ordering you to be there, as your senior officer.'

The uniformed officer at the entrance to the park knew both Ted and Mike by sight but Ted still held up his ID as the car Mike was driving was waved through. They'd been told the road was currently closed to all traffic except anyone involved in the case. They could drive down to a parking area and walk the short distance from there into the woods, where the latest body part had been found.

'I hope you don't think I'm treading on your toes, Mike. I know you're well up to this. I just wanted a look myself. Just in case anything jumps out at me.'

'No worries at all, boss. Any and all input gratefully received. We've not made much headway yet, have we?'

Mike parked the car where indicated and the two of them got out. Ted stood looking around him for a moment.

'Something like those London plane trees, for instance.'

'Come again, boss? I'm not much into gardening. I leave that to the missus. That's been a big help with her stress levels. Keeps them on a nice even keel. What are these trees, and what's significant about them?'

Ted pointed across the park to a line of trees next to a path.

'Those trees over there, with the patchy bark. I only know what they are because I was the sort of small child who had to know the name and purpose of everything. My dad was great. Always finding things out for me. And for himself. He was interested in everything. That's where I got it from. He went to the library a lot when he could. There were some of those trees growing in the road where my dad's house was. Still there. People moan when they shed their leaves and they pile up in their gardens, though.

'They can stand a pretty hefty pruning. They even pollard them in some places. Those over there have had a good trim. Quite recently, by the look of it. That's a job for a skilled tree surgeon, working at that height in a public open space and doing a proper job of it. Can you make a note to get someone to check with the council parks department if they ever contract out their arboriculture work or if they use their own employees.'

Seeing Mike's look, Ted laughed. 'I'm just showing off now. I told you, I was a precocious child who liked to know stuff. It's the posh word for growing and managing trees. We have body parts the Professor thinks were removed with a chainsaw and she said she might be able to match fibres left on the body to the type of trees the saw had been used on, if it had. Over there we have a line of trees which have clearly had a recent encounter with a chainsaw. Not far from where the latest body part was found. Coincidence?

'Right, let's go and see if there's anything else we might spot to give us another lead.'

The area where the latest remains had been found was taped off. Ted signed in for both of them and they were given coveralls before they entered the scene.

Doug, from the CSI team, was scene manager. He glared at them as they approached cautiously. Normally he had a lot of time for Ted. He'd given him Adam, the kitten, and they often chatted about cats, which Doug bred and exhibited. Today he looked decidedly disgruntled.

'You need to get whoever's behind this, boss. We're stretched too thin to cover all of these sites properly. Plus I've got people on the arson case as well.'

'I hear you, Doug. If it's any consolation, we're equally stretched, for the same reasons. We've no ID on the victim yet. But we are working on it, I promise you. So anything at all you can give us will be a bonus.'

His appeasing tone seemed to smooth ruffled feathers to a degree. He shared Doug's frustrations. They'd normally have at least an ID on the body by now. But with no head – yet – facial recognition wasn't going to happen. The DNA wasn't on record and so far there were no distinctive features to go on. No tattoos, no piercings, nothing to give any indication of identity.

'As you can see, boss, I've got Uniform searching higher up that bank you came down for any traces of who might have left this body part. That's because, from the slight indent in the soil where it was found, I think it's likely that the bag was thrown down here, rather than brought down and placed. There's a lot of confusion in terms of footprints where it was found, because I gather there was a bunch of teenagers here. I also hear one was Jo's son, so he at least had the sense to keep the others back once he realised what the find was.

'I can't tell you yet how long it was lying here before they found it. But I imagine it would be tricky for someone to trot through the park carrying a bin bag in broad daylight, without raising some suspicions. And public vehicles aren't allowed far enough down to get near to here. So somebody might have seen something.'

'I think I might just have a theory as to the vehicle in question,' Ted told him. 'Mike and I will have a look around here then get back to the nick to work on the idea. Thanks for all you're doing, Doug.'

Warren was busily mopping the chapel floor. The same monotonous humming under his breath.

Circle. Dab. Glide.

Circle. Dab. Glide.

He barely glanced up as the door opened and the chaplain strode in, stopping short of the point Warren had already cleaned. The prisoner still made no gesture to acknowledge his presence.

'Hello, William. Doing a good job there, as usual, I see. I hear you spoke to young Joey last night. I told the wing staff that I thought he was in need of a Listener and they put him on a 2052. Although I really hope he's simply troubled by the newness of it all, rather than actually suicidal. You can never tell, of course. Especially with the quieter ones. I told Joey when you were next on the rota, although I'm not supposed to do that, strictly speaking, because I thought you'd be the best possible person to help him.'

Now Warren lifted his pale eyes to the chaplain's face. 'Thank you, padre, that was a good idea. I think Joey and I made a connection, so I hope I can continue to help him. He seems a nice young man. Hopelessly out of his depth in here, poor thing. He spoke very highly of you.'

'Did he?' One of the chaplain's hands went up to his neck to fiddle with his dog collar. 'Good, good. That's good to hear.'

Warren was mopping again. Slowly. Rhythmically.

'Indeed. He spoke of the comfort your touch brings him. By the way, I've put in an application to speak to the Governor.'

'You have?' The chaplain's question came out as a squeak.

'Yes. You know I hate to complain but if it's not one thing it's another. This time it's my newspaper order being mixed up yet again. Surely I'm well enough known by now for it to be obvious I don't read the red top gutter press. That, plus a few other things I want to talk to him about.'

'Really?' A note of anxiety in the chaplain's voice now. 'If ever there's anything at all I can do to help you, William, I hope you know that you only have to ask. I think you know me well enough by now to understand that.'

Warren paused in his work and leaned against his mop, looking directly at the chaplain, who was shifting from foot to foot.

'Well, now you come to mention it, padre, there is another great service you can do for me. You've already helped me so much and I wouldn't ask if there was any other way. But I know I can trust you to do this small thing for me.'

Chapter Eight

There was a new face in the office when Ted and Mike got back in. Sitting next to Virgil, poring over whatever information he was showing her with rapt attention. She looked up at the sound of the door opening and sprang to her feet.

Ted decided Jim had been exaggerating when he'd said the new officer, DC Amelie Foster, looked about fourteen. She was more like sixteen at least. Everything about her was neat on first inspection. A smart tailored trouser suit. Hair pulled back into a severe French plait.

'DC Foster? Amelie, is it? I'm DCI Darling, this is DS Hallam. Welcome to the team.'

'Thank you, sir. I'm really excited to be given this chance. I've heard an awful lot about you.'

'Don't believe half of it, and make up your own mind about me. Virgil, have we got something new yet?'

'Strong possibility, boss, with a bit of luck,' Virgil told him. 'Bartholomew Byrne was living in a council flat. When he disappeared and the rent wasn't being paid, the council repossessed. They don't hang about these days, apparently, when it comes to bad debts. All his personal effects were bagged up and taken to a lock-up, in case he should ever reappear looking for them, but the flat is no longer his and the locks have been changed.

'I've arranged to go down there this afternoon and a keyholder will give me access. With a bit of luck, I can find something which might have his DNA on it which can then be compared to that of the body parts.'

'Nice one, Virgil,' Ted told him. 'Take Amelie with you. Amelie, what sort of things should we be looking for?'

He decided to test how far her theoretical knowledge was going to help her in the workplace.

Without pausing for breath, she started to reel off a list. 'Toothbrush, hairbrush, comb, unwashed clothing, especially underwear, bedding ...'

'Good,' Ted told her and made to head for his office, but she clearly wasn't finished yet. Jim had been right about her being keen.

'Sir, I know we don't have any fingers yet and that this man Byrne isn't on record, but should we also be looking for items like drinking glasses, mugs, that sort of thing? In case the fingers turn up at some point and we can get a match that way?'

'That's a valid point and it's certainly worth trying. Let's go for the DNA first because it will take time for those results to come back and that's most likely to give us the confirmation of identity we need. But bring back anything you think might be useful and relevant. Don't bother too much about an itemised inventory at this stage. We can sort that later. DNA samples are the priority. Let's concentrate first on anything likely to advance progress on the case.'

Amelie started talking the moment she and Virgil were in the car together and heading for the council lock-up.

'So that's the famous Ted Darling. He's not at all what I expected. Much shorter, for a start. I read up about him, when I knew I was getting this temporary posting. Have you worked with Ted for long?'

'The boss,' Virgil told her. 'We always call him the boss, even behind his back. You won't find a better one so he deserves that respect. And don't go off appearances. They can be deceptive. I've been with him a good few years now and I wouldn't willingly change.'

'He's very quiet, though. I thought he was ex-SFO? I was expecting some sort of Rambo-type macho man, I suppose. I knew he was gay, of course, from what I'd found out. I just didn't expect someone so small and quiet.'

Virgil gave a short laugh. 'The time to watch yourself is when he goes even quieter. He doesn't do shouting or reading the riot act. Very rarely, at least. But if ever he needs to jump on you, you'll know about it.

'Now, if you can read my scribble on that note, tell me which of these storage units we're supposed to be heading to.'

It was a depressing sight. The whole of one person's life, reduced to a few dozen heavy-duty plastic bags and slung into a lock-up on a council site. It didn't smell too fragrant in there, and that was before Virgil and Amelie had started opening the bags. A pervading musty odour of damp-infested fabric and stale socks.

Virgil signed them both in on a clipboard produced by the officious man who met them. He promised to phone the man as soon as they were finished, to come and lock the unit back up. At least they were able to park quite close to. If they did find a lot of stuff to take away for testing, they wouldn't have to lug it far. They'd also brought an ample supply of evidence bags of all sizes, with boxes to put them in. That way they could simplify things by arranging them in some sort of order.

Virgil spread out plastic sheeting so they could empty bags out without risking contamination of the items they contained. They both pulled on gloves, then Virgil produced face masks and handed one to Amelie.

'Really? Do we need those?'

'This stuff is going to be dusty. It'll make you sneeze. Believe me, I've drawn this short straw a few times. You can either put this on or you can explain to some grumpy sod from Forensics why you didn't and you managed to sneeze all over what might have been a good sample. The choice is entirely yours.'

Amelie laughed as she took the mask. They stood for a moment, looking at the task before them.

'How do you want to do this, then? How about if we move everything to one side first, then as we search each bag, move it to the empty side?' Amelie suggested.

'Sounds as good a method as any,' Virgil agreed. He was relieved that she didn't appear to be in the least bit bothered by the work they faced. At least she seemed to have no illusions about the glamour aspect of the job. Then he smiled to himself, thinking the boss would pull him up short for having been judgemental about his new colleague. Just because she was wearing a sharp suit, which looked expensive, didn't mean she was going to be too precious for the dirty parts of a police officer's work.

It was soon obvious she was keen to chat. It was natural she would want to know about her new team mates, even for a temporary posting. She kept up a barrage of questions, interspersed with a running commentary on anything she found which might be useful in the search for Byrne's DNA to compare with that of the body.

'Ugh, gross! What dirty type keeps used cotton ear cleaners in a bag in their bathroom? Still, I suppose they can extract something from those. And the world supply of used disposable razors. There should be plenty of skin cells and hair on them. They all look well used.

'Do you have a theory about why there were no internal organs in the abdomen found yesterday? If someone took off the fingers and lower leg because they were scarred, might they have removed the organs because they could help with identification, too? Suppose he'd had his appendix out? Or his prostate removed? Something like that.'

'I suppose it's possible. We're lucky with the pathologist we have. Professor Nelson. She's one of the best in the country. If we ever get most of the body together in one place, I imagine she'll do a standard post-mortem and find out details like that. In the meantime we'll try to get hold of Mr Byrne's medical records. That's routine in something like this.'

After a moment Virgil spoke again. 'I don't think personal hygiene was big on our Mr Byrne's agenda. Not judging by the kecks I've just found. They almost qualify as an offensive weapon.'

'Kecks?'

'Underpants. Skid-marks and all, plus something I'd rather not speculate on. Kecks is what we call them round here. But it can get confusing as some people use the same word for trousers in general.'

'I see. Thank you. I'm from Surrey, so I hadn't heard that one before. And it sounds delightful. I think we're probably going to go back with samples of every possible kind from our Mr Byrne.'

'You've probably covered it in training so I apologise if it sounds patronising, but when you bag items, you put your initials on the bag and give each one an individual number. Like this.'

He held out the bag into which he'd just put the underwear. Amelie took hold of his gloved hands in hers while she leaned over to read what he'd just written. She kept hold of him as she said, 'DT? I thought your name was Virgil Tibbs?'

Virgil grinned at her. 'That's just a nickname. My real name's Dennis, which I use for anything official. No one ever calls me that, except the wife. Especially when I'm in her bad books.'

Amelie was looking at him appraisingly. Virgil gently extricated himself from her hold and attempted to change the subject.

'Surrey's a long way down south. What made you come up to Stockport?'

'Putting as much distance as humanly possible between me

and an over-protective, cloying family.' She was rummaging through the contents of another bag as she spoke. 'Oh, look, here's a mobile phone. I wonder if it's an old one he didn't use and he had his newer one with him'

'Some people do go out without a phone. After all, if he was a bit of a loner, like it seems, he wouldn't have many people to call. Bag it up. It might tell us something. Although if there was no signs of a disturbance in the flat and this was his current mobile, it's possible he didn't have one with him when he disappeared, so we won't be able to pinpoint his last location. I know Maurice said it was examined when officers entered his flat, but probably no more than a quick look.'

'So, what about a drink when we finish the shift, after a lovely job like this?'

'We sometimes go for a drink at the end of the week. The boss is good about putting his hand in his pocket, too. Another reason we like him. Or we go for one if we get a good result.'

'I was wondering about the two of us? As mates, at the end of a shitty shift?'

Virgil went back to his rummaging, not making eye contact with her.

'No, you're all right, thanks. I have a wife and a little daughter to get home to. Another time, perhaps.' Then he paused and held up something he'd just found. 'The only photo we have to date of Mr Byrne, from the Misper poster, is his ID shot from his personnel file at work. Typically, it could be almost anyone. Here's a photo, from one of those booths, by the look of it, which looks a bit like him, though a bit younger. But he was supposedly a single man with no family other than a distant cousin.

'So who's the little girl sitting on his knee?'

Amelie looked up with interest and crawled closer across the plastic sheeting to study the photo Virgil was holding out to her. He wondered fleetingly if she needed glasses for distance and for some reason didn't like wearing them. This time, he was uncomfortably aware of her perfume. Subtle, with more than a hint of musk.

'There's something seriously pervy about that photo.'

'She could just be a relative we don't yet know about. A niece. A daughter, even.'

'Yes, but look where his hand is. That child looks about ten or so. That means she could well have been developing breasts. And feeling self-conscious about it. Whoever she is and whatever his relationship to her, there's something not right about him having his hand right over her boob.'

Ted made it to the dojo by the skin of his teeth in time for the junior self-defence club. He'd left Jo to wrap things up for the day, telling himself again that there was no point in having a perfectly competent DI if he didn't make good use of him.

He needed a lively workout. But first, he enjoyed working with the eager youngsters who all adored Trev and hung onto his every word with slavish devotion. Except for young Flip. He had eyes only for Ted, and the way his face lit up whenever he saw his hero arrive, especially when he wasn't expecting him, always lifted Ted's spirits.

Flip knew he had to concentrate on the session and not talk to Ted. But his eyes kept drifting to him while Trev was talking. Trev was reinforcing a lesson he and Ted often taught. No matter how good their self-defence skills were, it was always safer to avoid putting them to the test. It was even more vital for them to understand that, with the sharp increase in knife crime. Ted had the advantage of being able to show them his own impressive scar from a confrontation with a trained soldier wielding a knife.

As soon as the session ended, Flip raced over to Ted, breathless and enthusiastic, wanting to tell him about a new throw he'd learned in the judo classes his foster mother was paying for him to attend. Ted patiently let him try the move out on him a few times, not making any attempt to avoid being thrown, correcting Flip's technique until he'd almost perfected it.

The senior members of the judo club were starting to file in now, ready to get started. Flip's foster mother came over to retrieve him so they could clear the mat.

'Thank you for that, inspector. You're always so very kind and patient with Philip. That's why he looks up to you so much. He talks about you more than anything else.

'Right, come on now, Philip, time we were going home and leaving the inspector to his own training.'

The boy looked disappointed but said, 'Yes, mum,' willingly enough, and went off to get changed.

She saw Ted's querying look and smiled. 'Yes, the adoption has gone through. Philip is now officially our son.'

A vigorous judo session was exactly what Ted needed. Bernard, their coach, knew better than to pair him off with anyone other than Trev. Even so he had to step in at one point to remind him to tone it down a bit.

It felt good, after a long leisurely shower and a tasty supper, to be relaxing, feet up, watching some long and complicated film which Trev had chosen for them. It wasn't really holding Ted's full attention. It was just moving wallpaper for him. He even nodded off at one point, jolting awake to find himself even more confused.

'I thought he was dead. Didn't the sniper shoot him?'

'Ted, you're hopeless. The shooter missed the killing shot, and the baddy had a bulletproof jacket on. He was only winged.'

'At that range? With that calibre of weapon?' Ted scoffed.

He decided he needed another cup of tea before he went to bed. Trev was enjoying a glass of red wine so Ted rose quietly and went to the kitchen, Adam trotting behind him, faithful as any dog.

It was a nice night. Cold but dry, with stars readily visible, even with the light pollution. He took his mug of tea out onto the patio for a breath of fresh air, shutting the door firmly on Adam. If he let him out at this time of night he risked him playing silly beggars and not wanting to come back in.

Ted cocked his head as he heard the sirens. Fire appliances again. Three this time, by the sound of it. Somewhere down in the direction of the A6, he thought. This time they were closely followed by the sound of police vehicles. He got his mobile phone out, dialled the station and asked for the Duty Officer. He'd no idea who was on the relief rota, with Irene away on holiday and Roly still off sick.

'Inspector Patel,' a voice he didn't recognise told him.

'Evening, inspector, this is DCI Darling. I heard the sirens and wondered what was going on.'

'Evening, sir,' the man kept it formal as he didn't know Ted well. 'An empty building on fire – disused garage premises, according to early reports – just off Wellington Road South. Fire appliances in attendance and we've sent officers for traffic control as it's close to a busy junction. No further information as yet, but it's quite a blaze, by all accounts. I imagine there could have been old traces of petrol, oil, paint, perhaps, and goodness knows what else on the premises.'

William Warren was wide awake and staring at the ceiling of his prison cell. For once, it wasn't the loud snoring and occasional farting of his cell mate which was the problem. He was smiling to himself. Humming his refrain so quietly under his breath that his sleeping companion wouldn't hear him. Warren was always careful not to do anything to rock the boat or tarnish his image as the model prisoner who never caused any trouble.

He had good reason to smile. It was all going beautifully. It couldn't have worked out any better. He only wished he could have achieved all of this a long time ago.

But the stars were only just coming into alignment. And in

a way which exceeded his wildest dreams.

Things were working out perfectly. He just had to be patient for a little longer.

Chapter Nine

Ted was attending the morning Uniform briefing downstairs, leaving Jo to carry on with their own team one. Ted wasn't one of the breed of CID officers who had forgotten their own time in Uniform and thought they were above the 'Woodentops'. He knew he could do with their help with his current cases. He knew too that no-one was better placed to get the on-the-ground information which he vitally needed with both.

Things had started well upstairs with their newest member, DS Martha McGuire. She'd arrived on time, just, breathless and full of apology, having dropped her small daughter off at school. But she'd barely had time to be introduced to everyone before her phone rang. A call from her daughter's school.

Jo, the father of six children, had been understanding and allowed her to take it. Shortly after she'd arrived at school, the little girl had started vomiting and crying for her mummy. Martha's husband, another police officer, was on a shout and couldn't be contacted. Her mother-in-law, who was on standby for childcare emergencies, had had to take her car in for repair when it had started to show a steering wobble every time she braked. She could look after her granddaughter for the day, that was no problem. But she had no way of going to collect her.

'It's fine, Martha, happens to all of us from time to time. Go and see to your daughter and get back when you can. I'll explain to the boss what's happened.'

She needed no second bidding, already grabbing her coat and handbag, flushed in the face and gabbling a stream of apologies as she raced for the door.

Downstairs, Kevin Turner was addressing his officers. Ted was standing next to him, waiting for his turn to speak to them.

'More burglaries up Offerton, especially along Hillcrest Road. Attempted car thefts back on the increase there again, too. So anyone out that way, keep your eyes open, see what you can spot. Talk to your sources. See if anyone knows anything.'

'Has your place been done yet, sir?' one of the older officers sitting near the front asked Ted. Most of them knew he lived in Offerton.

'I've nothing worth nicking,' Ted replied, getting a ripple of mirth. 'I daren't even take my service vehicle home with me. I know what it's getting like up there. If they didn't try to steal it they'd key it.'

'Moving on,' Kevin continued. 'As you all know, because you've been first in line on the scene of them all, the Chief Inspector currently has someone dumping body parts all round our patch, as well as an arson case. Or is it two, now?'

'I called at the scene on the way in. Too early to tell for sure but the Watch Commander I spoke to is fairly happy there's a resemblance to the one last week. I should get confirmation later today, with any luck.

'And those cases are why I'm here. There's an outside chance that the person dumping the parts could be someone who does tree surgery, landscape gardening, that sort of thing. The Professor has confirmed the parts have been amputated using a chainsaw. I can't see someone walking through a park carrying a limb in a black bin bag without being noticed. So can you all please ask around if anyone's seen anything of note. Like a vehicle belonging to some sort of outfit that might do pruning trees. Anything at all like that.'

A stockily-built older sergeant in the front row, arms folded across his chest, hands in his armpits, put in, 'I've got a chainsaw in the garden shed, guv. Does that make me a suspect?'

It raised a few muted laughs. They all knew the DCI well enough to know he could take a joke.

'Fair point, sarge,' Ted conceded. 'We're getting a list of the contractors the council uses for parks and open spaces, but it's still an angle worth considering.

'The same goes with the first arson. There's nowhere to park very close to the first target building and the fire was started with a petrol/diesel mix. So someone would have had to carry a container of some sort to the site. There's just a possibility someone may have seen something. So again, could you all please ask around.'

'I'm not one of you clever detectives, guv, but if I was the arsonist, I wouldn't be seen carrying a jerry can of fuel. I'd put the can in something like a shopping bag to carry it.'

Kevin Turner looked at the sergeant. Eric Morgan. A reliable officer, with a good few years' service under his belt and a reputation for blunt speaking.

'Just for that, Sergeant Morgan,' he told him with mock severity, 'you win today's prize. I was about to say we've been asked to provide someone to make up numbers up in CID. To show them how proper policing should be done. So you're it.'

That raised a few more laughs. There was a lot of friendly banter within the nick between CID and Uniform. It wasn't always like that in other stations. But everyone knew Ted was a big believer in equality and wouldn't allow any hint of a them and us culture.

'We'd be glad to have you on board, sarge,' Ted told him. 'Now, coming back to our body parts. We don't yet have a positive ID. But this man is our most likely lead so far. Bartholomew Ignatius Byrne. Worked at the biscuit factory and had a council flat in Heaton Chapel, but he's not been seen in months. He had bad burns scarring to one hand, a foot and a lower leg, which are the parts of our body which haven't yet come to light. Our victim also had the fingers of one hand removed with tree loppers pre-mortem, as well as their genitals removed with a similar implement. I'm still waiting to hear if that was done while they were still alive.'

A few of the male officers shifted in their seats. Crossed and recrossed their legs at that piece of information.

'We're waiting on DNA confirmation, but this could be our victim,' Ted finished up, pointing to the photo of Byrne he'd pinned up. 'By any chance at all, do any of you happen to recognise him from the photo, which is admittedly not a good one? Or from his distinctive name.' He repeated it for emphasis. 'Bartholomew Ignatius Byrne. I doubt there are two of those in Stockport.'

'I live up that way but the name and the face don't mean anything to me. From the name, I'm guessing he was a left-footer. So we probably need to start looking at Catholic pubs and clubs, which isn't my scene.'

'Another reason we picked you, Eric,' Kevin Turner told the sergeant, lapsing into informality now he'd had his little joke. 'Heaton Chapel's your stamping ground, so maybe some of your contacts may know him or know of him. So for now, we'll let you go and join your new high-flying friends upstairs. Us humble types will go on doing all the donkey work while you grab the glory.'

The shift members gave the sergeant a round of applause as he stood up and went to follow Ted upstairs to start his secondment.

'Load of daft buggers,' Morgan chuckled. 'Happy to help, Ted, in any way I can. I don't know this man Byrne, but I'm sure I can find someone who does.'

He'd known Ted a long time. Enough to be on first-name terms when they were alone. But Ted knew he'd be formal as soon as they joined the rest of the team.

'We're hot-desking a bit at the moment, so just grab a place wherever you can find one for now,' Ted told him as they walked into the main office. Some of the team had gone straight out after the briefing but Amelie was there and Martha McGuire had just got back, looking hot and flustered. She hurried over to Ted as soon as he appeared.

'DS McGuire, sir. I'm so sorry about earlier on. My little girl was ill and ...'

'It's fine, don't worry about it. Superintendent Baker speaks highly of you and I respect his judgement. Everyone, most of you know Sergeant Eric Morgan, except probably Amelie and Martha. He's helping out for a bit. Our Mr Byrne lived on his patch, so he should be a great help to us in finding out more about him. We might, of course, find that he's still alive and well somewhere, but then at least we can rule him out of being our victim.'

Morgan looked round the room and singled out Amelie, who was on her feet, papers in her hand.

'If you're brewing up any time soon, Emily, love, mine's a tea, with two sugars. And leave the bag in. I like a proper brew.'

She visibly bristled as she retorted, 'I'm a DC, not the tea girl, Eric. And it's Amelie, not Emily.'

Morgan's grin was wolfish as he replied. He'd got just the reaction he was hoping for.

'And I'm a sergeant, love, even if I'm not a clever detective like you. So you need to address me as sarge, at the very least.'

Bright red spots appeared on her cheeks and she opened her mouth to bite back. Ted decided it was time to step in. He knew the sergeant was just messing about with a newcomer but they had plenty of work to be getting on with.

His voice was quieter than usual as he spoke, ensuring everyone had to pay attention to hear him. An old trick which he always found useful.

'All right, everyone. Please remember. We're original *Animal Farm* rules here. All police officers are equal and none are more equal than others. We have a lot of work to do and two cases to solve. So let's please settle down and get on with the job.

'Amelie, you work with Sergeant Morgan on finding out more about Mr Byrne, please. You're new to the area. He has the local knowledge. In particular we need to find out more about that photo found at the lock-up, and who the little girl in it is.'

At least Eric Morgan held the door of the office open to allow Amelie to go out in front of him. He grinned across at Ted and gave him a cheeky wink. He was obviously going to enjoy himself. But Ted knew he would also do a good job and show Amelie the ins and out of routine police work better than anyone else could, while he was at it.

'Jo, where are we at with the original file on the arson Warren was sent down for?' Ted asked him.

'On its way from the archives and should be on your desk later today, boss. At some point are you going to go and talk to Warren?'

'I'll read the file first, before I decide. We know it can't be him. He has the best alibi of all. But he might at least tell us who he's talked to about his fire-lighting methods. I did have an idea though. One I'd need to run past a few people first, starting with Jim Baker, before I take it further.

'You remember that homeless friend of mine? Martin Wellman. Got sent down for criminal damage and assault at the hospital when they wanted to discharge him from there. He's in the same prison as Warren, and doing anything he can not to get his sentence reduced. He doesn't want to be back outside and on the streets again, which he knows will happen to him eventually, one way or another.

'I'll need to talk to him, of course, and to someone with the right authority at the prison, although one of the assistant governors has helped us before. He was a big help with the Sorrento case, before you joined us, Jo. Anyway, I was going to ask if there's any way we can get Martin near to Warren. Try to suss him out a bit. Get a feel for what, if any, involvement, he has in the current cases. Assuming last night's one was also an arson.'

'There's something else we perhaps need to consider, boss. Something which occurred to me. And to Jezza, too. She came to me with it when I'd already been thinking it. Great minds think alike, and all that.

'Warren was sent down for a case which happened up near Preston. These copycat arsons, if that's what they are, are happening here in Stockport. Presumably there's a reason for the change of location.'

'And presumably you have a theory?'

'You personally have had a bit of publicity of late. Mostly, but not entirely, centred around you working on historical cases. Would it be too far-fetched to at least consider that whoever the arsonist this time is, they might have picked this area because of you? Because they want you to look into that original conviction?'

Eric Morgan had taken an area car for him and Amelie to go up to Heaton Chapel to start trying to find out more about Byrne.

'Does no harm for them to see a proper copper at work from time to time,' he told her with a grin. She was still quiet and prickly in his company. Not yet sure when she was being made fun of or not.

His first port of call was a café, as he said he hadn't had his morning cuppa. He was clearly well known in there as he was greeted on first name terms by the woman behind the counter.

'Morning, Brenda, love. This is Emily. She's new round here so I'm giving her the guided tour. What are you having, Emily?'

'My name's Amelie, Derek.'

He gave a shout of laughter. 'That's a good one. Well played. So what do you want?'

'A cappuccino?' she asked dubiously, looking around to

see what was available.

'And a frothy coffee for the young lady. On my tab. Do you know this bloke, Bren?

He held out an enlargement of the photo they had of Byrne.

'That could be bloody anyone. What's 'is name?'

'Bartholomew Ignatius Byrne.'

'Give over,' she scoffed. 'No one's called that.'

She squinted more closely at the photo. 'Looks like Bernie, that does. That's what everyone calls him. Not surprised, if his real name's such a mouthful. If it is Bernie, he's been in here a good few times but I've not seen him for ages.'

She called over her shoulder to a young man who was preparing food in the background.

'Hey, Tony, is this Bernie, do you reckon?'

He finished flipping bacon rashers then came over to look at the photo.

'Yeah, looks like Bernie. Not seen him in months.'

'You do realise there's a Misper poster of him in the caff window, don't you?' Morgan asked her.

'Why would I be looking in the window? I work here. Straight in, do me shift, then off home as fast as I can. So he's disappeared, has he? Done a runner or something?'

'That's what we're trying to find out. Do you know anything about him? Or do you know anyone who knew him?'

She made a face. 'Not really. I know he lived not far away but he seemed like a bit of a loner. I never saw him with anyone, but he'd chat to people in here sometimes.

'I do know he was a Cat'lic. Went to church up Reddish way, I think. He used to come in after church sometimes and he'd tell me that's where he'd been. Made a bit of a joke about it but you could see it was important to him, like. You could go and ask at the church. Someone up there would know more, for sure. Seemed like he was a regular.'

Warren was watching the news in his cell after bang-up. His

right to have a TV there was one of the privileges of the enhanced regime to which his exemplary behaviour entitled him. It was his TV and he fiercely guarded ownership of it against all comers. Anyone who happened to share his cell had to put up with his choices, which meant almost exclusively news and politics, with the occasional serious documentary thrown in.

Warren's interest was focused on the local news highlights. His current cell mate was trying laboriously to read one of Warren's newspapers which, by the amount his lips were moving on some of the bigger words, was proving challenging. He looked up when he heard the words 'serious fire' mentioned, in time to see film of three fire appliances tackling a big blaze in what the soundtrack said was a former car showroom and garage premises.

'Hey, Johnny, someone doing your old tricks, look. Unless you've been sneaking out over the wall at night. Not far from here, either, eh? Stockport, did they say? That's just down the road, ain't it? You've got competition, mate.'

Chapter Ten

Ted was desk-bound. Wading through the file which had convicted William Warren and seen him sentenced to a life term. The further he read, the more he was surprised that the case had resulted in even a majority verdict. Most of the evidence was circumstantial and Warren had vehemently denied any involvement, right from his first interview.

His damnation was clearly the inability of either of his parents to confirm his alibi. His mother because of dementia, which was substantiated by medical evidence, his father because on his own admission, he might have 'had a drink or two' and couldn't remember much of the crucial time-frame in question. There was seemingly no love lost between him and his son. Warren Senior was not about to back him up regardless. Ted made a note to look into that aspect, in case it was relevant.

His notes, scribbled as he read, focused particularly on the details of the circle of fuel with the extra dollops at the cardinal points. That seemed to be consistent between the blaze for which Warren had been convicted and the first one in Stockport.

Ted's phone started to ring as he read on. It was George Martin, the fire officer now investigating both suspicious incidents on Ted's patch.

'An update for you, Ted, since first thing this morning. Hugh's on the scene now, plus the fire dog and handler. I just thought I'd give you a heads-up.

'With this being an empty building, the floor was bare concrete in most places, especially in the workshop where the fire started. So no fibres to melt and spoil the pattern the arsonist left. I've not checked and measured in detail yet, but it certainly looks like another precise yard-wide circle with Hugh's famous dollops at north, south, east and west.'

'Is there much damage?'

'Once again, we got there in short order and had it under control soon enough. Probably a daft thing to say but from the times the fires have been set, they were clearly going to be spotted early on. So they weren't likely to cause a great deal of damage. I wonder if that was the intention. Is whoever is doing this trying to get attention rather than anything else?

'In an old motor workshop like this, there would have been traces of oil, grease, fuel, that sort of thing lying about. But like I told you last time, it's vapour that ignites, not the fuel itself, although that will burn off. Most arsonists would know stuff like that. They usually know their trade well.'

'How did they gain entrance this time?'

'Same as last time. Of course it's for your teams to confirm but it looks like a window pane was broken round the back to allow a catch to be opened. The window was left wide open again, giving our man a clear escape route, as well as leaving a better draught to help the blaze get going.'

'Man? So you think the arsonist is definitely male?'

'Statistically, it's far more likely to be a man. Fewer women than men are convicted of arson. The figures may be a bit skewed because arson gets used a lot as a method in the so-called honour killings. Although I've never understood what's particularly honourable about burning your wife to death just because she slept with someone else. If anyone took the trouble and strife off my hands, I'd be more likely to buy them a pint,' he ended, laughing.

'There's something else about that wide open window. You can't quote me on this as it's just a feeling. Nothing remotely scientific about it. Man or woman, they plan their exit carefully. Well in advance. Almost as if they're afraid of being caught in the building when it goes up. That's not typical arsonist behaviour. Usually they're fascinated by fire. Some of them get off on it. That's why they'll often come back to the scene to watch their own handiwork in action.

'This one is different. Whoever he – or she, possibly – is, it's like they can't wait to get away once they've done what they came to do. No sign of loitering to admire their skills. Not that we can detect so far, but your CSIs might be able to tell you otherwise, of course.

'Anyway, I just wanted to update you. We'll clear the site as soon as we can to let your Forensics in. Oh, and to save you asking, I haven't spotted any convenient cameras nearby.'

'Thanks, George, I appreciate it. We're checking CCTV all round, of course, and we've got officers out and about in the area, talking to people. Seeing what, if anything, they can find out.'

No sooner had he ended the call than his phone rang again. A look at the screen showed him it was Penny, the local newspaper reporter. He was tempted to ignore it but decided it would only be postponing the inevitable. If he didn't answer now, she'd find a way to track him down. She was nothing if not tenacious. Timid, in the way she always spoke to him, but determined. And a big improvement on her predecessor, Pocket Billiards.

'DCI Darling.'

'Erm, hello, Chief Inspector. It's Penny. Penny Hunter.'

Ted tried to keep it polite with everyone. It was how his dad had brought him up.

'Hello, Penny. What can I do for you?'

'Erm, I've been contacted by someone called David Mercado, from Gibraltar. Or rather, my news editor was contacted by him and passed it on to me. He's trying to sell us a piece ...'

'Yes, I know what he's been peddling and I'm afraid there's nothing I can say to you. A definite no comment. You'll need to go through the Press Office.'

'But I think there's another story behind all this,' she rushed on before he could bring the call to a close. He paused long enough for her to continue. Intrigued.

'Only, it's been hard to get any detailed information of what was going on in Spain ...'

'That's because it's an ongoing investigation, Penny, you know that,' he interrupted her.

'Yes, but from what we have been told or found out, you went over to interview a retired police officer and just by chance found one of Britain's most wanted criminals. I think that's the story we should be running, locally. Who cares if you and the others had a bit of a celebration after that? That's human nature.'

She sounded passionate. It was probably the longest speech Ted had ever heard from her. He paused, surprised. Knocking the police seemed to have become a favourite sport for the press of late. It was refreshing to hear of a reporter who was looking for another angle. He doubted she could persuade her paper to run with it. It didn't sound to him like the sort of thing which would sell papers. But he appreciated her sentiments.

'Thank you for the thought, Penny. But I still can't comment on any ongoing cases, so you really will have to speak to the Press Office.'

Only Jo and Martha were at their desks in the office. The rest of the team were all out, working with Uniform officers on trying to find witnesses to help with either case. Martha went out to do the midday sandwich run for them. Jo took advantage of her absence to bring Ted up to speed on the latest findings.

'How's Martha getting on?' Ted asked him before Jo started to speak.

'Good solid officer, but a bit out of date on some

procedural stuff. I need to keep checking up on that side of her work. I can see her filling Maurice's boots very well while he's off. She definitely has a caring, compassionate side.

'Anyway, back to our body. More or less full house now, I think. Most of a torso found in a lay-by on the edge of town not long ago. Again in a bin-bag, stuffed behind a litter bin along with all the other crap people dump there. We got lucky, in a sense. A motorist stopped to water his dog. He let it off the lead, because apparently it's usually obedient. It refused to come back so the owner went to look why and found it trying to gnaw at what turned out to be a human rib, still attached to the rest of them.'

'I'm so glad I ordered a bagel and not spare ribs for my dinner,' Ted told him.

Jo laughed. 'Yes, the poor bloke who owned the dog threw up his breakfast when he saw what it was. But he was kind enough not to do it over the evidence. I've diverted Rob and Jezza there to get his statement, and one from the dog, if it has anything to say for itself. Forensics are on their way too. Grumbling as ever at the volume of work. But I think this now gives the Professor pretty much a complete body to work with, so I'm assuming she'll proceed to a full post-mortem as soon as possible.'

'I'll give her a call. I need to speak to her anyway. Were there any internal organs this time?'

'Nothing. Just an empty shell. Thoracic cage, would you call it? Ribs and backbone, shoulder-blades and part of the spine. Apparently the head was removed and the spine sectioned with something resembling a chainsaw once again.'

'An ID would speed things up. Let's hope someone comes back with one, or at least a solid lead, from today's work, or we'll just have to wait for DNA results.'

'Any theories on the missing organs?'

'That's something I'm sure the Professor can help me with. If you've no objection, I might go to that PM myself. Then I can pick her brains at the same time.'

Jo laughed again. 'Sounds a bit grisly, in the context. Will we ever find the head, do you think? The killer, if there is one, or at least the depositor, must realise we'll be able to identify the body eventually, even without one.'

'There's a strong possibility whoever is involved is keeping the head and organs because they would either identify the victim or show the cause of death. A bullet to the head, for instance, tends to leave rather a lot of damage which is distinctive.'

He was speaking from personal experience of his Firearms days. Not something he talked about much at all but he had once had to shoot an armed and dangerous man holding a hostage.

'Fingers missing, possible gunshot wound to the head. Fingers and dangly bits possibly cut off while the poor sod was still alive. It's all sounding more and more gangland, Ted. A bit more London than Stockport. Let's hope we're wrong on that theory.'

Amelie and the sergeant found the parish priest at his church. He invited them into the vestry, which was a lot warmer than the body of the church, and with just a small hint from Eric, put the kettle on to brew up for them all.

'Yes, I know Mr Byrne. He's been a regular here for some time now, although I haven't seen him for quite a while. I understand he's considered as a missing person.'

'Hasn't been seen at his work for a few months now, which is apparently out of character.' Then, in response to the priest holding up a bag of sugar, 'Strong as you like and two sugars, please. Did you know much about him?'

'Not really. He didn't make his confession here, for one thing. Although you realise I couldn't tell you anything even if he had. He used to come often to services and take communion. He'd always stop for a chat afterwards, but that's about as much as I can tell you, I'm afraid. He was always on his own, too.'

'Do you know where he lived before he came here? Or which church he attended?' Amelie asked him. Morgan threw her a look she couldn't interpret as she asked the question.

'I'm afraid I don't know where he lived but he did tell me that he used to worship at the Hidden Gem.'

Seeing her blank look, he went on, 'St Mary's. Off Deansgate, in Manchester. It's a bit of an architectural gem, hence the nickname. I don't know if it was all that local to him but he did tell me he was a bit of a traditionalist. He liked the old church buildings more than some of the modern ones which, it has to be said, can look more like a library from the outside than most people's idea of a church.'

'Did he just come here on Sundays?'

'Mass every Sunday, without fail as far as I remember, but he'd often come during the week as well, depending on his shifts.'

There wasn't much more they could get from the priest. As they walked back to the area car, Morgan looked at Amelie and asked, 'Are you telling me you don't know where he was living before he came to our patch?'

'That information hasn't come out yet ...' she started to say.

He cut across her. 'You mean you haven't asked for it. Right, get your phone out and dial this number.' He recited it for her. 'Ask to speak to John in Housing and tell him you're with me. Ask him to find Byrne's last address before he got his flat here. Tell him I'm on my way there now with you and if he hasn't got it by the time we arrive, I'll arrest him for obstructing the police. Especially if he hasn't got the kettle on.'

Amelie wasn't sure from his tone whether he was serious or not. When she dutifully relayed the message and got a chuckle and a 'Tell him to piss off' in response, she assumed it was a standing joke between the two of them.

Another cup of tea. Another chat. This time full of easy

banter between the two men. Then Amelie and the sergeant were on their way up to the police station at Gorton, armed with an address on its patch where Byrne had been living before he moved into their area some years previously.

They stopped on the way. Another greasy spoon where the sergeant was welcomed as an old friend and where he put away yet more tea and a fry-up. Amelie suspected he had hollow legs, watching him tuck in. She, meanwhile, nibbled round the edges of a fried egg sandwich, the only remotely vegetarian food on offer, and sipped possibly the worst cup of coffee she could ever remember drinking.

Eric Morgan sought out a sergeant of a similar age to himself when they got to the police station. They clearly knew one another well.

'Does this bloke mean anything to you, Stefan? Lived on your patch for a while. Moved away about six, seven years ago, onto ours.'

'We got the poster too, of course,' the man said, looking at the copy Morgan was showing him. 'He never came to our attention and believe me, with a moniker like that, I wouldn't forget him. But if you've got his old address from round here, I can ask around and see what anyone knows or remembers about him. Anything else to go on?'

'Catholic. Practising. Used to go to St Mary's in Manchester. Bit of a loner by all accounts. No close family that we're aware of. That's why I need some local knowledge from you lot. There's also this other photo. I'll leave you a copy. Maybe that will jog a few memories.'

The other sergeant looked at it. The one from a booth, showing Byrne with the unknown little girl sitting on his knee. He grimaced.

'Look where his hand is, the dirty bastard. Right, if that's his game, I'll make this a priority. Whatever we find out, you'll have it as soon as I know it.'

It was late by the time all the team members filed back into the main office. Even without being told, Ted could tell by the general mood that there were no new breakthroughs.

'Time to call it a day, I think. Unless anyone has anything pressing, let's pack it in and start back fresh tomorrow morning.'

'Just before we knock off, guv,' Eric Morgan put in, 'Emily had a good idea while we were out. She got onto the council Housing Department and managed to track down Byrne's last address before he moved here. He lived up Gorton way and I have plenty of contacts at that nick. So we've been up there to put the word out that we're interested in anything at all they can dig up about his past history there. We showed them that photo with the kiddy, to motivate them.'

Amelie had been about to snap at him for getting her name wrong again, as he'd been doing all day. Then she saw the sly wink he sent her way when he'd finished speaking and as the boss was congratulating her on good work.

As everyone was standing up, getting their things together, she sidled over to the sergeant.

'Buy you a pint, sarge?'

'Aye, go on then Amelie, love. I reckon I've about earned one. Don't you?'

Soft humming. Over and over. So quiet it was barely audible, except from close to. The circle and dab movement of the mop in perfect time with the last notes of each line of chorus.

William Warren appeared so engrossed in his task and the music – always the same tune, over and again on a loop – that he showed no reaction when the priest came into the chapel. Until he spoke to him. Only then did he pause and look up with a bland smile.

'Oh, hello, padre, I was so absorbed I didn't hear you come in.'

'Hello, William. I must say the chapel has certainly never

been cleaner since you were put in charge of it. It's good to see someone take such pride in their work. How are you? How are things in general?'

'Never better, padre, thank you for asking. And I could say the same about you. Meaning no disrespect at all to the former chaplain, god rest his soul, but things are so much better here now. Everyone says so. Especially those I see in my role as a Listener.

'You have such compassion, padre. Always a kind and a guiding hand when it's needed. And the services you've so kindly done for me ... well, without them, I would have much less hope for my future than I have now.'

Chapter Eleven

Ted phoned Professor Bizzie Nelson before morning briefing the next day. He knew she was always an early bird and would have been at work for some time already.

'Ah, Edwin, good morning. I was about to phone you. I thought you might be in by now.'

She made it sound as if the morning was almost over. She'd told Ted once that she managed on little sleep. He'd wondered if her work patterns might slow down now her domestic circumstances were changing. Apparently not.

'Have you got enough body parts for a full post-mortem yet? I'm still waiting on DNA for a positive ID, but a cause of death would really help. We're treating it as suspected murder at the moment. If it's a lesser crime, I could scale the enquiry down a bit which would help with numbers for the arson cases we've got on at the same time.'

'I'm flattered by your faith in me, Edwin, but even I normally need a head and some internal organs to give you a definite cause of death. However, my young students are excited to the point of wetting themselves about this case. So I have promised them at least the basics of a post-mortem on it, which they can attend. I'm proposing to do it on Monday morning, although not my usual dawn start. The little chickadees, who are assigned to my care for the day on Mondays, don't arrive until nine. They all know by now not to dare to turn up even one second after the appointed hour if they want to be included in the fun and games. So if you want to send someone along, I can do it then.'

'I might come myself for this one.'

'Excellent! In which case, being frugal, I shall hand deliver your invitation to the handfasting, to save on a stamp. We're celebrating it at Beltane, which obligingly falls on a Friday. In the evening, so no doubt the merrymaking will go on well into the weekend. Feel free to come at whatever time you can and to stay as long as you are able. But I will quite understand if your work calls you away.'

As he rang off, Ted scribbled himself another note, to find out when Beltane was and what it represented. As he stood up, he put a hand into the small of his back to knead at a few muscles which were still protesting from the night before.

He'd managed to get to his karate club. He hadn't been for a while and it showed. His *sensei* knew him well. Had known him for years, since he'd first joined the adult section of the club. He could read him like a book. He knew the signs when Ted was under pressure at work and needed a particularly vigorous workout. He'd paired Trev off with his friend Mark and put himself with Ted.

He was graded higher than Ted, was taller than him, with a longer reach. More importantly, he kept his karate training up to date on a daily basis. The outcome was always a foregone conclusion, but it was just what Ted had needed to help him unwind.

Ted went out into the main office, where the team members were filing in and taking their seats. Martha was one of the first to appear, clearly anxious to make up for the day before. Ted looked to Jo to begin while he perched on a desk in the background.

'Rob and Jezza, anything to report from the scene yesterday?'

'Nothing of any great use,' Rob told him. 'The man who made the find seems perfectly on the level. He's from out of the area, just passing through on his way to visit friends in the

Lakes for a long weekend's walking and camping.'

'The dog looked like a shifty character though, trying to destroy evidence like that,' Jezza put in, half an eye on Ted to see if he was going to react. He let it go.

'The man gave us a full statement, then he went on his way,' Rob went on. 'We have his contact details. He reported finding the body part in the first place. I know that doesn't automatically rule him out, but I think it makes him a less likely suspect. That spot is a common dumping site for all sorts of stuff. You'd be surprised what else we saw there.'

'Virgil, what did you find out about council contractors for parks and open spaces?' Jo asked him.

'There are more than I thought there would be in the area and the council seems to have used most of them at some time or another. They put a lot of work out to tender these days as apparently it's more cost-effective then employing a lot of full-time staff. Bidding is competitive and these small firms are pretty ruthless in under-cutting one another to get the business.

'I'm looking at all sorts. Tree surgeons, landscape gardeners, gardening services. Anyone who might have reason to use a chainsaw and loppers. I've got a full list and I'm going through cross-checking which ones have definitely been contracted, plus any who bid and weren't accepted. I thought that was worth doing, in case there's some sort of a grudge thing going on here. Although I can't initially see how that fits with someone working in the biscuit factory.'

'Good thought, Virgil, well worth checking,' Ted put in. 'We mustn't take it as a given that our victim is Mr Byrne. If the DNA disproves that theory, then we'll need to be looking at other angles. And you might just have hit on one.'

'You mean like the Glasgow Ice Cream Wars in the 80s?' Jezza asked. 'They used ice cream vans as a cover for drug supply and organised crime, didn't they? Could this really be linked to something like that, do you think? It might explain the torture element, if it's gang warfare.'

Her encyclopaedic knowledge of the strangest things was down to the insatiable curiosity of her younger brother, Tommy, and his obsession with making his own version of *Trivial Pursuit.*

'Duelling chainsaws?' Virgil suggested. 'That sounds grim. I hope it doesn't mean there are more bits of other bodies still to come.'

There was an insistent buzzing from Maurice's jacket pocket. He put in a furtive hand, withdrew his mobile phone, glanced at the screen, then shot to his feet.

'Sorry, boss, it's Megan.'

He was already picking up the call as Ted told him to answer it.

'Yes, love. Are you all ... Are you sure?'

He sat down, heavily.

'Sorry, of course you are.' He got to his feet again, looking anxious, grabbing his things. 'Hang on, bonny lass, I'm on my way.'

He looked towards Ted. 'Boss, sorry, I have to go. My sons are about to put in an appearance. And they're a bit early.'

There was a cheer from the regular team members. Virgil cracked a comment which brought laughter.

'They can't be your sons if they're early, Maurice. You've never been on time for anything, let alone early.'

Maurice wasn't listening. He was heading for the door, fast.

'Drive carefully, Maurice,' Ted called after him. 'And let us know, as soon as you can.'

He turned back to the others. 'Right, everyone, settle down. What was Maurice working on, Jo, and have we got his notes to date?'

'Skiving, is what he was working on, knowing Maurice,' Jezza put in, which raised a laugh.

Steve was bristling with divided loyalties. He'd always fancied Jezza, even now he spent most of his time with

Océane. But Maurice had taken him in when he needed it and been more of a family to him than anyone ever had.

'I've been working with Maurice and I have the notes. We were doing the petrol stations around the arson sites, trying to find recent purchases of cans of fuel. Also the pubs round about the garage fire, as the recent one happened at a time when people would be coming out of pubs.'

Virgil laughed. 'Like Maurice needs an excuse to visit pubs in work time.'

Ted saw Steve go red and prepare to bite back. He slid off the desk to his feet, ignoring the odd twinge he felt in doing so and moved to stand with Jo. He didn't need to say anything for the team members to visibly settle back into serious work mode after the excitement of Maurice's departure. When they were quiet, he addressed Steve.

'Any leads, Steve? Anything at all that might be useful?'

'We found a young lad who'd been going into the pub late on, hoping to meet up with his mates and get a last drink before stop-tap. He said as he was coming round the corner he bumped into a tall man carrying what he said looked like a sports holdall.'

'Is there a punchline or is that it, lad?' Eric Morgan asked him. 'Only "a tall man carrying a sports holdall" isn't a lot to go on.'

'It's more than we had yesterday morning, Sergeant Morgan,' Ted reminded him. 'It's a starting point, at least.'

'Boss, should one of us start looking into what sort of sports clubs there are nearby? Try to find where the man might have been coming from?' Martha suggested.

'Might not be a sports club at all,' Eric Morgan put in. He was back in his familiar pose. Arms folded across his chest, feet pulled back under his chair. 'Suppose he'd been playing darts at his local and had a change of clothes with him for that.'

Martha McGuire was not about to be intimidated by the likes of Eric Morgan. She was his equal in rank, though with fewer years of service. She made up for those with valuable experience as a CID officer.

'Good point, sarge, so whoever does it can include pubs. As well as things like amateur dramatics or anything else we can think of which might involve people dressing up. Which of itself gives some interesting ideas. Steve's given us a good start with a likely time-frame. I'd say there's a good chance someone else could have seen this man and he's someone we should at least find and eliminate from our enquiries, if nothing else.'

She stopped suddenly, looking from Ted to Jo and back again, unsure if she'd crossed a line. Jo was quick to reassure her.

'You're right, Martha. We need to find this man, whoever he is. That task's yours today, if you want it. I can put someone else on CCTV.'

'I spoke to the Professor this morning. We've not yet had the DNA results from Mr Byrne's possessions confirmed, so still no ID on our body parts,' Ted told them. 'She's going to do a PM on what parts we have on Monday morning. I'll be attending.'

'Sir,' Amelie began, so hesitantly Ted half expected her to put her hand up. 'I've never been to a post-mortem. Would I be able to attend?'

'It doesn't really need two of us there,' Ted told her, then seeing her disappointed expression, he went on, 'I'll talk to Jo about who's doing what and let you know.'

The briefing finished, Ted went back to his office. He wanted to speak to the Security Governor of the prison where William Warren was serving his sentence for arson.

'DCI Ted Darling, from Stockport. You helped me out once before on a paedophile case and I'm hoping you can do the same again with a couple of recent arsons.'

'Hello, Ted. Happy to help again, if I can. What can I do for you?'

'You have a prisoner there, a William Warren, serving life for a fatal arson. I wondered if I could come and talk to you about him, and about a possible idea I have which might just help me for my own cases. And to interview him, at some point.'

'There are more than a thousand men in here, Ted. It would take some doing to know every one of them by name off the top of my head. But you're in luck with our Mr Warren. Usually the ones who stand out the most are the troublemakers. Warren is exactly the opposite. He's the perfect prisoner. Blends into the background. He's always the one everyone forgets about when they're talking about who's on which wing or doing which activity.'

'Yet you clearly know him and all about him.'

'Probably not all about him. We've always suspected he has hidden depths, but we certainly can't fault him on his behaviour since he's been with us. It really has been exemplary. The reason I know him is that he is one of our Listeners. That's like a Samaritans scheme for prisoners having a bad time. Someone to talk to, for help when they're feeling adrift. Especially the ones on a 2052, which is suicide watch.

'Warren wasn't a particularly religious man when he arrived but he rather got god in a big way since he's been here. A couple of years or so ago it all started. He does cleaning duties and he's now the chapel Red Band, which means he's in there often, keeping it spotless, by all accounts. He makes his confession regularly to the prison chaplain, too.

'Obviously if there's anything at all I can do to help you, I certainly will. What kind of thing is it you're after? Then I could perhaps start putting the wheels in motion ahead of us fixing a meeting.'

'The two arsons on our patch show the same very distinctive pattern of starting method as the one for which Warren was convicted. Including something which wasn't made public at the time. That means there's a possibility that someone who's spoken to Mr Warren and knows about those features is behind our arsons. So I'm going to need a list of anyone he might have spoken to.'

'Now that risks being quite a Herculean task, Ted, I'm afraid. As well as the many prisoners he's helped through the Listeners scheme, because he's such a model prisoner, we often put new arrivals in with him until they settle down. But we'll do our very best for you. Now, shall we look at diaries and see what we can do? Although I'm afraid I'll have to leave you with one of our police liaison officers for most of it. It's more their remit than mine and I'm usually snowed under.'

'Just promise you'll behave,' Ted told Trev, using his stern policeman voice, when he got up to answer the doorbell. 'Jim is already bricking himself at the prospect of having to dance with a gay bloke. So don't go camping it up and being outrageous or he'll run away.'

'Scout's honour,' Trev told him, lifting three fingers to his forehead in salute.

'You were never in the Scouts.'

'No, but I was in the Pony Club. And what fun those camps were. All those young boys, under canvas together, with all those raging hormones.'

'I'll deal with you later, once Jim's gone home,' Ted threw over his shoulder as he went to the front door, leaving Trev laughing his delight.

'Hello, Jim, come in.'

Big Jim stepped hesitantly over the threshold, looking uncomfortable and already out of his depth.

'I'm not sure about this, Ted. I don't know what possessed me even to think it was a good idea ...'

'Jim, trust me. It will be fine. You're doing something special for the woman you love and she'll be stunned by it. You're giving her the wedding she'll never forget. Just hold that thought.'

'Hi, Jim, come in. Ted tells me you need some help. Take a seat and we'll talk about what we can do to help you.'

Jim nodded a wary greeting to Trev, then sat down on the sofa. The cats had all been banished to the kitchen. After Jim's last attempt at dancing, Ted had decided he didn't want to risk his boss tripping over a curious feline and breaking his other leg.

Trev sat in the armchair, not too close to Jim. He knew his mischievous sense of humour made the man uncomfortable and he'd promised to try to behave.

'Tell me your expectations. What is it you want to achieve?'

'I want to learn a really easy dance, something slow, so I can take Bella round the floor a time or two on our wedding day. Without falling over or making a complete prat of myself.'

'And Ted tells me Bella likes country music and line-dancing, which is usually a bit lively. But I think we need something slow and smoochy, perhaps, for ease. Something really romantic. Tell me what it is you want to say to Bella with this dance.'

Jim shifted his position. 'I'm not good at talking about feelings and stuff.'

'We need to pick the right track, though. What is it about Bella whenever you look at her that makes you want to marry her?'

'Because I trust her,' Jim said simply. 'I look at Bella and I know she won't hurt me. Not like the ex-wife did.'

'Oh, that's gorgeous. That's perfect. And I know the very song.'

He opened his mouth to sing but Ted cut in rapidly. Jim was uncomfortable enough, without having to suffer listening to Trev murdering a tune.

'Find the song on your mobile then I can play it for you while you work out the moves and practise with Jim.'

'It has to be *When You Say Nothing At All*. It's country, it's slow, and it says all the things you want to say to Bella.' His fingers were flying nimbly over the keypad. 'The Alison Krauss version, obviously, not the Ronan Keating one.'

He stood up and handed the phone to Ted as the music began to play, then he began a slow, seductive sway around the room, holding an imaginary partner. Simple steps, moving to and fro, with the occasional turn.

'Something like this, Jim. Do you think you could manage that?'

Jim looked doubtful. 'I could try. It looks easier than bloody line dancing. But does that song make it sound like I think she talks too much? She does like to chatter on, so I don't want her to think I'm having a dig at her.'

'Try not to over-think it. Trust me. She'll love it.'

Patiently, Trev led him through the steps a few times, being careful not to get too up close and personal. Jim was clearly never going to make it to *Strictly Come Dancing*, but he was trying hard.

'Right, that's excellent, Jim, you've got the basics of it really well. You'll need to find time for a few more practice sessions, especially just before the big day. But now you need to try a few times with you leading your partner. I'm too tall to be Bella. You'll have to dance with Ted.'

Jim leapt back in horror, suddenly nimble on his feet. 'I can't do that.'

'Of course you can! You want it to be right, don't you? Look, put one arm round his waist, like that, and hold his other hand here, close to your chest. That's perfect. Just keep your hand off my husband's bum.'

'Trev, behave,' Ted warned him, seeing Jim's horrified look. 'Come on, Jim. I'm no more comfortable than you are, but just think how thrilled Bella's going to be.'

'If you ever breathe one word of this outside this room, Ted, you will find your career making a rapid U-turn. I can guarantee that. Right, let's bloody get on with it, then.'

Chapter Twelve

It was late on Friday evening before Ted got a text from Maurice. A photo of him beaming happily, a sleeping baby cradled in the crook of each arm. A brief message: 'Owain and Killian arrived safely. Mother and babies well.'

Jim had gone home long since. Ted and Trev were relaxing on the sofa, surrounded by sleepy cats. They were, as ever, watching a film chosen by Trev. He'd picked *Scent of a Woman*, clearly inspired by his dancing earlier, and had already rewound and replayed the tango scene three times.

He paused the film while Ted looked at the text then held the screen up so Trev could see it too.

'Oh my days, that is so cute! Just look at those little faces. Are you sure we shouldn't adopt a baby, Ted?'

Ted was worried for a moment, never sure whether his partner was joking or not.

'Completely sure, yes. With my hours? Is that what you really want, though?'

Trev had taken the phone from him and was looking at the happy scene, smiling.

'You know how fickle I am. Right now, yes, I'd love to have a little munchkin like this. As soon as it started screaming and waking me up at night, the novelty would wear right off.'

Ted seriously doubted whether anything would wake Trev once he was asleep. He'd never yet discovered anything that did.

'We should have a drink to wet the babies' heads. I've still got some wine. Do you want me to make you a Gunner? Something to do, to stop me feeling broody and wanting another kitten, at least, to satisfy the latent parent in me.'

'It's fine, I'll do it. You enjoy the film.'

Ted got up and headed towards the kitchen. His mobile rang. The ACC calling him. It must be something important for him to be phoning so late in the evening.

'Russell Evans, Ted. Sorry to call at this hour but I thought I should put you in the picture. You're at home now, I take it?'

'I am, sir.' Ted went into the kitchen and closed the door behind him, so he wouldn't spoil Trev's film-watching while he talked shop.

'Well, so am I and long since changed out of uniform so for god's sake stop calling me sir, you bloody dinosaur.'

Ted laughed. He couldn't rationalise, even to himself, why he stuck to the formalities. But he did, unless under orders not to.

'Right, you're not going to like this. Not at all. But the Chief has signed off on it, so it's a done deal and there's no going back on it.

'The Press Office had a call from that funny mousy little reporter from your local rag. Instead of wanting to do the whole "drunken cops on rampage on the Costas" stuff like that cretin in Gib, she wants to do the "local police hero spots Britain's most wanted whilst enjoying three days well-earned leave with his partner after a difficult case". And, yes, I know, that's stretching the truth a bit but don't they say never let the truth get in the way of a good story.

'Amazingly, her news editor has backed her and it's going to be for the local weekly and the parent evening paper. Plus the website, of course. On Monday. Hence me calling so late, to give you advance warning.

'I think the lass has a bit of a crush on you, secretly. Anyway, it's a godsend, from a PR point of view. So the Chief and I worked with the Press Office to put together a piece they're going with. The Chief's going to chuck in a commendation for you. Above and beyond the call of duty and all that malarkey. But that's just on paper. No need for a presentation because I know you'd fight that. We've given them the photo from your bravery award. Don't worry, not the one with your Trevor in, as I know that caused problems once before. Just a shot with you and the Chief and your prize.'

Ted started to speak, to protest, but the ACC cut him short. 'I told you, Ted, it's a done deal. If you don't like it, talk to your Federation Rep and arrange a meeting. But don't forget, you're on thin ice for having let your Trevor go with you on that raid. And yes, I know you said he stayed in the car the whole time, but still. So this is the best and the neatest solution all round.

'Like it or not, Ted, you're the GMP's new poster boy. Until someone else comes along to steal the limelight. So it's a case of sucking it up and saying nothing. Yes?'

There was nothing Ted could do to stop it from happening, if that was what had been decided at high level. And he knew it. It didn't mean he had to like it.

'Yes, boss.'

It didn't happen often, but right now he felt like something considerably stronger than ginger beer or green tea. But he hadn't touched a drop since his dad had died and he wasn't going to weaken now. He hated publicity, but he was clearly going to have to grin and bear it this time. Especially if it made the critical stuff go away. He wasn't bothered for himself. But he didn't like to give the press any more excuses to start bashing the police. Especially not when it spread to Josie Balewa.

'Trouble at t'mill?' Trev asked him, when Ted went back into the living room with his freshly-made Gunner.

'Not really,' Ted told him as he sat back down. 'Just the ACC letting me know the local press are running a piece on me on Monday, about the Spanish case.'

'More crap about me dancing with Josie? I'm really sorry, Ted. I shouldn't have turned up like that without asking you. I've caused you a lot of grief and I know you hate all this public attention.'

'I'm fine. Don't fuss. And this one's actually going to be a positive piece. A real PR job, about a local copper finding a most wanted criminal. The Chief's even sticking a commendation on my sheet to add weight to it.'

Trev turned to put his arms round him, smiling, pulling him closer in a hug so Ted almost spilled his drink.

'Ted, you are funny. You're the only person I know who pulls a face as long as a wet weekend when they get a big tick from their boss.'

'Now then, young ladies and gentlemen, I have a double treat in store for you on this wet and miserable Monday morning,' Professor Bizzie Nelson began, addressing the eager young faces sitting in the viewing gallery.

Ted was impressed, as ever, at the way she was with the students. She'd been right about them being punctual, for a start. He didn't recognise any of them from his previous visit when students had been present, and he was usually good at face recognition. They must be the latest intake. They all looked as keen and rapt as the previous lot had done. And they clearly already knew, and obeyed, her rules on punctuality.

Ted and Jo had decided between them not to let Amelie attend the PM. She was seconded to them to help with routine work. They both felt that, as stretched as they were with two cases running simultaneously, any training she needed should be on someone else's time and budget.

'Firstly, let me introduce you to Detective Chief Inspector Darling, from the local police. And secondly, as you all know, today I am going to attempt to do the impossible for him. With just this incomplete collection of body parts,' she gestured to the metal table she was standing next to, 'I am going to endeavour to tell him how this unfortunate person met their end.

'My usual rules apply. If you must puke at the sight, have the good grace to remove yourself first, or to clean up after yourself if you can't manage that. And if you behave sufficiently well and come up with some intelligent enough questions and answers, once I've finished you'll be allowed to come down here for a closer look.'

She moved to stand at the far side of the table so she was facing the students, with the remains on the table in front of her. That way they could see most of what she was doing at all times.

'Now, I think the Chief Inspector possibly thinks forensic pathologists have psychic powers. He has high expectations of what I can do for him. Perhaps he believes in magic and Father Christmas, too. But I am, as ever, going to do my very best, with what we have here.

'You've all studied anatomy by now so you will have observed that certain crucial parts – vital for arriving at an accurate cause of death – are missing. I'd like you all to think carefully and suggest which part would have been most useful in establishing cause of death. And here's a clue for the gentlemen amongst you. Yes, I know that's missing and no, I'm already fairly certain that its removal, although undoubtedly excruciatingly painful if it was done pre-mortem, was not the primary cause of death in this case.'

She exchanged a wicked grin with Ted. He already knew her sense of humour was near the knuckle. It was probably one of the reasons the students appeared to adore her so much.

An earnest-looking young man pressed the intercom first and suggested, 'The head, Professor? The brain would be able to tell you a lot. If it showed signs of being hypoxic, for example.'

One of the female students took over. 'The heart, also. That might give some indication as to what caused it to fail.'

'You are both correct, of course. Although a little gender stereotypical. A woman favours the heart, a man the head. Having been told he cannot choose that other part. So now I shall do whatever is within my modest skill set, working with what little I have to go on, to send the Chief Inspector on his way with as much as I can tell him for certain. Unusually, I might even provide him with a few theories based on what some might call hunches, but I would prefer to call years of experience poking around in dead bodies.'

'Jo, I just need to check something online before we catch up. I'll be right with you.'

Unusually for Ted, he hurried straight for his office rather than stopping to give Jo the results, such as they were, from the morning's PM. He was in a hurry to see what was on the local news website about him. Forewarned was always forearmed, as far as Ted was concerned.

With something of a sense of dread, he found the home page for the local newspaper and entered his own name in the search box. He was soon looking at a photograph of himself receiving his bravery award from the Chief Constable for an earlier case, when he had successfully tackled a man with a knife who had been holding a young girl hostage. Ted had to concede that Trev had a valid point. He didn't look thrilled to be getting it. He hadn't wanted to accept. Didn't enjoy the fuss and the limelight when he felt he was just doing the job he was paid to do. But he'd been backed into a corner that time, just as he was now.

The article could have been worse. He wasn't comfortable with the publicity, but hopefully it might put an end to any more.

He went out of his office in search of Jo.

'Sorry, Jo. And before I forget, I've got Josie Balewa and Jock Reid coming down tomorrow for a debrief after the Spanish case. Their part in it is wrapped up and we want a catch-up.

'Right, just briefly, in summary. Professor Nelson was at pains to point out that it's almost impossible to give an accurate cause of death with what little she has to go on. So, with many caveats, based on what evidence she could find, she thinks the victim might have been suffocated. Shortly after having his fingers lopped off but, thankfully, before having his genitals removed with the same tree cutters. She's based her conclusions on findings to do with what amount of blood was found in various remaining vessels, and what the oxygen saturation was in that blood.'

'So there's definitely a torture element involved in it all? If it was just about concealing the identity, it would have been enough to remove the fingers after death, surely? And conceal the head somewhere. Is there still no word on the DNA results from Byrne's possessions? And what about from the cigarette butt from the arson site?'

'Nothing that I've seen yet. It's not been a week for Byrne's things, with an intervening weekend, so I think we'd be lucky to get them so soon. I'll chase up the results from the cigarette, though. We should have had that report by now.

'What's happening about an inventory of the rest of his possessions, now we've extracted what we need for DNA?'

'Kev's put two of his officers onto going through everything and itemising it. I doubt Virgil will have missed anything significant, but it doesn't hurt to have belt and braces, just in case.'

'And no more body parts or fires while I've been with the Professor?'

'That's not like you, Ted. Tempting fate like that. If this was a corny TV cop show, it would be "cue fire sirens" as soon as you said that. But, no, nothing new on either case so far. Let's see what the day brings up, if anything.'

'You'd be surprised how many clubs there are dotted about Stockport,' Martha commented as the team got together at the end of the day. 'More than I imagined. And it doesn't help that on the night of the fire one of the pubs nearby was having a karaoke evening, with singers dressing up to perform.'

'Do people still do those?' Jezza asked in surprise. 'I thought it was a bit passé now.'

'Apparently so, and one pub finds it so popular they sometimes do a mid-week slot as well as a Saturday night one. Anyway, when I went in to ask if they'd had a tall man coming in with something like a hold-all, I got asked if I meant Elvis or Shakin' Stevens. And it didn't help that they had a drag queen on as well that night. One who looks quite tall and wears big frocks so always comes with a large bag.'

'As if things aren't strange enough with some bizarre torture and murder on our hands, we now have the possibility of a pyromaniac drag queen?' Jezza asked in disbelief.

'Let's not get ahead of ourselves,' Ted cautioned. 'But we do seem to have a torture element to the death of our victim. The Professor confirmed the fingers were removed while the person was still alive but not the genitalia. She also favours asphyxiation as the likely cause of death, although she remains guarded on that with so little to go on.

'Anything else from anyone?'

'Me and Amelie are still looking into Mr Byrne's background,' Eric Morgan put in. He'd clearly stopped teasing her now and they seemed to have reached a working understanding, at least. 'We've been to his old schools. No one left there who remembers him personally but they gave us the name of his old form teacher and we went and had a chat with him. Pretty much confirms what we already know. A bit wild when he was younger but definitely a reformed character after the firework incident. And we still haven't found out who the little girl is, but we'll keep at it until we do.'

The prisoner was absorbed in the local evening newspaper when the door to his cell opened.

'On your feet, Warren. Your Listener services are required.'

It wasn't until they were walking along the corridor, out of earshot of anyone else, that the prison officer told him, 'Young Barrow again. In a bit of a state. You seemed to have a good effect on him last time, so we thought we'd get you rather than whoever was on the rota.'

He unlocked the cell in which Joey Barrow was being held, ordered the second prisoner inside to vacate it and allowed Warren to go in. The other inmate would be moved to Warren's cell while he was in there undertaking his duties as a Listener.

Joey was sitting on his bed. Head down, clearly upset, sniffing noisily. He had a gauze bandage round one wrist.

'I can't hack it in 'ere, Mr Warren,' he said miserably. 'I can't, swear to god. There's blokes trying to get me to do stuff and I'm not into nuffing like that. I'm scared shitless. There's only you and Farver Archer I can talk to.'

'What happened to your wrist, Joey? Did you hurt yourself?'

The young man nodded, his voice wretched. 'I fought if I could get myself taken to hospital or somefing it might be better. Farver Archer came to talk to me, but then they put me back in here and I got scared again.'

'And was Father Archer able to comfort you, Joey? Did he perhaps put a comforting hand on you?'

Joey looked up, puzzled. His face was streaked with tears and snot. Warren took a tissue from his pocket and handed it to him.

'Well, he give me like a pat. When we were talking. He's kind.'

'Where did he touch you, Joey?'

Barrow put a hand on his own thigh. Made a clumsy

patting gesture.

'Because you know that if anything like that happens and if ever it makes you uncomfortable, you can always tell me about it. It's part of my role as a Listener. It will go no further. Unless any time you want me to help you to talk about it to someone else. Someone in authority. In case ever those little gestures of comfort started to trouble you in some way.'

Chapter Thirteen

'Nice piece about you, boss. And another commendation. You kept that quiet,' Jezza said at the start of morning briefing. 'We should take you out for a drink to celebrate. We could probably afford a Gunner between us, if we have a whip-round.'

Ted should have known he wouldn't be able to keep it quiet. It was on the force's own website now, as Trev had told him, clearly proud of his partner.

'It was just a PR exercise. And not of my choosing. Nothing to celebrate at all. Once we get a result on either or preferably both of our current cases, then we can raise a glass and I'll happily take a Gunner with you all. Anyway, we have Maurice's new twins to toast first, and that's far more important.'

'Speaking of which, anyone who's not yet chipped in for flowers for Megan and Maurice, I want to send them today, before they think we've forgotten them. So come and see me as soon as possible, please,' Jezza said, her tone stern enough for a couple of them to shift in their seats and mumble something.

'But back to the subject of your celebrity, boss, before I finally let it drop. If we suddenly get another arson right on our doorstep, will you then consider the possibility that someone is trying to get your attention because of recent publicity? You specifically. Not just the police in general. That it really is personal?'

'I'm open to any and all possibilities, Jezza. For now, I'd prefer a bit of solid police work rather than pure speculation, please. Jo?'

'Right, to work,' Jo told them all. 'We have the DNA results on the body parts now, boss, I think?'

'The ones for the body parts are just in, but still not yet those for the cigarette stub from the first arson, although I know Jo's been chasing those. Our body parts are a match for DNA samples taken from the possessions found at Mr Byrne's flat. We need to keep in mind that there's always a slim chance that someone other than Mr Byrne had been using the flat – someone we don't yet know about – but it seems improbable in the face of no evidence for it. So for now we go on the basis that the remains are his. Of course, still without the head, it's going to be very difficult to get a positive visual ID from anyone to confirm the hypothesis.'

'Jezza, I think you and Mike should go and try to track down the cousin in Wythenshawe,' Jo went on. 'She's the only next of kin we know of, so she should be informed first, for one thing. See if there's anything else at all she can tell us about him that might give us a lead as to who could be behind this. And don't forget we really need to know about that young girl in the photo. Who she is and what her connection to Byrne is.

'Eric, you and Amelie keep looking into his background. With your contacts, Eric, if anyone can find out more about him, it will be you.

'Virgil, how are you getting on with tree contractors?'

'Slowly. I wouldn't say no to a hand, if anyone's free. I've been cross-referencing where they've been working with the locations of all dump sites to see who's been nearest to those.'

'Steve, can you work with Virgil on that for now? We need to start talking to them all and eliminating any we can, as soon as we can.'

'Especially whoever pruned those London plane trees near the last drop site,' Ted put in. 'We don't yet have any update of what type of tree fibres were found in the wounds on the body, so there might be no link there. The professor did warn me that might take some time because it's specialised work. But clearly someone with a chainsaw has been working in that particular location recently so knows about it and about access to it.'

'What about the arsons, boss? What do we need to be focusing on for those?'

'I'm still waiting on reports to confirm if they were both the same pattern, but we'll start out as if they were. Meanwhile I'm making arrangements to go and see William Warren, to get a feel for whether or not he could have been innocent of the crime he was convicted of. If we're possibly looking at a miscarriage of justice. Now I've read through the file, I would say the evidence against him isn't very compelling. It is possible that it wasn't him who committed the original crime.

'I've also been on to the prison for details of who he's had contact with over the seven years he's been inside, and which of those people have since been released. They warned me it's going to be a substantial list, so there'll be a lot of routine work there.'

'I've made a start on known arsonists on our patch who are back out,' Jo told them. 'I'll widen it to the whole Force area, in case it's someone who's moved here or isn't living locally, just travelling here to start fires. That list will then need cross-checking against anyone who's had contact with Warren since he's been inside.'

'I've been looking some more into Warren's background, in case it would be helpful,' Rob O'Connell told him. 'The mother's in a home now, quite unfit to be questioned. I spoke to the manager and she says the lady doesn't know much about anything these days and hardly speaks. But the father is still alive, although he's moved since the fire. A lot of bad feeling from the neighbours, perhaps understandably, once his son was convicted. If you want someone to talk to him at some point, I can go, if you like?'

Ted nodded his agreement. 'Go and sound him out first,

Rob. See if, with the passage of time, he's had any more thoughts on the night of the fatal fire. Find out if he visits his son at all. See what their relationship is like.

'I know you're all working hard. But we're a week on in both cases, so we could do with something to show for it.'

'This is going to sound daft,' Jezza began. 'But I asked before whether there could be any link between the arson cases and the body parts, because of the burns injuries we know Byrne had. Now Martha's uncovered a drag queen in the vicinity of the most recent fire, and one of the limbs found had nail varnish on the toes. Is that putting two and two together and making twelve?'

'Can forensics give us any more on that toe nail polish from the body part, boss?' Jo asked. 'Do you want me to follow that up? See if we can't get at least a brand and the name of the colour?'

Sergeant Eric Morgan was observant. He never missed a thing. It was what made him a good copper. He may have appeared to be sitting quietly in his customary pose. But his eyes were following everything that was said. Every gesture which anyone made. He saw Amelie's glance dart from Jo to Virgil and back again at Jezza's words. She said nothing. But the sergeant filed that information away for later.

'Mrs Brady? I'm DC Vine, this is DS Hallam, from Stockport Police.'

Jezza and Mike held up their ID for the woman who had opened the door to see. They'd agreed on the drive over to Wythenshawe that Jezza would do the talking to begin with, although she always protested that she wasn't the tea and sympathy type. Hopefully, as a cousin of Byrne's who admitted not having been close to him and not staying in touch, the news wouldn't come as too much of a shock to her.

'Is it about our Bernie? Has he turned up?'

'Could we come in, Mrs Brady? Rather than talk on

the doorstep?'

'It's not good news, then. Yes, well, you'd better come in, I suppose. I don't want the nosy neighbours wondering why I'm having a visit from the police. You might not be in uniform but anyone round here can smell a copper a mile off.'

She looked Mike Hallam up and down with a critical gaze and added, 'Well, I suppose you could pass for an insurance salesman or a Jehovah's Witness, at a pinch.'

She led the way to the back of the house. A compact kitchen, neatly kept. She pulled out chairs by the kitchen table and gestured to them to sit down.

'I think you're supposed to offer to make me a brew, but I'll save you the bother, if it is bad news. Bernie and I weren't close, and I hadn't seen him for years. I'm sorry to hear if he's passed away but I'm not so grief stricken I can't put the kettle on. Tea or coffee?'

They both opted for tea and Jezza queried, 'Bernie?'

'It's what he always called himself, from being small. Well, with a name like he was saddled with, it's not surprising, is it? I can't imagine what possessed my Uncle Milo to come up with that. Bartholomew was too much of a mouthful and Bart wasn't cool enough back then, before The Simpsons came on TV.'

Despite her saying she wouldn't be affected by bad news, she was clearly skirting round the subject, busying herself with brewing up. Mike Hallam stepped in quietly.

'Mrs Brady, I'm sorry to have to tell you but remains have been found, the DNA of which has been matched to items from the flat where your cousin was living when he disappeared.'

'Do I have to come and identify the body, then? That's what you usually do, isn't it?'

Mike carried on, in the face of the grateful look Jezza gave him. She knew tact was not her strongest point, so she was more than happy to leave it to him to break the news gently.

'I'm afraid that won't be possible, Mrs Brady. We haven't

yet been able to recover all of Mr Byrne's body, so facial recognition isn't an option.'

'Bloody hell,' she said, as she put the teapot down hard. Jezza stood up quietly and took over from her while she went to sit down.

'It would help us a great deal if you could tell us if your cousin had any distinguishing features on his body, to help rule out any doubt about identity.'

'Well, there were the burns scars, of course. You probably know about those. His left hand and foot were badly burned when he was mucking about with a firework at a bonfire party. When he was a kid. He was always a bit wild, until that happened. That seemed to settle him down. Ta, love,' she added as Jezza put tea in front of her.

'Was it fire in particular that interested Bernie?' Jezza asked her. 'Or did he get up to other things as well?'

'He was a typical lad. Always up to summat. Until that accident. That turned him round, you could say. He got more into religion as a result of it. Probably because he realised how much worse it could have been. He'd been brought up Catholic, like all the rest of the family. But it became much more important to him, after that.

'So how did he die? What happened to him? Was it some sort of an accident?'

Again, Jezza looked to Mike to field that one.

'At the moment, Mrs Brady, we're treating it as a suspicious death. How long ago did you last see your cousin?'

'Heaven knows. Ten years, at least, for sure. Maybe longer. We used to do the whole exchanging Christmas cards thing that families do, but even that dropped off after a time.'

'Was there a reason for that? Did you fall out over something?' Jezza asked her.

'No, not really. We just sort of drifted apart, like.'

Jezza produced the enlargement of the photo booth picture. Byrne with the still unknown little girl, sitting on his knee. She put it on the table in front of the woman.

'Do you know who this girl is, please? Have you seen her before?'

The woman glanced at the picture. Made to push it away. Then pulled it closer and picked it up.

'I don't know who she is, no. But I can see why a photo like this might make you suspicious. A grown man with a little girl, and his hand where it is. It probably means nothing. Our Bernie was always a bit like that, from being a lad. A bit touchy-feely, you could say.'

'Was he like that with you?' Jezza asked her.

'Oh, good grief, you know what kids are like, growing up together. Show me yours and I'll show you mine. That sort of stuff. I never thought there was anything pervy about him. Not unless you're going to tell me you found a load of kiddy porn on his computer or something.'

'We didn't find a computer among Mr Byrne's possessions, Mrs Brady,' Mike told her. 'Do you know if he had one? We found a fairly basic mobile phone at his flat but we aren't sure is that was his current one.'

'We never did emails or anything, now you come to mention it, so perhaps he didn't have a computer. I haven't seen him for years, like I said, but he did phone me one time to make sure I had his mobile number. In case I ever wanted to get in touch, he said. Although I think we both knew that I probably wouldn't.'

'Do you still have the number, please? It would be helpful to our enquiries if we were able to at least trace where his phone was last used, if he had a different one to the one we found.'

She stood up and went to rummage in a handbag on the work surface. She took a phone out, scrolled through some entries, then read out a number which Jezza noted down.

'Mrs Brady, do you by any chance happen to know who your cousin was trying to throw the firework at when he was injured? Were you there at the time? Was it just a random thing or was he targeting someone in particular, for some reason?'

'Oh, I was there all right, love. It was me Bernie was trying to throw the firework at. Thank god it never hit me. Although I was sorry it injured him. Folks were telling him it was divine retribution.'

Once Jezza and Mike were in the car and heading back to Stockport, he remarked, 'You're determined there should be a link to the arsons with the Byrne case, aren't you? I don't see how there possibly can be. The time-lines don't fit.'

'I wasn't thinking so much about the current arsons. I just wondered if Byrne had a history of playing with fire. And then there was the firework incident. Trying to throw a firework at his cousin. That's a bit warped. It might even give her a reason to hold a grudge against him, over the years. Was that the first such incident he'd been involved in? Could somebody else have had a reason to kill him because of something he'd done to them? Something to do with fire.'

Ted was head down over paperwork, hoping to clear the decks before Josie and Jock turned up later. Trev had suggested inviting them round for a meal that evening, before they headed back to Bury. Ted wasn't keen. He tried hard to keep his work and home life as two separate entities. But Trev had insisted, and he could be persuasive when he wanted his own way.

'Please, Ted. I'd like to see them again. Josie's a riot. I don't know how she manages to have such a sense of humour, especially not when she's working on a case like that. Usual rules can apply; no shop-talk in the house. You can do all that at work before you get back here.'

Kevin Turner practically bounced into Ted's office, looking pleased with himself. Smug, Ted decided was a more appropriate word.

'Uniform to the rescue once more, Ted,' he told him. 'You

can thank me later with a pint.'

'Can't be this evening. I've got Josie and Jock coming down from Bury for a debrief then they're coming back to mine for supper.'

'You're taking work home? Won't Trev divorce you for that?'

'It was his idea. He's rather taken with Josie.'

'I saw that, on that dodgy website. Anyway, we might just have something of interest and importance for you. One of my officers, doing the inventory of Byrne's possessions, found a bottle of nail varnish. Old, almost empty and pretty much dried up. Only didn't the lower leg that was found have painted toe nails? I'm surprised whoever did the first search through for DNA sampling didn't pick up on it straight away. It can't be a coincidence, surely?'

'I'm surprised it was missed, too. I'll need to look into what went wrong there.'

'My officer said it looked like a possible colour match for the photos of the foot. We've sent it off for testing and cross-matching, but I thought you should know. That's nearly a week lost when that lead could have been followed up. Looks like someone needs a kick up the backside for missing that.'

Chapter Fourteen

'Right, goals for today. What do we hope to achieve?' Sergeant Eric Morgan asked Amelie as he drove them back up towards Gorton, to the address where Byrne had been living before moving to their patch.

'You mean before or after you've had the first of your several breakfasts?'

Morgan laughed. She was getting his measure. He patted his stomach as he replied, 'What can I say? I'm a big boy. And me mam always said I had hollow legs. We will stop for a brew on the way, for sure. Best way to make contact with the locals. Second best?' he asked her.

She hesitated. Not the sort of thing she'd learned in all the theory she'd studied to date.

'Local corner shop, where they still have them,' he told her. 'Especially a newsagent or an offy. They tend to know everyone and everything that goes on in their area. Even if Byrne hasn't lived round there for a while, we might get lucky and find someone who remembers him.

'It's the sort of routine shoe-leather work that us humble Woodentops get saddled with. And you'd be surprised how many times it's exactly what solves a case. If you watch crime rubbish on the TV you'd think we spend our time holding up the tape for you lot to enter a crime scene. At least with Ted Darling as your gaffer, you'll see him give credit where it's due.

'Right, so while I drive, why don't you search online for

what local shops there are in the area which are still open and we'll work our way through them.'

They got lucky at the second newsagents they tried. Amelie was learning a lot from watching Eric Morgan at work. People seemed willing to talk to him. There was a confidence and air of authority about him. A solid presence, deserving of some respect.

He started out by showing the woman behind the counter the picture on the Missing Persons poster. Asking her if she knew the face, if the name, or his nickname of Bernie, meant anything to her.

'Bernie? Yes, I remember him. Haven't seen him for a good while, though. I heard he'd moved away, but I don't know where to.'

'What about this one? Would you have any idea who the little girl with him is?'

She took the second photo from him and lifted it closer to her face to peer at it.

'Not very clear, is it? But I reckon that'll be Lucy.'

Still looking at the picture she raised her voice suddenly and bellowed, 'Bill! Bill! Come and see what you think to this photo.'

'What?'

'Deaf old bugger,' she muttered before shouting again, 'Come and look at this.'

'Who is Lucy?' Amelie asked her.

'Daughter of the neighbour up where Bernie was living. She used to come in here with him sometimes. He'd buy her sweets and stuff. Mother was some kind of a junkie, so little Lucy spent a lot of time with Bernie, bless her. At least he was nice to her.'

A man came into the shop from the back of the building, mumbling and grumbling to himself. He visibly started when he saw Eric Morgan, in uniform, standing talking to his wife. She thrust the photo at him and asked, 'This is little Lucy, isn't it? With Bernie?'

He hitched his glasses up his nose and looked at it in turn.

'Aye, looks like Lucy. What's this about, then?'

'Mr Byrne disappeared a few months back. Had you heard?' Morgan told them. 'We're just making some enquiries into his time living round here. Do you have a second name for this Lucy, and does she still live round here?'

'No idea, love, this photo's ancient. Must be, what, going on eight or ten years ago now, Bill, would you say?'

'About that, aye. I've no idea where she is now. The mother died, didn't she, love?' he asked his wife.

'She did, yes, poor soul. Overdose, I read. I don't know where Lucy finished up, though.'

'What was the mother's name?'

'Eeh, now you're asking. Bill, can you remember?'

'How should I know? I don't think I ever saw her.'

'Rob-something, perhaps? Robson? Roberts? Robinson? Some sort of a strange first name. Like a singer or something. Carly? Kylie? I honestly can't remember.'

'So what should we do next?' Eric asked Amelie, after they'd thanked the couple and gone back to the area car. He took a walk all round it before getting in, just checking that it was in the same condition as when he'd left it and still had all its wheels.

'After your second breakfast?' she teased him. 'I suppose we need to find out the mother's full name, when she died, and how she died, if it's relevant. Plus what happened to the daughter after she died. How do we do that?'

'Quickest way is for you to phone Stefan, who we spoke to yesterday. I'll give you the number. Ask nicely, remember to call him sarge and to say please, and tell him it's me that's needing the info. He can find it faster than we could by asking around.

'In the meantime, I'll drive us up to the address where Byrne used to live and we can go door to door there, asking about Lucy and her relationship with Byrne. If it was a dodgy one, someone will know. Whether or not they'll tell us is another thing entirely.'

It was good to catch up with Josie and Jock. Even though the subject matter – the child abuse case in Spain – was dark and difficult, Josie could somehow crack jokes as she spoke, without losing the respect. And she had plenty of good news for Ted in the shape of strong evidence against not only the wanted criminal he had found purely by chance, but also against the former senior police officer he had gone out to Spain to interview in the first place.

'You already know that Maxwell was thick enough to include himself in the porn films with the children. And now me and Jock have had the dubious honour of watching all of the many hours of film that were found, I can also tell you he was stupid enough to have himself filmed while he was killing one of them.

'As for your delightful friend, ex-Superintendent Shawcross, I'm pleased to tell you we found his fingerprints and DNA all over the cameras used for making the films and in plenty of locations in the house.'

Ted frowned. 'Of all the things Shawcross is, stupid isn't one which sprang to my mind in the contact I had with him. He's an ex-copper, after all. He must surely have realised that if anyone did ever happen to find that house and its dirty secrets, they'd also find those traces.'

Josie could be serious sometimes. She sounded earnest when she replied, 'It just makes me think that there are others higher up the system who are involved in all of this and who were supposed to be covering the backs of those lower down. In a sense, I'm glad me and Jock have handed everything over to the Met now as part of their operation. We've done as much as us humble urban types can do. I've a feeling it's going to get very dirty, the higher up it goes.

'And I'll tell you another thing, Ted, although no doubt it's occurred to you, too. That twat in Gibraltar. Mercado. You and I have both been round the block. We've seen it happen before. Especially me, a black woman from a council estate and you, a gay man from wherever ...'

'Miner's son from the Lancashire coalfields,' Ted supplied for her.

'Okay. Not everyone likes to see us succeed. As soon as we start getting near the big names behind a case like this, suddenly some pit-bull with a tripe-writer – pun intended – goes after us both and tries to get the nationals to do the same. I'm betting that's no coincidence.

'Next time I get a bit of leave, if you lend me your Trev – purely for interpretation purposes, you understand – I've a good mind to go out to Gib and start digging into this Mercado bloke.'

'Nice try, Josie, but I'm pretty sure they speak English in Gibraltar,' Ted laughed. 'Although I do think you may very well have a good point there with your theory.

'Right, as I warned you, I have one or two things to sort out here before we go back and eat, if that's okay with you. I thought perhaps, if you don't mind, you could go and wait for me in our local. It's not far and it's a decent pub. You go out of here and turn ...'

'Ted,' Jock Reid interrupted him patiently. 'We're coppers. We can find the nearest pub in the pitch dark. Besides, Josie's like a heat-seeking missile when it comes to the drink. We'll be waiting there, whenever you're ready.'

The two of them went off happily enough, leaving Ted to rejoin the team for a catch-up.

'I've had confirmation now from the FIO that the method of starting the fire at the garage was identical to that used in the previous fire,' Ted told them to begin with. 'And therefore also the same as the one for which Warren is serving time. Although no convenient stub left this time. I'll circulate the report but in summary, the circle of liquid was exactly three feet across, measured to the precise centimetre.'

'Inch, boss,' Jezza corrected him. Seeing from the look he gave her that he didn't seem to be in the mood for joking, she hurried on, 'What I mean is, if it's a precise yard, it will be measured to the inch, not the centimetre. And that might perhaps be significant. Might it suggest someone older, who thinks in Imperial for everything, rather than metric? A younger person might possibly have made the circle a precise metre.'

'It's a valid point to keep in mind,' Ted conceded. 'Although it could simply point to someone clever enough to know that and to exploit it.'

'Martha, how are you getting on with the tall-man-with-bag enquiries?' Jo asked her.

'Slowly, in a word. But I did spend some interesting time talking to a very nice drag queen this afternoon. I got some great make-up tips.'

There was a ripple of amusement, which Ted didn't seem to share.

'Did anyone know where you were going, Martha? I don't remember hearing that visit mentioned this morning. And that person is a possible suspect in an arson. Someone we know nothing about. There should have been a risk assessment on that visit, and two of you present.'

'Sorry, sir,' she looked uncomfortable as she said it. 'It was one of those spur of the moment things. Talking to someone else about the sighting, I just happened to get a lead about where the person was. I was nearby so I thought I'd make use of the time and go and talk to them. I should have called in first to check on what to do. Sorry.'

'Basic procedure, everybody, please,' Ted told them. 'I know we're stretched, with two cases, but we're getting slip-ups and it's not helping.'

'My fault, boss,' Jo said immediately. 'I should be across

everything and clearly I'm not. Has there been something else?'

'I'll fill you in when we've finished here.'

A few of the regular team members exchanged loaded glances. It was not like the boss to be in a mood. But he was clearly grumpy about something. Most of them were examining their consciences carefully, to see what they might have forgotten to do.

'Steve, what about your eyewitness to the sighting of the tall man?' Jo asked him. 'Has he been in, and was he able to give any more detail? Anything more we could be going on?'

Steve was always nervous about speaking up. Knowing the boss wasn't happy made him even more so. He had to pause to clear his throat a few times. Unusually, he even opted for calling Jo 'sir', which he never did.

'Sir, he came in and I spoke to him at length but I couldn't get anything more than he's already told us. He admits he'd already had a few drinks and that his memory was a bit fuzzy. He thought the man was about six foot, but he couldn't be sure. The only thing new he said this time was that he thought he must have been going to or coming from a fancy dress party. But when I pressed him he couldn't say what gave him that impression. Just that it was something he thought for a fleeting moment. Sorry, sir.'

'The drag queen still with their slap on?' Jezza suggested.

Martha shook her head. 'I doubt anyone would call the one I spoke to tall. Not out of costume anyway. They're nowhere near six foot, even with the heels that go with the frock. Although I can see they might look taller with the wig on and up on a stage. But I can't imagine them choosing to walk the streets with those shoes on. They did tell me how uncomfortable they are to perform in and how glad they are to get them off as soon as they're finished with a gig.'

Ted stood up from where he'd been perching, as no one seemed to have much else to offer.

'Jo, I'll come and find you in a minute. Virgil, Amelie, can I have a word with you both in my office, please?'

Ted led the way into the room and stood behind his chair. The other two followed him in, Virgil closing the door behind them, relieved that whatever the boss had in store, it didn't involve his famous kick-trick.

The fact that Ted's voice was even quieter than usual and that he didn't invite them to sit down, nor do so himself, was a warning trigger to Virgil. One or other of them had clearly dropped a massive bollock. He couldn't for the life of him imagine what it could be.

'Could either of you please explain to me why Uniform officers have just found a bottle of nail polish in Mr Byrne's possessions, when they were doing the inventory? The ones the two of you searched last week without, apparently, seeing it.'

Amelie replied immediately. Speaking quickly, her words tripping over each other in her eagerness.

'I don't remember seeing it in any of the bags I searched through, sir. And as you'll remember, I was looking out for things with hard surfaces which might hold fingerprints. Remember I mentioned coffee mugs and drinking glasses, that sort of thing.'

'Virgil?'

'Boss, I honestly don't remember seeing it either. I suppose it's just possible that it was in a bag which we both somehow managed to overlook.'

Again, Amelie cut in quickly. 'It can't be that, though, Virgil. Remember, I suggested we start by putting all the bags on one side of the storage container and only moving them across to the other side when we'd finished searching them. And we emptied each bag out as we searched it.'

Ted looked from one to the other of them, then said again, 'Virgil?'

Virgil spread his hands. 'Boss, what can I say? If I've screwed up, I'm really sorry.'

'DC Foster, can you leave us now, please?'

As soon as she'd gone out, closing the door behind her, Ted spoke again.

'Right, what really happened? And don't give me any more crap, please. I know you too well.'

'I really don't know for sure, boss. I did wonder if Amelie was short-sighted and should have had glasses on. I should have checked up on what she was doing though. Sorry, boss.'

Ted followed him out of the office then went to speak to Jo, to explain what had happened.

'It's one thing to make a mistake. It's another entirely to drop a team-mate right in it to cover yourself. I'll leave her with Eric for now. No doubt he can straighten her out a bit.'

'Bloody nuisance, though, losing nearly a week on what's clearly an important lead,' Jo told him.

This time the tempo of the mop was faster. The gestures staccato. Instead of a dab in the centre of the circle at each side of the corridor, it was more like a stabbing movement. The prisoner was humming, but just the brass bridge at the end of the chorus. Louder than usual. His lips were clamped in a tight line which emphasised the anger in his face.

The chaplain was late. Much later than usual. Warren was not pleased. He wanted to talk to him. Needed to talk to him.

And soon one of the prison officers would be coming to find him if he lingered here too much longer, waiting for him.

It was not satisfactory at all.

He plunged the mop into the bucket with such vigour that water splashed everywhere. Now he'd have to redo the whole section to get it perfect. At least it gave him an excuse for taking longer than usual. He could exaggerate the spillage. Claim to have tipped the bucket over accidentally.

He stayed on the brass section but this time his humming had a note of triumph about it. He was back in control of the situation. And Warren liked to be in control. That's why he found prison life so hard. Every moment of his waking day was controlled by someone else. He had no say in his own destiny.

It was killing him.

He needed a way out of there.

This time he made no pretence of being unaware of the chaplain's presence. He paused in his work and looked him in the eye as he approached, his eyes boring into those of the cleric.

'You're late today, padre. I was getting concerned. There are things I need to speak to you about. You promise me your help, spiritually and on a more practical level. Yet your efforts don't seem to be bringing me the results I need.

'I'm wondering if I should, after all, ask to have that long talk with the governor.'

Chapter Fifteen

'Some more forensic results in, which may or may not help us,' Ted told the team at morning briefing. 'It does give us another possible lead, which is going to mean a bit more legwork.'

After a riotous time the previous evening with Josie and Jock, Ted was thankful he'd stuck to his pledge never to touch alcohol again. He dreaded to think what Josie and Trev were feeling like this morning, the amount of wine they'd put away between them. He just hoped Trev managed to get himself up in time for work. One good thing was that somehow he seldom had to pay the price of the morning after the night before in the shape of a hangover.

Ted had enjoyed a few Gunners, watching the other two drink and dance the night away. Jock had been driving and had stuck to one bottle of lager which he'd made to last all evening. He'd told Ted out in Spain that Josie was not only his work colleague and boss but also the widow of a good friend of his. Which is why he was her self-appointed minder. Especially when she decided to let her hair down, as she certainly did in Trev's company, once more. The cats were banished to the kitchen again while the two of them reprised their dance routine from Spain in the confines of the compact living room.

'Firstly, we now know that the DNA from the cigarette found at the first arson site isn't a match for anything held on file. So it won't lead us to our arsonist. But once we have some suspects, it will make it easier to identify the correct one,' Ted went on.

'Secondly, we've got the preliminary report on the nail varnish from the toes of our victim, Mr Byrne. Not hugely helpful, I'm afraid. It's a cheap and cheerful brand, readily available in all sorts of shops, and the colour's been around for years. It's called Racy Rouge. It's not changed much since it was first introduced. The lab were able to state that this sample appears to be from an older batch because of some very minor changes in its composition since it was first introduced more than ten years ago.

'Now, because of an unfortunate procedural error,' Ted was careful not to look at anyone in particular as he said it, 'an old bottle of what appears to be the same varnish, in one of the bags of Mr Byrne's possessions in storage, was not discovered until this week and has only just gone off for cross-matching against the sample from the limb.'

Jezza opened her mouth to speak but Ted carried on, 'The reasons for the error are not up for public debate. It happened. It's been dealt with. We're moving on.'

Virgil had been stony-faced and unusually quiet since he'd arrived and appeared to be blanking Amelie. From Rob O'Connell's body language, it was clear that he also knew what had gone on. It made sense. He and Virgil were close friends both at work and in their social lives.

Ted didn't want any more time wasted on the incident. He certainly didn't want bad feelings between any of the team members to interfere with the case. He handed over to Jo to carry on.

'Mike, you and Jezza can start by talking to people where Byrne was working when he disappeared. See what you can find out about him there. His social life, who he mixed with, if anyone. Anything at all you can come up with.'

'It's going to be a doddle to drop into the conversation; questions about him painting his toenails,' Jezza put in, with her customary note of irony. 'I can't somehow see that being the sort of thing he'd talk about to his workmates.'

'I'm sure that was simply a facetious remark, Jezza,' Ted told her, 'but just in case, let me point out two things. One, we don't know if he painted his own nails or if that was done to him either pre- or post-mortem. And two, I'd prefer that information not to leak out into the public domain yet.

'Jo, I'm sure you were about to come on to it but we could profitably spend a few moments looking for motives in both cases, and from there to people who might have those motives.'

'Ahead of me as usual, boss,' Jo smiled. 'Mike, did you ever get anywhere with the owner of the first arson building?'

'Nothing to give us a solid motive. Poor bloke is gutted as he was hoping to sell the place. It's been on the market for ages but no takers. And his insurers are being awkward. Saying it wasn't properly secured so they're not going to pay out the full amount, if anything at all.'

'And I don't suppose, to make our job easier, the same bloke owns the second premises, too?'

'Steve's been on that one. Steve?'

Steve was clearly still a bit rattled by the atmosphere. He presented his findings, sounding anxious.

'Not the same owner as the old warehouse. He's equally upset. He'd also been trying to sell it and he'd finally had some interest in it when it went up in flames. And it's the same for him with his insurers. They're still investigating but they're already saying it won't be a full pay-out because the premises weren't fully secure. Sir,' he added, looking at Ted, anxious to please, as ever.

'Thanks, Steve. So, any ideas of motives for these arsons, for a start?'

'Do arsonists always need a motive, boss?' Martha asked him. 'Don't some of them do it just because they can? And because they get off on it? Which won't make our task any easier.'

'I've already told you what I think, boss. Someone's targeting you personally, because they've seen stuff about you in the media, they know you're in Stockport, and that you've worked successfully on old cases, with good results. You need to go and talk to Warren in the nick, soon as.'

Ted's tone was dry when he replied. 'Thank you, DC Vine, for your suggestion.'

'She does have a point, though, boss,' Jo said. 'Someone who met Warren inside, believes he's innocent and is trying to shake things up to get the case reopened, perhaps.'

'I'm on it. I'm hoping to see Warren tomorrow, and to talk to someone about my idea of a way to find out more about him and what he gets up to inside.

'So, moving on to people who might have a motive to want Mr Byrne dead, and not in a nice way.'

Eric Morgan had been sitting quietly up to now. 'If it suits, Jo, I thought Amelie and I might make a start on trying to track down this young girl, Lucy, from the photo. If that picture's anything to go by, and if he was a bit free with his hands, she might have grown up to be someone who held a serious grudge against him. Assuming she's still living round here somewhere, of course.'

Ted followed Jo into his office once the briefing was over and the team members were starting on their tasks for the day.

'I'm meeting with Jim and Debs on Friday afternoon for a progress report, Jo. So I'm hoping for some scrap of something, anything, which I can throw at them, on both these cases.'

'It's annoying about that nail polish. It might not have helped, but it was still a week's delay we could well have done without. Are you going to follow it up with Amelie?'

'Oh, I have a feeling I can happily leave that in Eric's capable hands. If I hear nothing via that channel then I will, yes. And I just wanted to remind you that I'm taking the weekend off. As in off, away, not to be contacted, not even in dire need. Or you might be retrieving bits of my body from wherever Trev decides to dump them if I let him down again.'

Jo laughed. 'Going somewhere nice?'

'It's more Trev's thing than mine, but we're going to watch his sister do horsey stuff. Then he's taking her off to Paris next week for half term. I say no contact but, of course, if there's anything urgent you can call me ...'

'We'll manage. Go off and have some fun. Hopefully our arsonist friend won't decide to burn the nick down while you're away.'

Instead of starting the area car once Amelie had sat herself in the passenger seat and fastened her seatbelt, Sergeant Eric Morgan hitched himself round so that he was facing her, his right arm leaning against the steering wheel.

'Right, young Amelie. There's a few ground rules we need to go over, before you go anywhere with me today.'

She opened her mouth to speak but he cut across her.

'I'm talking, you're listening. At least unless you really want me to go to the gaffer and tell him that I don't want to carry on working with you, and why.

'The problem is, you broke Rule Number One. And that is, whatever happens, you don't drop your team mates in the shit. That's what you did yesterday, isn't it? Let Virgil carry the can for your mistake. And because he's a nice bloke and probably felt sorry for you, being new to the job, he took it on the chin. But it's not on. Especially when you have a good boss like Ted Darling. If you made a mistake and owned up to it, he'd probably have sat down with you and gone over what you did wrong to make sure it doesn't happen again.

'Now you're going to have to go to him and tell him you not only made a balls-up but you also lied to let Virgil carry the can. And he's not going to like that. Not one bit. He expects his officers to act like adults and tell the truth.'

'But I can't do that!' She sounded horrified at the suggestion. 'He'll throw me off the team.'

'He might well do that and I wouldn't blame him if he did.

But I've known him a long time and you won't find anyone more fair. So if I was you, I'd try very hard today to make some sort of a breakthrough on this case, no matter how small. Then, when we go back, I'd go and talk to him, tell him the truth and hope he gives you another chance.'

He turned back in his seat and started the engine.

'How did you know?'

He gave her a smile and said, not unkindly, 'Because I've been a copper for years, love, and I've trained more probationers than you've had hot dinners. And I'm a dad and a granddad. So I know when someone's telling porky pies. Remember what I said. The DCI is a good boss. He's not going to be thrilled, but he will treat you fairly. And if you're worried about talking to him, I'll come with you, if you like. As long as you promise me it was a one-off and you're not going to make the same mistake again. Ever.'

It was lunchtime in the factory. Jezza was sitting down with the production line workers, almost all women, as they ate. Mike was talking to the management. They'd agreed to Jezza talking to their workers as long as it didn't disrupt the production run. One of them made Jezza a cup of strong tea. Others offered her a sandwich out of their lunch boxes, which she declined. Not all of them appeared to speak much English, so she was concentrating on those who did.

'So, what can you tell me about Mr Byrne? Bernie. Did you all know him?'

One of the older women spoke. 'Oh, we all knew Bernie. He were on quality control so he had to keep an eye on us lot.'

'He liked to have a nibble now and again to make sure standards was kept up,' another said, which brought a round of raucous cackling.

'Are you saying he was a bit free with his hands?' Jezza asked them, trying to make notes. This was clearly going to be hard work.

'He was a bloke, love. Aren't they all?'

'Unless they bat for the other team, like young Winston in packing. More's the shame, cos I definitely would. Have you seen the bum on him?'

More laughter, from all of them. Jezza could see she was going to have her work cut out. She needed to try to get one of them to act as spokesperson. She focused her attention on the woman who'd spoken first. 'Which team was Bernie on, then? Could you tell? Did he like the ladies? Or did he prefer men?'

'Take no notice of this bunch of mucky Marys, love. They don't get much excitement. Bernie was all right. Proper gentleman. This lot loved to tease him but he behaved himself. He had to come and talk to us and check up on standards. It was his job. But I never saw or heard him step out of line, in all the time I knew him, which was six or seven years, for sure. Ever since I started here.

'I heard he'd gone missing. We all did. So why are you asking all these questions now? Has he turned up? Is he dead?' She was nothing if not blunt.

'We're just looking a bit more into his background in connection with his disappearance,' Jezza told her, dodging the question.

'He is dead, then. Poor sod. God rest his soul.' The woman was no fool. She heard the true meaning behind Jezza's words.

'Can you tell me anything at all about him outside work?' Jezza was concentrating on the one woman now, leaving the others to chat and eat their food. 'Did he talk about himself at all?'

She shook her head. 'Private man, really. All I knew was that he was on his own. And a regular churchgoer, like me. Catholic. I never heard anything bad about him. He seemed a bit sad, like. As if he'd lost someone he cared about. Although he never said owt about it. Not to me, anyway.'

Having said his piece, Eric Morgan was back to exactly how

he'd been the day before. While he drove, he told Amelie what phone calls to make and who to speak to in order to get the information they needed for the next part of the enquiries.

First she got hold of the full details on the death of Lucy's mother. Carly Robson had indeed died of a drugs overdose, leaving her daughter Lucy, then nearly thirteen, to be taken into local authority care, as no relatives had been traced.

Thanks to more information from Stefan at Gorton, Eric and Amelie were now on their way to the Manchester Children's Services department, on the southern edge of the city. He'd supplied them with the name of someone to speak to. Amelie relayed the information to Eric as he drove.

'Lorraine, eh? I wonder how he knows her. Although I can make an educated guess. He's a bit of a lad on the quiet, is Stefan. But keep that to yourself.'

Stefan had clearly phoned ahead as the woman was expecting them and, no doubt having been primed, she had the kettle on ready and a packet of digestive biscuits open on a plate. She invited them to help themselves and made tea to their order. Then she sat back down at her computer.

'So, Lucy Robson. A sad case. The mother died of a drugs overdose, as you probably know. There was only her and Lucy. No father on the scene, and no family traceable, so Lucy was taken into care just before her thirteenth birthday.

'She was being looked after by a neighbour, it says here. A man called – good gracious, what a mouthful – Bartholomew Ignatius Byrne. The notes say they did seem very attached to one another. The girl cried when she was taken away from him. But as he wasn't a relative he clearly couldn't keep her with him.

'Lucy was placed in a home and she stayed there until she was sixteen. Again, because he wasn't a relative, Mr Byrne wasn't given details of where she was, so as far as I can tell from the notes here, the contact between them ended.'

'Do you have any record there of anything which Lucy

might have said about him?' Amelie asked her. 'About the relationship between them or anything? Or would we need to go to the home and try to find someone who'd known her in her time there?'

Lorraine was scanning the screen rapidly, speed-reading through the notes which appeared there.

'Everything I'm reading here says Lucy was a very quiet, rather withdrawn girl who was never any trouble, but showed no inclination to open up to anyone about herself or her feelings.

'Most children in care stay in the system and get support until they reach the age of eighteen. Lucy was very clear, from early on, that she intended to leave as soon as she was legally allowed to do so, at the age of sixteen. And that's exactly what she seems to have done. She didn't give any indication of where she was going and refused to give a forwarding address.

'Staff tried hard to get her to stay, to accept the continuing help and support available to her but she was adamant. She had somewhere else she'd rather be, and so she left. Apart from a few cards to the home saying she was fine, doing part-time work and continuing her studies, that's the last record we have of her, I'm afraid. We have no idea where she is now.'

Chapter Sixteen

'Are you eating the magic mushrooms or something, Ted? Only that sounds a bit far-fetched to me. Been watching too many bad cop shows on TV?'

Ted was on the phone to his contact, Jono, at the Metropolitan Police.

'It was something Josie Balewa and I were discussing yesterday when we were having a debrief about Spain. That it was strange for a copper with Shawcross's experience not to have covered his tracks better than he did. Almost as if he was expecting someone else to cover his back for him.'

'Yes, but realistically, it was a hell of a long shot that some copper from Greater Manchester would drop into Shawcross's local when he was having a cosy chat with one of Britain's most wanted. Like you say, he was a copper, so he'd have planned things to make sure the two of you didn't meet. He'd have done his homework on you. Found out you're not a drinker. So he wouldn't have expected you to nip into a bar on your way to interview him at his home as planned.'

'That's possible,' Ted conceded. 'But then we suddenly get this bloke in Gibraltar trying to smear me and Josie with the videos ...'

'Yeah, we saw those. Lovely mover, your husband.'

'Is there any bugger on the planet who's not seen that video?'

Jono laughed. 'Maybe some hermit living in retreat on an island which doesn't have internet. Seriously, though, Ted, you and Josie are both right about this whole mess going a lot higher than we've gone so far. So it is possible this so-called journalist is in someone's pocket and being paid to do a hatchet job.

'We're pretty flat out on this case, as you can imagine. It's like a bloody octopus, with the number of tentacles there are and where they take us. And as fast as we chop one off, another appears to take its place. But I'll put someone onto looking into the bloke in Gib. What's he called again, Meccano? He might just lead us to some bigger fish.'

'Mercado. David Mercado. His company's Mercado International Life and Finance.'

Jono laughed again. 'He didn't think that acronym out properly, did he? Unless he's taking the piss, of course. Anyway, I'll let you know if we find anything out about him. And seriously, Ted, thanks again. You bumping into Maxwell like that and finding his house was a big boost. I doubt we'd have got to him for ages without that chance encounter. Especially if there is someone much higher up taking care of this, which is what we've suspected for a long time.'

When Ted ended his call, there was a knock on his office door and Virgil came in. There was no hint of an atmosphere between them. They were both too professional for that. The earlier incident was done with as far as they were concerned.

'Boss, can I just run something past you, because Jo's out?'

'Of course. Take a pew. What have you got?'

'I've been looking into contractors who might use chainsaws and the like. I decided to look at all of them, not just those who've worked for the council. I've also run all of them through the system to see what that throws up.'

'Good. That makes sense. Anything interesting?'

'Possibly. One of the outfits, a small one, by all accounts, reported the theft of a load of equipment off their truck when they were doing some contracting work for Highways, a few months back. Only the kit stolen included a chainsaw, some tree loppers and a heavy-duty shredder. And I was wondering if such a shredder might possibly cope with things like amputated fingers and, erm, well, the other thing. I don't even like to think about that.'

'Does the time-line fit? With the length of time our body parts were frozen?'

'It does, boss. I've checked against the Professor's report and the theft was within the length of time she says is the maximum for the body parts having been frozen. And it's likely it was cut up before being frozen, so it would fit better in a domestic freezer. Easier to cut, too, unfrozen, I imagine.'

'What's the company?'

'They're called Tam Lee, from up beyond Offerton Green way. Small company, just two employees registered, one of whom is the company director. At the moment I can't find anything more about them at all. I haven't tried contacting them yet. I wanted to run it past Jo first, but he's out so I thought I'd ask you before I go any further.'

'You did right. This potentially complicates things. If someone stole those items, it could be anyone. Which means it's not going to be as simple as checking the equipment of all the firms in the area for any traces of human blood or flesh. Or even for a match to the same type of trees that were found in the wounds on the body parts. And of course, like Eric Morgan said, there's nothing to stop anyone owning a chainsaw or loppers. You can buy them at any big DIY or gardening shop.

'For now, can you pull out the file on the report of the theft and go through that. Just in case there's anything in it that we need to look into. Good work, Virgil, thanks.'

'Well, that potentially throws a bit of a spanner in the works regarding finding people with motives,' Jo commented, after Virgil had laid out his latest findings, once everyone was back in at the end of the day. 'If by any chance the tools which were stolen were the ones used in this crime, we're back to square one regarding who might have used them.'

'I've said all along that was a bit of a tentative idea. Like I said to the boss before, I've got a chainsaw in my garden shed. I've been tempted to use it on a few folks in my time, but I've resisted the urge. So far,' Eric Morgan put in.

'Have we checked if anyone has form for crimes involving a chainsaw?' Ted asked.

'No one on our patch, boss,' Jo told him. 'It's a big job to widen the search and track down anyone else with that kind of previous. It's already stretching us a bit looking into our friendly local arsonists who are out and about. Steve's been checking on those, whenever he gets a moment.'

'Sir, the MO in our two latest cases is very distinctive. I'm not finding any matches in any other cases. Not with exactly the same precise measurements, and the compass points. Not anywhere.'

'Jezza, you'll be pleased to hear my visit to Mr Warren tomorrow has been confirmed. It's just possible he might at least tell me what the significance of the yard-wide circle and the four compass points is.

'Steve, you're the online gamer expert. Is that symbol relevant to anything like that? Or to any film, or TV series? Anyone? It clearly means something very specific to our arsonist, but where does it come from?'

'I can ask Tommy,' Jezza said. 'Maybe it's something from Tolkien. The precise dimension of a hobbit's front door or something. If Tom doesn't know, he'll spend hours trying to find out and he'll love doing it. Plus his time won't come off your budget, boss.'

'Or something from *Game of Thrones*?' Martha suggested. 'I've never seen it but my sister is completely hooked on it. It's probably one of those daft things that belongs to some series or another which means nothing to any of us, but someone who's really into it would know straight away. *Star Wars*, maybe.'

'It's not from *Star Wars*,' Steve put in quickly. That was

one of his specialist subjects.

'Someone needs to talk to Warren's father, please, Jo,' Ted said. 'Soonish. It's just possible it's some strange family tradition. I suspect many people have bizarre rituals they do in their own household which wouldn't mean anything to anyone else. Send someone round to see if it has any significance to the father.'

'The four points could also be the old Catholic thing when you cross yourself,' Jo suggested. 'Spectacles, testicles, wallet, watch.'

'Except Warren's a recent convert to Catholicism,' Ted pointed out.

'Whereas Byrne was a lifelong practising Catholic,' Jezza put in, still doggedly sticking to her theory that there was some connection, albeit tentative, between the two cases.

'Suppose just for a moment that Warren really is innocent and was wrongfully convicted,' she went on. 'He's not going to be able to tell you what the circle means, is he? I mean, you've said yourself the evidence is thin, boss, and he was only convicted on a majority verdict. What if they got it wrong? What if the original arsonist has been away – perhaps inside for something else – and now he's back and doing exactly the same thing again because it's his thing? And whoever it is could be trying to draw attention to the Catholic connection and the link between the cases. '

'How does that tally with your theory that our arsonist is trying to get my attention, personally?' Ted asked her. 'I thought you said that was to get the original conviction looked at with a view to getting Warren released?'

'I hate the way you shoot down my best ideas with logic,' Jezza grinned at him.

'Are we doing any better with finding someone with a motive to kill Mr Byrne?' Jo asked.

'The people we spoke to at his workplace all seemed to think highly of him,' Mike told them. 'The management had no complaints about him. He was a good timekeeper, did his job well. Kept to himself a bit but everyone liked him well enough. Jezza found the same, talking to the production workers.'

Amelie was keeping quiet. Eric Morgan rightly deduced that she was worried about what she was going to have to say to the boss later on, and not wanting to draw attention to herself. He spoke up for her.

'Amelie and me identified the little girl in the photo but the trail ran cold on us. Lucy Robson. Byrne's next-door neighbour's daughter. The mother was a drug addict and sadly died of an overdose. Byrne used to look after Lucy for her and they spent a lot of time in each other's company. It seems as if it was innocent enough, too. When the social went in to take Lucy into care she was apparently very upset and wanted to stay with him. They couldn't allow it, of course, because he wasn't a relative or anything.

'She went into a home and was there for three years. She left as soon as she was legally allowed to. She never said anything about Byrne to the staff there, in all that time, but then it seems she was very closed. Didn't open up much about anything. There was certainly nothing on record to suggest that anything between them hadn't been right.

'She'll be around twenty now and the social have no idea where she went. She could have moved away, got married, changed her name. Died, even. Anything. We don't really have a lot to go on, but from what we've been told so far, there's nothing to suggest she would have a motive for killing Byrne.

'If it's all right with you, Jo, we were thinking of visiting the home Lucy was in tomorrow. Seeing if there's anyone there who remembers her and might know a bit more about her. Or if they can tell us who she was friendly with. Who she might have confided in.

'We may be on a hiding to nothing and it's possibly a dead-end trail, but in the absence of anything else so far, is it worth a shot?'

'Well worth it, I would say,' Ted said, looking to Jo, who agreed with him. 'If Mr Byrne's relationship with her was improper in any way, even if she never talked about it, it would certainly be a strong motive.'

'Boss, I'd quite like to do some more digging into the cousin Mike and I spoke to. After all, it was her Byrne was trying to throw the firework at when it went wrong. There could possibly be some history between them. Maybe he'd done other stuff like it before.'

Mike was shaking his head. 'I'm not buying that, Jezza. I'm not saying it's not wrong to chuck a firework, but to go from that to torturing and killing someone is a huge leap. Besides, Byrne himself was badly injured. Wouldn't that make her think he'd suffered enough?'

'No one from outside ever knows what's simmering underneath the lid when it comes to families,' Jezza retorted. 'We've not checked her out at all. We should at least do that.'

'I agree, Jezza,' Jo told her. 'Have a quick dig into her background, see what it throws up.'

'Boss, I keep thinking that because of the mutilation and torture aspect, there's a definite sexual element to this,' Martha said. 'I'm not just thinking about chopping off his member. But removing the fingers while he was alive? That makes me think it could be a punishment for what he'd been doing with them. That he'd touched the wrong person, in the wrong way.'

Jo wound things up. People started to gather up their things, log off on their computers. Ted went to his office to get his briefcase. Eric Morgan followed him, Amelie trotting at his heels.

'Have you got a minute, guv? Only Amelie wanted a word.'

Without being invited, Eric pulled the spare chair out and sat down, leaving Amelie standing in front of the boss's desk as Ted took his seat. She hesitated. Eric indicated to her to get on with it.

'Sir, I'm really sorry. It probably was me that made the mistake with the nail varnish bottle. I mean, I honestly don't remember seeing it, but Virgil wouldn't have made that mistake. I should have owned up straight away. I'm really sorry.'

'Can't remember seeing it, or didn't see it?' Ted asked, studying her hard. 'Amelie, do you need glasses?'

She nodded miserably. 'I'm supposed to wear them but I hate them. And I can't get on with contact lenses.'

'It's an operational requirement, DC Foster. You must know that. You must have worn glasses for an eye test before you were accepted. If you need them, wear them. I shall expect to see you in them tomorrow.'

'Tomorrow? You mean you're not kicking me out?'

'I'm short of officers. You're an officer. Please act like one. Turn up tomorrow, wearing your glasses as and when you need them. That'll be all.'

She hurried out of the office as Eric leaned back in his chair and laughed.

'I told her you were a pussy cat. Silly vain kid. She'll be all right, once she learns a few of the ground rules.'

Warren had been glued to the local television news at every opportunity he got. As well as reading the evening paper cover to cover and back again. He was trying to hide his mounting level of agitation. He didn't want to do anything to draw attention to himself. Not now. Not while things were finally, slowly, starting to move in the direction he wanted them to.

This time his mopping rhythm changed even more. He was back to humming the full chorus. It contained one word which was repeated three times. On the third time, he banged the mop down, hard, viciously, before carrying on.

To make matters worse, the chaplain was late again. Much later than usual. Soon Warren was going to have to go. The patrolling officer had already looked in on him to see if he was nearly finished. But he needed to talk to the chaplain before he was escorted back to his cell. He needed everything to be exactly as he had planned it, before tomorrow.

Finally, the priest came hurrying into the chapel, flustered, clearly out of breath. On the defensive. Apologising even before he reached where Warren was working.

'William, please forgive me, I am so very sorry I'm late. I know you will have been waiting to speak to me.'

Warren's eyes were steely. 'I'm disappointed in you, padre. I have to say that. You promised to do one small thing for me, yesterday. And you haven't done it. Have you?'

'William, something came up yesterday. I was called to give last rites to one of my old parishioners. Her own parish priest was away and there was no one else available. She was asking for me. The family contacted me to say she had very little time left. What was I to do? I am deeply sorry. Tonight you will have my undivided attention, I promise you that. And I can only apologise, once more.'

'It has to be tonight, then. No more excuses, padre. I have a very important visit tomorrow and everything has to be just right. Don't let me down again. Because I've been talking some more to young Joey. He confides in me readily. And he's in a fragile state of mind. You know he's already on suicide watch. If I was concerned enough about him, I might have to talk to someone about those concerns.'

Chapter Seventeen

The muted buzzing of his phone on the side table woke Ted. As he reached out a hand for it, Adam, curled into a ball on his chest, stretched out one paw, claws unsheathed, in protest.

Ted lifted up the phone. The screen told him two things. It was five o'clock in the morning. And it was the station calling him.

He gently lifted the cat off himself as he slid out of bed, putting him down on the pillow he'd just vacated and heading out onto the landing as he answered.

'Duty inspector, sir,' Patel's voice greeted him. 'Sorry to wake you but I have a note that you're to be informed personally of any suspected arsons on the patch. We've got an ongoing incident at an empty lock-up on the far side of town.'

He gave Ted the exact location before he went on, 'Initial reports from the fire crew attending suggested it was kids messing about and things got out of hand. Then the Watch Commander called in to log it as suspicious. They've been told to update us on anything with a particular burn pattern, in case it's linked to your case. He says it's early days yet, they've only just got things under control. But he said he's pretty sure it's the same pattern.'

'All right, thank you. I'm on my way up to Manchester this morning so I'll look in myself. Are Uniform attending?'

'They are, because of the early alert to another possible arson. We were hoping we might get lucky and find the perpetrator still in the vicinity, but nothing so far.'

'Right, I'll send a couple of my officers as well. We've no leads yet on this arsonist. It's about time we made some progress.'

He called Jo, who clearly dropped his phone trying to answer. Ted assumed the string of Spanish words he heard were not complimentary.

'Sorry to wake you, Jo, but I was woken by the duty inspector so I thought I'd share the honour. Our friendly neighbourhood arsonist at it again. Not yet confirmed but a definite probable. I'll call in on my way up to the prison but I thought it might be profitable to send some of the team now, see if they can spot anything early on. Maybe the arsonist will be hanging around for once. It's about time we got lucky on this one.'

He could hear Jo clattering about, a door opening and closing. He gave him the address of the incident and Jo gave an evil chuckle. 'I've a good mind to wake Eric up and send him. Remind him that we don't all have fixed shift patterns. But I'll go myself, while I'm already awake. It saves me the ritual of family breakfast and attempting to get all the kids ready for school at the right time. I'll give Jezza a bell. I'll be going almost past her place. I believe she has a live-in babysitter these days, for her Tommy. Nathan's pretty much a permanent fixture, isn't he?'

'He usually is, I believe. I might see you there if you've not wrapped things up and left by the time I arrive. I'll call Mike and get him to brief the team. I'll give him another hour or so yet. No sense in us all being awake at silly o'clock if we don't have to be.'

Ted went back into the bedroom. He knew he probably wouldn't go back to sleep now. It was just as well he had no such plans. Seemingly without waking, Trev had managed to spread even further across the bed than usual. Even Adam, curled up on the pillow, showed no signs of stirring a second time and relinquishing his spot. A definite case of no room at the inn.

Ted decided on another early morning run. A road run, this time. An hour or so steadily pounding the pavements of his neighbourhood could result in anything. It had been a relatively quiet area when Ted had first moved there with his parents. Recently, crime levels had gone up. As Kevin Turner had reminded his officers, burglary and car theft were sharply increasing. He might just spot something of interest at that time of day.

He ran for nearly an hour. He was just getting ready to turn up Lisburne Lane to head for home and a shower when he spotted an elderly woman in her front garden. It wasn't warm but she was wearing only a nightie and slippers as she stood by the front gate, looking anxiously up and down the road.

When she saw Ted approach, slowing to a walk, wiping sweat from his face with the towel slung round his neck, she called out to him, 'What day is it, love?'

'It's Thursday,' he told her. 'Are you all right? Are you waiting for someone?'

'What day is it, love?' she asked again.

'Thursday,' he repeated. 'Is there someone with you?'

'What time is it, love?'

Ted went closer to the gate, reaching for his mobile phone with one hand, his warrant card with the other. He couldn't carry on his way and leave what was clearly a confused and vulnerable woman alone. He could already see that the nightdress was sodden. She was in need of some attention, especially if there was no one with her.

'I'm a police officer. Do you need some help?'

'What day is it, love?'

She didn't seem alarmed as he opened the gate and took her as gently as he could by the arm.

'My name's Ted. Shall we go indoors? It's a bit parky, isn't it? Shall I put the kettle on for you?'

'What time is it, love?'

'It's early yet. Come on, I'll make you a brew.'

As he guided her towards the house, he dialled the station.

'It's DCI Darling. I've just found a confused elderly woman in a front garden near to Cherry Tree. No signs of anyone else present so far. I'll need a unit with a female officer.'

The smell hit him as soon as he stepped over the threshold. The woman tottered off towards the back of the house. Ted still had his phone in his hand with the call connected.

'I think there's a death, too. Hang on, I'll just check.'

He followed her into a small kitchen at the back of the house. A man was sitting in a chair by the kitchen table. He'd clearly been there for some time. The woman didn't react to the smell, nor to the sight of the body. She turned to Ted and asked again, 'What day is it, love?'

The unscheduled stop made Ted later than he'd intended before he set off for the scene of the latest arson. He'd stayed with the woman, made her tea, talking reassuringly to her, until the area car had arrived. He was pleased it was PC Susan Heap who was one of the first responders. She was the ideal person to handle the situation and arrange a place of safety for an elderly person as a matter of urgency. The woman had still not said anything other than repeatedly asking the day and time.

'Do we have a name for her, sir?'

'I'm not sure if she knows it herself, to be honest. The only things she's said to me the whole time have been to ask me the day and the time. I haven't started to look for post, pension books, or anything like that. I didn't want to leave her alone. I imagine the deceased is probably her husband, although she doesn't seem to acknowledge his presence, even. Perhaps he was her carer. She might not have had anything to eat since he died, in that case, but I didn't want to give her anything without knowing anything about her. I've made her a cup of tea, but that's as much as I've done.'

'We'll take it from here, sir. What a good job it was you who found her. I imagine there's some folk around who'd have taken advantage of the situation and come in to rob the place.' She was looking round the gloomy and outdated interior as she spoke. 'If there's anything worth nicking.'

Ted spent a lot of time under the shower when he got back to the house, trying to get rid of the stench of death. He couldn't decide if it was on him or if he just had the smell of it in his nostrils. He splashed on a bit more aftershave than usual, to be sure. An extra dollop, he found himself thinking. He wanted to know the significance of those additional splashes of fuel at the arson sites. Perhaps Warren might be persuaded to talk about them.

It was a different fire crew who were still on the scene when Ted arrived at the latest suspected arson scene. He found the Watch Commander talking to Jo.

'What have we got?'

'Boss, this is Brian. My boss, DCI Ted Darling. Too early to be sure of anything yet but distinct similarities to our other two fires.'

'You'll know already that we need to wait for the findings of the Investigation Officer, and he might well bring a dog in to work the scene. The details of the previous two fires have been circulated, of course, and I'm pretty sure we have the same circle pattern in there. Once again, it's a concrete floor with no carpeting or tiling to distort the image. Lots of refuse lying about so it went up like a torch and ignited all the old timbers.'

'Any signs yet of the starting method?'

Brian gave him what Ted's father would have called an old-fashioned look. 'Ted, we're the fire service. For miracles, you need someone with their collar on back to front. It's just possible the dog might find you something to show how it was started, but I can't guarantee it.'

The officer went back to his work and Ted turned to his DI.

'Jo, have we made any progress on checking possible

sources of dodgy cigarettes? The imported type which would carry on smouldering without being smoked?'

'I hope you're not implying that I, as a secret smoker, might somehow know the route for buying dodgy knock-off fags from Eastern Europe?'

'And I hope you're not telling me that a DI might be buying such things in a pub to avoid paying import duty,' Ted countered with a smile.

'Perish the thought. I've been talking to Kev about that one. Some of his officers know better than I do where that sort of thing goes on. He's putting a list together for us to work through. Meanwhile Jezza's having a wander about here looking for any possible eyewitnesses or any signs of anything. Although there weren't many folk around early on when the fire started. You're off to see the arsonist now?'

'I am. I'm not sure how long I'll be, or whether it will achieve anything, but it's worth a try. I'll see you later.'

He started to walk away, then stopped and turned back.

'Vicars and tarts.'

'Come again?'

'It was something Brian said just now. Someone with their collar on back to front. Martha found a karaoke in costume which took place near the first site, and the eyewitness said something about someone he thought was in fancy dress but couldn't say why. Could it have been someone dressed as a vicar? After all, the only thing different about them would be a dog collar. Can you give Martha a call and ask her to check on that, please?'

'It's nice to meet you, Ted. To put a face to the voice on the phone. But you're going to have to excuse me if I leave you in the more than capable hands of Katie, who is one of our liaison officers. I suspect my day is a bit like many of yours. Meetings, paperwork and yet more meetings.'

The Security Governor had dropped by to introduce

himself to Ted before hurrying away. They were in Katie Pilling's office. She invited Ted to sit down and made him the cup of tea he'd asked for when she offered him something.

'If it suits your needs, I thought we could go over the details you requested in here first, before you meet with Warren. Then I understand you want to see Wellman? Your email about your plans for him has been passed to me, with approval. It's not entirely regular but it doesn't go against any rules so it's something we could accommodate.

'Warren is a Listener, and one who is well regarded in that role. Wellman is a troubled prisoner and has been since his arrival. It's not his first stay with us and his behaviour is consistent with his last time here. So it wouldn't stretch credibility too far for him to have contact with Warren.'

'What can you tell me about Mr Warren?'

'He's vehemently denied his guilt ever since he arrived. That's not at all unusual. Practically every man in here is innocent, according to them. Wellman is one of the exceptions. Quite happy to admit his guilt and never misses any opportunity to behave in a way which risks prolonging his stay. It's almost as if he enjoys it here too much to leave willingly.

'Warren was a self-confessed atheist when he joined us, but then started attending chapel and is now a dedicated practising Catholic. He seems to have become much more religious since the former chaplain retired and Father Archer joined us about two years ago. Warren carries out cleaning duties and is our chapel Red Band, which gives him additional responsibilities and a certain level of trust, which he has never breached.'

'I imagine all of this has made for quite a long list of people who've had contact with him since he's been with you?'

'Oh, yes. I've been through all the records and pulled up everything I can for you. Cell-mates, people he's had contact with through the Listener scheme, plus any visitors. He has few of those. His father only visits occasionally. About twice a year on average.

'Warren does still have contact with a former prisoner, someone he got to know quite well. A younger man he helped a lot. He was virtually illiterate when he arrived and Warren took time to teach him to read and write. They became reasonably close through that. The nearest he's had to a friend, I think you could say.'

'I have to ask this, as a police officer. With no hidden agenda. I'm married to a man myself. Was there any more to their relationship than friendship, do you know?'

'Not as far as I'm aware. Although, of course, it is possible. Warren appears always to have been rather a solitary person. He doesn't seem to have formed any close relationships either in here or before his time with us.'

'Yes, I noticed the lack of character witnesses at his trial. I think the headteacher of the school where he worked said a few guarded good words about his time there but that was all. And he seems to have said it more in a way to exonerate himself and the school of any blame in the incident which killed two of their pupils.'

'That pattern of behaviour seems to have continued in here. He certainly doesn't go out of his way to make friends. I can't, of course, go into confidential details about any prisoner's medical records. That would be a breach of their Human Rights and believe me, Warren knows his rights inside and out and would be the first to complain. But I have been authorised to tell you that if for any reason Warren's – comportment, shall we say – gives you any cause for concern, there will be an officer outside the door of the room you'll be using who can come to your assistance.

'This next thing I'm going to say isn't on my brief, and I doubt you can do much about it anyway, but I'll mention it, for your information. Excuse me for being personal. I love your aftershave. But sometimes, strong scents can be a trigger for certain medical conditions.'

'Oh, sorry, is it as strong as that? I had a not very pleasant death to deal with before I came out. I couldn't tell whether the smell was clinging to me or not. Should I try to wash some of it off?'

She smiled at him. 'I think it's rather nice, but I just needed to make you aware. Now, I'll take you to a private room where you can speak to Warren. I know you mentioned wanting to try to keep your connection and meeting with Wellman as much of a secret as anything can be in here, so I've arranged for you to see him on another wing altogether afterwards, which is the best I can do.'

She led the way along several corridors to where a prison officer was standing outside a door, waiting patiently. Then she opened the door and invited Ted to follow her in.

The man sitting behind a table rose to his feet as they entered. Ted ran his eyes over him appraisingly. Medium height, medium build. Unremarkable, apart from strange, light grey eyes. Ted was finely tuned to body language. What he picked up from Warren was an almost excited anticipation, which surprised him. Not the usual reaction he got to an unexpected visit from a police officer.

'Warren, this is Detective Chief Inspector Darling, from Stockport Police, who has asked to speak to you.'

She turned to Ted as she left and said, 'Don't forget, there's an officer outside the door if you need anything at all.'

'Please sit down, Mr Warren.'

'Chief Inspector. This is indeed a privilege.'

Chapter Eighteen

'Mr Warren? Detective Sergeant O'Connell, Stockport Police. I wondered if I could have a word with you, please. It's about your son, William.'

The man holding the door ajar was unshaven, his shirt none too clean. His eyes were bloodshot, his look suspicious.

'What's he done now? Has something happened to him?'

'No, he's absolutely fine. I just wanted to ask you a few questions, if that would be all right?'

'You'd better come in, then. House is a bit of a tip, mind.'

He wasn't exaggerating. He opened the door slightly wider and led the way to the kitchen. The hallway was cluttered. Bin bags which didn't smell too good. Piles of newspaper. Empty bottles. Rob already knew this wasn't the house William Warren had been living in when he'd been arrested and charged. The family had had to move away from the neighbourhood when they became the target of hate crimes because of the fatal fire. Warren Senior had moved again since his son had been in prison, but Rob had tracked down his address.

As if reading his thoughts, the man said, 'Aye, I know it's not much. We moved away from where the fire happened. It got nasty, with the neighbours. Then I had to sell the next place too and get this shit-hole when the wife had to go into the nursing home. I couldn't cope with her at home any more.'

He tipped more newspapers onto the floor and pulled a chair up, inviting Rob to sit down and offering to put the kettle on. Rob didn't fancy anything which came from that filthy kitchen. Not even a boiled drink. He declined politely.

Warren sat down at the table, pushing dirty plates and cutlery out of his way.

'What's this about, then? Is Will trying for an appeal again? I've not seen him for a while.'

'I just wanted to go over a few details of the original case, Mr Warren. Anything you might remember. Perhaps something you'd forgotten at the time which came back to you over the years.'

'D'you not think I'd have give him an alibi if I could? He's my son, after all, even if we never really got along all that well. I just couldn't remember anything. And I didn't want to start lying, not even to try to help him. I know how clever you police types are. You'd have soon caught the lie and then I'd have made things worse.'

'Is there a particular reason why you and your son don't get along?'

'It's just like that sometimes. Our Will was always a cocky little sod. Thought he was better than everyone else, including me. He was always bright, always studying. He looked down his nose at me because I worked for the Royal Mail. In the sorting office. He used to tell his university friends I were middle management, but I weren't. That's just how he was. A bit of a snob. I weren't good enough for him.'

'Did he have many friends?'

'Well, I call them friends but they weren't really. Just other students he hung about with.'

'Girlfriends?'

The man shook his head. 'There were some lasses in the group but he didn't seem particularly interested. He weren't queer, though,' he went on hurriedly. 'Weren't interested in any of the lads in that way, either. Not from what I could see. Never did take up wi'anyone, even when he got older.'

'Do you remember anything about the night of the fire, Mr

Warren? Anything at all?'

'I didn't then and I still don't. You probably already know, but the wife, Edith, has Alzheimer's. Got it early too. I managed with her at home for a while, just about. But I admit it. It were bloody hard. Especially trying to hold a job down at the same time. Our Will stayed living at home, to help out a bit. It still weren't easy, seeing her like that. So I drank. To deal with it.'

'Can I ask you a candid question, Mr Warren?'

The man narrowed his eyes and squinted at him in suspicion.

'Aye, go on then,' he said guardedly, then went on, 'but I can guess what it is. You want to know if I think our Will were capable of starting a fire which killed four people, two of them only young lads. Do you know how much I wish I could say no, I don't believe it for a moment? The honest truth is, I don't know.

'Will were always very controlling, even as a little lad. He always got very angry when anyone crossed him. Especially if anyone touched anything of his. I suppose part of that were being an only child. He never had to share owt and he never learned how to. And there'd been a big row at school when he accused them two lads of keying his car. He didn't have any proof but he told them that when he got it he'd make them sorry they'd done it. It seems a lot of people heard him say that and it got took the wrong way.'

'Were you at the trial, Mr Warren?'

He shook his head. 'Couldn't leave our Edith. Having the Old Bill come round here and drag her only son away in hand-cuffs seemed to tip her right over the edge. She never really got over it. Kept asking and asking for him. Still does. Every time I visit her. And of course, she never saw him again. I had to give up work and look after her full-time until I could get her into a home. I read about it in the papers, like, but that's all.'

'So you perhaps know that the fire was started by pouring a

circle of fuel and setting light to it. Would a circle have any particular significance to William, that you know of?'

'I don't know. I didn't know the half of what went on in his head most of the time. Summat to do with chemistry, perhaps? A symbol for something?'

'What about music? What was he interested in?'

'Music? I've no idea. He played stuff in his room but it were just like noise to me. Some whiny classical stuff with violins, I remember. But loud rock too, with lots of thumping. I used to shout up the stairs at him to turn it down.'

'What about country music?' Rob was thinking about something Jezza had said during a briefing.

'Bloody 'ell, no. I never heard him play any of that shite. Not his scene at all. Thank the lord.'

'And was he a smoker?'

'Fags, you mean, or illegal stuff? Neither, as far as I know. I never saw him with any and his clothes and his room never smelled of it. Why are you asking all these questions, all of a sudden? Are you reopening the case? Is our Will innocent after all?'

'It's just routine, Mr Warren. Thank you for your time. I'll leave you my card. If you do happen to think of anything at all, please don't hesitate to contact me.'

'Like buggery it's routine. If someone has cocked up and sent the wrong man to prison, you should know that our Will makes a very bad enemy. Always has done, probably always will do. He won't rest until he's made whoever it were pay for their mistakes.'

'Mr Warren, I'm here to ask you a few questions about the crime of which you were convicted,' Ted began.

'Wrongly convicted, Chief Inspector,' Warren corrected him, his tone on the patronising side of patient, as he might have spoken to a pupil he thought was being unnecessarily obtuse.

'But you were convicted, Mr Warren, and you've so far not been successful in your attempts to launch an appeal against that conviction.'

Warren leaned back in his seat and studied Ted. He was unimpressed so far. Thoughts running through his head.

'Is this it? This insignificant little man who reeks of too much aftershave? This is what I've been building my hopes on to get the case reopened? I hope I haven't been wasting my time.'

'Please, Chief Inspector. You're clearly an intelligent man. I imagine you must be to hold your rank at what would appear to be a young age, if you forgive a personal comment. I presume you're graduate entry. So surely you're not going to insult my intelligence by pretending British justice has an unblemished record when it comes to wrongful convictions. Which case should I cite first? Timothy Evans? Stephen Downing? The Birmingham Six?

'I was in the unenviable and ethically questionable position of having to prove my innocence, rather than relying on the prosecution to prove my guilt. I was at home with my parents when the unfortunate fire took place. But I couldn't prove it. My mother was completely unfit to testify and my father … well, he dealt with my mother's condition by being drunk most of the time, except when he was at work.'

'You were heard to threaten the two boys who died, Mr Warren.'

'Oh, really, Chief Inspector,' Warren sounded disappointed now. The school teacher who'd thought a pupil capable of brilliance and had instead been handed a piece of sub-standard homework. 'On that basis I should have murdered several boys I taught. I've never tolerated what is now put under the umbrella of anti-social behaviour instead of calling it what it is – criminal damage. Those two boys keyed my car, which was quite new. I knew it was them and they knew I knew. I told them, forcefully, that when I had the evidence, they could look forward to spending rather a lot of time in detention. To go from that to making it into some threat to kill was such a tangential leap that neither I nor my defence team could begin to find a way to counter it.'

'Are you a smoker, Mr Warren?'

Warren was studying him, his light-coloured eyes analytical. The science teacher, watching the results of his latest experiment and being less than impressed.

'Let me see. This is either you trying to establish whether I had the means and the opportunity to procure what was used to start the fire. Because of course, I read in detail all the so-called evidence against me, including the type of ignition device used. Or this is you remembering a course on interview techniques. Ask a seemingly banal question to catch the interviewee off balance and to observe the body language to establish the norm for when they are telling the truth or not.'

Ted wasn't a chess player. But he imagined this was what it must feel like as a novice playing against someone highly skilled. He felt Warren was testing him the whole time, weighing him up to see whether or not he was a worthy adversary.

Ted's tone was mild as he responded, 'It's just a simple question, Mr Warren. With no hidden agenda.'

'If you say so.' He didn't sound convinced. 'In which case I shall answer it as such. No, I'm not, and never have been, a smoker.'

'Thank you, Mr Warren. What can you tell me about the circle of fuel which was used to start the fire? With the cardinal points marked.'

'How can I tell you anything about that? As I've said, repeatedly, it wasn't me who started the blaze. So I can't begin to speculate on the meaning behind any of it.'

'You must have some sort of an idea about it though, Mr Warren. You and your defence team would surely have discussed it, in preparing rebuttal to any evidence the prosecution brought forward in connection with that circle.'

'Or ring, possibly, rather than circle,' Warren corrected him. 'I'm sure you probably know that the Ring of Fire is a volcanic area of the Pacific Ocean. It means absolutely nothing to me. I did say at the time that it seemed more like the signature of a geography teacher, what with the ring and the cardinal points, than one which could be attributed to a man of science, such as myself.'

'Unfortunately for you, though, Mr Warren, both geography teachers from your school had perfect alibis, as you know. One was in hospital in traction after a rugby accident. The other had had to replace him at the last minute on a field trip up in Scotland. Otherwise he might well have been at home, and possibly without an alibi.

'Having ruled both of them out, did you or your defence team have any other theory on the meaning behind the circle and the four points?'

'I'm not sure where you're going with this, Chief Inspector. As I've already said, we were in the invidious position of having to prove my innocence, not simply to disprove my guilt. I know about the song of that name, of course. I wonder if you know, perhaps, that the phrase "ring of fire" in that context is allegedly a euphemism for the female genitalia. That theory didn't advance us in our defence any more than any other.

'May I now ask you a question, Chief Inspector?'

When Ted didn't immediately react, Warren ploughed on.

'What exactly is the purpose of your visit here today? Are you, in fact, reopening the case and re-examining the evidence on which I was wrongfully convicted?'

'I'm afraid that's not in my remit, Mr Warren. I'm merely making enquiries into some apparent similarities between various cases. That's all.'

Something in Warren's expression changed. As suddenly and perceptibly as a switch being thrown. The grey eyes became colder, harder. His jaw clenched. His anger was palpable.

He leaned forward. Put his elbows on the table which separated him from Ted who braced himself, alert to any sign of danger.

Then Warren lowered his head into his hands. His voice was quiet, muffled.

'I wonder if you'd be kind enough to call the officer, please. I have the most appalling migraine. They can be triggered by strong scents. I'm afraid your aftershave is overpowering. I need medication, and a lie down.'

'Honestly, Ted, don't worry about it. As I said, I can't discuss confidential medical matters with you but I did say it might possibly be an issue. Strong fragrance can trigger migraines. And the trouble with them is it's one of those conditions where it's not possible to say categorically whether an attack is genuine or not. I'm a sufferer myself. I can't tell you how many lessons I bunked off at school by using it as an excuse. Ironically, given Warren's profession, mostly science lessons, which I didn't enjoy.'

The liaison officer, Katie Pilling, was walking with Ted to another private visiting room where he would be meeting his childhood friend, Martin Wellman, who was doing time.

'I know you can't breach confidences either, but was your meeting with Warren of any use to you?'

'He's an interesting character,' Ted replied evasively. 'As you said, total denial of any involvement in the fatal arson. And to an extent, I agree with him. Conviction by default, in a sense. The prosecution wasn't very strong but his lack of an alibi, plus some of the circumstantial evidence, was clearly what swayed the verdict against him.'

They'd reached a room with another officer waiting outside.

'Same thing again here, Ted. Just tell the officer when

you've finished talking to Wellman and someone will escort you off the premises. I hope this interview is more fruitful for you.'

Martin looked up with a smile of evident pleasure when Ted walked into the room. He was in a minority of actually being quite happy to be inside. After his time living rough on the street, it probably felt like a decent hotel, with plenty to eat, regular showers and clean clothes.

'Hello, Ted. This is a nice surprise. I wasn't expecting to see you. They didn't tell me who my mystery visitor was. You're looking good. Love the aftershave.'

Ted grinned at him. 'Sorry about that. Covering up for a death I had to deal with. I hope the fumes don't knock you out.

'I'm here to ask a favour from you, Martin. Feel free to say no, of course, if you like. Do you happen to know a prisoner called William Warren? He's doing life for a fatal arson.'

'Johnny Cash? Everybody knows Johnny.'

'Why do you call him that?'

'He does cleaning duties. A Red Band. Model prisoner. Never puts a foot out of line. But he's got this habit of humming under his breath when he's doing the mopping. That Cash song, *Ring of Fire*. Not loud, or anything. Almost like he doesn't realise he's doing it. That's what got him the nickname, although most people don't call him that to his face. He commands a bit of respect.'

'I've just been talking to him. An interesting man, but he doesn't give much away. I need to try to find a way to get a bit closer to him. To find out more about him.'

'And that's where I come in? I know of him, of course, everyone does. But our paths seldom cross, unless he happens to be cleaning an area I'm being moved through. I don't see how I can help, really.'

'You know about the Listener scheme? Like Samaritans. Warren is a Listener.'

'But you know me, Ted. I like being in here. It's better than the alternative. I don't need any counselling or anything. I only get anxious when it's coming up to release time and I know I'm quickly going to finish up back on the streets again. It's only ever a matter of time.'

'Precisely. And it won't be long before you are coming up for release. So it would seem quite natural if you were starting to get anxious and were in need of someone to talk to. I just want to get a feeling for what he's like. Could you do it for me?'

'Helping out an old friend? Of course I could. The thing is, there's something I'd want in return. Something I'm pretty sure you're not going to like.'

Chapter Nineteen

Eric Morgan gave Amelie a nudge to present their findings at the end of the day. To allow her a chance to redeem herself by showing what she was capable of. She was wearing her glasses now. Tortoiseshell frames which gave her a studious look and probably cost a fortune, judging by the brand name on the side.

She stood up hesitantly and began to speak, her eyes on Ted.

'Sir, Sergeant Morgan and I have spent our time today trying to track down Lucy Robson, as she had seemed to have a possible motive for killing Mr Byrne. If he really had been indecently assaulting her, as the photo tends to suggest.'

Ted picked up immediately on the use of the past tense in relation to the motive theory and wondered at its significance.

'We haven't succeeded in finding her at all. Nor any clue as to where she might be now, or what name she might be using. But we did find a girl, Jennifer Bradley, who shared a room with Lucy at the children's home. What she said gave a bit of a different story to what we were expecting.

'She told us that when Lucy first arrived at the home she spent most of her time in tears, asking for Bernie. When Jennifer finally got her to talk, Lucy told her that Bernie was her next-door neighbour. The person who'd always looked after her and been kind to her when her mother was completely out of it on drugs and incapable of looking after herself, never mind her daughter. An older man, who used to make sure Lucy had food and spending money and whatever else she needed that she didn't get from her mother. Especially affection. He bought her nice things to wear and took her to get her hair done. That kind of thing. Like an uncle might do.

'But according to Jennifer, Lucy said the two of them were in love. That as soon as she was old enough, Bernie was going to come and find her and they were going to go off together and get married and start a family. They'd already had a pretend wedding.

'Because Bernie was a Catholic, he'd started taking her to church with him. Getting her prepared for first communion and confirmation. All that sort of thing. He got her a first communion dress, with a veil and everything. Picked it out and bought it for her himself. And you know those dresses look a lot like wedding dresses sometimes. They had a little ceremony the evening after her first communion, when she was still wearing her dress. Lucy said it was like a trial run for when she was old enough to marry him properly.'

'That is about the sickest thing I've ever heard.' Jezza's voice was full of disgust. 'What kind of a pervert was this bloke Bernie? Getting a young girl of – what was she then, twelve or so? – to think she was in love with him. Are you going to tell us they had a wedding night, too?'

Amelie shook her head. 'Lucy told Jennifer that they did often sleep together in the same bed, but that Bernie was always the perfect gentleman and there was no sex between them. He told her he would wait until she was old enough and it would be all the more special for both of them because they'd waited.

'Jennifer said that Lucy really did talk about him as if she was in love with him. Or sincerely believed that she was. Not afraid of him in any way. Infatuated, she said. And here's the really weird thing. Lucy told her that for their pretend wedding, and for her first communion earlier the same day, Bernie got her some nail varnish and spent a long time painting her toenails with it, very carefully, so they were perfect. None on her fingers, he told her, because that would attract too much attention and people might take it the wrong way. Just on her toes so they'd be hidden by her shoes and only the two of them would know. And yes, it was a bright red varnish, although Jennifer couldn't remember whether or not Lucy ever told her the name of the colour.

'While we're on the subject of nail varnish,' she went red in the face as she carried on speaking, although her voice didn't waver, 'can I just say it's entirely my fault that the bottle in with Byrne's possessions was overlooked. Nothing to do with Virgil at all. I was stupidly not wearing my specs because I hate them, so I missed it, completely. Sorry.'

She sat down hastily, now going bright red from the neck up.

Virgil threw her a broad grin of approval. Ted smiled at her in recognition. It couldn't have been easy for her to make the admission in front of the whole team.

'So if she really did think she was in love with him, where does that leave her motive to kill him?' Martha asked.

'Jilted lover?' Mike suggested. 'He never came back for her after promising he would. She felt abandoned by the man she thought she was in love with, so she went after him to get revenge.'

'That's a bit bloody drastic,' Jezza snorted. 'He may have broken her heart but did that warrant cutting off his todger? Not to mention chopping his fingers off while he was still alive.'

'Clearly we need to find Lucy Robson as a matter of some urgency. To eliminate her from our enquiries, if nothing else. Any ideas on how, anyone?' Ted asked them, giving Jezza one of his looks about her last remark.

'Guv, I thought Amelie and me could tackle that tomorrow. We need to go back and talk to the parish priest, now we know about the first communion. I find the clergy in general not all that forthcoming unless you know exactly the right questions to ask them. Someone may well have noticed Byrne being rather too close to the girl. Maybe tongues started to wag.

'If she'd really wanted to find him, the first thing she'd have done when she left the home would probably have been to go back to her old address and start asking questions. But before that, why wasn't she trying to make contact? Writing to him? Letting him know where she was and asking him to get in touch?'

'Do the dates tally? Had Byrne left there by the time she left the home?' Jo asked. 'And I agree with Eric. We need to find out if she made any attempt to contact him in the intervening time.'

'He left very soon after she was taken into care, and Amelie and me need to find out why. If it really was this big love affair, I can't believe he would just have gone away without trying a bit harder to find her. Something must have happened to convince him it was time to move on. Perhaps things were said after the mother died and that's why he decided to move away, sharpish. I suppose the mother's death was definitely a self-inflicted overdose, was it? If we knock on the right doors and ask the right questions, we might just find out what it was all about.'

'In the absence of any other suspect to date for Mr Byrne's death, we definitely need to find Lucy Robson,' Ted agreed. 'Even if it's just to eliminate her from our enquiries. And that's a good point about the mother. We'll check up on the circumstances of her death. Anything else on the Byrne case?'

'Boss, is it worth starting to ask to take samples from chainsaws and loppers from the various tree surgeons and the like we've identified?' Virgil began then, seeing Eric Morgan open his mouth, he hurried on, 'and yes, sarge, I know, anyone could have a chainsaw in their garden shed but we need to start somewhere. Otherwise we're just treading water on this one, it seems to me.'

'You've spoken to all of them now?' Jo asked him.

'All of them except this Tam Lee, the small outfit who had their kit stolen. I can't get hold of them at the moment. I've left a couple of short messages. Nothing too specific, just asking them to get in touch, but I've not yet had an answer.'

'Either run off their feet with work, or they've gone out of business,' Jo suggested.

Virgil shook his head. 'If they have gone under, it's very recent. There's no mention of it on the Companies House website.'

'Boss? What do you think?' Jo asked him. 'Time to take samples? I don't know much about chainsaws myself. Eric, would you routinely clean yours thoroughly after cutting up your latest victim?'

'Funny man,' Eric growled. 'I do clean and oil mine after every use, but I'm meticulous like that. Forensics could certainly still find traces of human bone and goodness knows what else though, even on one which had been cleaned, no doubt. But that's going to be one hell of a big job, isn't it, guv? You're in charge of the purse strings, but will the budget really stand a big operation like that based on what's pretty much just a hunch?'

'I'm talking to the bosses tomorrow, so I'll see what they say. It's something to keep in mind, but I'd much prefer us to find Lucy Robson first. If anyone knows Mr Byrne thoroughly, it must be her. And let's not rule out the possibility that when he lost her, he simply moved on to grooming another young girl.

'What's the latest on the arsons?'

'No vicars, boss,' Martha told him. 'Nor tarts, either. At least not in fancy dress. I checked at the karaoke pub, and at all the other pubs in the vicinity. I also did some door-to-door. I took a Uniform officer with me this time, in case I came face to face with a suspect. It occurred to me that someone might have been having a private party with that as a theme, but if they were, we didn't find any trace of it by asking around.

'I also got to thinking about that phrase from the witness. About thinking the person was in fancy dress, then not being able to say what gave them that idea. It could have been a parish priest going about his business, of course, going with the dog collar theory. Maybe, with the bag, going out to perform last rites or something. So if it's all right, I could try to follow that up tomorrow. Check with local Catholic churches, then working out from there.'

'Not just Roman Catholic,' Jezza corrected her. 'Church of England does it too.'

Seeing Martha's querying look, she went on to explain, 'Religion isn't my thing but my kid brother Tommy is a mine of sometimes useful information on anything and everything.'

'Thank you, I'll bear that in mind, although it will be more legwork, of course. I was also thinking of what type of person might be out and about carrying a bag and looking as if they might be in fancy dress. Apart from sports clubs, as I've drawn a blank on that so far. And I imagine most people doing sports change before and after them, rather than walk home through the streets in their gear. So they wouldn't look as if they were in fancy dress.'

'I certainly do for kickboxing,' Jezza put in. 'You wouldn't catch me even crossing the car park in nothing but a skimpy layer of Lycra. And it's a bloody good job our Maurice isn't here or he'd come over all unnecessary at me saying that.'

'I'm the same with weight-training,' Virgil agreed.

'I have, on occasion, had to come straight in to the nick from a martial arts session without changing first,' Ted told them. 'But not from choice and always with a top layer on and my belt in my pocket.'

'What about plumbers?' Amelie suggested. 'Could they be out on emergency repairs, in their overalls and carrying a bag of tools?'

Jezza sighed theatrically. 'Have you ever tried to get an emergency plumber round here? Especially out of hours?'

'No, but don't some insurance companies provide twenty-four-hour breakdown cover?'

Jezza gave her a patient older sister smile as she said, 'You've been watching too many adverts on TV. We could look at it, though. Anything's worth a shot.'

'I have another possible lead for us after talking to Mr Warren. He was not very forthcoming, it has to be said. Steadfastly maintaining his innocence. He did say one thing that might we worth looking at, though. Steve, perhaps one for you to read up on, see if it takes us anywhere. He talked about the other Ring of Fire. Not the song but the volcanic one in the Pacific Ocean. I asked him about the circle with the cardinal points marked, which was used to start the fires. He said it was more like the signature of a geography teacher. It's a long shot, but a possible one. The case notes already show it was neither of the geography teachers at the same school. But let's look into any former teachers from there. Or even supply teachers who taught geography.

'Once I told Mr Warren it was not my role to reopen his case, he lost all interest in me, pleaded a bad migraine, which may or may not have been genuine, and got taken back to his cell. But the liaison officer gave me details of all the visitors he's had, which is not many. He does get one every three or four weeks from a young man who shared a cell with him for a time. Duncan Dooley. Specialist subject, burglary.

'The interesting, and possibly significant thing about Duncan Dooley is that he's six feet one. So he could well be described as tall. And we have an eyewitness account of a tall man near the scene of our second arson. We need to track down Duncan Dooley and interview him. Find out if he has an alibi. I've got his address so Jo, can you sort that for tomorrow, please?'

Warren was lying on his back on the bed in his cell. One arm was crooked across his eyes to shield them from light. One leg was bent, the foot on top of the bed, the other leg crossed over it. The foot on that side was tapping against the wall, any sound muffled by his sock.

Almost inaudibly, he was humming his refrain. Every time he reached the word repeated three times, the foot tapped harder, staccato. His whole body was stiff with barely suppressed anger.

He'd carefully tucked the migraine medication he'd been given under his tongue and spat it out into the toilet at the first opportunity. He didn't want anything which would make him feel sleepy and clog his thinking processes. He needed a clear head to plan the way forward from here.

The spy hole in his door slid open and he heard a prison officer say, 'Chaplain for you, Warren.' Then, in an undertone which wasn't lost on Warren, 'You know this is highly irregular, chaplain, because of the risk of hostage-taking. I'll have to leave the door open with the bolt shot.'

Warren removed his arm from his face and opened his eyes as the lanky figure of Father Archer bounced in, his face lined with concern.

'I'm sorry if I'm disturbing you, William. I was just very concerned to hear you were having another of your nasty spells. I'll go, if you'd prefer to be alone. But when I heard you'd been excused cleaning duties I realised how much you must be suffering. So I just wanted to come and see if there was anything I could do for you. Anything at all. You know you only have to ask.'

Warren took his arm away from his face. His clothing had left creases there. He turned his head slowly towards the chaplain. The grey eyes were darker than Archer had ever seen them. They looked almost black. He unconsciously took half a step back under their impact.

'But I do ask you, padre. Repeatedly. You're simply not delivering. I had a visit today from some cretinous police officer with so much aftershave on it gave me a crippling migraine. He asked idiotic questions but showed no signs of recognising my innocence or of reopening the case.

'I can't carry on like this. It's affecting my health, as you know. It's killing me.

'You're just going to have to do better, padre. A lot better. If not, you're backing me into a corner and I shall have to take more drastic direct action.

'And believe me, you don't want to put me into that position.'

Chapter Twenty

'Is it this one? Half the number's missing off the door.'

Jezza and Mike Hallam were standing outside a terraced house, paint peeling off the front door which bore a single digit – the number two.

'Logically, number twenty-eight should be between twenty-six and thirty, but you never know,' Jezza grinned at Mike as she knocked on the door.

She knocked a few times before there was any sign of life inside. Neither Jezza nor Mike had any visible ID. But as soon as the door opened on a tall, thin man in his twenties, wearing nothing but a torn T-shirt and scruffy tracksuit bottoms, he clearly knew exactly what they were, if not who.

He tried to slam the door on them but Jezza was too quick, moving forward to block it with her shoulder as the man turned and bolted through the house.

'Get the car and drive round the back,' Jezza shouted as she sprinted out of the house in pursuit.

She could hear, but chose to ignore, Mike bellowing after her, 'Risk assessment, DC Vine.'

The man she was chasing, presumably Duncan Dooley, as it was his address and the fleeing figure matched his photo on file, sped out through the back door, trying to slam it behind him. The small back garden was barely a few strides of his long legs, then he was hurdling over a low wooden gate and running up a narrow passageway.

He may have had the advantage of height and leg length

but he was clearly not much of a runner. Jezza did a lot of it, whenever she could. She had the speed and the stamina. She'd easily outstripped Ted, a medium-paced distance runner, on the beach in Spain. She was determined, too. She may not yet have been closing on her quarry, but he wasn't gaining any ground and she was dogging his every move.

Jezza had her phone out and was relaying to Mike the direction the pursuit was taking her in. She didn't waste her time or her breath in responding to his increasingly irate orders to cease pursuit. She knew there was always the risk that Dooley would stop and face her and could be carrying a knife or another weapon. If that happened, she could either rely on her kickboxing skills, or she could put her sprinting to good use and leg it back the way she'd come.

At least, that's what she was planning on telling the boss had been her risk assessment when he read her the riot act later on, as he no doubt would. Mike Hallam would be obliged to report her conduct, but she was sure she could talk her way out of any trouble it might bring her. Especially if she caught their possible suspect.

Luck and timing were both on her side. Dooley had made a few turns into other alleys and small streets. As he made to dash across a bigger road, he ran straight into the bonnet of Mike Hallam's car, bounced off it and landed with a thud on the tarmac.

Jezza was on him in a flash. Holding him down carefully as she told him, 'Duncan Dooley? DC Vine, DS Hallam. We only wanted a cosy chat. There was no need to run for it. Stay still for me while I check you for injuries. Does it hurt anywhere?'

He was panting for breath now. Jezza was barely winded. Mike was giving her daggers as he got out of the car to join the two of them.

'Are you hurt, Mr Dooley? Do you need an ambulance?' Mike asked him.

Jezza had done a recent first aid update and was busy

putting it into practice, with a top to toe survey, asking the man questions as she worked.

'We really did only want to talk to you, Duncan. Nothing more than that,' she told him when she'd finished. 'Are you all right now? Do you think you could stand up?'

'Should we get him properly checked out first?' Mike was erring on the side of caution.

'He's fine. Aren't you, Duncan? Just a couple of minor scrapes from the road surface.'

Dooley was getting slowly to his feet. 'What d'you want with me?' he asked, with open hostility.

'Come on, we'll drive you home. Then you can make us a nice cup of tea and answer a few questions. You're not being arrested or anything. We just want to talk to you.'

Jezza saw him into the back seat and sat next to him while Mike drove them back to the house. Dooley maintained a sullen silence. He let them into his home and went to close the back door, which was still standing wide open from his hasty exit. He showed no signs of offering them a brew. Not even a seat. Instead the three of them stood there in the kitchen, looking at one another.

'What's this about?'

Mike left Jezza to do the talking. He got his pocket book out to take notes.

'Routine questions, nothing more. Where were you the Friday before last, in the early hours?'

'Work. I work nights in a supermarket. Stocking shelves, mostly.'

'What about last Wednesday? Evening, going up to midnight.'

'Work.'

'And yesterday? Early hours of the morning.'

'Work. Whatever this is about, it weren't me. I've got alibis for all those days. They fixed me up with a job, and this crappy flat, when I came out of prison. I don't want to go back there so I turn up for work and do my job. We have to clock in and out and the supervisor checks up on us all the time. You can't even go for a piss without him wanting to know where you are. You can ask him.'

'You shared a prison cell with William Warren, didn't you?'

'Yeah. So what? He was nice to me. Helped me to learn to read and write proper. That's why I got a decent job when I come out. Never had one before, 'cos I couldn't read well enough.'

'And you visit Warren sometimes, since you've been released?'

'Yeah, so what? Nothing wrong wi' it. Couldn't be, anyway. They watch us all the time, 'cos I'm an ex-con. Security cameras always locked on the table where I'm sat, and prison officers patrolling near us all the time, listening out. I'm not slippin' him drugs or nothing. I just like to keep in touch. He was the first person who helped me with reading. Everyone else just told me I were thick.'

'Do you wear a uniform for work, Duncan?'

'Yeah. With the name of the store on.'

'And how do you travel to and from work?'

'Bus.'

'Do you wear your uniform on your journeys? Do you ever walk through the streets with your uniform on?'

He narrowed his eyes at that question. 'I put a jacket over it, mostly.'

'And do you need to carry a bag with you for anything? Like a holdall, perhaps? Something like that. Maybe with a change of clothes in?'

'I'm not on the rob, if that's what you mean. I don't nick stuff from work and bring it back here. There'd be no chance of that, anyway. Like I said, they watch us like hawks all the time.'

'I never said you did, Duncan. I was just asking.'

'No, I don't. Have a bag. Anyway, that's all I'm saying for now. I've answered your questions. I ain't done nothing. Now I need to get some kip before work. And I could report the two of you. Chasing me like that and running me over. I could get compo or something.'

'You weren't exactly run over. You just ran out into the path of DS Hallam's car and fell over. But please feel free to make a complaint if you want to, Duncan. Here's my card with my details and a contact number. My senior officer is Detective Chief Inspector Darling. Give him a call at any time if you want to take this matter further, and thank you for your time and assistance.'

'We'll have to tell the boss,' Mike warned her as they went back to the car. 'Just to cover ourselves, in case Dooley does try to make waves. And you were bang out of order going after him on your own like that. Especially not listening to me when I ordered you to cease pursuit.'

'Yes, sarge,' Jezza told him with not a trace of remorse. 'And I'll talk to the boss, with pleasure. I know what a pussy cat he is really.'

'Thank you, Mike, that'll be all. Not you, DC Vine,' Ted went on as Jezza made to follow Mike who hurried gratefully out of the office. It hadn't looked to him as if the "pussy cat" had been purring, listening to what he and Jezza had had to report on their return to the office.

Jezza stood in front of Ted's desk, giving him her most disarming smile. He remained unmoved. His voice was ominously quiet when he spoke.

'Jezza, this was total recklessness on your part. You know perfectly well you should have called for back-up and not made a move until they arrived.'

'I did a risk assessment, boss. There was a chance I wouldn't even have caught up with him but I thought that if I could keep him in sight, I could at least guide DS Hallam as to the way he was going. And if he had stopped and pulled a knife, I thought I could probably kickbox it out of the way then run off. You know I'm a fast sprinter, boss. I outran you easily in Spain.'

'It's not the appropriate time for smart answers, DC Vine. What if the suspect had produced a firearm? Or if he'd been deliberately leading you towards friends who would back him and might well be armed? Your risk assessment was completely inadequate for the situation. You put yourself at risk, as well as DS Hallam, potentially. Not to mention possibly injuring someone who might well have been innocent of any crime.'

Jezza put her drama training to good use and tried to look as contrite as possible as she responded with, 'Noted. Sorry, boss. It won't happen again.'

'It certainly won't, Jezza. We're at full stretch at the moment, as you well know. But as soon as there's a lull, I'm going to refer you for further training in risk assessment and management. And that is non-negotiable. That'll be all.'

'That's a bloody big gamble to take, Ted, with no guarantee of getting anywhere,' Big Jim Baker complained when Ted put forward his idea about testing chainsaws and loppers for any traces of human remains. 'It would make one hell of a hole in the budget, and might not produce a single solid lead. I think it might need to be a last resort option.'

Ted was talking to his two bosses at the end of the week, to bring them up to speed. He wanted everything to be neatly tied up, as far as possible, before he sloped off for two days away with Trev.

'If we had a few more officers we might make better progress. We're handling two biggish cases with the size of team we'd usually have for one.'

'Cheeky bugger. You know what resources are like. You've got Maurice back soon so I was going to ask you who you wanted to let go, Martha or young Amelie.'

'Neither of them,' Ted said firmly. 'Jim, we really are at full stretch. Is there no one else you can bring in, even for a few days?'

'I have to say that I agree with Ted, Jim,' the Ice Queen told him. 'It's not a lot of officers for these two cases. We'll be starting to come under scrutiny soon for lack of progress. It's a vicious circle. We all know that. Progress is unlikely without more personnel on the job.'

'I suppose I could ask Leona Rakale if she could spare either Charlie Eccles or Graham Winters for a few days. Both of them are useful officers now, since you knocked them into shape a bit, Ted.'

'What about Leona herself? She's excellent.'

Jim snorted. 'You've already got three DSs on the team. Four would be just taking the pi... taking the pee.'

Even Big Jim clearly felt obliged to moderate his language slightly in the Ice Queen's regal presence. He said 'bloody' so often and so naturally he clearly no longer considered it as a swear word.

'All right,' he growled, 'you can keep Martha and Amelie for now and I'll see who Leona can spare for you. How's the young lass shaping up, anyway?'

'A shaky start, but Eric Morgan's got her well and truly under his wing. We'll make a proper copper of her yet. And at least she has the courage to own up to her mistakes.'

'Ted, it's this weekend you're away, isn't it?' Debra Caldwell asked him. 'Is Jo in charge in your absence?'

'He is. I've told him I can be contacted if it's urgent ...'

'Nonsense. None of us is indispensable. He's an experienced DI. I'll make sure he knows he can call me if anything untoward happens. But there's no reason why you shouldn't have two days off occasionally.'

'It's a pound to a bloody penny that as soon as you swan off, we'll get a towering inferno of a blaze plus a load more body parts strewn all over the patch,' Big Jim said gloomily.

Trev was in the kitchen when Ted got home, not too late, as he'd promised. He was determined that Trev was going to get his full attention all weekend, even if some of it was to be spent watching his sister compete.

'Supper's nearly ready and I've already done our packing for the morning. I know it needs to be an early start to get down there in time for Eirian's first class, so I thought I'd try to be organised.'

Ted stepped over the herd of cats and went to put his arms round his partner to pull him close. He saw Trev wince in evident pain and was immediately concerned.

'Are you all right? Have you hurt yourself?'

Trev grinned ruefully. 'This was my big idea to give you a surprise Valentine's present. It hasn't turned out quite like I hoped it would.'

Instead of his usual tight jeans he was wearing a loose pair of sweatpants. He half turned and gently pulled them partway down. Near the top of his left hip was a recent tattoo, looking red and angry. It was a heart with a broad arrow diagonally through it and the word 'Moondance' across it.

'I wanted to do something special. To show how much I appreciated you dancing with me in front of your whole team when I know how much you hate that sort of thing. I'd no idea it would hurt this much, though.'

'A tattoo? You always said you didn't like them. Is it meant to be this red? It's not infected or anything, is it?'

'It better not be. I went to a really posh place. Expensive. She's given me some cream to put on it. I just thought it would be a romantic gesture. Do you hate it?'

'No!' Ted said, slightly too quickly. 'It really was a lovely gesture. It puts my effort to shame. I was going to show you tomorrow, when we were having dinner together at the restaurant. But I'll get it now. I'm always telling you I'll make it up to you when I let you down – again – and this was my pathetic attempt to do that.'

He opened his briefcase, took out two folded A4 sheets of paper, put them down on the table and pulled the chair out for Trev to sit down. He did, and started to read. Then he looked up at Ted, his blue eyes shining in evident delight.

'Trail riding in Corsica? Ted, this looks absolutely amazing! I've never been there.'

'I got Océane to phone them for me to ask about it in French so I got all the info properly. They've got some quiet horses suitable for novices like me, and some better ones for experienced riders like you. It's not luxury accommodation, though. It's basic B&B, a couple of nights in hostels and one night under canvas next to a river. But I thought we could have a few days at the coast in a nice hotel afterwards. I haven't booked it yet. I thought I'd check with you first, in case you don't like the idea.'

'Like it? Ted, I absolutely love it. It's so kind and thoughtful. And at least halfway up a mountain in Corsica even you can't be summoned back to the nick at short notice.'

Chapter Twenty-one

Warren exuded good spirits. He was in the front row of the small congregation in the prison chapel, singing his heart out. He had a good voice, although he seldom let it be heard anywhere else inside the prison walls. He'd sung in the choir at school as a boy, though never in a church choir. Neither he nor his family had ever been remotely religious. His conversion to Catholicism was relatively recent. Since the arrival of the new prison chaplain.

Father Archer, by contrast, didn't look good at all. He was pale. Dark rings under his eyes spoke of insufficient sleep. When Warren went up to receive communion, the chaplain's hand trembled visibly as he placed the host on his tongue.

Archer always made a point of standing in the doorway as the prisoners were leaving the chapel to be escorted back to their cells, as he would outside any parish church. Although some of the prison officers tutted to themselves at the delay, he insisted on shaking each man by the hand with both of his and speaking to every one of them in turn. He knew all the members of his congregation by name and addressed them by their first name. Prison staff used surnames only.

Warren always managed to engineer things so he was the last to leave. The officers on duty were getting impatient by that point. When he stopped to say, as he did after every service, 'Lovely service today, padre. Thank you so much. Bless you,' one or other of them would usually snap, 'Move it, Warren. Now,' to which Warren would respond with a beatific smile and a 'Coming, Mr Smith. Bless you for your patience.'

It pushed buttons, as he doubtless intended, but it was borderline. Not worth making a fuss about. More than one of them had discovered that if they did take him on over it, it could provoke one of his attacks which would delay all of them even more and require too much paperwork to be completed. Simply not worth the hassle.

Warren was making plans as he was escorted back to his wing. He had some free association time before lunch. He preferred to spend any such time alone in his cell, reading or watching his television. He wasn't much of a mixer. But he was planning on issuing another visiting order for young Duncan. He enjoyed the visits he made. He was looking forward to seeing how his young protégé was getting on.

Ted managed to make it to just before he joined the M5 motorway before he gave in to temptation and phoned Jo. He'd left Trev at the hotel where his sister would be joining him for the night, after she'd seen to her horse, before they flew out to Paris the next day.

It had been a relaxed and enjoyable weekend, even if Trev was hampered by the discomfort from his new body art. Eirian had done well, coming third in her class. Even Ted, who only knew the basics about riding, could see how much she and her horse, Blue, had come on since he'd last seen them perform together.

Equestrian events were always a time of mixed emotions for Trev. They reminded him of what he'd had in his previous life, and of what he'd lost. But he was visibly proud of his younger sister, offering her any help and advice he could. It was typical of his generosity that he put his own feelings aside to be there to support the sister he hadn't known about until relatively recently.

As on a former occasion, he'd seen people he'd known from his younger life, but had gone out of his way to avoid most of them, other than to nod and exchange a polite, restrained greeting. The setting opened old wounds which were as raw and painful as the new one on his hip.

'You're meant to be off duty until tomorrow morning, Ted,' Jo reminded him when he answered.

'You know me. I can't keep away. I just wondered if there was anything I needed to know about before then.'

'There is, and it's not good news. Another arson, in the early hours of this morning. Again not far from Wellington Road. And a fatality in it, this time.'

Ted swore under his breath. Something he seldom did.

'And before you say anything, no, I shouldn't have called you about it. You weren't on the rota for today so I left you to enjoy yourself. We're handling it.'

'Sorry, yes, I know you will be. How many casualties in total?'

'Just the one fatality as far as we know, but it was quite a big blaze. It took longer to attend this time because the Fire Service were dealing with other incidents at the same time. Typical aftermath of a Saturday night. It had quite a hold by the time they got there.

'Details are a bit sketchy at the moment but we have some survivors who've given us information. Another derelict building. One which was being squatted this time. Three older teenagers, well off their faces with god knows what, who'd been sleeping upstairs, but thankfully, somehow, managed to get themselves out of there. One of them had got up to go for a slash, realised what was happening and managed to rouse the others enough to drag them out.

'He told our officers that there was an older man, someone he described as a tramp, who used to sleep in the cupboard under the stairs. They said he was very strange. A heavy drinker. Didn't associate with them at all. He swears he tried to get him out, but the whole staircase was ablaze by the time he'd helped the others to safety and he couldn't get near. Fire crew confirmed they found human remains in the cubby hole.'

'Do you think our arsonist knew there were squatters this time? Pretty callous to walk into an occupied building and set fire to it. Taking quite a risk, too. If anyone had survived, they could have seen whoever it was. Unless whoever started the fire was counting on no one getting out.'

'Apparently it was well known locally that this place was being squatted. Pretty obvious, too, from the outside of it that it wasn't secure and people had been coming and going.'

If he hadn't been driving, Ted would have been tempted to bang his head against the steering wheel in frustration.

'Tell me there's some good news in all of this, Jo.'

'There's some good news, boss. Big Jim came in to see how we were doing. He's agreed extra staffing. We can keep Martha and Amelie and we can have Graham and Charlie as from tomorrow. Eric can stay and Kevin's sorting out a couple more officers to work with us until we make some sort of a breakthrough.

'I've had everyone available out all day trying to find any eyewitnesses. As you can imagine, the small hours of a Sunday morning are not traditionally a time for people to be out and about. So we've pretty much drawn a blank so far, but we might have more luck tomorrow morning.'

'I'll be back in about three hours. I'll come in.'

'Seriously, Ted, there's not much we can do at this stage. Not until the Fire Service have finished and we can get our circus on site and start looking for some pointers. Why not go home and come in early in the morning? Then we can decide who we need to put on what, and how we're going to make some sort of progress with so little to go on.'

'On your feet, Warren. Chaplain's asking for you. Extra cleaning duties.'

That was unusual. Warren didn't normally clean the chapel on a Sunday. He had extra time allotted to do it on a Monday morning, after it had been used for service the previous day. He liked to have it looking spotless before the regular Monday evening meetings for the Listener group.

Warren knew there was no point in asking the reason or debating the issue. He'd long since learned that as a prisoner he had no control over his life and no say in what happened to them. It was the part of prison life which he found hardest to deal with.

He carefully slid his bookmark between the pages of his current read, laid it neatly on the bed where he'd been lying and got to his feet, smiling pleasantly.

'Yes, Miss Gee.'

She marched him at a brisk pace from his cell to the chapel in stony silence, pausing only for him to collect his cleaning equipment on the way. He knew she was even less likely to engage in any sort of dialogue with him than some of the other officers, so he didn't even waste his breath making the effort.

'Warren for you, chaplain,' the officer announced as she followed Warren into the chapel.

She stopped and looked around her, frowning at the disarray. The chapel was bare of many of the ornaments of a normal church. Devoid of almost anything which could be picked up and turned into a potential weapon. Fights were not unusual in the chapel, where prisoners from different wings came together and drug deals could be struck. Or scores settled between rival factions.

There was a solitary, sad-looking plant in the corner in a cheap plastic pot. A *tradescantia*, Wandering Jew. The chaplain's ironic attempt at humour. It had ended up on the floor, scattering compost everywhere. A small patch of dark brown liquid was slowly being absorbed by the contents of the plant pot.

'What's happened here, chaplain? Trouble?'

'I'm so sorry, Miss Gee. I was about to have my coffee but I spilled it then managed to slip in it and knock over the *tradescantia*. And I'm sorry to spoil your afternoon off, William, but I thought it needed cleaning as soon as possible in case it stained the floor.'

'Right, well, I'll leave Warren to do it and come back to collect him later.'

'Thank you, Miss Gee,' Warren said to her retreating back, inwardly seething at being talked about rather than addressed directly.

She'd barely left the room when the chaplain began to speak, his voice low, words tumbling over one another in his anxiety.

'I heard it on the early local news this morning, William. There was a fatality. A person is dead. That was never meant to happen. You promised me that. You said he would take care of that.'

Warren glanced towards the door to check if the officer was safely out of earshot.

'Hush, padre, calm yourself. An unfortunate accident, that's all. Tragic, but unforeseeable.'

'But you said we could trust him. You said it would be damage only. Empty buildings. Never anything more than that. I can neither condone nor accept this turn of events. You must see that. I have to talk to someone.'

Warren had set down his mop and bucket and now looked directly into the chaplain's eyes, his stare hard and calculating.

'Now that would be very unfortunate, padre. Very unfortunate indeed. Because, you see, I've been thinking more and more that I should risk breaching a confidence and talk to someone. About the things young Joey has been telling me. Disturbing things. Very similar to those of which Duncan Dooley spoke to me when we shared a cell. The very same things which led me to seek you out and talk to you in the first place.'

The cats came swarming round Ted as soon as he opened the

front door. All of them, for a change, not just Adam, his hero-worshipper. He shut the door carefully behind him to avoid any escapes and led the way to the kitchen, picking up the envelope from the floor just inside.

'And you can all stop trying to give me the guilts. You know perfectly well you've had visits and fresh food and probably lots of cuddles,' he told them sternly.

It hadn't been worth getting a live-in pet-sitter for one night away. Nor had Ted got his mother to come up, knowing Trev was going to be away all week and he would be too busy, with two big cases, to spend any time with her. And that was before he'd found out both cases involved a fatality.

Instead he'd booked a local pet sitting service who had come in both days, using the spare key Ted had given them. They had, as instructed, pushed it through the letterbox before leaving on their final visit. Ted disliked having strangers in his personal space, especially when he wasn't there. But he'd vetted the company thoroughly, interviewed the sitter they were going to send and he'd never had a problem with them before when he'd used them.

Trev had left a sticky note on the kettle before they'd left the previous day, knowing it was the first place Ted would head for when he got home. Amazingly, the cats hadn't removed or eaten it.

'*Ffoniwch dy fam*. She worries. Xx'

Ted could still remember a few of the Welsh words and phrases he'd learned from his mother as a small boy. He could certainly work that one out. An instruction to phone his mother. Trev was getting good at Welsh. He hoovered up learning languages.

It was late in the evening for Ted to call Annie now, but he took his phone out to send her a reassuring text. It rang as he did so. Trev.

'Safely back?'

'Just got in. And seen your note. Yes, I'll text her in a

minute. It's getting a bit late to call.'

'Phone her. You know she won't sleep until she hears you're home. She knows you're driving back today so she won't settle without hearing that you're safe. You know what she's like.'

'Is Eirian with you yet?'

'She called to say she's in a taxi on her way here. And yes, I told her all the things you said to tell her about safety in taxis. I think she's scared the driver so much he might just drop her off and not ask for a fare.

'Anyway, now I know that you're back in one piece, I better go. She'll be here soon and perhaps the sight of me standing outside waiting for her might be the clincher for the poor driver. Kiss all the boys and girls for me. See you soon. Love you.'

'You too. Have a lovely time and don't do anything I wouldn't approve of. Either of you,' Ted added, more in hope than anticipation.

Trev was still laughing when he rang off, as Ted found his mother's saved number to call her as ordered.

Chapter Twenty-two

Ted arrived early to read up on the latest arson, then to sit in on Kevin Turner's morning briefing before his own. He was going to need the help of Uniform more than ever, with both cases going as slowly as they were. The days of beat bobbies and regular patrols were largely gone, but the Uniform officers had greater contact with the goings-on within their patch on a regular basis than CID officers often did.

'We need eyewitnesses. Even if it's nothing more concrete than our tall man in what might have been fancy dress from the earlier case. Please can you ask your contacts. Especially anyone in and around the area of yesterday's fire. We don't have an ID yet on the victim. The youngsters who were in the building only seemed to know him as Dirty Len, if that means anything to any of you.'

An older PC sitting at the back nodded. 'I know Len. I've had to move him on a few times for begging and getting aggressive with it. Always claimed to be ex-Forces. Invalided out with PTSD and down on his luck, but I don't know how much of it was true. I'll ask around. I know folk who might know. Pity, if it was him. Whatever his story was, he clearly had some serious mental health issues. Not helped by the booze, when he could get his hands on it.'

'Was he known to us? Any record?' Ted asked him.

'Not as far as I know, but like I said, I only ever knew him as Dirty Len. I tried to chat to him a couple of times, to see if I could do anything to help. Sometimes the lights were on but no one was home, if you know what I mean. But if he really was ex-Forces, there's a chance his DNA might be on military records somewhere, so you might be able to get a match that way.'

'Was the nickname a reference to a personal hygiene issue? Or some indication about his behaviour. Indecent exposure?'

'Guv, from what I ever saw of Len, he had trouble standing up straight. Doing that long enough to undo his flies and put himself on show for someone to see sounds unlikely.'

'Thanks, Keith. Any idea of what regiment he might have served in? Or where he could have seen action? Regimental tattoos or anything?'

'Afghanistan's the most likely, I would guess, from the age I'd put him at. I don't think he was all that old. He just looked it. And as for tatts. I don't know when he stopped serving or when he finished up on the streets, but I reckon he's been a stranger to soap and water for most of that time. I couldn't tell you for sure if he was IC1, IC3, IC4, IC6 or something in between.'

Ted went straight from there to the morning briefing for his own team. They'd had to move from the main office to the briefing room to accommodate the larger numbers. Big Jim Baker was attending. It was Ted who signed off on the decision logs for both cases, but Jim held the purse strings. Wherever he could, he needed to ensure best value for money without loss of efficiency.

Maurice Brown was back from his parental leave, looking as if he'd hardly slept at all during the two weeks, but beaming with pride and showing photos of the twins to everyone. They still hadn't toasted the twins' arrival. Ted and Maurice had agreed between them to leave it until the following week when they might finally have some better news on the two cases.

Ted fed back the information he'd just picked up about the victim and asked Eric Morgan if he'd known the man.

'Contrary to rumour, guv, I don't know everyone on the

patch. I know of him. Passed him a time or two. But if anyone knows more about him and his background, Keith will find out for you.'

'Mike, have you or Jezza checked up yet on Duncan Dooley's existing alibis after you spoke to him? Can you two concentrate on those for now? And Jo, can you please send someone else round to speak to him about yesterday's fire?'

'We haven't yet, boss. The personnel manager we needed to speak to was off, but we'll chase that up first thing.'

Jim Baker was too sharp a copper to miss a trick. He picked up on the detail straight away.

'If Mike and Jezza have already had contact with him, why don't you two go again?'

Jezza was always prepared to meet potential trouble head on. Even if it came in the shape of the Big Boss.

'Because he didn't like the look of my friendly smiling face the first time, sir. So he legged it, tripped over DS Hallam's car bonnet and is threatening to lodge a complaint.'

'That's all we bloody need. Ted, let me have a full written report on that, so we cover our backsides. And whoever goes this time, for god's sake be diplomatic. We don't want him screaming police harassment as well.'

Jezza opened her mouth to speak, saw Ted's look and wisely decided to shut it again. Ted continued, 'I've got all the lists of the prisoners who William Warren has had contact with in the time he's been inside. They're going to have to be gone through carefully and cross-checked. Visitors are few and far between. Mostly his father, a couple of times a year, and Duncan Dooley more frequently. So if he is persuading someone on the outside to start fires to try to clear his name, those two are the most likely. Rob, you spoke to Mr Warren Senior. Could it be him?'

Rob shook his head. 'I'd be surprised, boss. For one thing, his visits are scarce so it's hard to see when they could have come up with such a plan between them. But I'll go and talk to him again and I'll check his alibi for all of the dates.'

'The most time-consuming thing is going to be the fact that Warren is what they call a Listener. Like a Samaritan. Someone for troubled prisoners to talk to. He's only been doing that role for a couple of years but he's already clocked up quite a lot of them. He seems to be good at it. He's taken on more responsibility for helping to train new Listeners.

'The prisoners he sees in his Listener role, it's always one to one, in their cell, so they could be saying anything to each other in those sessions. We need to go through that list and start by checking anyone else on it who's now been released, then looking at their alibis for the arsons. Charlie and Graham, that might be one for you to start with, as you're new to the case.

'It seems Warren only got into religion a couple of years ago when the current chaplain started there. The chaplain, Father Archer, seems to be more approachable than the old one, and he's been a driving force in building up the Listener scheme, which is where Warren got involved.

'Now, my old school-friend, Martin Wellman, who's serving time for assault, is going to help out by trying to get close to Warren through that scheme. He'll let me know what he can find out, if anything.

'Of course, at some point soon, one of us is going to need to talk to the chaplain to see if he knows anything useful. More importantly, if he's prepared to tell us, or if he's going to claim the sanctity of the confessional.

'And speaking of priests and issues of confidentiality, are we any further forward in finding Lucy Robson, either through the church or through other means?'

Eric Morgan shook his head. 'Not really, guv, though not for want of trying. Amelie and I went to see Byrne's old parish priest again, and then back to his last one, to see if we could find out anything, even gossip, to tell us why he might have moved away without trying to contact Lucy.

'We also went back to the home to see whether they could tell us if she'd tried to contact him. If she'd ever had chance to slip away by herself, for any reason. The type of relationship seemed to be news to them. They'd thought he was just a kindly neighbour who looked after her when her mother couldn't. They did say the girl who told us about it, Jennifer, wasn't usually one to make up stories. Certainly not ones on that scale, at any rate. But we're a bit back to square one with Lucy because they never saw her again after she left and they never had any contact with Byrne in the first place.

'They had a few cards from her to start with. Saying she had a part-time job working with animals, and doing some training. But then even those dried up. Postmarked in the Manchester area, but that's all they could tell us. And no, they didn't keep any of them.'

'And what about the landscape gardeners and tree surgeons?'

'Making contact with all of them gradually, boss. General enquiries, checking their location at the time of the various findings of body parts,' Jo told him. 'We're slowly getting through them. There's just this Tam Lee that's proving a bit elusive. No response at all to various phone messages.'

'Right, I'll take that one,' Ted was keen to find an excuse to get out of the office for a bit. 'I'll have a run out up there and see if there's anyone at home.'

He looked round the room at the team members, then said, 'Amelie, you come with me for this. Let's see if we can't run down the mysterious Tam Lee.'

Ted handed Amelie the keys to his service vehicle and asked her, 'I take it you're safe enough to drive now you're wearing your glasses?'

'Yes, sir.'

'Right, you drive, I'll direct you. It's not far and I know the way.'

Ted liked to see how people drove. It told him a lot about them. He didn't make small talk, simply gave directions, so as not to distract Amelie. She was competent and careful. Which was just as well, as the lanes they were taking got narrower the further off the main road they went.

They found the property they were looking for easily enough. A small isolated cottage, with a pocket handkerchief front garden and a track at the side clearly leading to the rear of the property. A wooden board on a post by the front gate announced, '*Tam Lee. Tree surgeon. Landscape architect/gardener. Free estimates. No job too small,*' followed by a mobile telephone number. The one which had so far failed to get any response.

Amelie tucked the car carefully into the end of the track so it was off the road and not likely to hamper any traffic. It would also effectively block in any vehicles round the back, which might have advantages.

She made to follow Ted through the front gate, but he stood aside for her to go first, hoping she wasn't a militant feminist who might object to the gesture on principle. Ted's dad had brought him with old-fashioned values. They tended to stick. Amelie thanked him, with no sign of taking offence. They walked the few short steps to the front door and knocked. Several times.

'What now, sir?'

'Boss is fine, Amelie, especially out of the office. Come on, let's take a look round the back while we're here, then we haven't had a wasted trip.'

This time Ted did put himself in front. He had no particular reason to expect danger but as the senior officer, and a former SFO, he prepared to lead the way to see what might be waiting for them behind the house.

The land behind was surprisingly extensive. The plot was not particularly wide, but it seemed to go on for quite some way back from the road. At the end of the track was a large timber building which clearly served as a garage and workshop. The doors were standing open, showing a tidily organised space with a concrete floor.

Further away from the house, the land was divided up into small paddocks. The first one held a couple of white goats. Behind that, Ted could see two spotted pigs happily snuffling in the dirt.

In front of the first of the animal enclosures, a woman was pegging washing out on a line. The space between them and her was filled with chickens scratching and pecking the ground, as well as a goose and gander, who started to kick up a fuss as soon as they spotted intruders.

'Oh my god, I hate geese. I'm terrified of them,' Amelie said in a low voice, tucking in close behind Ted, even though he was no taller than she was, so not much of a shield. 'I'm sorry, sir.'

'It's fine, Amelie. Just stay behind me. You'll be fine.'

Ted walked forward calmly, looking straight at the gander who waddled closer, hissing ominously. Ted wasn't worried about geese. Had it been a dog, especially a big one, he would have wanted to hide behind Amelie.

The woman turned to look at them and called out, 'Watch out for the gander. He likes to get behind you and peck your bum if you're not careful.'

That made Amelie change her position rapidly and scuttle in front of Ted so he was protecting her from behind.

'We're looking for Tam Lee. Is he here?' she asked.

'No,' the woman replied, going back to pegging out the washing.

Amelie frowned. 'The board outside says this is his address. Will he be back at some point?'

'No, he won't.'

Ted picked up on the inflection immediately, but decided to wait to see how Amelie would get on. It was good training for her, if nothing else, dealing with a hostile witness.

'I don't understand. How can we get in touch with him, then, if he doesn't answer his phone and he isn't here?'

Ted decided to intervene. 'I'm sorry for the confusion. Tam Lee is a woman, I take it. Is it you?'

'Give the man a coconut,' she said, hanging out the last of the washing. 'No, it's not me. But yes, Tam is a woman. Just imagine. A mere woman capable of doing tree surgery.'

She turned to look at them with a critical eye, which lingered a moment longer on Ted.

'Who are you, and what do you want? Tam doesn't like people just turning up here out of the blue.'

'DCI Darling and DC Foster. Stockport Police,' Ted told her, pulling out his photo ID, as Amelie did the same. 'We wanted to talk to Ms Lee about the reported theft of a number of items of equipment, including a chainsaw.'

Her eyes narrowed in suspicion. Now she was facing them, Ted could see how painfully thin she was. Dark circles under her eyes. Sunken cheeks. Teeth which appeared prominent and made her face look skeletal. There was fine down on her cheeks and jawline. It was hard to estimate her age because of how she looked. Early twenties, perhaps.

'Why did you need to come out here and ask about it? Tam's already spoken to some police officers about it. You need to speak to her.'

'We're looking at it in connection with other cases which might possibly be linked in some way. When would be a convenient time for us to come and talk to Ms Lee about it, please? We have tried leaving messages but we haven't had a response.'

'Tam said she got pissed off waiting for you lot to do something. It's been ages since the stuff was taken. She said you kept her waiting long enough to get a crime number to give to the insurers so she could claim the money to buy replacements. That's probably why she doesn't want to talk to you any more.'

201

'Hopefully we can do something to restore her faith in the police service.' Ted took out one of his cards and handed it to her. 'Perhaps you could get her to contact me, whenever it's convenient. And please pass on my apologies for the lack of progress. May we have your name, please?'

Amelie was hovering, trying to pick up clues from Ted about what she was meant to be doing. As he asked the question, she whipped out her pocket book and stood, pen poised, glad that there was something she could do.

'Cyane,' the woman replied, then seeing Amelie hesitate, she spelled it slowly.

'Is that a first name or a second name?' Amelie asked her.

'First name. Second name is Lee. Would you like me to spell that out for you? Tam and I are married. So we have the same surname.'

There was no hint of sarcasm in the way she said it. More like someone trying to be helpful. Something in the way she spoke made Ted wonder if she was younger than he'd first thought.

Amelie flushed but wrote it down without saying anything.

Ted thanked her and stood looking round him.

'It's a nice place you have here. Quiet. I've driven down here a couple of times but never really looked. I live in Offerton.'

'We like it. It's very quiet. We don't like visitors dropping in.'

'Nice looking pigs, too. Are they Gloucester Old Spots?'

She looked at him in surprise for a moment before the shutters came down again and the wariness was back. She nodded briefly.

'Right, we won't take up any more of your time, Ms Lee. Thank you for all your help, and it would really be helpful if your wife would be kind enough to give me a call at some point.'

She had thrust his card into a pocket without looking at it, so he wasn't optimistic.

He stood aside to let Amelie go first as they left, mindful of the warning about the gander's preferred method of attack, but they regained the car in safety. Ted stayed quiet until Amelie had successfully backed out into the narrow road. Then he asked her, 'What did you make of that?'

'She was very passive-aggressive wasn't she, sir? And she mostly told us about what Tam thought or said, not so much about herself. Why do you think she seemed hostile towards us? Fear of the police? A dislike of people in general?'

'I don't know. But I certainly think it would be worth our time to have a look a little more closely into Cyane Lee and her background.'

Chapter Twenty-three

'Have you heard of *Betula nigra*?'

Ted was used to Bizzie Nelson's abrupt and sometimes cryptic openers. He'd only just arrived in his office, early, as usual, and was busy shaking the worst of the rain from his trench coat. Even in the short sprint from his car to the nick, he'd got a good soaking. It was bucketing down outside.

'Black something, but I don't know what. Animal, vegetable or mineral?' Ted asked her.

'A tree,' she told him. 'More commonly known as black birch or river birch. Not exactly rare but certainly not common. The sort of thing the Victorians loved to collect to plant in the arboretum no self-respecting stately home owner was without. It has a distinctive flaky cinnamon-coloured bark, said to resemble peeling skin.'

'And that's what's been found on our body parts?'

'It is indeed. It doesn't usually require much maintenance in the form of pollarding or the like. But it may well require attention in the event of something like disease or storm damage. Small traces of it were found on our body parts, together with some much more common trees. Particularly traces of *Fraxinus excelsior*, the ash tree. Diseased traces, in that case, to be precise. You've probably heard of the dieback disease which is affecting the native ash? It's feared it might attack as much as ninety-five per cent of them. Infected trees need to be removed as a matter of priority and it's widespread, so those fibres are unlikely to help you pin down an area, like our more rare friend might.

'However, dealing with dying ash trees is highly specialised work. Ash trees snap quite easily even when healthy. Diseased ones can shed limbs or even collapse completely. So attending to them is a job for a skilled tree surgeon, not just anyone armed with a chainsaw. Particularly in public areas with the inherent risks. And it's a very common tree. Or was until the numbers started to be decimated. There are still several millions of them left, though.'

'That's great news for us, Bizzie, thank you. If we can find out where those black birch trees are growing and who does their maintenance, we might finally be on to something with the body parts.'

'Excellent, I'm happy to have helped. Now, onto your unfortunate victim from the latest arson. I understand there's no ID on this one yet?'

'Not yet, no. All I know is that he was a homeless man known locally as Dirty Len, who might possibly have been ex-Forces, and also might have had PTSD. We're hoping that if that's true, we might get a DNA match through military records. But anything at all to come out of the PM will potentially help us, so we need you to work your usual magic, please.'

'I'm planning on doing it first thing tomorrow morning. Who are you sending along?'

'I might take it myself, if nothing else comes up in the meantime. I'm feeling a bit detached from the case at the moment.'

'Splendid. I'll look forward to seeing you. At least I know I don't have to remind you what I mean by first thing. I shall see you here tomorrow, then.'

Once all the team members had arrived, Ted went out to join them. Time to pool findings and ideas to see what progress, if any, they were making. He kicked things off with news of their visit to Tam Lee's premises the day before, then mentioned the update from the Professor on the tree fibres and the two different species isolated and identified.

'Jo, we now need to find out where in our area these trees grow and who's been contracted to do any work on them recently. Start locally, but we may have to spread the net wider if they don't grow close to us here. We need the date of any such work, and we need to start by comparing that to the date when Tam Lee reported her equipment missing. She may just be cold-shouldering us because she didn't get the prompt response she wanted. If such work was done prior to her reporting the theft, then she becomes a person of interest to us and we'll need to up our efforts to speak to her.

'I think we need to attempt to rule her in or out first, before we consider examining all the equipment of other firms. She may, of course, have nothing to do with our body parts. It could be the person who stole her equipment who's responsible. But let's try to establish that for sure.'

'Sir, I spent a lot of time yesterday, after we got back, trying to find out about Cyane Lee, as you asked, since she's our only connection to Tam Lee at the moment,' Amelie told him. 'I don't think I made any mistakes in checking, but the weird thing is, she doesn't seem to exist. At all. Not on our records under that name. Not on the electoral roll. No National Insurance Number. No driving licence or passport. Nothing. And she's not the other company employee registered with Companies House, either.'

'She's not Tam Lee, is she?' Jezza asked, voicing what a few of them were thinking. 'The same person, just messing you about for some reason?'

Ted looked across at Amelie. 'Would you like to tell us your thoughts on that, Amelie? Just say what you think. Don't be worried about getting it wrong. I'd be interested to hear your opinion.'

She looked awkward. 'I'm trying not to be judgemental here, sir, because I know you don't like it, and it's generally not a good way to work. But I don't see how Cyane can possibly be Tam Lee, the tree surgeon. She looked ill to me. Incredibly thin, and not in a strong and wiry sort of way. Weak. Exhausted, perhaps. I honestly thought she looked as if pegging out the washing was about the limit of her physical capabilities. I'm really struggling to picture her going up ladders with a chainsaw.'

Ted nodded his approval. 'Thank you. That was my impression too. And it wasn't judgemental. I was asking you to give your opinion.'

'But boss, what if the illness is recent? That might explain why Tam Lee isn't responding to messages on her business number.' Jezza suggested.

'It would have to be a pretty dramatic illness to lay her low like that, from what Amelie said, if that really was Tam Lee you were speaking to,' Virgil put in. 'According to the council, she did some contract work for them just last month. That was diseased ash trees, too. Although no mention of the other one. That timeline doesn't fit, anyway. Tam Lee's equipment was reported stolen some time ago so the chainsaw she's using now must be a replacement.'

'We need to speak to her as soon as possible,' Jo reiterated. 'If she's not going to come to us, we'll have to go and find her. Virgil, can you check with the council if she's contracted for any more work for them? If so we'll track her down that way. And at the same time ask them if they have any black birch trees, or if they know where any grow.

'And I agree with the boss. We really need to find out about this Cyane. Amelie, you've made a good start but we need to widen the net.'

'If she's as ill as that, we could check GPs' lists. Maybe even the hospitals,' Jezza suggested. 'Her details must be recorded somewhere, with someone. What sort of age is she? Any signs of children about the place? If there are any, we could also check local schools to see if she's known there.'

Amelie looked at Ted to see who should answer that. When he nodded to her, she said, 'No children's clothes amongst the washing and no toys anywhere about. Age-wise I found it hard to tell because of her appearance. But I'd put her somewhere around early twenties. Sir?'

'I agree with you. Very hard to be sure, but I'd say that was a fair estimate. Although something about her made me think she could be younger than she looks.'

'Guv, I've made a bit of progress about Byrne and Lucy Robson today,' Eric Morgan began. 'Following on from talking to the priests yesterday, who told us seven shades of bugger all, I did a bit more digging round his old area. Where he was living when he was involved with Lucy. And according to a near neighbour, she did try to find him, not long after she went into the home.

'She turned up on his doorstep one day, after school, hammering and shouting through the letterbox. Only he'd moved away. Did a bit of a moonlit flit, the neighbour said, without leaving a forwarding address. She said little Lucy was absolutely distraught. She took her in and comforted her, then when her other half got home from work, he drove her back to the home. She made him drop her off a couple of streets away and leave her, so they didn't know where she'd been or why.

'It took all my considerable charms, plus a few cups of tea,' the sergeant winked at Amelie as he said that, 'to get her to tell me what she clearly knew.

'It turns out that Byrne had a visit from two pillars of the Union of Catholic Mothers. Not long after Lucy's first communion. You know the type. All folded arms and lips pursed in disapproval. I ran them down eventually, with the neighbour's help. Or one of them, at least. Blood from a stone might have been easier, but eventually she told me there had been,' he made exaggerated quotation marks in the air, 'concerns about the closeness of his relationship with Lucy. They hadn't approved of the first communion dress he bought her, or the way he'd had her hair done. They didn't like how she was so clearly besotted with him, and so on.'

'Genuine concerns, d'you think, or just mean-spirited, interfering old biddies?' Martha asked him.

'Interesting question, especially as one of them was called Biddy. Whether or not they were right, they certainly put the fear of god into Byrne. He seems to have packed up and moved on in days. Without leaving a forwarding address. So when Lucy came looking for him – and let's face it, that does tend to suggest their concerns were justified – he'd moved on and the trail had gone cold.'

'Thanks, sarge, that's helpful. See what else you can dig up for us, please.

'Now, onto our arsons. Professor Nelson is going to do the PM on our fire victim tomorrow morning early, so I'll take that one.'

He saw Amelie's face fall at that news so he told her, 'When the Professor says early, Amelie, she means six o'clock and not one second after. And you'd need to be back here by nine as I'm sure Jo has plenty for you to be getting on with. But if you want to come, and you understand that no one is ever late for the Professor, you can do.

'So, any updates?'

'Boss, Steve and me went to see Duncan Dooley, and to check up on his alibis,' Maurice told him.

'I bet you made Steve drive so you could get some kip, bonny lad,' Jezza teased him.

'Aye, and why not? I need some chance to catch up. Anyway, we checked his clocking in and out times and we spoke to the management. Seems pretty certain that he couldn't slip away during a shift for more than five minutes without someone noticing. So then we went to see the lad himself.'

He looked across at Jezza as he spoke again. 'I don't think you're getting a card from him this Christmas, bonny lass. We had to swear an oath you weren't with us before he let us in.

But he did and he says he was on a night off on Saturday, which we've already checked and confirmed from the rota at work.

'According to him, he met some mates for a jar or three at the pub, then went for a curry. He said he got pretty off his face so he went home about midnight and didn't get up until two in the afternoon.

'We went to the pub to check his alibi ...'

'Of course you did,' Jezza interrupted him, never passing up an opportunity to tease her good friend.

'They remember seeing him there,' he went on, ignoring her, 'and his mates. So did the takeaway. They were a bit lively apparently. We've got the name of all the mates but we've only caught up with a couple so far. They alibi him. Their story is the same as Dooley's. Exactly the same as his. Only the lass behind the bar in the pub, who knows him by sight, didn't think he was drinking as much as the others, and not as much as he usually does.'

'So he has a tight alibi for three of the fires but not for the fourth. The fatal one,' Jo said. 'Boss, if for some reason it is Warren who's behind these fires, trying to clear himself, is it possible he's using more than one person on the outside to set the fires? Having told them about the signature pattern?'

'Rob and I have been sifting through the people he's had contact with who've since been released,' Mike told them. 'It's not as bad as we first thought. Just because they were banged up in Manchester doesn't mean they're from the area or have stayed here, of course. A couple have died, some are back inside, some have gone back to where they came from. We're working through the rest of them for now.'

'And hopefully my friend Martin will make contact with Warren soon, so he may well have something to tell me.'

'Martin, is it? My name's Mr Warren. I'm one of the prison Listeners and I'm here to see if I can help you in some way. Is it all right with you if I sit down just here? You're quite comfortable with that? Because I want you to be comfortable. It's not always easy, making the first step. But I'm here to listen, and not to judge you in any way.'

Martin was eyeing up the insignificant-looking man with his strange light eyes. When Ted had first asked for his help, he hadn't been sure if he was up to the task. This man was used to talking to people desperately unhappy inside prison. Some of them even suicidal. The 2052s.

He'd solemnly sawed away at the inside of his wrist with a plastic knife, the only weapon available to him, as he'd seen others do. It had been seen to and bandaged, but he hoped it gave him some sort of badge of credibility. He hesitated, not quite sure where to begin. He'd only gone along with the scheme when Ted, reluctantly, had agreed to his condition for doing so.

'I suppose most of the people you talk to are finding it hard coping with being banged up,' he began tentatively. 'I'm a bit different. I don't mind being inside. I've been homeless. Even when I've been inside before and they've fixed me up with a hostel room when I got out, it's never worked out for me. I've always finished up back on the streets. And that's a hard life. Dangerous, too. It's cushy in here by comparison.'

To his surprise, once he started, it was easier than he'd imagined. Warren sat still and quiet. A somehow reassuring presence, as Martin began to try to put some of his concerns into words.

When he paused, Warren asked him, 'Are you a religious man, Martin? We have a very good chaplain here. Always a kind word. A supportive hand. And he carries on his help once prisoners have left here and are in need of guidance. He still sees some of those I've had contact with through the Listener scheme, for instance.'

Martin was about to say it wasn't his thing. But something told him he might be of more help to Ted if he played along with Warren for now. After all, his remit was to find out as much as he could about the man. And the pay-off was going to be big enough, if he could come up with the goods for Ted.

'It's never been my thing before. But I think I'm in need of some help and guidance. Maybe spiritual guidance. I don't know how to go about it, though. They've got me down as an atheist because that's what I've always called myself. Would it look odd if I suddenly ask to start going to church?'

'You can leave everything in my hands, Martin. No problem at all. I'll be happy to help you find your way. Father Archer is a kind and warm-hearted man. He's a Catholic but he provides help and comfort to all religions and those with none. His gentle hand may be just what you need to lead you to the right path.'

Chapter Twenty-four

Ted was always punctual. Obsessively so. He arrived ten minutes before the appointed time for the post-mortem. He found Amelie waiting for him at the top of the steps down to what Bizzie always referred to as her lair in the bowels of the hospital.

'Morning, sir,' she said brightly, although she looked freezing. 'Thank you for giving me this opportunity. I really appreciate it.'

Ted wondered how long she'd been standing there in the cold, waiting for him. He couldn't fault her on her enthusiasm for the job, for sure.

'It's certainly not everyone's idea of a fun start to the day. But it is a useful training opportunity for you. Professor Nelson is very good, especially in a teaching role, so you'll learn a lot.'

Once again he stood aside to let her go first, still talking as she went.

'Sir, I wondered if I'd be able to talk to you about something before we go back to the station? Only I had an idea, but it might be completely stupid. I didn't want to say anything in front of the full team.'

'Never worry about that, Amelie. Everyone is always welcome to throw in ideas, even if they are wild. But I usually stop for a bacon barm and a cuppa on the way back from a PM, so we can chat then, if you like?'

'Thank you, sir. I don't actually eat breakfast and I'm a vegetarian. But I promise not to cramp your style if that's what you enjoy.'

It somehow sounded as if there was a hint of reproach there. Ted liked his rituals, though. He wasn't going to let her guilt him out of his bacon butty.

'Ah, here you are, Chief Inspector,' Bizzie greeted him, somehow managing to imply he was late instead of bang on time, having sorted Amelie out first with coveralls. He was grateful to her for not calling him Edwin, as she usually did. No one at work knew his full name, much less used it, and he preferred to keep it that way. He made the introductions.

'Pleased to meet you, ma'am. I'm looking forward to this opportunity. It's my first PM.'

'Well, whatever you do don't puke anywhere near me, please,' Bizzie told her breezily. 'And don't call me ma'am. It makes me sound like royalty, which is not something I welcome. Professor is fine, or Prof, if you must, but preferably not.

'Now, shall we get started? As ever, I went to the scene before we recovered the body, to see if that gave me any clues I might need. Your poor crime scene manager was almost tearing his hair out with the volume of work he's currently juggling. And the big problem with fire is that it does often destroy quite a lot of forensic material which might otherwise be of use to us. It tends to have something of a cleansing effect. So it's up to me and my humble skills to give you absolutely any and all clues I can.'

Amelie was staring in fascination, hanging on to the Professor's every word. Ted found himself wondering if he'd been that keen at his first PM.

'To save some time, I decided to make something of a start while I was waiting for you,' the Professor continued, again making it sound as if they'd arrived late. 'And I can promise you something fascinating which might, I hope, give you a good chance of an early ID on this unfortunate victim.

'You can see immediately that our poor customer is in a somewhat foetal position. That can sometimes be related to the cause of death. Extreme heat may cause muscles and tendons to contract, for instance. But in this case, having visited the scene myself, I can rule that out. Whether from choice or necessity, this man – because I have determined gender; it is a man – slept in an extremely cramped cubby hole under the stairs. It can't have been comfortable, so I would speculate that he chose to do it for some feeling of safety in seclusion.

'Having been told there was talk of PTSD, I decided to start some investigations for evidence to corroborate that theory. Or possibly not. Some of my magic devices led me to look further and I was too impatient to wait for your arrival.

'You can see here,' she pointed with a scalpel, 'that I have made a start on accessing the skull. Scalping him, if you will. So now I'm going to carefully fold back the flap to show you what I found underneath.'

Ted and Amelie peered, fascinated, at the part of the skull exposed by her actions. Set into it was a fairly large piece of metal. The Professor touched it lightly with her scalpel.

'Titanium plate, in case you were wondering. Which indicates that this gentleman has undergone some quite radical surgery, as a result of illness or serious injury, no doubt. He may well have been diagnosed with PTSD, but I'd say it's more likely than not that once I start prodding around inside his head, I am going to find evidence of some significant damage.

'Now, DC Foster, I don't want you to think that we work magic for you on every single post-mortem. Your DCI can confirm that is sadly not the case. But I am pleased to be able to tell you that in this case, we have had a little bit of luck on our side.

'It's already gone off for forensic analysis, to see if it can tell us anything, so I can't show it to you. But amongst this man's scant possessions was something which he clearly treasured. A military cap badge displaying wings topped by a crown and a lion. Do you happen to know what regiment that is, DC Foster?'

Amelie frowned. 'I'm afraid I know very little about the military. But wings would tend to suggest something to do with flying. Something a pilot would wear, perhaps?'

'An intelligent guess. But no. This is from those extraordinary troops who, when travelling in a perfectly serviceable aircraft, simply can't wait to leap out of it. The Parachute Regiment.'

'Do you want me to leave the window down so you don't have to inhale the fumes of my breakfast?' Ted asked Amelie as he returned to his car with his meal and the cappuccino she'd asked for. She reached for her purse to pay him but he waved the gesture away as he got in and sat down. He was in his own car. It hadn't been worth going in to collect his service vehicle so early on. Amelie's car was parked behind his. She'd joined him to tell him her idea.

'No, it's fine, sir, but thank you for offering.'

'Like I told you, there's no need for sir all the time when we're out of the office. Now, what was it you wanted to talk to me about? But please remember, you can always say anything that's on your mind in a team briefing. No one will mock you. Or if they do, they'll have me to answer to.'

'You know how sometimes you see something but don't register it at the time? Then something happens later that gives you a sort of light-bulb moment?'

Ted nodded, his mouth full of breakfast.

'And then sometimes you start putting two and two together but you're not sure if you're making four or forty?'

Another nod.

'All this stuff about trees was new to me. I'd never really heard or thought about it before, so I looked some of it up online last night. Then I remembered. The road where the children's home is. The one where Lucy went after her mother died. That has trees along it and they'd been cut right back when we visited. I remembered thinking how ugly they looked like that. Now I realise it's good for them, really, and they'll grow back healthier and stronger because of it. So perhaps it's a regular thing. Every few years or so, or even annually.'

Ted took a swallow of his tea. Wondering where she was going with all of this, but prepared to listen to what she had to say.

'So that means that a tree surgeon or similar must have worked on them. And that got me thinking about Tam Lee again. And about Cyane.'

She hesitated, sounding unsure again.

'Go on,' Ted told her, his tone neutral.

'I was thinking about names. And what we do to them if we're not keen on them. When I was younger, I went through a phase of only answering to Amy.'

Ted could relate to that. He wasn't keen on Edwin, his father's choice, nor his mother insisting on calling him Teddy. Darling had been enough of a challenge, throughout his school days.

'I know what you mean. My partner's teenage sister is now going by the third name she's used since I've known her, and that's not been long.'

'So then I wondered what a young person might shorten Lucy to. Lu, Lulu. Or perhaps Cy. So I know it sounds completely crazy, but could Lucy Robson now be Cyane Lee? And could she just possibly have met Tam Lee when she was working on those trees outside the children's home?

'You can see why I wanted to try this on you first, boss, before making a complete idiot of myself in front of the whole team, with how far-fetched it sounds.'

Ted had finished his roll now and wiped bacon grease from his mouth and fingers with a paper napkin.

'When you've been in this job a little longer, Amelie, you'll find out that nothing is ever as far-fetched as it sounds, and that every potential lead like this is worth following. Even if only to eliminate it. We'll head in for morning briefing now and you can share your thoughts.

'And at some point, remind me to share with you mine when I

saw those Gloucester Old Spots happily snuffling over the ground.'

'So, two things to follow up on as a matter of priority. Finding out if our arson victim is ex-Army and if, therefore, his DNA is on file with them, for confirmation of his ID. And secondly, let's test out Amelie's theory of a possible link between our missing Lucy Robson and Tam Lee. If Lucy could possibly now be going under the name of Cyane Lee.'

Ted cut across as soon as he saw Jezza's mouth open. He knew she could be scathing and he didn't want to discourage Amelie. There was just a possibility she was on to something.

'And before you say anything, DC Vine, we can't overlook any idea at this stage.

'Jo, it might be an idea for you to try talking to the Parachute Regiment's records people. You know the military tend to like a bit of rank. Perhaps a request from a DI might be favourably received. If you get stuck, ask the Super if she can pull some strings. If our victim is a former serviceman, we need to know.

'And with that in mind, I'm going to talk to her now about a press appeal for witnesses, in both cases. There's just a chance that if the public get wind of a possible service veteran killed in an arson, they may be more inclined to come forward with witness sightings. It's something else that's worth a shot, in the absence of much else at the moment.'

The Ice Queen was in agreement with him when he went downstairs to her office after the briefing had finished.

'I don't like to sensationalise anyone's death. But sometimes if people can relate on some level to a victim, it does make them more inclined to come forward with information. We'll have to brace ourselves for the usual deluge of false alarms, and probably false confessions. But I agree. It's well worth trying.

'Leave it with me. I'll talk to the Press Office and get it sorted as soon as possible.'

Her desk phone rang before Ted had got up to leave.

She listened, said, 'Yes, he's here,' then handed the phone to Ted, saying as she did so, 'It's Sergeant Baxter, for you.'

Bill Baxter had been retired for some time now, working as a humble civilian on the reception desk. But most officers from the top down afforded him the courtesy of still using his old rank.

'Yes, Bill.'

'There's a man here asking to speak to you in person, Ted. Asked for you by name. Won't speak to anyone else. He says to tell you it's about historical child abuse. Says his name is Mr Lloyd.'

'I don't know a Mr Lloyd, as far as I know. Has he said anything else useful?'

'We've had this conversation before, Ted. Several times, if my memory serves me correctly. I am not your PA. I don't know who he is,' Baxter replied, although he could make an educated guess at the visitor's identity, just by looking at him. 'Either come and talk to him or tell me to send him on his way and I will.'

'Yes, sarge, sorry sarge,' Ted told him. Bill had known him longer than anyone else in the station and wasn't in the least intimidated by his rank. 'I'm on my way.'

He handed the phone back to the Super, chuckling. 'That's me put in my place very firmly. Apparently there's someone to see me at the front desk, so I'd better go and see what it's about.'

He walked through to the reception area where Bill nodded towards a tall, dark-haired man, standing looking out of the front window, his back towards them. He turned as Ted approached him.

Ted stopped dead in his tracks as he found himself face to face with Trev's father, Sir Gethin Armstrong. The man took a step towards him, hand outstretched in greeting.

'Please excuse the subterfuge. I wasn't sure if you'd agree to see me. Lloyd is my middle name.'

Ted's normal good manners had deserted him as he stood

looking at that hand. He had no inclination to shake the hand of the man who had hurt his partner so badly.

Bill's voice, from behind him, had a touch of reproach about it as he said, 'Interview Room 1 is free, Ted, if you want to use that one.'

That was the vulnerable witness room. All soft furnishings and muted colours. Not a hard chair in sight anywhere.

Sir Gethin had dropped his hand by now, realising Ted wasn't going to shake it. He stood, looking awkward, as he said quietly, 'Please, Ted. I would really appreciate your time, and your help. I let my son down appallingly all those years ago. I have new information. I desperately hope it's not too late to make amends.'

Ted hesitated a moment longer, weighing him up. If his years as a copper had taught him one thing, it was to know when someone was sincere or not. Armstrong seemed to be. Ted wasn't at all happy with the situation. Especially not with seeing him without Trev's knowledge.

Reluctantly, he turned, saying, 'I can give you a few minutes,' and led the way to the interview room.

'Take a seat. And I have to say, I'm not at all comfortable discussing anything with you without talking to Trev about it. He's away ...'

'I do know. He's taken Siobhan Eirian to Paris with him. That's why I chose this week. I knew he would do everything in his power to stop you from talking to me.

'What I did was unforgivable. A father's duty is to protect his children. Always. Above all else. And to believe them. I failed to do both. But as I said, new information has recently come to my attention. About the person Trevor Patrick was having a relationship with. The one he thought he was in love with.

'I've now found out the person I thought of as a valued friend and colleague was nothing but a filthy, perverted paedophile. And with your help, I would like to see him brought to justice for it.

'I know my son will never forgive me, and I don't blame him. I don't deserve it. But if I can at least do this, I might one day be able to start forgiving myself.'

Chapter Twenty-five

'Tam Lee?' Rob O'Connell called up the ladder to the figure near the top of the tree. 'DS O'Connell, DC Tibbs, Stockport Police. Can we have a word, please?'

The ladder was clearly the starting point for the ascent. The person they had been told was Tam Lee was much higher up, working at the top of the tree's canopy, wearing a safety harness and hard hat and holding a chainsaw, which was not yet running. She shouted back down to them.

'Just a bit busy at the moment, officer. And if I were you, I'd shift your arses sharpish because I need to start dropping these branches. Jimmy, can you clear the area, please.'

'I did warn you,' the man at the foot of the ladder told them with a shrug. 'You'll have to shift now. She means it about dropping branches.'

'And I mean it about wanting to speak to her. Now,' Rob told him, then bellowed back, to cover the sound of the chainsaw she'd just started up, 'Now, please, Ms Lee. You've been giving us the run-around for too long. We either talk now or I'll arrest you for obstruction. Up to you.'

'She won't hear you, with the saw running, and her ear defenders on.'

Rob was no fool and he wasn't prepared to be played like one.

'You must have a way of contacting her,' he told the man she'd called Jimmy. 'It's a safety requirement, working in a public area like this. In case you need to stop work urgently.

What is it? Walkie-talkie? Mobile phone earpiece? Whatever it is, get her down here. Don't make me send DC Tibbs up there to get her.'

Virgil was good at looking menacing. He was by nature mild-mannered, easy-going. A bit of a practical joker. A doting father to his little daughter. But all the time he spent on body-building gave him an ominous air to those who didn't know him.

Jimmy seemed to take the threat seriously. Rob had been right. They did have radio contact.

'You better come down, Tam. They're not going to go away until you do.'

There was a pause. Then the chainsaw stopped. After some fiddling about, the woman started her descent, swift and agile, chainsaw held firmly in one gloved hand. She put it carefully down on the floor, pulled off helmet and ear defenders, and looked at Rob and Virgil. A glare of open hostility.

'We've been trying to get hold of you, Ms Lee. We have left several messages,' Rob began, after he and Virgil had presented their ID, which she barely looked at.

Rob put her height at about five five, age somewhere near forty. Stockily built. He'd lay odds that she was more than capable of handling herself.

'Have you found the equipment that was nicked?' she asked him.

'Not yet but ...'

'Then the discussion is pointless. So why don't the two of you just piss off and let me get on with my work.'

Virgil silently took a step forward, putting himself between her and the ladder.

She eyed him up and down and said, with open scorn, 'The tough guy, eh? Just remember who's nearest to the chainsaw. Look, what is it you want?'

'Just a few moments of your time, please, to answer some questions. Perhaps you might like to answer them in private.'

Rob looked pointedly at the man with her who was hovering in the background.

'A few minutes. That's all you're getting. Then I'm going back up there. I've been pissed about enough already by you lot. Jimmy, go sit in the wagon and have your brew and a biscuit. And don't drop bloody crumbs all over the seats again.'

'Before you go, can I ask your name?'

'Jimmy Crick,' the man told him, as Virgil noted it in his pocket book. Crick, J. was the second name listed on the company registration which they'd found online. He estimated him at late thirties. Around six foot. Slightly built but with a suggestion of wiry strength about him.

'And don't make him mad by calling him Jiminy Cricket. He's sick to death of that by now. About as sick as I am of people assuming I must be a bloke. Tam is short for Tamara, if you must know. Which I never, ever use. Right, what d'you want? Clock's ticking.'

'Do you know a Lucy Robson?'

'No,' she replied brusquely, with not so much as a flicker. 'Next question?'

'Do you know what *Betula nigra* is? Have you ever worked on any?'

'What kind of a bloody stupid question is that? Of course I bloody know. I'm a tree surgeon and a landscape architect. Do you know what the Police and Criminal Evidence Act code is? That's sounding unlikely.'

'Could you just answer the questions for us, please, Ms Lee?' Virgil rumbled in his deep voice.

She gave an exaggerated sigh. 'Yes, I know what *Betula nigra* is. Yes, I have worked on some in the past, but not recently, and not round here. Anything else, or can I get on with the work I'm contracted to do? Because it's costing me money, standing here talking to you.'

'We won't keep you much longer, Ms Lee,' Rob assured her. He checked his notes in his book, asking her to confirm her address, then going on, 'The equipment which you reported stolen – a chainsaw, a shredder and some tree loppers – was taken from your vehicle while you were doing contract work. Is that correct?'

'You know all this already. I gave all the details to the Dibble when I first reported it. And two of yours were round at my house on Monday, asking the wife some questions about it.'

Again, Rob made a show of looking at his notes. 'Your wife. That would be Cyane Lee? Does your wife work, Ms Lee?'

'She's a telephone sex worker,' the woman told him with such a straight face Rob couldn't work out if she was being serious or not. 'Now is that it with the idiot questions? Can I get back to the job I'm being paid to do?'

'Thank you, Ms Lee, you've been very helpful,' Rob told her as the two of them turned to go. Then Virgil stopped and looked back at her.

'Just one more thing ...'

'Oh god, spare me the Columbo routine.'

'How long have you and Cyane been married? And was it a church wedding, or civil?'

'Civil partnership,' she told him, picking up the chainsaw. 'Couple of years ago. Now, can I get on? Or do you want me to tell you all the details of our wedding night? Lots of Cy's callers seem to get off on it, so you might enjoy it, too.'

'Nice one, Virgil,' Rob told him as they walked back across the park to where they'd left their service vehicle. 'Because for any kind of lawful marriage, they'd have had to produce birth certificates. If we can track those down, we can find the name Cyane Lee was given at birth. And I'll bet you anything it wasn't Cyane.'

'I don't know how much Trevor has already told you,' Sir Gethin began.

'We have no secrets,' Ted told him shortly.

'But as a police officer, you must know that any testimony can be ambiguous.'

'He told you he was gay. You both told him he was disgusting, to get out, and never darken the doors again,' Ted retorted. 'I'm finding it hard to see any ambiguity in that.'

'Terrible things were said that night. There was so much misunderstanding. I can only speak for myself when I say that what I tried to convey was my disgust at the things I was being told about someone I had thought of as a friend and valued colleague. Someone I'd brought into my home.

'I should have believed my son. I simply found it all too difficult. Beyond my comprehension. I appreciate that it sounds like a pathetic excuse. But that's how it was.'

He paused and looked around the room, his eyes lighting on a water dispenser in a corner.

'May I please get myself some water? I knew this was never going to be easy. I fear it may well be even harder than I imagined.'

Ted sprang to his feet, glad to have something to do. He was getting angry already and they'd only just begun. He'd phoned Jo to tell him he was talking to a potential witness about another case and was only to be disturbed in case of emergency.

He drew off two cups of water, put them on the low coffee table between them and sat back down. He watched Armstrong take a sip of the drink. Waited for him to continue.

'Trevor Patrick was always precocious. He was fluent in two languages before most small children were fully articulate in one. He could have had any career he wanted. With his language skills, Intelligence, and Six in particular, would have welcomed him with open arms.

'I had a close friend who worked in that area. We were at the same school, but he was older than I. Harvey Warboys. A frequent visitor to our house. Impeccable pedigree. Eton,

Cambridge. The right type. There were rumours about him, though. It seemed to be an open secret that he was a bit of an old queen. At school he'd been known as Whoreboys, but you know what public schools are like for nicknames.'

'I don't. I went to the local comprehensive.' Ted was only just succeeding in staying polite.

'I'm sorry, I didn't mean to be offensive. Nicknames are common in the circle in which my family and I move. Thankfully, I understand that my daughter has at least dropped her vulgar school nickname recently.

'Back to the story of my son. And my shame in how I reacted.

'Growing up, Trevor showed all the normal healthy interest in girls.'

He saw Ted's face darken and went on hurriedly, 'I'm sorry, Ted, I don't mean to be offensive. I know from my daughter how strong a relationship you have with my son, and I didn't mean to imply that it was in any way abnormal. It's just how we were back then. How we thought, in the circles in which I moved. It may well have been the turn of the century, but some of us were still out of our depth with such things.

'Trevor saw girls, regularly. One I remember in particular. Henrietta, she was called. I could see they were getting very close. Too close. I did the responsible father thing. I sat down with Trevor. Told him I expected him to be a gentleman, obey the law, and wait until they were both sixteen. But I also told him what he should do if he couldn't stick to that.

'I was anxious about how it would work out. Worried that he might impregnate a friend's daughter. Then one evening, he came into the library, where my wife and I were reading, and announced that he was gay. His relationship with Henrietta was simply him experimenting, he said. To be sure of who he was. That he'd been having a torrid relationship with Warboys and that's what he wanted.'

He paused for more water.

'We were both shocked rigid. Aoife, my wife – Lady Armstrong – particularly so. She'd been brought up an extremely strict Catholic. She'd wanted Trevor to follow her. She had plans for him as a choirboy. Except, of course, he's spectacularly tone deaf, without even realising it. So she'd tried him out for an altar boy.

'Then this bombshell. Completely out of the blue, as far as I was concerned.

'I did the fatherly thing, of course. I went straight round to see Warboys. To have it out with him. He denied everything. Laughed it off. Admitted he did see other men, but said he was always discreet about where and who. Assured me that he was in no way interested in under-age boys, and certainly not in my son. He had no explanation as to why Trevor would concoct such a story.

'I went back to confront Trevor. I did what no father should ever do. I took someone else's word over that of my own son. The things which were said that night were dreadful. Inexcusable. I packed him off to live with my sister, Gwenllian, up here in Manchester. I supported them both financially, but I asked her not to tell him that. You know the rest.'

'So now you're saying you believe Trev, after all these years? What's changed?'

'I finally did what I should have done immediately. I spoke to other people in the same circles. It was difficult. It's not the sort of subject easily broached over drinks at a social event. And not something people speak freely about. But it's not as if I don't have the contacts.'

Ted remembered Trev once telling him that his father could get hold of almost any information he wanted or needed. That had included their home telephone number. Armstong's contacts included the Spooks of the Secret Intelligence Service, MI6.

'I discovered other, identical tales. Distraught young boys, convinced they were madly in love with Warboys. Trevor was fifteen; always mature for his age. But it was still a crime. Some of those boys were as young as thirteen. One was twelve.

'I now know of at least two of them who took their own lives because of what happened to them.

'I don't know if Trevor would ever agree to testify in court about any of it. But there are a number of us, now. Parents of Warboys' victims, who are coming together to get justice.

'Warboys is still very much alive. In his seventies. Retired long since and living the high life on a very good pension. It's time he was called to account. In a court of law.

'So will you help us, Ted? Will you advise me now on what to do next? How to proceed? And will you go further than that? Because if anyone could ever persuade Trevor to testify about what happened, it will be you.'

'Padre. You're late, again. I'm going to have to go very shortly and there are things we need to talk about.'

Warren had been mopping the same section of the chapel floor, over and over. No humming this time. No leisurely swirl of the mop. All his gestures were sharp, angry. The classic signs of a control freak sensing his grip on things slipping away from him.

The chaplain looked worse than ever. If he had slept at all since Sunday, it had certainly not done him a great deal of good. He appeared haggard. Wrung out. A haunted man.

'I'm sorry, William, I can't help you any more. It's gone far beyond what I agreed with you. Too far. I'm sorry. You said you could control things. That we could trust him. But he's betrayed that trust. It has to stop.'

'We can't stop now, padre. We've come so close. It would be a very bad move for both of us. We just need one more push and we're there.'

His eyes had an intense manic gleam to them now which chilled the chaplain to the bone.

'I can control him, and I will. He just made one small mistake. He won't do it again.

'Besides, I've been talking to a new convert I'm going to send your way. Martin. He's very much in need of your kindness and your guiding hand. I'm confident that he's just the right person to get us all back on track. Back within sight of our objective.'

'Hey, you,' Trev's voice in Ted's ear when he answered the phone, jerked him awake from where he'd been starting to doze off in front of a political programme on the TV. 'Have you had a good day?'

'So-so.'

'Ted? What have you been up to?'

Trev knew him so well he could instantly pick up on his mood, even from a few hundred miles away.

'Nothing. Just work stuff. Difficult cases. Anyway, what about you two? Are you having fun?'

Trev laughed. 'You are such a rubbish liar. Something's clearly bothering you, more than the usual work stuff. But yes, thanks, we've had a billirant day. Laurence arranged for us to go riding with friends of hers, then they invited us for a meal. Eirian's gone to bed, poor love. She's exhausted.

'Are you sure you're all right?'

'I will be. Once you get back. I'll tell you all about it then. We'll sit down and have a long talk.'

'Can I please speak to Ted Darling? I seem to be speaking to someone boring and middle-aged. Usually when I get back from any time away, the last thing on earth you want to do is sit down and talk,' Trev told him.

'True. But after that, we'll sit down and talk.'

Chapter Twenty-six

Ted was on the phone to Doug, the senior Forensics Crime Scene Manager, first thing in the morning before the team briefing. Doug was having a hard job of it, trying to oversee all the crime scenes at which they were currently working. Which was why he didn't start off with the usual cat conversation.

Doug listened in silence to what Ted had to say. After Ted had finished, he was quiet for a moment. Then he said, 'Boss, have you fallen off the wagon? Or have you been sampling seized drugs? You've had a few wild theories before, but I have never, in all my career to date, heard anything quite so far-fetched. And I would never have expected to hear it from you.'

'I know, Doug, I know. But it's so wildly improbable that it might be true.'

'Well, you know my motto from our side. The impossible we do today; miracles may take a little longer. It's theoretically possible, at a pinch, apart from the blindingly bloody obvious stumbling block. How in the name of all that's holy are you going to get a search warrant for this job? With absolutely nothing to go on except a hunch?'

'Aah. You spotted the obvious flaw in my cunning plan. I'd have to convince Jim Baker, for starters, and that's not going to be easy.'

'That's the understatement of the decade. And even if you do get a warrant, have you any idea of how big an operation this would be, and what other outside agencies we would need to bring in? The RSPCA for one, I imagine.'

'But if all of that could be overcome, is it even feasible?'

Doug sighed. 'Anything is feasible, with a bit of luck and a following breeze. But this is about as far from a guaranteed result as anything I've ever worked on. Not to mention the minor inconvenience of me not having enough people to work the scenes we already have without a big circus like this would be. But if you can get the go-ahead – and that's a mighty big if – my team and I will, as ever, give it our very best shot. With the caveat that nothing is guaranteed.'

'Thanks, Doug, I appreciate it. And I haven't said anything to anyone else about this yet ...'

'I'm not surprised,' Doug interrupted him. 'They'd have you carted away and sectioned.'

Ted laughed. 'I know. I'm clutching at straws here and hoping it doesn't come to a gamble like this would be. And I don't suppose there's anything on the Paras badge from our arson victim, yet?'

'Miracles, boss. Remember? Always hard to lift anything of much use from something like that. But once it's been exposed to the high temperatures of an intense fire, almost impossible. You'll have to look elsewhere for inspiration on that one. And don't worry. Your secret's safe with me.'

DC Charlie Eccles was the first to speak at the start of the morning briefing. When Ted had first worked with him, he'd not shown a lot of promise because of the way his senior officer at the time had run his enquiries. First pick a suspect – any suspect – then look for anything and everything in the shape of evidence with which to stitch them up. He was doing better since Ted had sorted him out. Charlie, and Graham Winters, had been working on the lists Ted had brought back from the prison.

'Boss, the most obvious common denominator in these is the priest, Father Archer. But that might be too obvious, because he runs this Listener scheme that Warren's involved in. And it's through that scheme that Warren got to know this Duncan Dooley lad who still visits him. They put Dooley with him in his cell when he was having a hard time of it.

'Some of them would be referred direct to Warren by prison officers on duty. But some of them, at least, would have been chapel-goers. So is it worth trying to find out, from prison records, which of them were RC and/or went to the prison chapel?'

'We certainly need to speak to the chaplain, boss,' Jo put in. 'He's not likely to tell us very much, but we should at least talk to him. Do you want me to take that one? As another practising Catholic, I might at least know the best way to ask him things.'

'We should definitely speak to him,' Ted agreed. 'Thanks, Jo. Duncan isn't looking like much of a possibility, with tight alibis for most of the fires. Plus his DNA is on file from his burglaries and we didn't get a match for him from the cigarette stub found at the first fire scene.

'Who do you want to take with you, Jo?'

'As there's no perceived threat involved in talking to him, as far as I can see, I'd rather go on my own, boss. I doubt it's going to be easy to get him to say much, if anything, but I might manage better on my own. I'll see if I can visit him in prison, perhaps in the chapel there. It might give him a relaxed environment to talk in.'

Once again, Eric Morgan had encouraged Amelie to present their findings from the previous day. Virgil's list from the parks department had shown that Tam Lee had been the contractor for dealing with tree maintenance along the road where the home Lucy Robson was sent to was situated.

'When the boss started talking about pollarding and the like, I remembered I'd seen trees like that when I first went to the home with you,' Amelie had told the sergeant as they drove there.

'Well spotted, young Amelie. I must have seen them subconsciously without registering it. We'll make a proper copper of you yet.'

The manager wasn't free, but another member of staff, who had known Lucy in her time there, had agreed to talk to them. It hadn't taken much prodding from Eric Morgan for her to put the kettle on and break out the biscuits.

'This is a strange question,' Amelie began in an apologetic tone. 'It's about Lucy again. Lucy Robson. I know when we came before no one seemed to know anything about her involvement with this man Byrne.'

'No indeed! But, as you can imagine, we've all been talking about it since we heard of it. Lucy was always a funny little thing. Very closed. Polite enough and no trouble but very hard to get her to open up about herself at all. A very private little person. Self-contained, you might say. Not very bright, and a bit immature, which is why we were all even more surprised to hear of her involvement with an older man like that.'

'By any chance, have you ever seen the people who come to see to the trees in this road? I think they get cut back every couple of years or so.'

'Well, that's a strange question,' the woman commented. 'But now you come to mention it, I did notice one time when they were here that it was a lady with the chainsaw, doing the high up work. She had a young man with her helping, like, but it was clear that she was the boss. I thought it was unusual to see a woman doing that kind of work.'

'She's done it for quite a few years now in this area, according to the council records,' Amelie told her. 'So they must be pleased with her work. Is it possible, do you think, that Lucy might have met her somehow, when she was working in this road?'

The woman frowned. 'I don't really see how. I mean, the

tree people tend to come in the daytime, when Lucy would have been at school. I can't say I noticed, if she ever did meet them.'

'What about in the school holidays?' Amelie persisted. 'Perhaps she might have met her then?'

'Well, it's possible, I suppose. Like I said, Lucy didn't share much with us. And it's four years or so since she left us. Is it important for you to find out? I could ask the other staff and perhaps let you know?'

Amelie summed up for the team on what they'd found out the day before, then finished with, 'I gave her my card and told her to get in touch if she heard anything, sir. But it seems to indicate that we can't rule out a link between Lucy and this Tam Lee, dating from her time at the home.'

'Sir,' Steve spoke up next. 'I've been trying to find any recorded change of name for Lucy Robson. There's no deed poll enrolled in her name with the Royal Courts of Justice. But she could well have done it unrecorded, and that might be enough for her. And of course there's no requirement to register a change of name by marriage. Speaking of which, I haven't been able to find any recorded document of an official wedding ceremony or civil partnership between Tam Lee and Cyane Lee either. I tried under Lucy Robson and Cyane Robson just in case, but nothing.'

Maurice Brown was stifling yet another expansive yawn when Jezza gave him a shove. Then she started to speak.

'Boss, something Maurice and I started looking at yesterday, which is showing some promise, to do with this stolen tree surgery equipment.

'Question: how do we know it was ever stolen in the first place?'

Blank looks.

Jezza made one of her noises of annoyance. 'If anyone says "because she filed a report on the theft" they seriously need to go back to basic training. I've been going over the statement she made when she reported the theft, with the help of my trusty assistant. When he stayed awake long enough. There are anomalies, which may or may not be significant.

'First off, the circumstances of the theft. She arrived on site with this bloke who works for her, though not in the same vehicle. Jimmy something. I couldn't read the spider-scrawl of whoever took down the details.'

'Crick,' Virgil supplied helpfully. 'Who doesn't like to be called Jiminy Cricket. And who can blame him?'

'Right, so Tam Lee and Jimmy arrive at the place where they have some trees to cut down and dispose of to improve visibility and therefore road safety. It's a rural area. Not many houses. But it's a main road, with quite a volume of traffic. Hence the need for the work. So they go to do a recce.'

She looked round at them expectantly, but no one reacted.

'Well, there's the first thing which makes no sense. Have you any idea what a professional chainsaw costs?'

Eric Morgan put his hand up and said ironically, 'I know what I paid for mine, miss. A bloody lot of money, and it's not professional standard.'

'Exactly! The chainsaw itself cost more than eight hundred quid, without even mentioning the other kit. Would you really go and leave that unattended? And why would it need both of them to do the recce? They must have seen the site already to quote for the work. Is it likely things would have changed that much?'

Ted was impressed, as usual. Jezza had a way of picking holes in things which often advanced them in a case. He found himself regretting once again her stated preference to stay as a DC, while being pleased she wanted to remain with the team.

'Next, according to the council, they finished the work contracted for well within the allotted time. In other words, the so-called theft of their equipment didn't slow them down at all.'

'So they had spare kit with them which didn't get nicked,' Mike Hallam suggested. 'If there are two of them working, they might well have two of everything. Another chainsaw they took with them, perhaps?'

'Seriously? Like I said, you're looking at about eight hundred quid a pop. It's a small firm. Could they afford two of those? And why leave one on the truck? Why not take both with them? Or one of them stay with the vehicle and the kit, at least. Something just doesn't add up here.'

'Rob, tell us what you made of Tam Lee when you spoke to her. How did she come across?' Ted asked him.

'A bit glib, boss. An answer for everything. When we asked her about Lucy Robson she denied knowing her and said it without a flicker, but I don't know. There was something about her. Virgil, what do you think?'

'Like you. Not a hundred per cent convinced about her. I think we could do worse than try getting to speak to Jimmy Crick on his own, to get his version of what happened with the so-called stolen kit that day. He may possibly tell a different story.'

'If there's even the slightest hint of an insurance fraud here, I want to know about it as soon as possible, please. I'd really like to get a thorough search done of Tam Lee's premises, but at the moment I don't have anything at all to justify a search warrant. And I still want us to find out more about Cyane Lee. We don't know anything about her and I have a feeling we need to. Let's check with the school Lucy Robson went to, for instance, to see if it could be the same person.'

Amelie opened her mouth to speak but changed her mind and said nothing.

Virgil risked a joke. 'Boss, Tam Lee said Cyane was a telephone sex worker. I could try finding some cards and ringing round a few of them.'

'Much as I admire your selfless devotion to duty, Virgil, I think we'll pass on that line of enquiry for now. We've got

Jimmy Crick's home address, from the company listing, haven't we? I think the best idea might be for you and Rob to pay him a visit after work, since he already knows you two by sight. See what you can get out of him about the alleged theft incident, without Tam Lee being there to cramp his style.

'You might have seen or heard already on the local news that the appeal's gone out about our homeless victim, still known to us only as Dirty Len. Let's hope that brings us some results. Jo, anything from military records on that yet?'

'They were surprisingly helpful, boss. I've arranged a cross-match check to see if the DNA from the body matches anything they have on record, but they warned it could take a while. They also said, which is slightly more hopeful, that head injuries of the sort the Professor found on the victim might make it easier to trace, if the man really was ex-military. They'll let me know what they can dig up.'

The movement of the mop was calmer again. Purposeful. The wielder back in control. Or at least feeling himself so.

Glide, circle, dab.

Glide, circle, dab.

Warren was once more humming the refrain. Softly, under his breath. Over and over.

The chaplain came hurrying down the corridor. Breathless. Agitated.

'William,' he started to speak before he even reached where Warren was working.

The prisoner raised his head and let a slow smile form.

'Hello, padre. You seem to be in a great hurry for something.'

'It's been on the radio, William. The man who died. They think he might have been a homeless veteran ...'

'Hush, padre,' Warren told him calmly. 'Surely you must know by now that the walls in here have ears. You don't want to be saying anything like that where you might be overheard.'

He didn't look in the least concerned, which served only to increase the chaplain's anxiety.

'But William ...'

Warren's face changed. Like slipping on a mask. Closed. Stony.

'I said hush. Get a grip of yourself. What's done is done and cannot be undone.'

'But you don't understand, William.' The tone of the chaplain's voice went up. Anguished. 'There's a policeman coming to see me tomorrow. He wouldn't say what it was about. Just that he needed to speak to me. Here. In the chapel.'

'Is there now? Well, that's only to be expected. I just hope he's slightly more intelligent than the one who came to speak to me. All you need to do is to keep calm and say as little as possible. Exactly as we discussed.'

'But ...'

Warren cut across him again, speaking calmly. Conversationally.

'I was called to see young Joey again last night. Such a disturbed young man. So very vulnerable. Once again he spoke so warmly of his one-to-one sessions with you, padre. How the touch of your hand calms him and brings him relief.

'And then there's Martin now, too. I've referred him to you. He's an older man, of course, but so very distressed and disturbed, although trying to hide it. I sense there are deep-seated mental health issues there. I think he's going to be another one who will benefit enormously from some time alone in your company.'

Chapter Twenty-seven

'Thank you for agreeing to see me this morning, father. I'm Detective Inspector Jo Rodriguez, from Stockport Police. This is a nice chapel you have here. Very restful.'

'Thank you. It's pleasant enough but, of course, very different to the churches I've been used to. It has to be plain and unadorned. You'd be surprised at how enterprising the prisoners can be in making a weapon of the most unlikely items.'

His laugh, as he said it, was high-pitched. Nervous.

'Oh, not much surprises me these days, father. Not in my line of work.

'My family and I are regulars at St Joseph's. I do like a nice, traditional church building. I know it's not about the outward and visible sign, but I find some of the modern buildings a bit cold and impersonal.'

'Please do sit down, Inspector. You're practising, then?'

'Very much so, father, when my work allows it.'

Jo was working hard to create a relaxed rapport between them, but the chaplain's nervousness was evident. Jo had no way of knowing whether that was his normal behaviour. He may simply have been shy by nature. He'd known many perfectly law-abiding citizens become nervous wrecks in the face of an unexpected visit from the police. No matter how calm and polite the officers were.

'Please feel free to call me Jo. Inspector is a bit impersonal for an informal chat.'

Again, the nervous little laugh.

'Very good. Thank you. Jo it shall be. Is that short for Joseph, like your parish church?'

'I have a Spanish father, so it's actually Jorge. But that's a bit harsh on the throat if you're not used to the pronunciation. Growing up in Bolton, it was quickly shortened to Jo.'

'I hope you understand, right from the start, Jo, that I cannot breach the sanctity of the confessional. Anything which a prisoner may say to me in confidence must remain that way. I'm sorry if that interferes with your enquiries, but it's something on which I'm not prepared to compromise.'

Jo laughed. 'Oh, I expected no less, father. It's a relief to hear you say it. To be honest, there are things I may well confess to my parish priest which I certainly wouldn't want to get back to the mother of my six children.'

He was still working hard to make the priest more at ease. It wasn't having much visible effect. He decided simply to plough on.

'You've possibly heard or seen on the news that we're currently investigating a series of arsons in Stockport. The most recent of which involved a fatality.'

'Indeed. I heard it on the local news. That poor man, God rest his soul. I understand it's thought he might have been an ex-serviceman?'

'It's one of the lines we're following up to try to identify the victim, yes. Now, I know you know a man called William Warren, who is serving time here for an arson which killed a family of four.'

The chaplain probably didn't realise that in response to the question, he wiped the palms of his hands, the fingers of which showed a slight tremor, against the thighs of his trousers. But Jo spotted the gesture immediately and logged it away in his mind for future reference.

'Yes, yes, indeed. William is an absolute stalwart of the Listener scheme and is our chapel Red Band. That shows his trusted status and gives him a little more freedom of movement than most prisoners. As you can see, he does a wonderful job of keeping our chapel spotless.'

'A recent convert to the faith, as I understand it, isn't he? He was not a believer before you came here; is that right?'

'Well, yes, that's true. But then many people find their true path later in life, don't they? And I'm so pleased that William did, because of the great comfort he now brings to others.'

'Do you have any idea what gave him his road to Damascus moment, father?'

The priest shifted uncomfortably in his seat. His struggle with his conscience was evident. He didn't want to lie to a police officer – certainly not in the chapel – but it was clear he wasn't comfortable with telling the whole truth.

'It began with a very troubled young man who was sharing his cell. A lapsed Catholic who was completely at sea in here. William very kindly took him under his wing and asked to see me about reintegrating D... the young man in question, back into the flock. That's how he got started.'

'The young man in question being Duncan Dooley, I take it?'

A flicker of surprise, and perhaps something else, showed on the chaplain's face. He clearly hadn't realised how much Jo knew already.

He nodded, not risking saying too much. Not trusting his voice.

Jo switched topics, watching the chaplain's body language for anything it could tell him.

'Do you ever stay in contact with former prisoners, father? Once they've left here?'

More moving about in his chair. Another subconscious wipe of his hands on his trousers.

'It would be a breach of confidentiality for me to tell you who I see as part of my pastoral duties.'

'I think we both know that it wouldn't, father,' Jo told him pleasantly. 'I'm not asking you to betray any confidences. Simply to confirm or deny whether you still have any contact with former prisoners.'

The chaplain was starting to go red now. A flush spreading up from under his clerical collar to his cheeks.

'Well, of course, a great many of the men who serve their sentences here are not from this area. So once they are released, they often move back to where they came from and we lose all contact.'

Jo was starting to feel that changing water into wine might actually be an easier task than this interview. Keeping his tone patient, he persisted, 'But some of them may well stay in this area. So I'll ask you again, father. Are you still in contact with any prisoners you met inside this prison?'

The priest nodded miserably and hurried on, 'Not many. Just the occasional one in need of continued spiritual guidance from someone they know and are already comfortable with.'

'Thank you, father. And is one of those prisoners Duncan Dooley?'

'So we have the triangle, right there,' Jo told the team as they got together at the end of the day. 'A direct link between Warren, the chaplain, and this lad Dooley, who's now on the outside.'

'And who just happens to be another six-footer, I would say,' Jezza put in.

'That's what his records show, yes,' Jo replied. 'But don't forget he has rock solid alibis for all of the arsons except the last fatal one.'

'But perhaps that explains the escalation,' Jezza pressed on. 'The first three were being done to get attention. There may be more than one arsonist at work. The first one doesn't have the bottle to endanger life. When that doesn't work, after three arsons, a second person takes over and takes more drastic action.'

'We need to talk to Dooley again. More formally, this time. Let's have him in and ask him about those meetings he has with Father Archer.'

'Boss, he told me and Mike that because he's an ex-con, he's watched like a hawk when he visits Warren inside. Security cameras on him. Is it worth trying to get hold of the camera footage, depending on how long they save it for? And then getting a lip reader to see if there's anything of interest being said between Warren and Dooley on those visits?'

'Anything's worth a shot, Jezza. I'm just not sure what information can be passing between those two, though. If the chaplain is involved, and that's a big if, Warren has ample opportunity to talk to him direct. He's a trusted prisoner. Does the cleaning, spends a lot of time in the chapel so he has plenty of chances to talk to the priest. What information does he need from Dooley? Jo, what did you make of Father Archer?'

'Nervous. Very. Definitely a man struggling with his conscience.'

'So is he our arsonist?'

'Boss, call me indoctrinated, but I'm really struggling to imagine a priest setting a fire which risked killing anyone. Damage to a property, at a pinch, if they thought they had valid motives to do it. But setting light to a building with squatters in it? I'm really having difficulty with that. Unless they genuinely believed it was empty, like the others were.'

'Like I said, perhaps the priest did the first three but it was someone else for the last one,' Jezza reiterated. 'Someone without that sort of a conscience. We need to start looking at the chaplain's alibis, surely?'

'And his motives. I got the impression that he's eager to please, particularly to help those under his pastoral care. He could possibly have set the early fires, under the belief that he's helping Warren to prove his innocence. But I still think Warren would have to have a very powerful hold over him to get him to do anything like that. He seemed genuinely upset at the news of a fatality, and the possibility that it might have been an ex-serviceman.

'So what could Warren possibly have on him to blackmail him into doing it? I've checked the chaplain's background, of course, and there's not a hint of anything. Squeaky clean.'

'Hopefully my friend Martin might just be able to pick something up from his contact with the chaplain. Get some idea what he might be being blackmailed about, for instance.'

'Boss, can I just add something?' Martha began. 'Only Jackie and I went back to try again with our only witness to date to this tall man carrying a bag.'

She looked towards one of the Uniform officers who'd joined them to help with enquiries.

'We recorded it all, so we could show we weren't leading the witness. I went through an interview technique of getting him to concentrate on just one aspect of the person he saw at a time. I was particularly trying to pin down the detail about what he'd said about fancy dress, but it not looking like fancy dress.

'We'd already been round all the churches in the area but we hadn't managed to find any priest who might have fit the bill. No home visits, no sneaky nip into a pub for a swift one before closing. Not even any six-foot priests. Nothing. So we went back to the fancy dress idea.

'Long story short, because it took us a while. I was getting him to concentrate on the person's collar. Shirt, tie, roll-neck, that sort of thing. Jackie's good at sketching, so she did some drawings to show him, until he found the thing he was trying to describe.

'Boss, it was a clerical shirt. The sort a priest would wear. Without the white collar bit, which just slips in, I think. So not a dog collar as such but a shirt which would usually have one on it.'

'So do we pull the chaplain in for questioning, boss?' Jo asked him.

Ted hesitated.

'We might be overplaying our hand if we do, at this stage. We've nothing much to go on yet, only circumstantial evidence. Jo, what was his state of mind? Is he about to do a runner, do you think, or can we leave him for the weekend to see what else we can get on him?'

'Promise not to karate kick me if I've got it wrong, but I didn't get the feeling he was on the point of bolting. Could we discreetly keep him under obs for the weekend? After all, Sunday's his busy day. So unless something panics him, he might not let his parishioners down.'

'Sort a rota out then, please, and let's make sure we know where he is and what he's doing at all times. Then we can review the situation on Monday morning.

'What about Tam Lee and her sidekick? Where are we on that?'

'Boss, Virgil and me tried to find Jimmy Crick last night with no luck,' Rob O'Connell told him. 'He must have gone out somewhere straight from work. I discussed it with Jo and we decided to try him this evening, rather than hang about all night. With the weekend coming and the weather as bad as it is out there now, we figured he might just knock off a bit early this evening. We'll go round to his house now and see what he has to say for himself.'

'Right, good work, everyone. I'll be in in the morning, Jo. Let's see if we can't pull a few more leads together before Monday. And Maurice, I've not forgotten we owe you a drink. But for goodness sake go home and try to get some sleep. We'll do the drinks next week when we might just have made a bit more progress.'

Ted went to his office when they'd finished and spent some time sorting emails and messages. He was just getting his things together, ready to go home and face another barrage of reproachful looks and allegations of feline abuse from the cats, when his phone rang.

'Ted, you have to be the jammiest bastard I've ever encountered.'

Jono, his contact at the Met.

'And you must have some friends in bloody high places.'

'News to me if I have. What are you talking about? And you must be a mind-reader. I was about to call you. You go first, though.'

'I was going to put someone onto digging into the no doubt murky past of this so-called journo friend of yours from Gibraltar, but we've been a bit flat out. You know what it's like. Then not all that long ago, I got a mysterious phone call. Some bloke – he didn't say who, nor where he's from, but he seemed to know the ins and outs of a duck's arse about your man in Gib – to say there was a bike courier on its way over with a file for me.

'It arrived, but I'm still none the wiser about its provenance. Heavily redacted, with all mention of sources removed. But it's bloody dynamite, Ted. Stitches up that Mercado bloke like a bloody kipper. Names, dates, places, and most importantly of all, the full money trail. It shows a very strong, clear link between him and his supposed property exhibitions and some of the names on the guest list for those child porn parties with your other good friends, Shawcross and Maxwell.

'Seriously, though, Ted, who are you connected to? This is the kind of file I'd expect to see coming from the Intelligence service. It would have taken us poor plods weeks, if not months, to put together anything as detailed as this. And seemingly coincidentally, it lands on my desk just a few days after you start having trouble with the little scrote in Gibraltar who's implicated in it up to his arse and beyond. Which means we can jerk his chain and bring him in, for sure.

'So who the hell is watching your back for you, and why? Who do you know in the Spooks? You jammy sod.'

'Can you copy me in on it all at some point, when you get chance? And I honestly don't know any Spooks. At least, I don't think I do. Although I'm very grateful to them, and I'm certainly not going to look a gift-horse in the mouth.'

He didn't know anyone capable of getting that sort of information at such short notice. But he did know a man who could.

He wondered if the dossier was Sir Gethin Armstrong's idea of thanks in advance, an apology for the past, or a bribe to ensure Ted persuaded Trev not only to testify but perhaps also to agree to some sort of a reconciliation with his father. He wasn't about to mention any of that to Jono, though.

Whichever it was, Ted was grateful to get Mercado off his back once and for all, to let him get on with trying to wind up both of the cases he and his team were battling with.

'Anyway, what I was about to call you about is connected to your big historical child abuse case and it's a bit delicate. My partner Trev was a victim of another predatory paedophile you might not yet have heard about. His father came to see me about it and he's in touch with parents of other victims. The thing is, I haven't yet spoken to Trev about this latest development – he's in Paris until tomorrow – and he's not going to like it. He hasn't spoken to his parents for fifteen years and I don't know yet if he will agree to testify. And if he even does, I want to make sure it's someone who'll handle the whole thing with kid gloves. Someone whose discretion I can rely on.'

'Shit, Ted, I'm sorry to hear that. Count on it. If and when he's ready to talk, I'll sort it all out myself. Now I know the kind of company you keep, it will be a case of anything to keep you happy.'

Chapter Twenty-eight

'Here's our boy,' Rob announced, as a battered white van turned into the road where he and Virgil were parked, watching and waiting.

'Can I be bad cop?' Virgil asked him, as they opened the doors and grabbed coats to drape over their heads against the deluge. 'I like being bad cop.'

They sprinted across the road and came up behind their target just as he was putting the key in his front door. He didn't hear them until the last minute because of the volume of the rain drumming down and spilling noisily from a gutter which was in need of unblocking.

'Hello, again, Jimmy. DS O'Connell, DC Tibbs. Remember us? Can we have a quick word? And can we come in, please? Only it's pissing down out here, in case you hadn't noticed.'

Jimmy Crick had opened the front door and stepped inside. His look towards the two wet officers standing on his doorstep was not exactly welcoming. He was interrupted by a small child, face smeared in chocolate spread, coming running down the hallway, shouting, 'Daddy, daddy!'

Ignoring Rob and Virgil, who took advantage of his distraction to step into the house behind him, Crick bent down to pick her up, swinging her high in the air as she laughed in delight. A woman's head appeared round the doorway of a room at the end of the passage. She frowned as she saw the two men standing there, Virgil trying his best to look looming and menacing but was unable to stop smiling at the little girl who was staring at him.

Crick turned back and nodded at a room on the left.

'We'll go in there,' he said, then carried his daughter to hand her back to her mother, before returning to talk to Rob and Virgil.

'You might as well sit down, but I can't give you long. My daughter likes me to do her bath or she won't settle. What's it about?'

Rob was doing the talking, Virgil once more trying to look tough, without the distraction of the child to smile about.

'We're still making enquiries into the missing equipment. We've now heard what Tam Lee had to say about it, but we need some details from you, please.'

'I don't see how I can tell you any more than Tam did at the time.'

'But you were there at the time of the theft?'

'Yeah, but I didn't see what happened or anything.'

'I see you have your own van. Do you travel to jobs with Tam or go separately?'

'Depends where we're working. We might meet up in the middle, if that works best.'

'And what about on the day of the theft?'

Rob was still doing the questioning while Virgil made notes.

'I got there first. Tam was a bit behind me. She said we should go and have a look at the site first to see what kit we needed with us as we were going to be working a bit of a distance from where we could park. We did that, then when we got back to where we'd parked and went to get our kit, Tam saw straight off that the tarp was pulled back on her truck and some of it was gone.'

'Some of it, but not all of it?'

'Yeah, we reckoned whoever it was must have heard us coming back and legged it. They'd took Tam's chainsaw, the big loppers and the shredder.'

'How do you operate a shredder if you're working off grid? Aren't they mostly electric?'

'There's a genny on the truck, so we can run electrics. Sometimes we might need lighting.'

'They hadn't taken the genny?'

'They hadn't taken anything except those three things. It meant we could carry on with the work, at least. I had my chainsaw in the van, Tam sometimes carries a spare, and we still had the ladders and some other kit. Tam phoned the police, but no bugger came out or anything. So we just cracked on with the job with the tools we still had.'

'Was it unusual, to leave expensive kit unattended like that? And for Tam to arrive after you?'

'Sometimes we have to leave it, although we try not to. Mostly Tam gets there first but she said she'd forgotten she needed diesel so she had to make a detour.'

'Did you see for yourself that all the kit was on the truck when she arrived? And whether or not the tarpaulin was secure?'

Crick frowned, looked from one to the other of them. 'Well, no, not really, but ...'

'Thank you. Now, have you met Tam's wife, Cyane?'

'What's all this about? What has Cy got to do with the stuff getting nicked?'

Virgil spoke up this time. 'Just routine, Jimmy. Have you met her?'

'Only a couple of times. She's not what you might call sociable. Keeps to herself.'

Rob took over again. 'And is she a telephone sex worker, like Tam told us?'

Crick gave a snort of laughter.

'Is she buggery! That's just Tam's sense of humour. She gets pissed off with people in general. She gets a lot of stick over being a lezzer. Doesn't bother me, like, but some people make a big deal about it. Plus people always think she must be a man to do the job she does, and with a name like Tam. That really boils her piss.'

'So what does Cyane do?' Virgil, again.

'Helps keep the books straight for the business, Tam told me. She does a little bit of painting, too. Nothing much. Just greetings cards, that sort of stuff. Local scenes. One or two shops take them and sell them. Tam goes round pushing them and supplying them. Cy doesn't go out much. Only occasionally, and local, mostly. Tam takes photos of places for her on her mobile and she paints from those. On the weekends Tam takes her out further afield to do sketches. Some visitor attractions sell her cards, I think, when she draws their places.'

'Did you happen to go to their wedding?'

'No. No one did, as far as I know. Like I said, Cy is very private. They just had some sort of ceremony at their place.'

'And do you happen to know how they first met? Did Tam ever tell you?'

'She didn't need to. I was there. This funny young girl used to stop and watch us work on her way home from school. A teenager, but a bit out of the ordinary. Quiet. Young for her age. Not a lot to say for herself. But she seemed fascinated by watching Tam go up the trees with the chainsaw. They got talking one time, and it led on from there.'

'Thank you, Jimmy, you've been very helpful.'

'Enjoy bath-time with the little one,' Virgil told him with a broad grin. 'Mine will be asleep when I get home but I might manage a sneaky cuddle without waking her.'

Jimmy looked at him in surprise. 'And here was me thinking you were bad cop. The tough guy of the two of you.'

'What we need to do next is talk to someone where Lucy Robson went to school. See what subjects she studied,' Ted began, after listening to Rob and Virgil present their findings on Saturday morning.

Not all of the team were in. Jo had sorted out rotas to allow for a twenty-four hour watch to be kept on the chaplain. He'd apparently shown no signs so far of going anywhere other than the prison, his home and his parish church. He was still being kept under observation.

'That was good work, the two of you. Interesting on several points. Firstly, him calling Tam's wife Cy. That fits nicely with one of your theories, Amelie, about a teenager possibly shortening Lucy to Cy. And secondly because it indicates that there is no independent corroboration that the tools were taken from the truck. That they were ever on it when it arrived at the site.'

'So what are you thinking, boss?' Rob asked him. 'That it was an insurance fraud? In which case, does that give us the grounds you need to get a warrant to search Tam Lee's premises?'

'At the moment I'm speculating, rather than thinking. Wildly speculating, in fact, which you know isn't really like me. But we're not making the progress we should by going the orthodox way, so let's try some lateral thinking. See if that gets us anywhere.

'All of this is hypothetical. But let's just suppose for a moment that, for reasons at present unclear to us, Tam Lee and/or her wife Cyane, who may or may not be Lucy Robson, murdered Bartholomew Byrne. They used a chainsaw and loppers to torture and dismember him and put most of the remains in the deep freeze. The body parts which were most likely to lead to an early ID of the body were disposed of separately. And thoroughly. Some may possibly have gone through the heavy-duty shredder, although there's another possibility I'm not prepared to share yet as this is already all too far-fetched.'

Amelie's face lit up at those words. Once again she looked on the point of saying something but contained herself.

'First, Tam Lee disposes of the equipment which might

incriminate them. Where, I'm not sure at the moment, but I doubt it was conveniently stolen. Then once they think the heat has died down, and enough time has elapsed, Tam Lee starts chucking away the body parts from the freezer as she goes out on her various jobs. And I'm betting the freezer was also going to be disposed of afterwards, although I did notice one in the garage when we went there.

'How am I doing so far?'

There was silence for a moment. Then Jo stood up, walked across the office and stood in front of Ted.

'I don't know who you are but I'm arresting you for impersonating a police officer. The DCI Darling I know would never come up with anything as wild as that.'

Even Ted had to laugh at that.

'Yes, I know. I warned you it was crazy. But it is at least a possibility. So, without letting it cloud our judgement, or leading us to make assumptions, and in the absence of absolutely nothing else to go on, let's see if it has legs. No pun intended.

'I highly doubt we're going to get anything at all from the school about Lucy Robson over the weekend, so that will need to be first thing on Monday. In the meantime, we need to try to figure out what Tam Lee might have done with the equipment to get rid of it, if it wasn't stolen as she said.'

'Sir, I don't think it's quite as far-fetched as all that,' Steve began, hesitant as ever. 'I've been playing about with some geographic profiling, based on the body part locations. I did that in my own time, because it wasn't authorised,' he said hurriedly, justifying his actions. 'Océane helped me because she's really into that stuff.

'It would be best to show it on a big screen but I can quickly run you off a copy of what we've been looking at.'

The printer started to whir almost as he spoke and began spitting out copies. Virgil was nearest to it. He collected them and passed them round.

'It's not the sort of case this would usually be used for. It would be more usual for a serial killer, tracking their crimes and estimating their possible home location. But Océane did a few tweaks to see if we could get it to give us any help at all.

'You can see from the pinkish shading a possible home location for the perpetrator based on the spread pattern of the dump sites. We also factored in known sites where Tam Lee was working on the dates the parts were found.

'One thing which stood out to us both as something worth looking into is to do with the date when the equipment was meant to have been stolen. On that day, Tam Lee was working out towards the ring road, near to Bredbury. Not very far from where she lives is a council tip. It opens at eight in the mornings. From the tip to her work site that day is a ten-minute drive.

'Is it just possible, do you think, that she simply dumped the stuff at the tip then claimed that it was stolen?

'Another thing. We found an arboretum which has these black birches, *Betula nigra*, growing there. The same type as the fibres on Mr Byrne's body. They had some storm damage around six months ago which needed tree surgery. Tam Lee was the person who carried it out. So her chainsaw might well have had fibres from that type of tree lodged in the chain. Microscopic traces, which even a thorough cleaning might possibly not be able to eliminate entirely.

'I have to stress that this method we've used isn't scientifically proven for this type of case. It's based on Rossmo's Formula, which is used for serial killer cases. But it does give an interesting hypothesis.

'Based on all of the information I've mentioned, and the locations we entered, the software indicates a strong possibility that the person involved lives somewhere within the Offerton area.'

Steve looked directly at Ted now as he asked, 'And doesn't Tam Lee live near Offerton Green?'

Ted had told Jo first thing that he fully intended to leave at midday. Trev's train didn't get in until after seven that evening but Ted wanted to make sure the house was clean for his return. He'd been neglecting it in favour of work. He also wanted to go shopping to get something in for their supper.

It was well after two o'clock when Jo finally chased him out of the office and told him he'd carry out his earlier threat of arresting him if he didn't go and leave him to it.

Ted arrived at the station early but the train was running almost to time so he didn't have long to wait before he saw Trev alight, then break into a run as he saw his partner there to meet him. Trev swept Ted almost off his feet in the ferocity of his hug.

'We've had the most billirant time but I've missed you. And the boys and girls, of course. How are you? How's everything?'

'Fine,' Ted said evasively. 'How's the tattoo? Still sore?'

'Really painful, despite the cream several times a day. I am never, ever doing that again.'

He had an arm draped round Ted's shoulders as they walked back to the car. He was eyeing him astutely, always finely tuned to his moods.

'But what about you? What is it you've been up to that you're not telling me about? And don't tell me it's nothing, Ted, because I know you far too well.'

'Let's get home and then we can talk.'

'You're starting to worry me now. Talk is usually the second thing on the agenda when one of us gets back from time away.'

The drive home was short but the atmosphere in the car was tense. Ted left Trev to go in and see the cats while he put the Renault away. Then he followed him indoors, dreading what his partner's reaction was going to be.

'Your father came to see me, while you were away.'

He opted for the direct approach. He knew he couldn't keep anything from Trev for long. As soon as he said it, he saw the muscles along Trev's jaw tighten and his eyes darken.

'Well, I hope you told him to piss off.'

'I didn't know that's who it was. When Bill phoned me from reception, he said it was a Mr Lloyd asking to see me.'

'That's his middle name. He always was a devious bastard. So then did you tell him to piss off, when you saw who it was?'

Ted went to him and put his arms carefully round his waist, trying not to put pressure on the healing tattoo area.

'No, I didn't. Because I'm a police officer, and he came to report a crime. Look, let's sit down and talk about this like adults. I'll put our supper in the oven – it's just a ready meal, but it's one I know you like – and I'll open the wine I got for you. Then I'll tell you everything.'

Chapter Twenty-nine

'Ted Darling, you wild and crazy man, remind me one more time why I love you so much.'

They were sitting near the top of Kinder Scout, close to the waterfall, sheltering as best they could amongst the rocks. Trev had to raise his voice to make himself heard above the howling wind which was making the Downfall defy gravity, sending great clouds of water into the air to form a mist. Ted was doggedly trying to pour coffee from his flask into two cups without losing too much of it in the process.

He paused to look at his partner as he said candidly, 'I have no idea why you do.'

He'd long since given up trying to rationalise what had brought them together in the first place, let alone kept them so for more than eleven years. He was afraid of spoiling the magic by over-analysing.

They'd sat at the table until gone midnight the previous evening, talking. Ted was never keen on face-to-face personal discussions indoors on difficult subjects. His preference was for the top of a mountain or a windswept upland. It had been as hard for him as for Trev. He'd been trying to persuade his partner to do what he'd not found the strength to do himself – to his eternal shame. To talk to the police about the man who had abused him.

Ted had been a young schoolboy when he was raped by a teacher. Trev had been fifteen; mature beyond his years. But Warboys was still breaking the law when he'd slept with him, and as Ted had patiently explained, his actions had caused two of his vulnerable victims to take their own lives. That news had moved Trev to tears.

As difficult as the discussion was for both of them, Ted had been in policeman mode. An officer talking to a victim about their options on whether or not to testify and how it would go. He'd been calm, persuasive. Trying not to let the fact that the victim was his partner influence the way he would handle the situation.

Trev had started out angry. Clearly feeling hurt by what he saw as Ted's betrayal in agreeing to speak to his father once he'd found out who his mystery visitor was.

Halfway through the bottle of wine, he'd mellowed enough for them to discuss things calmly. Once the bottle was empty, he'd agreed to testify.

'Will I have to go down to London to give a statement?'

Ted shook his head. 'Someone will come up here to speak to you. They'll probably ask to use our vulnerable witness facility.'

'And can you be there? Because I need you with me, if I'm going to do this.'

'It would be unusual, but I'm sure I can swing it, if that's what you want. I already spoke to my Met contact, Jono. I needed to tell him about the rest of the cases, and particularly about the two linked suicides. I'll talk to him again to make sure he sends someone suitable, and I'll ask him if I can sit in.'

'There's a bit more I need to tell you, too. Something Sir Gethin did for me.'

Ted was careful not to refer to him as Trev's father. Now his partner was calm he didn't want to risk lighting the blue touch paper once more. He was hesitant to mention what Armstrong had done, all too aware that it sounded like a bribe. But he hadn't been exaggerating when he said he and Trev had no secrets. Anything as big as that he simply couldn't contemplate keeping from him.

Trev listened in stony silence while Ted explained about the mysterious file on Mercado and his business.

'I'm happy you've got that scandal-monger off your back, Ted. I really am. But I hope you realise you've sold your soul to the devil by letting Mr Lloyd,' he placed heavy sarcasm on the name, 'help you. One day he's going to expect a pay-off.'

'But in the meantime, I've booked the day off tomorrow. Another Do Not Disturb day, so we can spend some quality time together. Do something to help us chill out a bit.'

Trev was now laughing hysterically among the rocks near Kinder Downfall, watching Ted's battle with the coffee. It was a special place for both of them.

'When you said we could chill out, I hadn't really imagined risking getting exposure was on the agenda. I'd thought more of a leisurely morning in bed with fresh croissants and hot filter coffee. God, Ted Darling, some days I have no idea why I put up with you and your mad ideas. But I do love you, though. You're very good for me.'

'Mrs Hughes? DC Vine, Stockport Police. Thanks for making time to see me so quickly. I really appreciate it.'

'You're very welcome. I do hope I can help you. I was Lucy Robson's form teacher in her last year with us. We could go and talk in the form room. It's not being used at the moment and it might be more private than the staff room.'

She turned and led the way along a corridor and up some stairs, opening a door onto a classroom on a mezzanine level. Large windows must have made it bright and sunny on a day when the sky was not as leaden as it currently was. She pulled out two chairs and invited Jezza to sit down as she did the same.

Jezza studied her before she began speaking. Firm but fair was the phrase which sprang to mind.

'I wanted to find out a bit more about Lucy in connection with a case we're working on.'

'She's surfaced then, has she?'

Jezza added 'astute' to her first impression.

'I'm sure you will have found out by now that she left here quite abruptly,' the teacher continued. As soon as she turned sixteen. You also probably know she should have started recognised training or carried on with part-time training whilst working, until she was eighteen.

'When she didn't come back to school after the summer break, we contacted the home where she lived, to ask about her. They said she'd left them and moved away. They'd heard from her, saying she was working and studying part-time, so there was no immediate concern for her welfare.

'I'm afraid Lucy became yet another young person who slipped through the system. The unfortunate truth is that neither the education system nor the care system has the resources to keep tabs on everyone, and to follow up on people like Lucy. Especially when there didn't seem to be any grounds to do so.'

'What sort of a person was Lucy, in her time with you?' Jezza phrased the question carefully so it didn't imply anything.

'A funny little thing,' Mrs Hughes told her. 'As you can imagine, I see a lot of children, so it tends to be the ones who are a bit different who stand out in my mind. The ones I remember. Lucy didn't have an easy life, of course, but you'll know that already, I'm sure.

'She was always very immature for her age. Way behind her classmates in social development. A below average student who struggled a bit but tried hard. She was very easy to influence, too. Some girls would get her to do things for them which got her into trouble, not them. She lacked any form of judgement of people's behaviour or motives. She only ever saw the good in people. Very child-like.

'I took her for English for part of her time here. Her creative writing efforts really were what I would expect to see from someone much younger. More the sort of thing I'd associate with someone at primary school, Year Six, than a teenager. And the theme was always the same. Fanciful romance. The stuff of fairy tales. Damsel in distress is rescued by kindly older man who then sweeps her off her feet and marries her. Always the same theme, recycled to fit whatever the actual subject was. And always the happy ever after. Wishful thinking, no doubt.'

'What about other subjects? How did she do with those?'

'Struggled, basically. Generally low marks, but she scraped along somehow.'

'Special needs?'

'She was never statemented. Nor put in any particular pigeon-hole. She could read, write and do very basic maths. But she did struggle, especially socially. Very few friends her own age. She always tried to befriend older people. She'd hang round teachers, trying to chat to them. That sort of thing.'

'What was she like physically?' Jezza asked, thinking of Ted and Amelie's description of Cyane Lee's extreme thinness.

'Always a skinny little thing. Looked as if a strong puff of wind would blow her away. She hadn't had the best of starts in life, of course. Because of her mother, we were told.'

'Eating disorder?'

'Not as far as I know. It wasn't flagged up to me, as her form teacher. I suspect she'd just got used to going without when she was little and it had become her norm.'

'Were there any subjects she was better at that others?'

'She liked to draw and paint. Her style was certainly naive, like she was, but it was pleasing enough. In fact, I put one of her pictures on the wall in here, just to encourage her, when she so seldom did anything worthy of much attention. I'll show you.'

She stood up and went to get a small painting from the wall, but Jezza stopped her.

'May I please borrow it, just for a short time?' She was

putting on gloves and reaching for an evidence bag as she spoke.

The teacher eyed her shrewdly. 'So you're hoping to find her fingerprints on the painting, then? Is Lucy in some sort of trouble?'

Jezza didn't reply immediately. She was carefully lifting the small, framed picture off the wall. It was a simple landscape, mostly in shades of blue. A lake, sky, and a line of green grass, with tall trees. Jezza's eyes were on the bottom left corner where the artist had signed their work.

A simple two-letter signature, in black paint.

Cy.

'Thanks for arranging this for us,' Martha McGuire told the prison police liaison officer, who was showing her and the man she'd gone there to meet into a room with facilities to watch security camera footage.

He had introduced himself as Todd Rosser, a lip reader, there to see if he could make out anything of the recording of William Warren's last visit from Duncan Dooley. There was also a prison officer there to manipulate the equipment for them.

'I'll leave you to it for now,' Katie Pilling told them. 'The officer will let me know when you've finished and I can arrange for you to be escorted out. Oh, and Martha, I've been asked to pass on a message to your DCI. Please could you tell him that Martin Wellman would like to speak to him as soon as he can arrange to visit.'

'What I'd like to do first, please,' Rosser told Martha, 'is just to watch the tape through, perhaps a couple of times, before I give you any feedback of what I think is being said. It's a bit like listening to someone speaking with a broad regional accent, where it takes you a while to tune in and understand what they're saying.'

'The other problem you're likely to have is that the

cameras aren't trained on Warren and Dooley the whole time,' the officer warned them. 'Depending on who else was visiting at the time and needed an eye keeping on them, the camera might have moved about a bit. You may be lucky, though, as Security had been told there was police interest in Warren and his visitors.'

Martha was glad she had an expert with her. She couldn't make out anything from watching Warren and Dooley, no matter how hard she concentrated on the way their lips moved. The lip-reader was busy making rapid notes, so he was clearly picking up something from it.

After the third run-through of the relevant sections of the tape, the officer fast-forwarding through any parts which didn't feature Warren and his visitor, Rosser turned to Martha.

'Right, not the easiest to work with, I'm afraid. Both of them seem highly aware of the likelihood that there are cameras trained on them and they're tending to keep their heads down more than would normally be the case on a visit, I imagine.

'Also the younger man has a habit of swallowing the end of his words so the interpretation of them is likely to be ambiguous. One phrase he uses several times, though, is something like "welly row". The same word shape as row a boat. And one word he also says a few times, which is sadly harder to read, is either "tosser" or "dosser".

'Is the older man the boss, in some way? Does he have a hold over the younger one?'

'I'm afraid I can't go into any details about our investigation, Todd.'

'Let me put it another way, then. The older man is the boss of the younger one, as he's clearly giving out the orders. They are firm, clear, repeated and unequivocal. He tells him several times, "you'll have to go back to see him again and tell him what he needs to do". He also says, more than once, "just remind him what's at stake if he doesn't".

'I'll transcribe all of my squiggles into something resembling English as soon as I get back to my office. Then I can email them straight to you. Does that help you at all?'

'Enormously, thank you. More than I imagined it would. I have to confess it looked an impossible task to me. I'm not sure how you managed to get anything out of watching that. I could never have made anything of it in a month of Sundays.'

Todd stood up, packing away his notebook, and smiled at her.

'I'm sure there would be very many aspects of your job I wouldn't be able to do without years of training, either.'

Warren was taking out his frustrations on his mop and pail once more. He wouldn't get to see the chaplain until later that evening and then it would be hard to find any time to talk to him one-to-one. Archer's role at the prison was not full-time but was divided between there and his other duties as curate in his own parish. He deputised there for the parish priest, filling in during his absence, taking services and confessions as needed.

There was another Listeners' meeting that evening, for the existing ones, with some of the new volunteers coming along to hear more of what was involved. But a prison officer would be present at all times and would soon jump on Warren trying to get any individual attention from the chaplain.

And he didn't dare risk staging another of his seizure episodes. He kept those for special occasions. He knew some of the screws already had their suspicions about their authenticity. He had to make himself reserve them for times of dire need, or when he wanted to make a point.

His humming was as angry as the stabbing of his mop as he finished his cleaning of the corridor.

He had to find a way to get some time alone with the padre, and soon.

He had to.

Chapter Thirty

'Welly row has to be Wellington Road, surely, near where the car showroom fire was?' Mike Hallam said, once Martha had finished presenting her findings at the end of the day.

'Logically, yes,' Ted replied. 'Especially as the last one so far, the one with the fatality, was also not far from there.'

'The other reason I thought they might mention it, boss, was with an eyewitness account from near to the showroom. Whoever the man with the clerical shirt was, he'd know he'd been seen by someone.

'We're fairly certain the arsonist for the first ones can't have been Duncan Dooley, because his work alibi seems tight. Although of course he doesn't have an alibi for the fatal blaze. But it does seem, on the face of it, that that's what Warren and Dooley were discussing. And as we've said before, the third part of the triangle with those two is the prison chaplain. He knew Dooley inside prison and he has regular contact with Warren.'

'He's still in touch with Dooley,' Rob O'Connell told them. 'Archer was at his home today. He doesn't work at the prison every day. He does stuff in his parish. And not long ago, just before me and Virgil handed over the relay of obs on him, he had a visit from Dooley, who was with him for nearly an hour.'

'Time to pull the chaplain in for further questioning, boss?' Mike asked. 'Check out his alibis in detail and get a sample of his DNA. See if it's a match for the cigarette stub.'

'I still think, from having spoken to him, that if he is setting these fires, he must be under some considerable pressure to do it. Blackmail, for sure. And it is just possible that he's simply being told the locations to set fire to, without having any idea whether or not the places are occupied,' Jo put in.

'Warren certainly can't be doing a recce of anywhere from his prison cell,' Rob continued. 'But Dooley could be picking the sites and acting as the go-between.'

'That would fit with Warren telling him to go and see someone and remind him of what's at stake.'

'And tosser is surely dosser,' Jezza put in. 'That might have been how they described the homeless man who was the casualty.'

'Speaking of him, we now have a confirmed ID on him, through military records,' Jo told them. 'Leonard Baines. Ex-Parachute Regiment, seriously wounded on active service and invalided out after a prolonged stay in hospital which involved putting a titanium plate in what was left of his skull. He got a medal for his pains, but he also finished up out on the streets, a broken man.

'I've been talking to the Super and the Press Office. There's a press release gone out today, naming the victim. Next of kin have been informed. An ex-wife who's not seen him for years. With luck it should make the early evening news, with an appeal for witnesses. People might be more likely to want to help with the death of what we can now confirm is an Army veteran.'

'So do we haul the chaplain in, boss?' Rob asked him.

Ted thought for a moment. 'I'd like to give it another day. If we've got him under surveillance, he's unlikely to go far. I'd consider it to be a calculated risk that's worth taking in the circumstances.

'There are two things I'd like to wait for first, to see how they pan out. One is that there's a strong likelihood that the news of the ID on the fatality might rattle our arsonist more than somewhat. Bad enough if they weren't expecting anyone to be in the building at all. Far worse if they now discover they've killed a military hero.

'The second point is my friend Martin. As you know, he's been trying to get closer to both Warren and the chaplain, to see if he can pick up on anything going on between them which may give grounds for blackmail. It's possible, for instance, that Warren's got him to start smuggling stuff in to prison for him. Nothing too serious, but enough to make sure the chaplain would be in big trouble if it ever came out. Martin's asked to see me, so I'm hoping he has some news for me. I'm going tomorrow morning, first thing.

'As long as we're happy the chaplain can't disappear overnight, I'd sooner wait and see what that visit brings me.

'So, what else?'

He could see that Jezza was itching for a chance to say something.

'Boss, a productive visit to the school, I think. I picked up a small painting which Lucy Robson did while she was there. She signed it Cy. So, Amelie, you were on to something there. I've sent it off for fingerprinting. If we ever get the chance to get prints from Cyane Lee, we can get them checked to see if she and Lucy are the same person.

'Another thing about Cyane. Again, sorry if I'm spouting stuff you already know, but art isn't really my thing, other than finding out stuff for Tommy, so this was newish to me. Lucy's painting uses a lot of blue. I took a photo on my phone before I sent it off, if anyone wants to look. It's the greeny-blue colour sometimes called aqua. It's also called cyan, without the E. Amelie, you've written it as with an E ...'

Amelie was on the defensive immediately. 'I got her to spell it for me; that's how she spelled it.'

'It wasn't a criticism. Adding an E is a way of making a name feminine, of course. It's also the name of a water nymph in Greek mythology. Lucy's form teacher said she was always very immature in what she wrote. Maybe not a reader of Greek myths, but she might have chosen cyan, after the colour, and just added the E because that's how she thought it was written.

'So, boss, can we bring her in and question her? Can we ask to take her fingerprints, so we can rule her in or out as Lucy? Because that would give us the link we need to Byrne, if she is Lucy Robson. A word of caution, though. Her teacher said she was always emotionally very immature. Easily led. She was never given a statement of special needs but she could be classed as vulnerable, so how do you want to handle her, if at all?'

'Boss, if it helps, I did recent update training in interviewing vulnerable persons, as part of my return to work package. I'd be happy to interview her, unless anyone else is more qualified?' Martha suggested.

'If we do bring her in, I think it would be a good idea to keep her well away from Tam Lee. When me and Virgil talked to Tam, it's clear she's a strong character. Controlling, perhaps? When you were telling us about your visit to see Cyane, boss, some of the things you reported her saying sounded very like Tam's way of speaking.

'We've checked Tam Lee out and she has form, though not recent, for getting a bit physical. It never came to much because there was always sufficient doubt over whether she was just defending herself, or whether she liked starting trouble.'

'Lucy's teacher said she was always very easily influenced,' Jezza confirmed. 'And it certainly sounds like it, with her relationship with Byrne. Surely, these days, most girls, even as young as eleven or twelve, know it's not normal behaviour to be sharing a bed with a much older man. Even if he never touched them, which I find hard to believe.'

'Yes, I think the way forward now is to bring Cyane in, hopefully without alerting Tam Lee, and to ask her some questions about Lucy Robson. Show her the picture on your phone, and the signature, and see what she says about it. Martha, yes please, can you take that. And Maurice, can you go with her? We've no reason to believe she'll be bothered about the presence of a male officer, have we?'

'I'd say the reverse, boss,' Jezza responded. 'If she really is Lucy Robson, she seems to relate well to older men. Daddy Hen could be just what's needed to get her to talk.'

'Make sure you get her written consent to give fingerprints, and the three of us will have a talk at some point, to see what needs covering. If at all possible, we need to get hold of one of these cards painted by Cyane Lee, to compare with the one from school. Particularly the signature.'

Eric Morgan gave an exaggerated sigh and unfolded his arms to pick up an evidence bag from the desk he was sitting at.

'Guv, you should know by now, if you want a job doing properly, you give it to Uniform. Me and Amelie have already got one of the cards, on our rounds. So even if she doesn't consent to fingerprints, with any luck, there should be something on this. It's in one of those little cellophane pockets and we picked the one from the back of the display, so hopefully it's not been pawed already by every man and his dog.'

'Nice one, sarge, good work,' Ted told him.

The sergeant laughed. 'Oh, you've seen nothing yet. Me and my young oppo have been on a roll today. It's not all cups of tea and meal breaks, you know. Amelie, love, you tell him. It was your idea, so you should get the credit.'

'The sarge and I thought we'd take a run out to the tip which Steve highlighted. Just on the off chance. We didn't for a moment expect to find anything, but it was worth a shot. I couldn't see why anyone would take the risk of dumping the stuff there in case they were seen. But then, we thought if it was dropped off early morning, it could well be quickly covered over by other things being added. So by the time anyone was sorting through, the person who'd dumped it would be long gone. There are cameras there but they don't always work, we were told. So we gave it a go. And it paid off.

'We talked to a couple of the people who work there. They said no one was allowed to help themselves to stuff they saw there. Anything decent was pulled out, done up and sold.

'The sarge is very good at knowing when someone's lying and making sure they know he knows.' Amelie's look towards her partner was admiring. 'He could tell straight away that one of the men knew immediately what we were asking about. Eventually he told us he'd seen the chainsaw straight away. It had been dumped early on, wrapped in a big sheet of polythene, so he'd pulled it out and put it straight in the boot of his car, before anyone saw him. He clearly realised it was worth a lot of money.

'The best news of all for us is that he stashed it in his garage and didn't immediately do anything with it in case it was too hot to handle. He thought he'd keep it for a while then sell it on, so we were able to recover it. We checked the serial number, and it's the same one Tam Lee reported missing.

'It's now on its way to Forensics in the hope that, if it's not been used since, there might be traces of *Betula nigra* tree fibres, and maybe even of Byrne himself. It was still wrapped in the polythene sheeting, so that's gone for testing as well.'

'So with evidence of an insurance fraud at the least, does that get you enough for your search warrant of Tam Lee's place, boss?' Jo asked him.

'You know the final decision isn't mine, but I'll talk to the Super and to the Big Boss and see what they say. Favourite for me would be to have Cyane in here talking to Martha and Maurice, and at the same time bring Tam Lee in but keep them separate. Rob, you and Virgil talk to her again, as you've already made initial contact.

'Then if we get that warrant, we could get Forensics on site and the search started while they're both here, safely out of harm's way.

'Finally, things are starting to go the way we need them to.'

Ted was feeling upbeat and optimistic as he drove up to Manchester. The Ice Queen was sorting out their warrant to search Tam Lee's premises. Ted had had a long phone discussion with Doug, from the CSI team, over what they hoped to get out of the search, and what they could legitimately look for, based on a suspected case of insurance fraud.

Above all, Ted wanted them to get into the big garage and workshop he'd seen on his visit, round the back of the small house. If Byrne had ended his days at the property, that was where Ted suspected it might have happened. Mention of the chainsaw being found wrapped in a sheet of polythene made him think that it might have been spread on the floor in there to catch all traces of what must have been a bloody and gruesome killing.

Because the chainsaw was the only one of the allegedly stolen tools which had come to light, it gave scope for a thorough search of the premises in an attempt to find the missing loppers and shredder. He was also anxious for Doug's team to get a look inside the large freezer he'd spotted in the corner of the building. He suspected that was where Byrne's dismembered body had been stored before it was scattered and dumped. He imagined it would have been thoroughly cleaned out of all traces visible to the naked eye. With someone as skilled as Doug on the case, if there was the smallest hint of any lingering sign of the presence of a body, he and his team would find it.

'You look pleased with yourself,' Martin greeted him when Ted was shown into the same private room they'd used before. One of those reserved for legal visits, which were not subject to the same amount of scrutiny as regular ones.

Ted put his briefcase, which had been searched on entry,

down on the floor next to the desk and sat down opposite Martin. They were alone in the room, with an officer on duty outside.

'Things are slowly turning in the right direction on another case, I hope. So, you wanted to see me. Have you managed to find anything out for me?'

'I did as you asked. I got god. I saw Warren a few times on the Listener scheme and he put me in touch with the chaplain. And that's the key word, right there. Touch. Father Archer's a nice chap. Obviously caring and considerate. But he is a bit touchy-feely. I can imagine that his actions, even though they're innocent enough, could be open to misinterpretation in a place like this.

'Archer's so well-meaning it's almost painful. He wants to be friends with everyone and to make everything right. Make the bad go away. Funnily enough, we used to see people like him in the hotel trade. They'd bring all their so-called friends in for meals and drinks. Treat them all to whatever they wanted, then often not even have enough money left to get themselves home again.

'Afterwards, Warren was very interested in anything physical – anything at all – which happened between me and the chaplain. Archer does have an unfortunate habit of patting you on the thigh when he's trying to give comfort. Like I said before, I've been with plenty of blokes and I know the signs. It's not him making a pass or coming on to you. It's an incredibly naive man, trying to offer support.

'Warren really gets off on being told stuff like that, though. It's clear that's what he wants to hear. He wasn't interested in anything else I told him. Just, did the padre touch me? Where did he touch me? How did it make me feel? All that sort of stuff.

'Does that help you, Ted, or do you need more from me? Only time's running out for me, a bit. I'm getting near the end of my sentence. Time to call in that favour.

'It's been nice having contact with you again but that's not going to be able to happen for quite a while now. So goodbye, and thank you. For being my friend.'

Ted stood up and put his briefcase on the table between them, making a show of opening it and looking inside. He didn't want to see what happened next. His reactions were too fast. He needed a distraction.

The thump to the side of his face rocked him on his feet. He let himself go down like a ton of bricks, knocking over the chair, which wasn't fixed down, unlike the table, in the process. Martin was standing over him shouting loudly, a wide grin on his face, a mischievous wink towards Ted's prone form.

'You always were a stuck-up bastard, Ted. Lording it over me ...'

He didn't get much further before the door burst open and the alarm went off, all available officers in the vicinity immediately being summoned to assist.

'Back against the wall, Wellman, and don't move!' the officer from outside shouted as he rushed over to Ted, glancing down at him while keeping a careful eye on Martin. 'You all right, sir? What was all that about?'

Ted was feeling his jaw, getting carefully to his feet.

'I've no idea. I thought we were friends, but he just lost it and went for me.'

Other officers had appeared by now and Martin was being hustled out of the room, heading for the Segregation Unit.

'I'm afraid there's a ton of paperwork you'll need to fill out before you can leave, sir. Sorry about that. I'll show you where, and we'll get you checked out and photographed. Are you sure you're all right?'

Chapter Thirty-one

'Cyane Lee?' Martha held out her ID card and put on her most reassuring smile. 'DS McGuire, DC Brown, from Stockport Police. As you know, we're investigating the theft of items of equipment belonging to your partner, Tam Lee. I wondered if you'd mind coming with us to the station so we can ask you a few questions about it?'

Cyane Lee's thin face peered at them around the front door. They'd had to knock several times before she opened it. The pallor of her face made her brown eyes look darker, almost black.

'I don't go out,' she told them. 'Only sometimes. With Tam.'

'We'll take you there and bring you back. We hopefully shouldn't need to keep you for long. We've got the car outside. If you want to confirm we are who we say we are, you're welcome to phone the police station to check.'

Cyane looked past them at the black car which Maurice had backed into the driveway to avoid obstructing the narrow lane.

'That's not a police car.'

It was Maurice's turn to smile at her now. To dial up the Geordie charm which made him so good at speaking to people. He could see straight away that the reports were true. Her responses had nothing adult about them. Without appearing to patronise, he told her, 'It's a special CID car we use for important undercover work. But it has blue lights and a siren. I can show you, if you like?'

Her face lit up at that, showing the child-like quality they'd heard about.

'I'll get my coat,' she told them, disappearing inside.

Martha stepped over the threshold to keep an eye on her. It would interfere with how they'd planned things to go if Cyane phoned Tam to tell her what was happening.

Cyane appeared so eager to see the car and its flashing lights that Martha had to remind her to shut and lock the front door before they left. Maurice gave a short flash of the blue lights and a quick blast from the siren before they set off. If they were to earn her trust enough to get her to talk, it was important to be honest in what they told her, right from the start.

She climbed happily enough into the back seat, as instructed. As Martha slid into the front passenger seat and Maurice started up the car, they exchanged a look which spoke volumes. This clearly wasn't someone functioning on full adult level.

They went with what they'd discussed with the boss about the interview – to talk to her in a witness room to start with, whilst recording the conversation, with her agreement.

Martha began by showing her the photo Jezza had taken of the painting from the school.

'Is it all right if I call you Cyane, or is there something else you prefer to be called? And do you mind if we record our conversation?'

'Cy is fine. I like Cy. That's how I sign the paintings. Cy. In black ink. Like that one. I did that one.'

'Are you sure this is one of yours, Cy?' Martha held her phone closer to her. Cyane took it from her with both hands and looked closely.

'Yes, that's mine. Look. You can see where I signed it. C.Y. Cy.'

She handed the phone back. Martha took it carefully, holding it by the opposite end to that which Cyane had touched. She put it on the arm of the chair she was sitting in.

'Have you always been called Cyane?'

'Cy,' she corrected. 'I've been Cy for ages.'

'Were you ever known by another name?'

The young woman's face took on a look of cunning as she said, 'No.'

'Because you see, Cy, the person who showed us this picture, the one you said you painted, told us that it was painted by a pupil at the school where she works. Someone called Lucy Robson. Are you Lucy Robson, Cy?'

No response.

Martha changed tactics, all the time trying to be as patient and non-threatening in her questions as she could. Maurice sat quietly for the time being, although Cyane didn't seem in the least troubled by his presence.

'Do you know a man called Bartholomew Byrne, Cy? You might know him as Bernie.'

Her face lit up immediately at the mention of his name. She turned her attention to Maurice and smiled at him as she said, 'I know Bernie. We're going to be married.'

Martha shot a look at Maurice, its meaning clear. Cyane clearly related well to him. He should carry on with the questioning while he had her attention.

'I thought you were married to Tam, pet?'

She smiled at him as if he'd made a silly suggestion.

'Oh, that was just a pretend wedding. Like I did with Bernie, the first time. Tam's always known I was going to marry Bernie. She even helped me to look for him.'

'And did you find him? When did you last see him?'

'Yes we did! A few months ago. We were driving along, coming back from a trip out and there was Bernie. Just walking along the pavement. He must have been looking for me, just like I've been trying to find him ever since I lost touch with him. And Tam's always helped me. She's been wonderful about it.'

'Did you stop and talk to him?' Maurice asked her.

'Yes! It was fantastic. We picked him up and took him back to the cottage with us. For tea. I was so thrilled to see him again. I'd nearly given up hope of ever finding him.'

'And when was this exactly?'

She frowned, trying to remember. 'A few months ago, I think. I can't remember exactly. Maybe about four months. I'm not sure.'

Martha put in a question. Cyane barely glanced at her, her eyes fixed on Maurice.

'How did you know Bernie?'

'He was my neighbour. Before my mam died.'

'When you were Lucy Robson?' Martha asked gently.

Still looking at Maurice, she nodded in response.

'And didn't Tam mind? About you and Bernie? You'd been living with her, as her wife, for some time, hadn't you?'

'Oh, she always knew I was just waiting for Bernie to come back. She didn't mind at all. That's what's so good about Tam. She takes care of me and helps me.'

'So after you had tea, what happened then, Cy? Did Bernie go home? Did you see him again?'

'I got very tired. With all the excitement. I do get tired quickly. Tam said I should go to bed and she'd run Bernie home. I gave him a big hug and told him I'd see him again soon. He said he had things to sort out but he'd definitely come back as soon as he could. He's not been yet, though, so I expect things just took a bit longer to sort than he thought they would.'

Martha caught Maurice's eye again. She didn't yet know him well. She hoped he would be sharp enough to catch on. Then she spoke. 'I'm going to need to take a short break, to go and make some phone calls.'

She picked her phone up carefully again, still looking at Maurice. He gave an imperceptible nod. Message received. Her mobile could be their only source of confirming Lucy Robson's new identity by fingerprints, if she didn't give consent to have her prints taken.

'I'll arrange a drink for you, Cy. Would you like some tea? Or coffee?'

'Just water, please.'

'I'll get a woman officer to bring them in,' she told Maurice, again hoping he would understand her meaning. She was potentially leaving him in a vulnerable position with someone immature and clearly obsessed with older men. For that reason, she left the door of the room wide open when she went out.

She carefully picked up her phone and slid it into her pocket. Cy wasn't even looking at her as she did so. The significance of her own actions was clearly lost on her.

Drinks and a chaperone arranged, Martha sprinted up the stairs and went in search of Jo.

'Is the boss back yet? I need guidance, so perhaps you or he can help me,' Martha asked him.

'He's still up at the prison. He phoned to say he was delayed. I'll help, if I can.'

Martha gave him a run-down of what she'd learned so far and ended, 'She seems to have latched onto Maurice for now, so I've made sure there's a female officer with them. But I'm worried about continuing the interview, even low-key and as a potential witness, not a suspect. I know it doesn't say so anywhere on paper, but I really don't think she's operating at a sufficient intellectual level to be interviewed on her own. I think she should have a solicitor present, at the very least. But I don't want to let her go if the search of the property is under way, clearly. We can't take her back there while it's ongoing.'

Jo put his phone on speaker as he called Rob O'Connell, so they could both hear. Rob answered, asked them to wait a moment, then they heard the sound of a car door opening and closing.

'We've just arrived back at the nick with Tam Lee in the rear seat. She went totally apeshit when we showed her the warrant. In the end we had to cuff her for our own safety. We're just about to bring her in and start interviewing her. The search team's on their way to the property now. We've liaised with them to let them know Tam and Cyane are out of the way.'

'Lucy,' Martha told him. 'Cy's confirmed that she is Lucy Robson. I've had to suspend questioning her for now because I'm not happy she's competent to make informed judgements.'

'Right, Rob, you and Virgil bring Tam Lee inside and start questioning her. Keep her well away from Lucy, obviously. Does she know we've got her here?'

'In the end we had to tell her that she wasn't at the property. She was going hysterical, thinking of the search teams turning up there with Cy home alone. We said we'd moved her to a safe place, but she's not stupid. She'll guess she's here.'

'Rob, Lucy's told us that Bernie was at their house, a few months ago. Lucy got tired and went to bed. Tam told her she was going to drive him home and Lucy's not heard from him since.'

'Now that's interesting. Jo, d'you want us to make it an interview under caution now? Put it to her that we believe she's the last person to have seen Byrne alive and see what she has to say to that?'

'Yes, that's the safest bet. I'll come down and observe in a minute. Martha, what do you want to do about Lucy for now? Is she all right where she is? And do you see her as a suspect for killing Byrne, or being present at the time?'

'She certainly seems to be all right. She's really made a connection with Daddy Hen. And no, I honestly can't see her having the physical strength for one thing, unless she's dropped weight dramatically since then. She's skin and bone. She's asked for water to drink. She looks as if that's what she lives on. But I'm not at all sure about her mental capacity.'

'Right, can you get on to anyone and everyone – children's services, social services, anyone you can think of – and check thoroughly that she's never been classed as special needs. It's possible she was diagnosed after she left school, although I doubt it, if it was never picked up before. But I don't want to go any further with her until we know that for sure. We need to cover our backs.'

'Martha, do you think there's any possibility she's putting it on for effect? That she's really as sharp as they come and just stringing us all along?' Rob asked.

'I honestly don't think so. For one thing, she took hold of my phone without any prompting. If she was really bright and cunning, she'd have known she'd give us her fingerprints on a plate by doing that.'

'I'll try again to get hold of the boss. I'm betting he'll want to go straight to the search site, so we'll crack on here for now. We've got some indication now that the house is the last known sighting of Byrne before his death, so I think he'll probably want to look at expanding the reference terms of the search, which might need an additional warrant.'

'Tamara Lee, you're now going to be interviewed under caution in connection with our ongoing enquiries. I've issued you the caution. Do you understand it?' Rob asked her.

'No comment.'

'Do you want to have a legal representative present while you're interviewed?'

She was sitting looking belligerent. They'd removed the handcuffs and she now sat with her arms folded on the table, leaning forward.

'As I don't intend to say anything at all other than no comment, it would be a waste of time.'

'Initially, we wanted to interview you about items of tree surgery equipment, which you reported as having been stolen from your vehicle.'

'No comment.'

'In particular, about a chainsaw,' Rob pressed on before she could open her mouth to decline to comment again. 'I have to tell you that the chainsaw has now been recovered.'

She didn't speak. Tried to keep her expression neutral. She couldn't control the slight flicker of her eyes at the news.

'It was found at a council tip, not very far from where you live.'

'And of course no one else lives anywhere near a council tip,' she couldn't stop herself from saying in a sarcastic tone.

'We wanted to talk to you in the first instance about a possible fraud in relation to that reported theft.'

'Theft. It happened. The stuff was nicked off my truck. Jimmy can confirm that.'

Virgil spoke up, his voice a deep rumble, in keeping with his bad cop image.

'Unfortunately for you, he didn't. He could only say that you told him the kit was on the truck when you arrived on site and you said it wasn't there when you got back from looking at the day's work. It's not a reliable enough corroboration of your statement.'

'The news doesn't get any better, either, I'm afraid,' Rob told her. 'The chainsaw has now been sent away for forensic testing in connection with a murder enquiry we're conducting. We spoke to you before about fibres from the *Betula nigra* tree. You've admitted having previously worked on such trees, and we've found at least one location, with dates, where you've done so. We've asked the lab to test specifically for those fibres, as well as for any other significant traces which might show up on that chainsaw.'

'So? I told you I've worked on *Betula nigra*. You can't clean every bit of everything off a chainsaw. But it was nicked months ago. Anyone could have done anything with it since I handled it last.'

She'd clearly decided to abandon her earlier resolve to say nothing.

'You've tried, have you? To clean all traces of something off your chainsaw?'

'You always clean your tools down at the end of the day. Whatever job you're doing,' she told him scornfully.

'Do you know someone called Bartholomew Byrne? Also known as Bernie?'

'No comment.'

The shutters were back down on her face. They were clearly in for a long session.

Ted asked to see Doug as soon as he arrived on site at Tam Lee's property, before he'd even donned his coveralls. Mike Hallam was already there, with Jezza, Charlie and Graham. There were Uniform officers helping. It was going to be all hands on deck to get the search completed in the shortest possible time.

Ted was heavily reliant on what Forensics could get from the scene to bring him any sort of a result from the case. Time and cost constraints meant he couldn't simply ask the investigators to search for anything which might prove useful. It needed to be carefully targeted if they were going to get anywhere.

Doug looked at Ted keenly as he came to the tape which closed off the suspected crime scene. He stayed on his own side of it.

'Have you been in the wars, boss? Looks like a tidy bruise you've got coming there.'

Ted shrugged it off. 'A prison visit that got a bit lively. It's nothing. But I have an update. We've now got a witness who puts Mr Byrne here, at this property, a few months ago. Possibly four months. And at the moment, that's the last sighting we have of him. So for now, finding any and all traces of his presence here supersedes the possible insurance fraud.

'You've seen that big garage place round the back. I spotted it when I visited and I'd favour that for a likely murder scene. I'd explain the lack of immediately visible traces on the concrete floor by the big polythene sheet the chainsaw was found in, which has already gone off for testing. So could you start in there, please?

'And you've seen the layout now, and the animals. Are the RSPCA here to help?'

'They are, and fortunately it's Rob O'Connell's Sally who's in charge. So at least she knows you're not completely insane, although your idea would tend to suggest you might be.'

'But is it theoretically possible?'

'Anything's possible, boss. I have to say this will be a first for me, if you're right. It will certainly be a novel experience, that's for sure.'

Chapter Thirty-two

Ted went to find Jo as soon as he got back to the station. Jo looked up from his desk, saw the bruise forming on the side of the boss's face, and opened his mouth to speak. Ted cut him short.

'I don't want to talk about it. Prison visit didn't go quite according to plan, that's all. Where are we up to here?'

'Maurice is babysitting Cyane Lee, who has now admitted she is Lucy Robson. We're trying to check out her special needs status as none of us are happy that she actually knows what's going on. She's taken a real shine to our bonny lad, Maurice, so we've made sure he has a female chaperone with him at all times. For his sake, more than hers.

'Rob and Virgil are still questioning Tam Lee, who's not giving much away. Any signs of anything from the search that's going to give us grounds to charge her with something, even if we have to bail her?'

'Early days yet. Doug wants to keep the teams working as late as they can. He knows we're desperate for something to build a case on. We don't want to let either Tam or Lucy go back to the house until the search is finished, so we'll need to have a plan of where to put them for the night if that becomes necessary.'

'If we can, I'd favour keeping them separate. We might get more out of them that way. Tam loses it completely whenever Rob mentions anything about us talking to Lucy by herself. She does seem to be the controlling one in the relationship.'

'I'll go down in a minute and have a look how it's going. You and I should get together again later on to review any new developments, so we can make some decisions on what action to take.

'And where are we up to with the chaplain? Any news on him? Because Martin was able to give me a very strong probable blackmail angle for him.'

'Was it Martin who …?' Jo risked asking. But the boss could make a clam seem talkative when it suited him.

'Not up for discussion, Jo. Martin told me that when he'd seen Warren, who'd fixed up for him to have a one-to-one with the chaplain, all Warren was interested in hearing about was whether or not the chaplain had touched him. And if he had, where, and how had it made Martin feel.

'Martin's my age, so not a young man like Duncan Dooley. But he is vulnerable. He has some issues. Any hint of the chaplain behaving at all inappropriately towards him could make big waves.

So what's the chaplain been up to, if anything? Any change in his usual behaviour?'

'All quiet on the Western Front so far. Going to and from his prison and parish business, seemingly as normal. And of course no more arsons since the fatal one – if that's not tempting fate.'

'I think we should perhaps haul him in soonish. Although it will depend if things suddenly kick off on the Byrne case, as a result of the search. We need to see what he says to the allegations Martin made. Perhaps that, and the news of who the arson victim was, will loosen his tongue a bit, if he is involved. I'd prefer to pick him up from his home rather than at the prison, so perhaps later this afternoon, when he gets back from work, if we're not tied up on anything else. I might go myself for that, depending on how things at the search site are going. Meantime I'll go and listen to what Tam Lee has to say for herself.'

Not a lot, seemed to be the answer to that, when Ted went downstairs to watch the interview over the monitors.

Rob O'Connell was doing a good job with her. Ted couldn't fault him on his procedure or his tenacity. For the moment it wasn't getting him anywhere. Most of his questions were met with a stony-faced 'no comment'. The only time she spoke more was whenever either Rob or Virgil made reference to her partner. Then she went on a rant.

'You shouldn't be fucking talking to Cy on her own. She doesn't operate like a normal adult. She's emotionally retarded. She won't understand what you're asking her about and she'll finish up saying anything she thinks you want to hear.'

Rob and Virgil had worked out a rough outline to the interview between them before they had begun. They weren't expecting to get much from her, if anything. Virgil took over.

'Tell me about Bartholomew Byrne. Also known as Bernie. When did you last see him?'

'Who? Never heard of him.'

'Cy tells us the two of you ran into him, about four months ago, and took him back to your place for tea.'

'I told you, Cy will say anything she thinks you want to hear. Her head's full of fairy stories. And she's obsessed with bloody tea parties.'

Rob came back at this point. 'She says that you and her are married. Jimmy Crick confirmed that. Are you living in a full relationship with Cy?'

Tam leaned back in her chair, folding her arms and looking at him with distaste.

'Have I asked you who you're shagging? I'm a lesbian, not a pervert. I told you, Cy is on a child's emotional level. I took her in because she has no one. I look after her. That's it.'

'So you maintain the man known as Bernie has never been to your house?'

'No comment. Can I go now? I have work to do.'

'And you still claim that your chainsaw, loppers and

shredder were stolen off the back of your truck some months ago?'

'No comment. Can I at least go for a piss and have a cup of tea? I'm spitting feathers here.'

'Chaplain wants you, Warren. Urgent Listener business, he said. In the chapel.'

Warren stopped his mopping and humming and made to go with the prison officer.

'Bring your kit with you, Warren. How long have you been here? You should know by now you can't leave anything lying around. It'll only end up being used as a weapon.'

'Yes, Mr Young. Sorry, Mr Young.'

Warren bent meekly to pick up his mop and pail. In his mind, Young died a grisly death, his body warped and contracted by flames licking ever higher. Consuming flesh and bone, while Young writhed in mortal agony on the ground at his feet.

'Warren for you, chaplain,' Young announced as he shepherded Warren into the chapel.

Archer was on his knees in front of the altar. He crossed himself as he finished praying and stood up, turning to face them both. He looked even worse than before. A haunted man. His face was grey, eyes red-rimmed, with dark bags under them. Clearly sleep deprived and suffering inner torment.

'Thank you, Mr Young. William, I need to talk to you on an urgent Listeners' matter.'

As soon as the door closed, the chaplain began to speak, not even suggesting they should both sit down as he usually did.

'It's gone far enough, William. I've wrestled with my conscience and I've decided the only thing I can do now is to give myself up to the police and tell them everything I know.

'The man who died was not just an innocent soul who didn't deserve an ending like that. He was also an ex-serviceman. I've seen it on the news. A man decorated for service to his country.'

'Padre, calm down,' Warren told him, trying to keep his voice as restrained as possible. 'It was a dreadful accident. Nothing more. Totally unforeseeable. Look, let's sit down together and talk about this sensibly. You're clearly stressed and you've obviously not slept. Come and sit down.'

Archer was like a man sleepwalking, but he allowed himself to be led to a chair. He sank into it, his exhaustion clear to see.

'I can't go on, William. I really can't.'

He put his head in his hands. The picture of abject misery.

'The guilt is too much to bear.'

'I understand, padre. I really do. I was also deeply affected by the news when I saw it on television. So tragic. But none of us could have known the man had picked that very night to sleep in a derelict building. A dreadful coincidence.'

'You said we could trust Duncan. You said it would only ever be empty properties, with no risk at all to life.'

'The best laid plans, padre. Sometimes even divine intervention doesn't save the innocent. We just have to hold our nerve for a little while longer, until everything settles down again. There's nothing to be gained and everything to be lost by you suddenly confessing, when you really have no need to. No one can prove anything against you. Not even by insinuation.

'On the other hand, if I were to go to the governor with the things Duncan and Joey, and now Martin Wellman, have told me about their private meetings with you ... And of course, what they say backs up my own experiences with you.'

He left the sentence unfinished, the air heavy with menace. Archer looked at him with beseeching eyes.

'But I haven't done anything wrong, William. You know that.'

'It's hard to see how it's possible to justify one man

touching another on their thigh. High up. Close to their genitals. Not for any perfectly innocent motive.'

Archer dropped his head into his hands once more, his shoulders moving in what may have been a silent sob. Then he raised it again and looked at Warren.

'I'm going to go home shortly and spend the evening in prayer, asking for God's guidance. By tomorrow I shall have reached a decision with which my conscience can live.'

Ted was in Jo's office with him and Jim Baker. The Big Boss had come over for a progress report and to give the final decision on what to do about both Tam Lee and Lucy Robson.

'We're going to have to move Lucy somewhere soon or she's going to want to marry Maurice,' Jo told him. 'She doesn't seem to have any appropriate filter on her reaction to older men.'

'We've nothing to arrest either of them for at the moment, unless you're hoping for a miracle from the search,' Jim Baker cautioned.

It was late afternoon. Doug and the teams had been on site since early that morning, but it was still optimistic to expect anything of any real use to them so soon.

As if on cue, Ted's mobile phone rang. The screen told him it was Doug calling.

'Now then, boss. How's young Adam? I forgot to ask you this morning.'

He was clearly feeling in a much better frame of mind if he wanted to talk about cats. Hopefully it meant there was some good news to come. Ted was champing at the bit for an update but made polite small talk, briefly.

'Good. Well, three things for you,' Doug went on. 'First, a search of the kitchen revealed a good supply of some fairly heavy-duty sleeping pills. Not prescription. Bought off the internet, I would say. But strong enough to knock out an elephant.

'Secondly, I asked the lab to fast-track the earlier results and they have done. They've come back with a match for Byrne's DNA on the plastic sheeting which was wrapped around the chainsaw, as well as on the chainsaw itself.

'And thirdly, you were right. As usual. After much scratching about in the pig-pen, once the brutes had been removed by the RSPCA, we found what look like fragments of bone. Plus a tooth. A molar, to be precise.'

'Human?'

'Well, unless you know any vets in the habit of putting amalgam fillings in the teeth of the animals they treat, then yes. Definitely human.'

'Tam, stop! Please stop!' Lucy was twisting round in the front passenger seat of the truck, half wriggling out of the seatbelt. 'It's Bernie! Walking down the pavement there. It's Bernie. I knew he'd come and find me one day. I knew it.'

Tam looked carefully in the rear-view mirror before braking and pulling the truck to the side of the road. Traffic was light, so as soon as she had a gap she started backing up the way they had come.

Lucy had wound her window down and was shouting out of it as they drew closer to a man walking along, his head down.

'Bernie! Bernie! Wait on, Bernie. It's me. Lucy.'

Whether it was her voice or the sound of the vehicle reversing, engine whining, which alerted him, the man slowed his pace and turned back. Lucy was by now leaning so far out of the window that Tam reached out a hand to grab hold of the back of her jacket to stop her falling out. As soon as the vehicle slowed enough, Lucy flung open the passenger door, shrugged off Tam's restraining hand and raced up to the man, leaping at him and flinging her arms round him.

His mouth opened in surprise. 'Lucy? Is it really you?'

Then he swept her off her feet and swung her round, hugging her close, his face split by a smile of evident delight.

Tam parked the truck and got out. She stood for a moment, watching the two of them, both of them laughing, shedding a tear or two. Their joy at being reunited was obvious to see. Tam's face was a stony mask as she watched and waited for either of them to pay her any attention.

'My little Lucy. I tried to find you. Many times. They wouldn't tell me where you'd been taken. And then I had to move away. I never thought I'd see you again.'

'I'm Tam,' she stepped forward possessively. 'I'm Lucy's wife.'

Byrne let go of Lucy and stepped back, surprised. Lucy laughed. A child-like sound.

'Oh, it's only pretend. Like I did with you that time. Tam knows I'm going to marry you. And now I've found you again, so I can do. Can't I, Tam?'

'Of course you can, love. And I'll be your bridesmaid, just like we always said. Look, Bernie, if you don't have to be somewhere, why not come to the house with us now? Have some tea? I can run you back to wherever you need to be afterwards. It's no bother. And you must know how much Lucy has been looking forward to seeing you again. I've heard nothing but Bernie this, Bernie that, ever since I've known her. Come on, hop in. Lucy, love, you squash up in the middle. We'll be there in two ticks, Bernie. It's not far.'

'Poor thing. She was that excited about finding you again it completely tired her out. I think she'll sleep like a log tonight. Look, I'm in the middle of framing some of Lucy's pictures for her. We sell some of them, to get her a bit of pin money. Come into the workshop before I run you home. You can pick one out to take with you. She'll do you lots more, now you're going to be together again. But take one with you for now, to keep her in your thoughts.

'They're on the end of the bench there, look.'

Bernie strode eagerly in front of Tam, heading for the tidy pile of prints and frames, ready to be finished off. He never heard or suspected a thing. Never even sensed her quietly pick up the heavy hammer from the workbench. The first thing he knew was the terrible crushing pain as it made contact with the back of his skull and laid him full-length on the concrete floor, out cold.

When he came to, the pain and confusion gave way to panic. His mouth was stuffed with a gag and his whole head was encased in a clear plastic bag, tied tightly round his neck. Every ragged, panic-stricken breath he drew emptied it of a bit more of the oxygen his brain and body were desperately craving.

He was sitting in a rush-bottomed kitchen chair, his lower limbs tied tightly to its legs, his wrists lashed securely to the wooden armrests at either side.

Tam Lee was standing in front of him. Her face was expressionless, her voice quietly conversational.

'I've painted your toenails for you. So they look nice. Just like you used to do for Lucy. She told me all about that, too. She always buys the same muck to do them herself, to remember you by. That revolting Rucy Rouge stuff.'

She stopped talking for a moment. When Bernie saw the heavy-duty tree loppers in her hand he tried to scream, making the plastic bag stick to his face as he drew breath to do so. The front of his trousers darkened as he lost bladder control.

'Four years Cy has been with me now. Four years of me having to listen to her gushing on about you and how one day you'd come back and marry her.'

She closed the jaws of the loppers round the little finger of his right hand and started to apply pressure.

'Four years of listening to every sick detail of what you used to do to her with these hands.'

As the cutters closed, Byrne passed out. He was dead – suffocated – before she'd reached and removed the thumb.

She'd found a large sheet of polythene at the back of the

garage and spread it carefully over the floor before she began. When she untied the body, she allowed it to slump to the ground, onto the sheet, before going to get her chainsaw.

She worked as quickly and efficiently as she would on any tree. When she'd finished, she went for a shower, put all her clothes in a bin bag, then went into the bedroom she shared with Lucy.

Still naked, she slid between the sheets and moved her body close to that of her sleeping partner. Arms folded around her, hands gently stroking her sleeping form.

When she woke in the morning, dressed and went downstairs, she left a note for Cy.

'Hello, sleepyhead.

'You were fast asleep when I got back from dropping Bernie off so I didn't wake you.

'I'll be home at the usual time tonight.

'Love you lots,

'Tam.

'PS I've fed the pigs. They won't need any more today.'

Chapter Thirty-three

Big Jim Baker was back, talking to Ted and Jo about the latest developments.

'Have we got enough to at least arrest her on suspicion? For insurance fraud and for the murder of Byrne, if nothing else? That tooth's going to be hard to explain away,' Ted said.

'She'll try saying it's one of her own, or Lucy's, no doubt.'

'And she'll know that we can't just look in their mouths like horses, Jo,' Jim grunted.

'But we can ask Lucy which dentist they use,' Ted put in. 'If we can track down the right one, we might even be able to get a look at their dental records this evening. Otherwise we risk running out of time to hold her for anything. Insurance fraud, maybe, but we're hardly going to get a remand in custody on that, which is what I'd prefer to get.

'We won't get DNA from the tooth until this time tomorrow at the earliest, for a positive ID. But we can at least pre-empt her attempts at a smoke screen. We'll do better with the chainsaw, though. Hers were the only prints found on it, so we can show strong evidence that she was the last person to handle it. The bloke who picked it up at the tip left it wrapped in the sheeting once he'd seen what it was. And there are traces of Byrne's DNA on the chain. That's going to be even harder to explain away than the tooth.

'Doug's quite happy to work on half the night if he has to. You know what he's like, especially when he knows we're up against the clock. We hoped he might find something of interest in the freezer, as we know the body parts were frozen in a domestic one. And in a sense he did.

'I noticed a chest freezer in a corner of the garage. Doug says it was empty, switched off, and smelling strongly of bleach. He tried switching it back on, out of interest, but the motor wouldn't run. We've been wondering all along why Tam, or whoever it was, dumped the body parts so close together in time. It could well be that the freezer broke down so she needed to get rid of them quickly. No doubt the freezer would have ended up at the tip as well, in due course.'

'Is she likely to crack and confess?' Jim asked.

Ted and Jo replied almost in unison.

'Doubt it.'

'If we arrest her for something now, we can start the clock for the twenty-four hours. So who's going to interview her? Will you leave Rob and Virgil on it or bring in fresh troops?'

'I thought I might have a go myself,' Ted replied. 'Rob and Virgil have done a great job. I can't fault them. But it's got us nowhere, so it's perhaps time for a different approach.'

'D'you know what? I think I might sit in with you,' Jim told him. 'It's been so long since I did any proper coppering I've forgotten what it's all about.'

'The dream team back together again?' Jo commented. 'Now this I have to see. I'll watch via the monitors, if neither of you objects?'

'First we need to sort out the dental records, and anything else we can think of that she might try to use as an excuse. If we can block every avenue of evasion, she might finally realise the best option would be to admit it. Ted, make sure she gets a solicitor. Even if she says she doesn't want one. I want this done by the book so we don't lose our chance on a technicality. We all know that happens far too often.

'It's likely to be a late session, so we'd better warn our nearest and dearest. I'm glad of the excuse, if I'm honest. Bella has a wild idea that I should try again with the line dancing malarkey. Not bloody likely, after the last time.

'And I'm betting anything, Ted, that you're looking for a chance to avoid your Trev seeing that bruise that's coming out on your face. Because he's going to want to know how that happened to you of all people. Probably as much as the rest of us do.'

Ted gave a guilty grin. 'You know me too well, Jim. But just remember – I know your secrets too.'

Jim covered the moment by pulling out his phone. Ted and Jo did the same.

'Bella, love. It's James. Sorry, but I'm going to be late tonight. Something's come up. Yes, I know, I was looking forward to it, too.'

He winked at the other two as he said it.

'Sofia, *mi querida*, it's your darling husband Jorge.'

Jo held his phone away from his ear to avoid the loud torrent of Spanish which immediately assailed him. His wife clearly knew from his tone why he was calling her.

'Trev, it's me. Look, I'm very sorry but it's likely to be a late one tonight. We're on the clock to charge or release. But I will make it up to you. Promise.'

As all three of them finished their calls, the other two looked at Ted.

'How many times have you promised him that?' Big Jim asked him.

'I've lost track,' Ted confessed. 'But I'm taking him on a proper holiday this year. Something he's going to love. We're going, come what may.'

It was a long session and a tough one. On the advice of her solicitor, Tam Lee was even more determined to say nothing more than 'no comment' to every question Ted and Jim Baker put to her. Occasionally she tried to be clever and respond, but her legal advisor jumped in to stop her whenever she could.

Ted was speaking quietly as ever, his tone patient and reasonable.

'You see, Ms Lee, the problem we have, on both counts, is that there are no fingerprints on the chainsaw, which you reported as stolen, other than yours. And as you know we have those on record from your previous offences.'

Tam Lee shrugged and managed to say, 'So the thief wore gloves,' before her solicitor silenced her, reminding her she didn't need to say anything at this stage.

'But that wouldn't work, of course,' Ted continued. 'Anyone handling it after you would have effectively smudged your prints, if they were wearing gloves. Or if they weren't, they would have left their own prints. We didn't find any others. And no glove prints. Which leaves a strong probability that you were the last person to have handled that chainsaw. This means that you reporting it stolen and making a claim, as you've already admitted you did, is a potential case of insurance fraud.'

When she opened her mouth to speak this time, the solicitor put a restraining hand on her arm. Tam yanked it away from the contact and glared at her.

Jim Baker took over, his voice a deep growl in contrast to Ted's quiet and seemingly hesitant tone.

'Now we come to the murder of Bartholomew Byrne. Also known as Bernie. The man with whom your partner, Lucy Robson, was having an inappropriate relationship before she met you.'

'Told you. Never heard of him,' she said, throwing a defiant look at her solicitor. 'And Cyane Lee is my wife. Whoever Lucy Robson is, she's not my partner.'

'The person you call Cyane Lee has admitted to us that she was formerly called Lucy Robson. That she lived, after her mother died, in a children's home. That home was situated on a road lined by trees. Trees which the council tell us you were paid to maintain.'

Tam made a dismissive gesture with one hand, but Jim Baker ploughed on.

'And unfortunately for you, the man you work with, Jimmy Crick, has already told us that you met Cy when she lived in that children's home. She lived there as Lucy Robson, although she liked to call herself Cy.

'Cy, or Lucy Robson, consented in writing to giving us her fingerprints. They were compared to prints taken from a painting done by Lucy Robson which is displayed in her old form room at school. The prints match. We therefore have proof that your partner Cyane is indeed Lucy Robson.'

Tam shot to her feet, her face dark with anger. Even her solicitor looked anxious. Ted rose instantly.

'Sit down please, Ms Lee.'

He said it as quietly as ever. But there was something about the way he said it that made her hesitate, then sink slowly back onto her chair. As she did so, the solicitor edged her own chair a little further away from her client, as surreptitiously as she could.

'I've told you. You shouldn't be speaking to Cy without someone with her. She'll say whatever she thinks you want her to.'

Ted resumed his seat and took over the questioning again.

'Ms Lee, can you explain, please, why we would have found a human tooth in the pig run at your property?'

'You really don't have to answer any questions, Tam,' her solicitor told her again.

Tam shrugged. 'I can answer that easily enough. The boar gets a bit arsey sometimes. He head-butted me while I was bending over to feed him. It knocked my tooth out.'

'Which tooth was that?'

She made to reply but her solicitor cut in. 'Is there a point to this line of questioning, Chief Inspector?' Then, to her client, 'I strongly advise you to make no responses at this time.'

'There is a point, yes. Because, of course, it's possible to check with dental records to establish certain facts. Which dentist do you use, Ms Lee?'

Ignoring further warnings from her solicitor, she glibly trotted out a name different to the one Lucy Robson had given them.

'The problem is, Ms Lee, that Lucy has already given us the name of a dentist you both use.'

She looked on the point of exploding again. Ted carried on calmly, 'And we have already spoken to that dentist and had access to your dental records. The tooth which we found contained a filling, and not a recent one. Your dental records clearly show that the corresponding tooth in your mouth has never been filled. Certainly not long ago enough for it to be a match.'

'I would like to request some time alone with my client. Now, please.'

Jim Baker spoke again. 'I think that's a good idea. I also think that we've now reached the threshold where we can arrest Ms Lee on suspicion of the murder of Bartholomew Byrne, and of attempting to defraud an insurance company by falsely claiming theft of property.

'Ms Lee, I won't, at this point, object to your release on police bail. However, your home is currently a crime scene so of course you won't be able to return there. We'll arrange for somewhere for you to stay tonight and there will be a watch on that location at all times. You are not free to leave it. You'll be brought back for further questioning at some point tomorrow, when we expect to have further results from forensics. I have to warn you there is a strong possibility that you will be charged with both offences.'

'Where's Cy? I need to be with Cy. She'll be worried and confused.'

'She's been moved to a safe place and is being looked after there. I'm afraid that at this point you won't be able to see her.

There is a likelihood of her being called to testify against you.'

This time Tam shot to her feet so abruptly her chair went over backwards. Her solicitor leapt up at the same time and jumped to the side. Ted was only seconds behind Tam in timing and moved to stand squarely in front of her.

'You need to calm down, Ms Lee. Now. You're not helping yourself.'

For a moment she hesitated, looking for all the world as if she was about to throw a punch at him.

'A charge of assaulting a police officer really isn't what you need right now. That could very well get you a remand in custody.'

'You can't make Cy testify against me. She's my wife.'

'Not officially though, is she?' Ted said reasonably. 'You may have had a ceremony but there's no record of a marriage between you which would be recognised by a court of law.

'I think what you need to do now is to have a long talk with your solicitor and consider all your options very carefully. We'll then arrange for you to be taken somewhere to stay for the night. Any items you need will be found for you, but you are not free to return to your home, nor to attempt to make any contact with Cyane, also known as Lucy Robson. Do you understand that, Ms Lee?'

Ted had chosen Virgil to go with him to visit the chaplain. An arrest, if it came to that, would be a good tick for him and he hadn't had one in a while. They met up at the nick early and took Ted's service vehicle. They wanted to catch Archer at home before he left for work at the prison.

By the time Ted had got home the previous evening, Trev had been in bed, fast asleep. Only Adam had noticed him creep in.

With Ted's early start, there was no chance of Trev having been awake, which meant he'd not yet seen the bruising to his face, so he hadn't had to explain himself. He felt bad enough about the statement he'd given about the incident. But he'd promised Martin a favour in return for his help, so now his friend would be comfortably locked away for longer. Most prisoners were keen to get out at the end of their sentence. A few, like Martin, whose circumstances were bleak on the outside, were quite happy to stay where they were.

At least Martin would plead guilty, which meant that Ted wouldn't have to give evidence in court and risk perjuring himself.

The chaplain's car was still outside his house. Graham and Charlie's car was parked in the road. They were keeping an eye on the property. Ted and Virgil went over to tell them they'd arrived to arrest him.

'He's gone to the church, boss,' Charlie told him. 'We can see him come and go well enough from here. I don't know much about vicars but perhaps he goes in for a chat with his Big Boss before he goes to work at the prison.'

'I don't either. But I think vicars are Church of England and he's a parish priest because he's a Catholic. Either way, you could well be right. We should go and see. Although if it comes to an arrest, I'd prefer not to do it inside the church. Can you two wait here for now, just in case?'

'I thought you were an atheist, boss,' Virgil said as the two of them walked the short distance to the church entrance, up the steps and through the graveyard to the front door.

'I am. I just don't think it would be very good PR to arrest a priest in his own church. And I'm trying to avoid any more bad press, if I can.'

He tried the latch on the heavy studded oak door, which opened immediately.

'He's not afraid of getting murdered in his own cathedral, then, leaving the door unlocked while he's in there alone,' Virgil observed.

Ted smiled at the literary reference. 'Wasn't that an archbishop? And I don't think we're quite knights in armour, acting on the king's presumed orders.'

It was dim inside the church, and chilly. Not many lights on, the heating clearly turned down low to save costs. They could see a figure, kneeling at the communion rail in front of the high altar, deep in prayer.

Ted and Virgil approached quietly, not wanting to startle the person they took to be the prison chaplain. As they got nearer, Ted asked, 'Father Archer?'

The priest jumped up so abruptly he didn't cross himself. He had clearly been absorbed in his prayers and hadn't heard them coming.

'Sorry to startle you, sir. Are you Father Archer? DCI Darling and DC Tibbs, from Stockport Police. We wondered if we could have a word with you, please?'

Ted may have been a non-believer but he was polite enough to afford the man the courtesy of his religious title.

The chaplain looked at them calmly. His expression was more one of relief than anything Ted would have expected to see there.

'Good morning, officers. You've actually saved me a journey. I was about to go to the nearest police station and hand myself in. I've just been talking to my boss,' he pointed towards the high vaulted ceiling of the church, 'and it seems to be the only honourable thing I can do.

'I have been a very stupid and weak man. I've allowed myself to be blackmailed into doing something which I thought was for the greater good. It's all gone horribly wrong and has ended in the tragic death of an innocent man.

'I imagine you want me to come with you to the station? Would you allow me first to lock the side doors, please? I can lock the main one on our way out. It's terrible to say, but otherwise people will come in and try to steal anything they can carry away.'

Ted nodded and Archer moved first to a door opening off to the side of the pulpit. Ted and Virgil had him in their sights at all times.

'This is the vestry,' he explained, producing a large bunch of keys and locking the door. Then he moved towards another one further down the church, closer to the main entrance. 'And this is just a storage area, for anything and everything.'

He was walking down the side of the nave, Ted and Virgil moving parallel to him in the centre aisle. He still had the bunch of keys in his hand but when he got to the door, he yanked it open, shot through and slammed it shut behind him.

Chapter Thirty-four

'I don't know about you, mate, but I could murder a bacon banjo.'

Graham Winters looked at Charlie Eccles and asked, 'What's a banjo?'

Eccles chuckled. 'Army-speak for a bacon butty with a fried egg. Nice crispy bacon. Egg fried so it's still runny. So you get the yolk dribbling down your chin when you bite into it ...'

Graham was no longer listening to him. He was leaning forward in his seat, looking up through the top of the windscreen as he said, 'Bloody hell!'

Then he was wrenching his door open and starting to run. Charlie saw what he was looking at and all thought of his breakfast deserted him.

'Shall I call back-up?' he shouted after Graham as he started to follow him.

'Charlie, we are the back-up.'

Ted reached the door first, grabbing at the handle, hoping the chaplain hadn't had time to turn the key. It opened easily but Ted's heart sank when he saw the spiral stone steps, heading upwards. He couldn't have read the situation more wrongly if he'd tried and he felt like kicking himself. Instead he put his head down and sprinted for all he was worth up the steep staircase.

Archer was tall, with long legs, and he clearly knew this

flight well. Ted was hampered by his shorter legs and not knowing the feel of the ancient treads, with their varying height and depth. He stumbled a few times. Nearly went down on his knees. He could hear Virgil behind him, swearing and puffing. Clearly not a runner.

The door at the top of the steps was wide open, giving access to roof space at the foot of a spire. It was enclosed by a stone balustrade. Disconcertingly low.

Ted stopped abruptly. Archer was standing right by it, the low barrier barely reaching above his knees. He was holding out one arm, the hand raised, in a warning gesture.

'When I told you I had planned to give myself up, I'm afraid I wasn't being quite truthful, officer. In a sense, I am giving myself up. But to God. It's up to him to decide what my just punishment should be for what I've done.'

As he spoke, he was feeling behind him with his free hand to locate the top of the stone wall. He lowered himself cautiously until he was sitting on it. As he started to swing his legs over it, his attention was distracted for a split second.

Ted took advantage of it. Moving as fast as he could, he dived towards him and grabbed hold of whatever was accessible. One hand closed on an arm. The other grabbed a fistful of trouser leg.

Ted was short and slight. Archer, although not heavily-built, was a good eight inches taller. The additional weight, combined with the force of gravity, was slowly pulling the two of them over the edge.

Then Virgil was beside them, still cursing, grabbing each man with a powerful hand. Flexing his knees and hauling.

Virgil regularly worked out with weights. In the gym, warmed up, he could bench press close to his own bodyweight. Standing up, perilously close to a long drop, and hampered by his work suit presented far from ideal conditions.

He dragged the boss back from danger first so he could then concentrate on pulling the priest back up. Ted safe, Virgil used all of his strength on slowly hauling Archer up higher. Ted grabbed one of the flailing legs until, between them, they dragged him over the wall onto the floor where he curled into a miserable ball, sobbing.

It was the chaplain's legs pedalling frantically in the void which Graham had seen and which had brought him and Charlie running as fast as they could.

Virgil glared at Ted then recited, 'Matthew Archer, I am arresting you on four counts of arson and for the murder of Leonard Baines. You do not have to say anything. But, it may harm your defence if you do not mention when questioned something which you later rely on in court. Anything you do say may be given in evidence.'

'Bloody hell, you two,' Charlie paused to catch his breath, leaning forward to put his hands on his thighs. He was another one not used to running. 'You scared the shit out of us, from down there. I thought you were a goner for sure, boss.'

'Sorry, everyone. That was irresponsible of me.'

'There's worse news, boss,' Graham warned him. 'In the shape of passers-by with mobile phones. I reckon your little adventure will be all over social media already.'

Ted put a hand to his brow. Lowered his head. Said 'Shit' quite distinctly.

Virgil took charge. 'Right, Mr Archer, on your feet, please. We're going to take you to Stockport police station now, where you'll be interviewed about the offences I've already put to you. You'll be able to call a solicitor, if you have one. If not, one will be found for you.'

Virgil got his cuffs out. The priest was already holding out his arms in a meek gesture.

'I'm going to admit everything. Plead guilty. Whatever it is I have to do. This is all new to me. But it was me who set those fires. I don't deny anything. And please accept my sincere apologies for putting you both in danger. It was wrong of me.

Thank you both for your efforts to save me. Clearly God decided that I was taking the coward's way out and that I should instead face my punishment through a court of law.'

'You shouldn't say anything more now, Mr Archer. Not until we've got back to the station and you've had the chance to take legal advice.'

They were starting to make their way back down the steps now, Charlie and Graham in front, to prevent the chaplain from making a break for it, and to ward off any onlookers who might have gathered to see what was happening.

As they neared the door at the bottom, still standing open, Virgil took off his jacket and made to drape it over Archer's head to conceal his identity. The priest brushed away the gesture, saying he was prepared to own up to his crimes.

'It's a legal thing, Mr Archer. Letting your identity be made public could interfere with any trial process. And that seems to be what you want, so this is the best way.'

There were some onlookers, though not many, and mercifully no signs yet of any press photographers. They walked the chaplain the short distance back to the vehicles, then Graham and Charlie went off in search of their breakfast.

Virgil saw Archer installed in the back seat and shut the door, then turned to Ted, still angry.

'Boss, I have to say, while it's just the two of us. That was the most bloody stupid thing I've ever seen you do. If any of us had done it, you'd have kicked us halfway round your office and back again, then put us straight on risk assessment update training.

'Imagine what would have happened if you'd been with someone who doesn't work out with weights. Someone the size of Amelie, for instance. You and the vicar would both have gone over the edge. The other person too, most likely. And how the hell would I have explained that to Big Jim and the Ice Queen? Let alone to your Trev.'

Ted let him finish his rant. He stood there and took it in

silence. He didn't even pull Virgil up on his use of nicknames for the two Supers, as he would usually have done. He deserved it. He'd acted purely on instinct, not based on any analysis of the dangers. The only thing which had been going through his mind was not to let Archer take the easy way out after what he'd done. Whatever his motives had been.

'You're absolutely right, Virgil, and I can only apologise. And thank you for stopping me falling. Right, so shall we get Mr Archer back to the station? Get him booked in and see what he has to say for himself? With any luck, we might get enough forensic results in today to charge Tam Lee with Byrne's murder as well. That should be cause for a few celebratory drinks, I think.'

Ted was hoping the video hadn't made it to social media. Or if it had, that it wouldn't show him clearly enough for anyone to have recognised him. He was trying to convince himself that because of camera angles it would have all been just a vague blur of indistinguishable figures.

He left Virgil to book Archer in and made to go back to the office to find out what was happening. He'd barely gone up two steps before the Ice Queen appeared from her office, looking at her most officious.

As soon as she said, 'Chief Inspector. A word, please,' he knew he was out of luck.

At least she didn't leave him standing in front of her desk like a naughty schoolboy, as she'd been known to do in the past. And she did offer him coffee, which he accepted gratefully.

'So we have a suspect under arrest for the arsons?'

'We do, and he's admitting everything. We had to keep advising him to say nothing without legal advice, but he wanted to talk. Basically, he admits to having an unfortunate habit of putting what's meant to be a comforting hand on the leg of men he talks to. Warren got wind of this and has been using it to blackmail him into setting fires in a bid to get his own case reopened.

'He'd probably have got out early for good behaviour anyway, but he was hell bent on clearing his name. Although it's fairly obvious he was guilty all along.

'Duncan Dooley, who shared a cell with Warren, has been helping out by finding suitable sites for the chaplain to start fires in. Archer was insistent there should never be any risk to life. We'll bring Dooley in shortly and see what he has to say.

'Whether Leonard Baines' death was a tragic accident, or whether it was malice on Warren's part to put the pressure on, I don't yet know.'

'And from what you do know so far, you definitely think Warren was guilty of the original crime?'

'Without a doubt, I would say. The case against him was weak but it looks certain it was him. And that his ring of fire was an attempt to implicate the geography teacher, who was lucky enough to be handed an unforeseen alibi at the last moment.

'Warren seems like a nasty, dangerous piece of work without a conscience. He spots weakness and exploits it to his own ends. I'd like us to go after him for conspiracy to murder and hope he gets a consecutive sentence so he stays out of harm's way for a very long time. I think the chaplain would testify against him now, after what happened with the last fire. Dooley might, too, if there was a sniff of a lower sentence for him if he did.'

'Well, that's good work, from you and all the team. However, I should just warn you about that video.'

'Ahh,' Ted said. 'I was hoping it wouldn't be possible to make much out, from the angle.'

'I'm afraid you're out of luck there. It's perfectly possible, for anyone who knows you, to recognise who it is who dives in to try to stop Archer going over the edge. And that it's DC Tibbs who saves both of you. I think you probably owe him more drinks than anyone else when you celebrate the arrest. But I doubt you've heard the end of it. And I shall look forward to your written report with full details of your risk assessment of the situation.'

It was late afternoon and Warren was still mopping the chapel. A couple of times a prison officer had looked in to see what was taking him so long. He'd been lucky that it hadn't been the same one both times or he'd have been ordered out and back to his cell.

The second time, he made a great show of scrubbing at an invisible stain on the floor with his mop, and said, 'I don't know what they've been up to in here, Ms Weaver. I think someone's been tap dancing in clogs or something.'

'Time to go, Warren. Move it.'

'I was just hoping for a quick word with the chaplain. Listener business I need his advice about. But I haven't seen him yet.'

'You won't be seeing him, either,' she told him. 'You'll hear about it soon enough, so I might as well tell you. Chaplain's been arrested. I don't know what for yet. But just think. With a bit of luck, he might even finish up being your future cell mate. Then you'll have all the time you need to talk to him.'

She laughed at her own joke.

Warren stood frozen for a moment, staring at her in disbelief. Then he opened his mouth to let out a howl of anguish. He only had time to fling the mop at her before she dived for the alarm button and the strident siren rang out, bringing officers sprinting from anywhere nearby.

The bucket full of dirty water was next, hurled at the altar. Warren was screaming by now, froth flying from his lips as he turned his attention to the *tradescantia* plant, flinging it towards the door, through which officers were streaming. Chairs followed, as he kicked and flung anything near enough to himself, his mouth wide open, making almost inhuman sounds.

Everything happened very fast. As soon as the first reinforcements arrived, Gemma and two others leaped for Warren. Gemma grabbed the nearest flailing arm, announcing 'Lock on' to the others, indicating a blocking movement in place, pressing on nerves which would cause Warren intense pain if he struggled.

Another went to control his head to avoid him butting them, barking a, 'Head down, Warren,' order at him. When Warren failed to comply instantly, the three officers took him down to the floor so hard and fast his breath whooshed out of him audibly.

'He totally lost the plot when I told him about the chaplain,' Gemma told her colleagues.

They would now transfer the safely restrained Warren from the chapel to the Segregation Unit, where he'd be given a medical assessment and no doubt sedated.

'Quite a downfall for the model prisoner,' she went on, then added, with an ironic smile, 'I guess the chapel is going to need a new Red Band now, not just another chaplain.'

For once, Ted was dreading going home. He'd delayed it as long as possible. He'd also spent the day avoiding phone calls. The number he'd missed from Trev left him in no doubt that he'd seen the incriminating video. He knew he should call him, to put his mind at rest. He also knew Trev would have called at least one of the team members, quite probably Virgil, to find out exactly what had gone on.

There were a couple of calls from Big Jim with no message left, which didn't bode well. Most worryingly of all, one from the ACC. Ted was clearly going to get it in the neck from so many quarters when they finally caught up with him. He preferred to keep a low profile for now.

It had been a good day for results, though. The chaplain

hadn't stopped talking since he'd arrived at the station and his testimony gave them plenty on which to go and arrest Duncan Dooley. Ted had phoned the prison about another visit to Warren but had heard the news that he was currently in their infirmary, heavily sedated.

'I shouldn't tell you this, but I will,' Katie Pilling, the liaison officer told him, after he'd given her a brief outline. 'From what we know of our Mr Warren, this is him building up to an unfit to plead, if you're looking at charging him with anything.'

They'd had better, if unexpected, luck with Tam Lee. In the face of yet more forensic evidence – a DNA match on the tooth to that of Byrne – she'd finally admitted to killing him. She had a new solicitor. Clearly the woman she'd had before was put off by her violent outbursts. She now had an older man from the same firm who'd been there, seen it, done it, and wasn't going to be intimidated by anyone. On his advice, she'd spoken, with no trace of emotion, of having killed the man she'd seen as having abused her partner. She'd been remanded in police custody for the night and would be up in front of magistrates first thing in the morning with a strong recommendation that bail should be denied.

All she'd been interested in was where Cy was and if she would be properly looked after. They were only able to tell her that social services had been informed of the circumstances and were doing their best to find her supported housing. But they warned the waiting lists were long so there was no guarantee.

Trev was lying in wait as soon as Ted put the key in the front door.

'Ted, where have you been? Why haven't you answered any of my calls? I've been going frantic. I saw the video. I had to phone Virgil, who told me all about it and … oh my god, what happened to your face?'

Ted gave him an apologetic hug. 'I'm fine, don't fuss. I'm

sorry I couldn't call you back. You know what it's like, with three arrests and all that entails. I should have found time to send you a text, at least. Sorry. I'll ma...'

'Ted, if you say once more that you're going to make it up to me, I swear I'm going to divorce you.'

The team would be losing its extra members at the end of the week, once they'd turned in all the paperwork on the cases they'd worked on. They had a get-together on the Friday after work in The Grapes, before they all went their separate ways.

Ted and Maurice had decided between them to save the drinks do for the twins, and the surprise reception for Rob and Sally, until the following week, with only the regular team members and their other halves present.

Amelie had clearly been sad to be saying goodbye. She'd drunk slightly too much and gushed incessantly to Ted about how much she'd appreciated him giving her a second chance after her earlier mistake. It was Eric Morgan who'd offered to see her home. An unlikely bond had developed between the two of them. Ted hoped she'd find another sort like Eric wherever she went next. She had the potential to be a good officer, with someone to keep an eye on her and carry on showing her the ropes.

Trev had excelled himself on the baking front for the joint party. Both Sally and even Rob had been moved to tears at Maurice's generosity in sharing the occasion with them.

'Howay, man,' Maurice told him. 'We all know what it's like to be short of brass. And you're saving yours for the best reason of all – having a kiddy of your own. Have I shown you the latest photos of Owain and Killian?' he asked, getting his phone out.

He had, several times, but Rob was not about to say so, not in the face of his kindness.

Ted put an arm round Trev and hugged him later in the evening, once most of the spread he'd prepared had been demolished. The tattoo site had settled down now so he was no longer wincing at every touch. Ted wasn't usually demonstrative in public but Trev wasn't about to complain.

'Thanks for doing this. The cakes were stunning. I really don't deserve you. Especially when I let you down and worry you all the time. I know you don't believe me but one day I fully intend to make it up to you.'

'Now you two,' Jezza told them as she came over to them. 'Trev, it's time to hand over custody of your husband to me for the weekend. I promise to look after him and to keep him off the top of bell-towers.

'Come on then, boss. When you suggested whisking me away for a weekend, I was hoping for the sands of Southern Spain again, not a wet weekend in Warrington doing risk assessment training together. As you can probably tell, I've had the odd drink or two, so you'll have to drive. At least we're taking your service vehicle, not your little Dinky toy. I'd never live that down, if I saw anyone I know.'

Ted shook his head in mock despair. 'DC Vine ...'

The End

Made in the USA
San Bernardino, CA
30 July 2019